'Transported back to ancient Ireland, *The Morrigan* took me on a breathtaking journey brimming with fury and longing. In her own words, The Morrigan weaves a tale rich with magic, and visceral with female rage, as resonant now as in the age of Gods and Goddesses, and the warring tribes of Ireland. Captivated from start to finish, I dreamed of The Morrigan and her lust for vengeance long after I read the last page. Stunning!'
Anya Bergman, author of *The Witches of Vardø*

'*The Morrigan* is a haunting corvid's cry of rage and feminine fury. Fall under the spell of this bewitching retelling of an enduring Irish myth'
L.R. Lam, author of *Dragonfall*

'Kim Curran's *The Morrigan* will do for Irish mythology what Madeline Miller did for Greek. I fell in love with her lyrical prose and the way she brought the complex layers of the Morrigan myth to life in all her fierce fury and glory. An absolute triumph'
Amy McCulloch

'Breathtaking in scope, blistering in truth, *The Morrigan* is a beautifully dark tale of rage, power and love. Razor-sharp, profound and intensely moving, this is more than a retelling. Kim Curran's writing is lyrical, brutal and sublime – a stunning story of sisterhood as relevant today as it has ever been. I adored it!'
Miranda Dickinson

The Morrigan

The Morrigan

KIM CURRAN

MICHAEL JOSEPH

PENGUIN MICHAEL JOSEPH

Penguin Michael Joseph is part of the Penguin Random House group of companies
whose addresses can be found at global.penguinrandomhouse.com

Penguin Random House UK,
One Embassy Gardens, 8 Viaduct Gardens, London SW11 7BW

penguin.co.uk

First published 2025
001

Copyright © Kim Curran, 2025

The moral right of the author has been asserted

Set in 13.5/16pt Garamond MT
Typeset by Falcon Oast Graphic Art Ltd
Printed and bound in Great Britain by Clays Ltd, Elcograf S.p.A.

A CIP catalogue record for this book is available from the British Library

HARDBACK ISBN: 978–0–241–71273–3
OM ISBN: 978–0–241–71274–0

Penguin Random House is committed to a sustainable
future for our business, our readers and our planet. This book is
made from Forest Stewardship Council® certified paper.

To my father, Malachy, who told me the stories.
And my mother, Deirdre, who taught me the truth of them.

'Fuil os a chind ag eigmigh
Caillech lom, luath ag leimnig
Os eannaib a narm sa sciath,
Is i in Morrigu mongliath.'

'Over his head is shrieking
A lean hag, quickly hopping
Over the points of their weapons and shields –
She is the grey-haired *Morrigu*.'

~ Annals of Leinster

A Note on Pronunciation

There are a multitude of ways to pronounce Irish names and places, depending on regionality and the quirks of early translators. I have stayed closest to how I was told the stories growing up.

Characters

the Tuatha Dé Danann (*too-ha day dan-nan*) **– Tribe of Danu**
the Morrigan (*mor-i-gan*) – goddess of fury, also called Badb (*bive*), Nemain (*nev-in*) and Macha (*mack-ha*)
the Dagda (*dag-da*) – chief god of the Tuatha Dé Danann
Ogma (*oh-mah*) – champion of the Tuatha Dé Danann
Manannán mac Lir (*mon-an-nawn mack ler*) – god of the sea
Nuada (*new-ah-dah*) – King of the Tuatha Dé Danann, and later Nuada of the Silver Hand
Ernmas (*ehrn-vass*) – mother of the Morrigan
Ériu (*air-oo*), Fódla (*foh-lah*) and Banba (*bahn-va*) – triplet sisters of the Morrigan
Brigid (*bridge-id*) – a younger member of the Tuatha Dé Danann
Bres (*bress*) – a half-Fomorian son of Ériu and husband of Brigid
Dian Cécht (*dee-an-keht*) – physician and healer
Airmed (*arr-med*) – healer daughter of Dian Cécht

Cian (*cee-uhn*) and Miach (*mi-akh*) – sons of Dian Cécht
Credne (*creg-na*) – the tribe's blacksmith
Crón (*crone*) – the tribe's whitesmith
Goibniu (*guv-noo*) – the tribe's carpenter
Firgol (*feer-gol*) – a druid
Lugh (*lu*) – half-Fomorian grandson of Dian Cécht and
    later King of the Tuatha Dé Danann
Cermait (*cer-mid*) – son of the Dagda
Buach (*boo-ock*) – one of the women of the tribe and Lugh's
    wife
Mac Cécht (*mack keht*), Mac Cuill (*mack cu-ill*) and Mac
    Gréine (*mack gray-nuh*) – later Kings of the Tuatha Dé
    Danann
Meche (*mec-ha*) – son of the Morrigan

the Fir Bolg (*feer bulg*)
Eochaid (*uck-hid*) – King of the Fir Bolg
Sreng (*sr-ng*) – champion of the Fir Bolg
Niet (*netch*) – great-great-grandfather of both the Fir Bolg
    and the Tuatha Dé Danann

the Fomorians (*foh-more-ee-ans*)
Indech (*in-deckh*) – King of the Fomorians
Balor (*bah-ler*) – champion of the Fomorians
Ethniu (*e-hnu*) – daughter of Balor, and Lugh's mother
Rúadán (*rou-awn*) – young son of Bres and Brigid
Domnu (*dov-nu*) – the Fomorians' goddess

the Milesians (*mill-ee-zhans*)
Mil (*mill*) – King of the Milesians, a people from the south
    of the world
Íth (*ee-th*) – brother of Mil

Amergin (*avergin*) – poet and new leader of the Milesians

Áed Rúad (*eye-dh roo-ad*) – one of the three High Kings of Ireland and father of Macha

Líadan (*lee-a-dan*) – Áed's wife and mother of Macha

Macha (*mack-ha*) – daughter to Áed, later High Queen and the Morrigan in another form

Cimbáeth (*kim-baw*) and Díthorba (*jee-hur-vah*) – Áed's cousins and joint ruling kings

Lugaid Laigdech (*loo-ud lie-deckh*) – a chieftain killed by Áed

Rechtaid Rígderg (*reckh-tad ree-derg*) – son of Lugaid

the People of Connacht

Medb (*mave*) – Queen of Connacht and once wife to Conchobar

Eochu Feidlech (*uck-hu fedleck*) – Medb's father and once King of Connacht

Tinni mac Conri (*tin-ee mack cun-ree*) – Medb's second husband

Ailill mac Máta (*al-il mack maw-ta*) – Medb's third husband

Finnabair (*fin-ahv-ir*) – Medb's daughter

Ferdiad (*fair-dee-ah*) – a warrior and Cúchulainn's best friend

Fráech mac Idaith (*fray-ukh mack idah*) – a young hero and love of Finnabair

Amadán (*ah-madin*) – Ailill's fool

Nad Crantail (*ned crandil*) – a warrior

Láríne mac Nóis (*law-ree-ne mack no-ish*) – a warrior of Munster

Mesgegra (*mess-geg-ra*) – King of Laigin

Calatin (*cal-a-din*) – a warrior of Mide, slain by Cúchulainn

Ethnea (*e-hnee*), Ethlend (*e-hlend*) and Ethnen (*e-hnen*) – Calatin's three daughters

Cú Roí (*coo ree*) – King of Munster, slain by Cúchulainn

Finnbhennach (*fin-ve-nack*) – a white bull

the People of Ulaid

Conchobar (*kon-kho-var*) – King of Ulaid

Cathbad (*kath-vad*) – a druid

Cúchulainn (*koo-chull-in*) – the king's nephew, also called Sétanta (*shay-dan-da*)

Deichtre (*dech-tin-e*) – Conchobar's sister and mother of Cúchulainn

Fergus mac Róich (*fer-gus mack roh-akh*) – formerly the king

Deirdre (*der-dra*) – a young woman promised to Conchobar

Leabharcham (*le-vor-kham*) – a poet and Deirdre's guardian

Naoise (*nee-sha*) – a young warrior and Deirdre's husband

Daire mac Fiachna (*dah-rah mack fee-uck-na*) – a cattle lord of Cooley and owner of the Brown Bull

Rochad mac Faithemain (*ruck-had mack fah-he-vahn*) – a young warrior

Súaltam mac Róich (*soo-al-dav mack roh-akh*) – the human father of Cúchulainn

Éogan mac Durthact (*oh-wen mack dur-tha*) – King of Fernmag

Others

Buchet (*bu-khad*) – a cattle lord

Odras (*od-dras*) – wife of Buchet

Crunden (*crun-den*) – a farmer and husband to Macha

Fir and Fial (*feer / fee-al*) – Macha's children with Crunden

Scáthach (*scaw-ha*) – famed warrior and teacher of warriors

Aífe (*ee-fa*) – Scáthach's sister

Uathach (*ou-hock*) – Scáthach's daughter

Locations

Murias (*mur-ee-ass*), Findias (*fin-dee-ass*), Goirias (*gwir-ee-ass*), Falias (*fah-lee-ass*) – four cities in the north of the world, once occupied by the Tuatha Dé Danann

Mag Tuired (*moy-tura*) – the plain of pillars and locations of two battles in the west of Ireland

Árainn Mhór (*ar-ran vore*) – an island off the west coast of Ireland

Tír na nÓg (*teer na nohg*) – land of the young, the other world to where the Tuatha Dé Danann pass over

Ulaid (*ull-lew*), Connacht (*con-ockht*), Laighin (*lie-in*), Mumhain (*moo-an*) and Mide (*mee-da*) – the five provinces of Ireland

Cruachan (*croohan*) – Medb's fort in Connacht

Emain Macha (*ev-in mack-ha*) – Conchobar's fort in Ulaid

Tír Eoghain (*teer oh-win*) – land to the south of Ulaid

Mureteimne (*mwir-hem-na*) – birthplace of Cúchulainn

Dún Scáith (*doon sky*) – Scáthach's fortress in Alba

Finnabair Sléibe (*fin-ahv-ir shlay-va*) – a mountain named for where Finnabair died

Miscellaneous

the Stone of Fál (*faal*) – the coronation stone for the King of Ireland

Uaithne (*ou-an-ha*) – the Dagda's harp

fidchell (*fih-hel*) – a game of strategy similar to chess

geas (*gyass*) – a magical binding, an obligation or prohibition

the Gáe Bulg (*gay-bulg*) – a many-barbed spear

Samhain (*sow-win*) – the festival marking the end of the harvest season and beginning of winter

Cailleach (*kyle-yeukh*) – a witch

Prologue

They called me the Morrigan and a great many things besides. Phantom Queen. Battle Crow. Hag. But the Morrigan will do. I was one of the Tuatha Dé Danann, a tribe of people they would later call gods. Our story has been told a thousand times. A thousand times a thousand. And each telling a wound. With each version they stripped me away, like willow whittled to strips. They twisted my story in with the story of the land; named rivers for where I washed my feet, mountains for where I laid my head, leaving nothing of me behind. They wove me into the tales of a boy hero, made my life the weft to his warp, a small embellishment to his most mighty of deeds. I was the seductress who tried to woo him. The crone who tried to warn him. The crow that guarded his death.

How little they knew.

It was bad enough when it was the poets showing off their skills reciting my prophecies from memory. But then Ogma showed them how to write. And write they did. The calves they slaughtered for skin to fill with black ink to tell the story of their God. They tied me up with him, too, placed my life in a timeline that led to his birth. Or wrote me out entirely because I didn't fit their narrative. I was too messy. A warrior *and* mother? A seductress *and* crone? Poet *and* prophetess? No, no, no. Be neater. Be smaller. They reduced me to an old woman wailing for the dead. But I was so much more than that.

I was magnificent. I was multitudes.

Trying to tell my story is like trying to hold the smoke of a forest fire in your hands or force an ocean into a cup. I resist. I re-form. How could they succeed when even I didn't know who I was from one moment to another?

I was the storyteller for my people, the documenter of their deeds. Yet no one has told my story. But I will try to tell it now. In my own words. My own voice. Shrill though it is.

It begins, as all the best stories do, in darkness.

I.

Of my time before our voyage, I remember little. My first
real memories are of the sea and the creaking of the masts,
the taste of salt on my tongue and the wind in my black
feathers as I scattered myself to the air to watch the three
hundred-strong armada of the Tuatha Dé Danann cut
through the dark waves like talons through flesh. I don't
know if we had sailed for seven years, seven times seven,
or seven times seventy, only that we were, at last, on our
way home. We had been in the north of the world learning
arts and magic and a people more skilled, more shining,
never had existed. Why we had left the land those many
generations past, no one would tell. But I know why we
returned. The land called to us, a song sounding deep in our
bones that no magic or arts could match. Home.

My mother, Ernmas, would tell me stories of the land as
she plaited my hair in nine thickly woven strands. Her voice
would call me down from the air and I would sit at her feet,
in the form of a child, and listen to her tales of a land more
beautiful, more fertile, than any in the world. I have only
fragments of that time. Her voice, soft and deep. Her smell,
of milk and grain. And a feeling that, like an anchor, called
me back to the ships. Love. A fierce, animal love I knew
from the moment my heart fluttered in her belly. There had
been, she would tell me, three of us, a trio of wriggling baby
girls fighting inside her. But when the birthing came, only
I arrived, screaming.

'Hush, my warrior babe.' Warrior she called me. For she believed I had fought my sisters even before birth to live.

I can still feel them inside me sometimes, my lost sisters, whispering to me. And so, as I lived where they had not, I channelled them, became them, lived the lives they should have lived. Maiden, mother, crone. Warrior, poet, queen. Everything a woman could be, I became it all for them. And more.

At night, my mother would wrap me up in soft animal furs and my sisters, Ériu, Fódla and Banba, the triplets born five years before me, would curl themselves around us and she would whisper stories till at last we slept. In the day, she stood at the prow of the lead ship, pointing the way, her face slick with salt water and eyes shining with hope, while my sisters sang the winds that caught our sails and hushed the waves that crashed at our sides and tugged at the oars. All the while I circled overhead, watching. My sisters and I shared a mother but not a father. Theirs had been one of our kings, left behind, and like him they were quick to laugh and warm of heart. Oh, how I longed to be as light and happy as they were.

Who my father was, well, that depends on who is doing the telling. Some say it was an old god we left behind. Others say it was a druid who charmed my mother into bed with his words. Me, I don't much care for whom. After all, who truly knows who their father is? Fathers don't push you out of their belly, covered in blood. One grunt and they've done their job. No, I'd take mothers over fathers. Mothers and kings.

One day, as the early light of morning turned the grey clouds golden, I saw what we had been waiting for. Land. A moment later, my mother and sisters saw it too, and the cry went up, taken from lips to lips. *Land. Land. Land.* Those who had been sleeping jumped to their feet, and oars that had lain still were taken up again, dragging us through the waves towards the shore.

The first of the fleet emerged from the dark cloud I'd created to hide our approach and thudded into the seabed with such force that a mountain was formed in its wake. Hundreds of ships came in behind it, like a school of whales beaching themselves on the rocks. We landed on the west of the land and by the time the ships had come to a halt, we'd carved a chunk out of the coast.

'We're home,' the Dagda said, gazing up at the grey cliffs obscured by mist.

The Dagda was our great father, a giant even by our standards. Arms like the oak-felled oars that had brought us here and a belly like the two pigs he had carried with him all the way. The long journey had done nothing to wither his flesh, and he was as plump and rosy-faced as the day we set sail. With a smile that lit up the gloom, he grabbed his staff in one hand and his cauldron in the other and leapt over the rails of the ship, splashing into the waters. He laughed, diving through the waves like a bull seal, the salt water slicking his golden beard.

Nuada, who was our king at the time, chosen for his skills with navigation, shook his head at his irrepressible brother. By rights, he should have been first ashore to claim the land for the tribe. But he was a generous man and a good king, unthreatened by the Dagda's antics. He knew he had his brother's loyalty. He had all of our loyalties. His only weakness then was a tendency towards vanity, which he tried to hide. Though I often caught him looking at himself in the reflection of his bronze sword, flexing his lean muscles and delighting in the way they moved under his shimmering skin.

'Wait for me, brother,' Nuada shouted, diving head first into the waves like a salmon come home to spawn.

Ogma, the last of the brothers, leant over the edge of his ship and dipped his fingers in the water. He brought them to his mouth, licking the brackish tang from his fingertips.

'What sweetness is this? You can keep all the mead of Gorias. Never a more welcome drink has passed these lips than this.' Honey-tongued, sweet-mouthed they called him. He did love to talk.

'No time for words, brother,' the Dagda called back. 'Get your arse on to land.'

Ogma shrugged, and stepped off the deck and into the water, as if he were stepping into a stream to cool his feet.

One by one, the rest of the tribe followed, jumping off the ships and into the waves. My mother and my three beautiful sisters. Credne, Goibniu and Crón our smiths. Druids, poets, warriors, craftsmen. Each more skilled than the last. Then came the beasts: our bone-white horses and red-eared cattle, too beautiful to leave behind. Some rode the animals to shore, holding on to their manes or their horns as they kicked up the foam of the waves with their hooves.

'We're home,' they said. 'We're home.'

They were giddy with the relief of it, splashing water at each other like children, throwing seaweed into the air. Years of wandering at sea and, at last, they were on solid ground. This land had been ours once, but we had left and gone searching the world. And now we had returned.

Only Dian Cécht, our healer, seemed unhappy to have arrived. He didn't like getting his robes wet and demanded to be carried above the waves by the oarsmen. Eight oars were laid over each other to create a litter for Dian Cécht, and he was ferried to the land.

While all made their way to shore, one of the youngest men of the tribe waded away from the land, deeper into the waves that crashed against the rocks. On our way here, he had spent more of his time in the sea than on the boat, just as I had spent more of my time in the air. While the others looked ever south, their eyes straining to see a hint of land, he gazed across the waves to where the clouds and sea became one. He swam with the fish and wrestled with squid that followed our boats and was never happier than when being dragged through the waters on the fin of a whale.

'Manannán,' the Dagda called after him. 'Where are you going?'

'I want to see what's beyond,' he shouted back.

And with a smile, he disappeared beneath a wave as high as a fort wall. It would be a hundred years before I saw him again.

I was last to step foot on the land, long after the others had wandered deeper into the oak forests that covered everything but the shores. I took on the form of a red-haired girl on the brink of womanhood. I tried to mirror the likeness of my mother, but where she was all soft curves like rolling hills, I was made of angles, as sharp and jagged as the cliffs. I looked at my body, at the edges of me, marvelling in how there was now a line between where I ended and the world began. For the first time, I felt contained. I took an experimental, wobbling step forward, and walked on to the land.

Pain. Stabbing, piercing pain set my senses alight. And as the blood from the cuts on my soles seeped into the ground, I awoke. I sometimes wonder if I didn't truly exist till that moment, my toes flinching against the needle stabs of the shale. That all before that moment had been nothing but a story my mother had told me.

As I stepped foot on the shore, I had my first vision of a time not yet come. I saw my family, their golden bodies slicked not with salt water but with blood. I saw the land's future stretching out ahead, clearer than I had seen anything across the waves. A future of war and blood and oppression. A future of pain.

I would later become used to the jagged, splintering undoing that came with a prophetic vision. It would become so familiar that it was often hard to know when I was experiencing the present or seeing the future. But that first vision terrified me.

I breathed in, gasping, taking my first conscious breath as a woman, lungs aching with the cold air, nostrils burning with the scent of rock and moss and salt. My heart punched in my chest, a pounding in rhythm with the thrumming of the earth below me. I dug my fingers deep into the cutting soil, talons retracting into soft fingertips, and knew why we had spent all those years journeying, knew the meaning of the word my family had been crying out over and over. Home.

2.

They say King Eochaid of the Fir Bolg, the people who called the land theirs then, dreamt of our coming: dreamt of a great flock of black birds coming from the depths of the ocean to settle on the land. He awoke, sweat-slicked, shaking in fear, and called for his seers before the dream vanished like mist. They puzzled over the meaning of it for days, while on the other side of this island, unbeknownst to them, Nuada set us all to work building a new fort on top of an ancient hill.

The magic and skills each of the tribe had learned became magnified with this new purpose. Or perhaps it was because we were now home that our powers expanded? The Dagda had always been strong as ten men, but now he could flatten hills with a stamp of his foot, raise mountains with a hand.

'Would you look at this,' he shouted, laughing as he stuck a finger into the cold, hard soil and stirred it like you would stir stew.

'That's nothing,' my mother said. She laid her hand over his and out of the soft, dark soil he had turned, tall green shoots burst forth.

My sisters fell to their knees and copied our mother. Ferns and bracken unfurled between their fingers. They marvelled at what they had done, staring at their hands and the new power they held, and laughed as they summoned up life from nothing. Barley, grass, wheat all grew under their soft touch.

'Sister,' Banba, the youngest of the triplets, called to me. 'Come. Come, see what you can grow.'

My sisters all looked alike: each one graceful and golden-haired, with pale, soft skin and rosy cheeks. Their hips were wide and their breasts heavy. It was said they could make even a crone fertile. And yet, as alike as they were in appearance, they were different enough in character. Ériu was cunning and careful, always waiting to make her move. She had been impulsive once, when a prince on a boat of silver seduced her to shame. She gave herself to him without ever knowing his name and he left her with child and without a word. During the pain of the birthing she swore to all the gods she would never act without thinking again.

Fódla was a dreamer, with a head filled with thoughts of tomorrow and tomorrow. Though she often found that when she reached the place she had been dreaming of it bored her, and she was quick to find a new dream.

Banba, the youngest of the three, was a little reckless, a little wild, though she fought hard to hide that from the others. She had a simmering temper and none could predict when it would erupt. Sometimes, she could resist even the most ruthless of teasing and other times, she would explode like a cracked stone in a fire and beware any in her way. I liked her best.

I knelt beside Banba and touched one of the green shoots she had caused to rise from the earth with the tip of my finger, curious to know how it felt. As soon as I touched it, it shrivelled and sank back into the soil.

'What have you done?' Ériu, the eldest, said, swiping my hand away, for fear that I might curse her creations, too.

'I . . . I don't know,' I said, looking at my hands as they had looked at theirs, only I looked at mine in dread.

'Just stay away from the crops,' Fódla said. She went to lay her hand on my arm in reassurance, and then stopped. If I cursed plants, perhaps my touch might curse her too.

I slunk away from the tribe to the edges of our encampment and there, I tried again, hidden so my attempts could not be seen or mocked. I took on the form of my sisters, turned my sharp, granite features soft and beautiful, and shook out my wild dark red hair to golden strands of silk. I did as they had done. Laid my hands on the soft, damp soil and called to the earth below. The soil remained dark and still. I curled my fingers into the dirt, dragging, clawing at it, and my calling became a silent scream. A single spiked shoot burst out of the soil like a spear. A single yellow flower like a tiny star breathed open. I reached out to touch it and it bit like a snake. One of the plant's barbs had pierced the flesh of my fingertip. A bead of blood blossomed and fell to the ground. I smiled at my creation. A plant that could make you bleed. That would do.

'Make way, oh, my family, make way!' Ogma the honey-tongued cried out.

He carried a giant yew tree thrown over one slim shoulder, its gnarled bark and splayed branches dragging behind him. He spun, sending red berries flying, and the tribe had to duck beneath the whipping branches. 'Never a tree more beautiful have I beheld,' he said, spinning in the opposite direction, forcing the tribes to their knees again. 'Or had the strength to be holding.'

'Put it down,' said Brigid, another woman of the tribe. 'And stop with your messing.'

Brigid was light and delicate, her limbs as slim as a child's. She had a soft, round face and hair the colour of a hot coal and was, it was believed, the most beautiful of the women of the tribe, though I found little appealing about her. Her skill was with healing of animals and she could breathe a spark into a roaring fire.

Ogma threw the tree to the ground and jumped up on it. He slapped the wood beneath him, as though he was slapping a woman's backside. 'The spears we can make from this mighty tree will shred flesh and shatter bone.'

Brigid laid a hand on the dark bark and stroked it as you might a beast felled after a hunt, gentle and grateful. 'You should have left it in the earth. We have no use for spears.'

'Not yet,' said Nuada. 'But soon enough.'

He was right. Playtime was all well and good, but battle was on the way. I could smell it in the air.

On the ships here, we had been equal. Sharing the work, the food, the stories. Men and women had rowed alongside each other, tended to the ropes together. And yet now, it seemed, there were men's jobs and women's jobs. Men took up roles that needed strength, building walls, chopping down trees; though two women working together could easily do in half the time what one man took a day to do. Women tended to the animals, the gathering of food and weaving, tasking themselves with the patience required for growing and crafting, though any man of the tribe could have done the same. But this line they drew to divide up daily life seemed to make them happy. Each of them knew on instinct their role and where they belonged. Each of them but me.

I was the only one, it seemed, with the skill to change my shape.

'How do you do that?' Brigid asked me as I shifted from a grey she-wolf to a girl.

I shrugged. I no more knew how I changed my shape

than I knew how I breathed air into my lungs. I thought it, and it happened.

'Does it hurt?' she asked.

'A little.' That was a lie. It hurt more than a little as my bones broke and mended themselves in new shapes, as tendons tore and restitched. But I was accustomed to it.

That this power was mine alone only made me feel less sure of myself, as if my ability to become anything meant I was nothing. There were no edges to my power. I had no domain that was mine alone.

'Shame it's not much use to anyone then,' Brigid said.

We worked in the day and told stories at night. But I was no good at any of it. Any wall I tried to build collapsed as soon as someone laid a hand on it. Any cloth I wove, came undone in an instant. I had been forbidden from going near the crops. And as for stories, I knew only prophecies of death and darkness, which none of them wanted to hear.

I tried to change as they were all changing. I grew into a young woman. I wore the shoes Goibniu made for me, crafted from the softest calfskin, but they strangled my feet so I would tear them off me as soon as they were strapped on and instead walked barefoot. I tried to bind my hair in intricate patterns as my sisters did, but it always unravelled and returned to the same nine plaits. For a shapeshifter, I was remarkably unbending.

I couldn't settle as they had done. I was too restless. Too wild. There was a nameless hunger swirling in my belly, and nothing I could eat or drink could quench it.

'Give over,' Brigid said, taking a break from her weaving to pull an apple out of my hand.

I had been helping my mother unload apples from the boats; great woven baskets full of them.

'That's for the stores,' Brigid said. 'We'll have nothing left for winter if you keep eating your way through it like a locust.'

Brigid was one of the Dagda's daughters, younger than me by decades, though she often spoke to me like I was the child.

'Stores? Why do we need stores when we have the Dagda's cauldron?' I said.

We had brought with us four treasures from the islands of the north, each gifted by the wisest of druids to protect us. The Dagda had been given a cauldron by the druids of Murias, which never went empty, no matter how many mouths it fed, though the joke went that he was the one doing most of the feeding from it. From Findias, Nuada had been given the Sword Undefeated, a blade that shone as though made of light. Once drawn, he had been told, it must slay whoever it was raised against, and there was no escaping its wrath. Manannán had been gifted the Spear of Striking from Goirias: as thick as his thigh though light as a hair. No battle could be won against he who held it and it never missed its mark. Though he had taken it with him into the waves. And at last, from Falias, we had been given the Stone of Fál, a pillar the size of a small child. It would, the druids said, cry out the name of the rightful ruler of our homeland. And true enough, when Nuada had been crowned, the Stone had cried his name like a woman in ecstasy.

'We can't rely on the old magic for ever, Badb,' Brigid said, her smile an upturned triangle.

They called me Badb then. Crow. Brigid thought it was clever and cutting, but it didn't bother me. I liked crows. More than I liked Brigid. Crows were cunning and vengeful. Never forgetting. Never forgiving.

Brigid was gentle and sweet and soft. Everything she did was graceful, her steps like dance, her voice like twittering birdsong. Around her, I felt clumsy and loud. I tried to grab the apple back, but she pulled it out of my reach, laughing like a brook. My talons itched under my skin; my teeth lengthened.

'Hush,' my mother said kindly, laying a cool hand on my cheek. The heat of rage that flickered in my chest was snuffed out like a candle flame. My mother was the only one of the tribe who could soothe me. They said she could calm angry oceans and quench volcanoes, but the only use she ever made of that power was to quieten my anger. 'Go take care of the horses,' she said. 'And my darling girl, try to be happy.'

That is all she wanted for me, from me. Happiness. For her, happiness was such a simple thing, which bloomed as easily as flowers and grains. She always smiled as though she knew a delicious secret. If only I'd known it, then perhaps I too could have been happy.

I left the rest of the tribe at their work and headed out to where the horses had been settled to graze. They didn't turn away from me or roll their big eyes at my restlessness, for they were restless too. Energy coiled in their tight muscles ready to burst forth. In those early days, the only time I felt at peace was when I ran barefoot with the horses as they got used to the soft, wet turf under their hooves, my heart pumping in time with theirs. Whenever I stopped running, the hunger caught up with me.

It was cold, this new land of ours, a cold that cut through to your bones. Ice covered the earth and rain came at you sideways, each drop a needle to your cheek. I heard some of the men talking of going home, longing for the warmth of their hearths and women back where we had come from. Dian Cécht could often be heard complaining about how he missed the conversation of the old druids, for he believed none here to be his intellectual equal. Even Nuada gazed back out over the waters to the west. But there would be no returning. I would make sure of that.

I waited till all were asleep and flew back to where the ships rose and fell with the crashing waves. I put torch to the sails and with a kiss of breath sent the blackness across the land to let the Fir Bolg know we had returned. I wanted them to come, armed and angry. I wanted there to be battle. For I knew that if the tribe spilt their blood for the land, it would bind them to it, as I was already bound.

They awoke to the smell of charcoal and heat like a summer's day as one hundred ships were devoured in flames.

'Who could have done this?' Nuada said, staring at the black, smoking wreckage of what had once been our armada. 'Who destroyed our beautiful ships?'

'Whoever they were,' Dian Cécht said, 'they have condemned us to this land for ever.'

'Well, I guess there's really no going back now,' the Dagda said, slapping Nuada on the shoulder.

And as the black clouds rolled east, Eochaid, the King of the Fir Bolg, knew his dream of invasion had been made real.

At last, on the morning of the thirtieth day since our landing, a figure appeared on the horizon as the sun rose. With my keen eyes, I saw he carried a mace as tall as himself and wore armour made from toughened calfskin. A champion if ever I saw one. Behind him stood a band of warriors, their weapons sheathed, but sharp no doubt. I blinked and images danced behind my eyes like shadows cast from firelight. Spears. Battle. Blood. My mouth watered as if I had not eaten or drunk for days.

I opened my eyes. 'They are here.'

'The fearsome Fir Bolg come at last,' the Dagda said, brushing dirt from his hands.

'What do you think they want?' asked my mother, lifting a pale hand to shield her eyes from the sun's beams.

'Same as us,' Nuada said, joining us at the edge of the camp. 'The land.'

'Will they fight us for it?' I asked, my palms prickling with sweat.

'They will,' Nuada said.

'But they're our family,' Brigid said, her pink lips trembling in worry. 'Didn't you say they were our family and would welcome us?'

We and the Fir Bolg were kin from way back, all of us great-grandchildren of Niet. While we had gone north to become enlightened, they had gone south and become slaves, forced to heft bags of soil day and night, earning them their name. Men of Bags. Whereas the Tuatha Dé were light and lean of limb, they were heavy and strong as bulls, with skin like leather and skulls like rock.

'And tell me, fair sister,' the Dagda said to Brigid, 'who fights more than families?'

'Bres,' Nuada said, calling on one of the younger members of the tribe, 'go speak with them. Tell them we will allow them to keep half of the land – the rest is for us.'

I spat my displeasure on the ground and stood aside as Bres walked forward. Bres was only half Tuatha Dé, born of my sister Ériu and the prince who seduced and then abandoned her. Years after his birth, Ériu learned the truth about his father, that he was one of the Fomorians,

17

our ancient enemy from lands beneath the sea, and her shame burned afresh. None dared speak the name of the Fomorians in her presence, for fear of her cool wrath. Her hatred of his father didn't stop her loving her son, however. And in truth, Bres was loved by all but me. He was one of the most beautiful of the tribe, and so naturally Brigid had made him her husband, two beautiful fools together. Bres was so beautiful that all things in the land would come to be measured in how like Bres they were. A horse you would keep for stud would be called Bresly, a field ripe and ready to sow would be Bres-like. Perhaps Nuada thought a beautiful face would win them over. But a fair face often hides a wicked heart.

'Why him?' I said, sneering at Bres. 'I will talk to them, for wasn't it me who summoned them here?'

Nuada turned to me. 'You burned the ships?'

I met his stare, silent and unashamed.

'No,' my mother said, her hand pressed to her chest as though in pain. 'Tell me it wasn't you.'

I didn't understand. 'This is our home. The home *you* promised us. Why would we have need of the ships?'

She shook her head as though ashamed of me.

'It is done now,' Nuada said. 'But it is clear she can't be trusted. Bres will do the talking.'

Bres called for his chariot and three of his men, and they rode to meet with the Fir Bolg. I grabbed a spear and ran behind them, hopping from one foot to the next, eager for it all to begin.

Up close, the Fir Bolg didn't look much different from us. A little squatter perhaps, a little heavier. It was in their movements where the similarities ended. The people of my tribe were swift, as if their bones were made of air. Whereas these men of the Fir Bolg moved as if still weighed down by the bags they had carried during their enslavement.

'Welcome, long-lost brothers and sisters. I am Sreng, champion of the Fir Bolg.' His voice was unlike ours too. It was deep as an echo in a cave.

'And I am Bres, of the Tuatha Dé.' Bres bowed in greeting, his arms flowing back like swan's wings, but never taking his eyes off Sreng's face.

'What brings you to our land?' Sreng asked, unflinching.

'It is *our* land,' Bres replied, straightening again. 'Though I suppose we can share it.'

Sreng laughed, though there was no wit in it. 'You can, your arse.'

'You wouldn't laugh if you had my gift of prophecy,' I said, seeing again the flickering glimpses of what was to come. I felt my pulse quicken as I saw Sreng, broken, on his knees. A hunger I could not name gnawed in my belly and I dug my talons into my palms to stop myself from clawing at his skin.

Sreng looked me up and down; his eyes seemed to drag at my clothing as if trying to see beneath it. 'A tribe that sends armed women and pretty boys to do their talking is not one to be feared. Why don't you fuck off back to where you came from and fuck your prophecies while you're at it.'

'Ah, it has come to this so soon,' Bres said with a sigh. He put Nuada's offer to them. 'Give us half the land or prepare for war.'

Sreng didn't need to consult. He had the answer ready. 'We choose war.'

He returned to his king and I sharpened my spears for their heads.

3.

Nuada had the tribe ready themselves. For three days, Credne, our blacksmith, set the forges blazing and the ringing of swords and spearheads being struck cut through the air. Dian Cécht prepared his healing herbs, bragging about how he could bring any of our fallen warriors back from the dead. And the Dagda played his harp to keep spirits light and courage strong.

For three days, the men stretched their limbs, checked and rechecked their shields. Their bellies bubbled with fear and excitement, eager to face the Fir Bolg in battle. I, however, needed no armour, no spears. I had my claws and my cry.

'Why are we waiting?' I asked Nuada. 'The longer we prepare, the readier they become. Let me go, my king, let me bring destruction down upon them as they sleep.'

He laughed at me, clicked his teeth at my battle lust. 'Hush, Badb. The battle will begin when we are ready and when it does, it will be glorious.'

He wouldn't think the battle so glorious if he'd known what was to come. Hundreds of our people slain. His own arm hacked from his shoulder and a new king on the throne. I saw it all, but I stayed silent, for I hungered for the fray as I had never hungered for anything. Only the blood of my enemies could quench my thirst and I knew it made me a monster.

Nuada turned from me and instructed his men to ready themselves. I couldn't wait that long. My hunger was rapacious. While the leaders put their heads together and talked strategy, I flew over our enemies, showering them in blood, screeching so they could get no rest night after night. They set their sorcerers against me, and I laughed. Their arts were no match for mine. By the time the Fir Bolg set out, they were weak and exhausted. Sleep, the greatest weapon that warriors forget to keep sharp.

Perhaps it was to humour me, or because he trusted my power of prophecy, but Nuada had me choose the location of the battle.

'After all, you've seen more of the land in your night-time flights.' He wagged his finger at me, as if I was a naughty child sneaking out to play, rather than a creature of fury wearing down our enemy so that our people might stand a chance in the slaughter that was to come.

The Dagda smiled across at me, his lips glistening beneath his thick beard. We sometimes shared a bed, and he knew better than to unleash my ire. And yet, he wasn't going to contradict Nuada either. I closed my eyes and reached into the future that lay ahead. I saw it clearly, the blood and bones, the wails of the dying, and all around the battlefield I saw broken pillars, like old men's teeth, remnants from a people who went before all of us. Had I spoken a different name, would the battle have gone differently? Had I told him to meet the Fir Bolg in a southern valley or atop a hill in the north, would the hundreds who were to die, have lived? If I'd chosen a riverbank for our battle, would there have been less slaughter and would Nuada have remained whole? All I knew was that the land was hungry for blood and so was I.

I looked across the gathering and saw my mother's face. Her expression was one I could not read. Pride at my finding this new place among the tribe? A gentle warning to hold my tongue? It was as inexplicable to me as the reading of the clouds.

'Mag Tuired,' I said. The Plain of Pillars. And our fate was sealed.

The armies lined up on either side of the plain, man after man like a forest of flesh, ripe and ready for slaughter. The ancient pillars looked on. We sent our poets out first to recount the deeds of our champions, each trying to outwit, out-astound and out-terrify the other side.

'My man once crushed a hundred warriors with nothing but his little finger.'

'That's nothing, mine once strangled a hundred times a hundred warriors with naught but one of his nose hairs.'

It was never long before the battles were left behind and their balls came into it.

'Our man's balls are so big they shake the earth when he drops his breeches.'

'Well, our man's prick is so huge, it drags behind him all the way from one end of the land to the other.'

Battles have been won with words. A poet's skill can save a thousand lives. But not today. Wits were too equally matched. Deeds equally worthy. Balls equally huge. The poets returned and the champions stepped forward. King Nuada himself was to lead the charge, neither precious enough, nor cowardly enough, to stand at the back. His armour shone like salmon skin as the sun rose over the plain, the ragged pillars sending shadows chasing after the assembled hosts, an echo of what was to come.

We were evenly matched in strength and in number, though the Fir Bolg had weapons the like of which we'd never seen. Hooked shields, venomous spears and sharp swords with blue blades. Black armour that swallowed the light. Our weapons were made of bronze and though they shone like the sun at dawn, they blunted easily.

'Bring me back their weapons,' Credne said, filled with envy at their arms.

'Go out there and bring them back yourself, smith,' the Dagda spat back, tightening the straps on his armour. It was shaped like the lean muscles of a youth, and the flesh of his stomach squeezed around the edges.

'But then, who will be here to patch up your breastplate when you burst out of it?' Credne placed both hands on the Dagda's fine gut as if cupping a woman's pregnant belly.

The Dagda poked him in the backside with his shield for his cheek.

'Do you hear that, my friends,' Ogma said, flicking back his long blonde mane and raising a hand to his ear.

We heard nothing. The hammering of metal and the stripping of spear shafts had stopped at last.

'That is the lull before battle. The hush before death. Soon, our ears shall ring with moans and the hiss of dying breaths. We will hack their limbs. We will take their heads. And where their blood shall spill, flowers shall be made.' He paused, pleased with himself. 'I really should write some of these down.'

As a black night became a grey morning, the armies assembled for the counting. Warriors faced each other across the ice-covered plain, their breath like dragon smoke. Some were glad for the cold, for it hid their shaking fear. Our satirists got to work then, stirring up the battle lust.

'Who among you will bring shame to the tribe? Who will be first to shit their breeches and run? Is it you? You?' They pointed at the assembled tribe.

'Not I,' the warriors cried out in reply. 'Not I.'

'Then get out there and prove yourself a warrior!'

The tribe lined up and I pushed my way to the front. Shoulders pressed against shoulders. I could smell the sweet tang of sweat from the warriors around me. I heard their hearts beat and their breath come heavy and fast. And then came the moment Ogma had spoken of. A quietening. Hearts that had been thudding skipped a beat, breaths that had been panting were held. The fear that had been shaking limbs and drying mouths faded as we focused on the space between us and our enemy. The space between us and death.

The horn sounded. Feet like thunder, roaring like an ocean, the warriors of the tribe moved across the plain. Blade met bone, shield met skin, and the battle began. Limbs were hacked, heads cracked, flesh opened up like flowers, petals falling to the earth. I danced over the host, hopping from spear to spear. I leapt on to the back of their chariots and flung the charioteers off into the mud. I sank my teeth into their flesh and my talons into guts. I was in every strike and every stab. In every cracked bone and shredded tendon. I sucked in the screams of the dying and spat them back out and my shriek could be heard in every corner of the land.

I sank the nails of my thumbs into the eyes of a man, blood pouring down my hands like the juice of a ripe fruit, and I laughed as he screamed in pain. I was made for this. Not for building or growing. Not for storytelling or for song. This. Battle and death and blood.

My mother fought too, as women did then. Though she stayed at the rear, slinging stones and blinding our enemies.

'Badb! Come, stand with me,' she called out as I scudded above, but I ignored her calls.

My sisters stood on the cliffs with the druids, singing up a storm and spitting curses on the warriors below. They too called as I swooped over their heads, gesturing to a place by their sides.

'Stand with us, our sister. Add your voice to ours.'

I closed my ears to their cries and dove into the fray. I tore limb from torso, head from neck; none who stood in my path lived. The cold, hard earth churned into bloody mud. There were no sides any more, no them and us, just the wild eyes of the man in front of you, come to kill you before you can kill him.

Nuada unsheathed the Sword Undefeated and walked forward, swinging the blade in great loops either side of him, carving up the air and any man unwise enough to be in his path. While Sreng, champion of the Fir Bolg, armed with his giant mace, its tip made from a fallen star, took down nine men with each sweep.

The two champions made a path through the slaughter to each other. Sreng rolled beneath Nuada's sword and came up, his mace swinging. With a wet, tearing sound, the mace struck Nuada's sword arm, cleaving it clean from his shoulder. Nuada stood dumb, looking down at the stump where his beautiful, precious arm had been. Sreng raised his mace over his shoulder, ready to finish the deed and end the battle. But Aengaba, one of our allies from the north who had followed us here, jumped forward, taking the blow on his own back. His spine was turned to dust under the power of Sreng's mace, his heart crushed like an egg. The Dagda and fifty of his men dragged Nuada from the field, while the melee closed in around them. And all the time, I circled overhead, singing rage.

I saw Eochaid, King of the Fir Bolg, stumbling around

at the edges of the hordes. Our druids had put on him a mighty thirst and he was scratching at his throat, desperate for any drop of liquid. I saw him press his face into the mud and suck at it. He scooped up handfuls of horse piss and brought them to his lips. But nothing could quench the dryness of his mouth. Driven mad by it, he staggered away from the battlefield in search of a drink, but no stream could quench it, or river soothe the burning dryness. I found him, bent over a puddle, trying to cup handfuls of grey water into his mouth. But every drop fell between his fingers, bringing only dry, cracked skin to his parched lips.

I jumped on to his shoulders and whispered in his ear. 'You should have run when you dreamt of our coming.'

I tore his throat open. At least he wouldn't be thirsty any more.

The battle was won but not yet over. They had lost their king and were in disarray. It wouldn't be long before it was a total massacre and Sreng knew it.

The Dagda knew it too and took pity on them. 'Come,' he called out. 'Enough blood has been spilt this day. Let us make peace.'

Sreng looked around at the host. He was a champion, not a ruler, and yet with King Eochaid dead, rule had passed to him. He could see it in the eyes of his men, in the shaking heads of the women. Enough. We've had enough. Let no more die today.

'What do you offer us?' Sreng asked.

'We offered you half of this land when we came and you chose war,' Nuada said. 'We could drive you into the sea. But, in honour of how well you have fought, we will give you one fifth of this land for the one fifth of my body you took when you had my arm off. Choose your portion.'

27

Sreng chose a province in the west and the Fir Bolg never bothered us again.

After the battle the Dagda's cauldron overflowed and Ogma moulded history with his tales, but the battle lust clawed at me still. The bodies of the slain were not yet cold and I longed to fight again. I knew, now, the source of that hunger that had gnawed at my belly and the restlessness that made my bones itch. I knew my purpose. I had been made for war.

I travelled the battlefield, stripping bones of flesh and skulls of eyes. Those on the edge of death, I freed of their pain. I drank from the pools of blood spilt on the soil. I feasted till I was sick with it.

In my scavenging, I came across a twitching body; pale, soft-limbed, lying face down and using what little strength it had left to try to free itself from the mud. I rolled the body over, ready to suck that last drop of life from it, and found myself staring into the blinking eyes of my own mother.

The side of her head had been crushed, her jaw broken. White bone stuck through the flesh of her face, and yet I knew her. How could I not know her? Her eyes moved wildly, as if looking for attackers still coming. Blood bubbled from her lips as she tried to speak.

'Fight,' I shouted at her, as though her dying was a choice she had power over. 'Don't leave me.'

She raised a hand to my cheek, its curves settling against the hollows of my face. Her touch had always been cool, but now it was ice cold. I had been too occupied with my feasting to have noticed she wasn't among the revellers in the court. I'd not even thought to look for her, for I believed that she would always be there, like the mountains that looked down at us or the earth beneath our feet.

'You were astonishing,' she croaked and I felt a flush of pride hotter even than the rage of war. 'Terrifying.' I saw it in her fading eyes. Fear.

'Don't try to speak. I will take you to Dian Cécht,' I said, pulling her into my arms. 'He can heal you.'

She shook her head and the effort sent her coughing.

'So much power,' she said when she could breathe again, and I think she was no longer aware I was with her. 'I never knew how much. If I'd only known. I should have . . .'

Her eyes snapped into focus again and she grabbed my arm, her fingers finding strength to dig into my flesh. 'Your voice is your power. Never turn it on our people. Never.' Her dying words were a binding. A geas. Break it and destruction would follow.

Her hand fell limp and slid from my arm and her eyes went blank. Around her body, white flowers burst into bloom and the ice that had covered the ground melted away, as she gave the last flicker of her life to the land.

I held her to my chest as my heart burst behind my ribs, pressing my lips to her face, and kissed and kissed her, as if I could breathe life back into her broken body. I could have prevented this. I should have prevented this. I should have stayed by her side, rather than throwing myself into the battle. The only men I should have killed were the ones who set their sights on her. This was my fault. The ecstasy I had felt in the undoing of men, in the tearing and shredding of flesh, was gone, replaced with an aching pain deeper than the seas that crashed against the rocks. I sobbed, and with each sucking breath I drank in anger and agony as if drawing it up from the soil around me. I cracked myself open and felt not only my mother's pain, but the pain of the land itself. I felt it all. Every pinch, every slap, every heart broken. Every punch, every broken bone, every skull crushed. My mother's pain and the pain of every woman who had been and who was to come. I drowned in their agony. A thousand years of fury flooded into me, filling me from my head to my fingertips. The anger and anguish of uncountable women swirled inside me like a hurricane. When I could take in no more, I breathed out, and my breath became a howling shriek. The screech of every cry let out in the dark and every whimper kept silent in the day. I wailed and my wailing became a storm. Crows spiralled and danced on the currents, looping above my head, gathering up the strands of my red hair till I rose above the land, my hands dripping my mother's blood on the soil.

When there was nothing left in me, when my throat was raw to bloody and my lungs empty of air, I fell to the wet, sucking mud on my hands and knees next to the body of my mother. Where there had been a hungry gnawing, there was now a swirling, howling storm inside me. I wanted to fight and scratch and rend and tear. To crush and break and flay. My very essence was rage. I was mad with it. A thousand years of battle wouldn't be enough to drain it. And yet there was no enemy left to fight. There were no more warriors to face. No more battles to be won. The Fir Bolg had been defeated. Peace had been made. And I was alone with my pain.

Before, the fury that had consumed me was formless. Untamed. Now, it was distilled and flint sharp. And it had a name. Grief.

4.

It was a week before I could face returning to the tribe, days and nights spent deep in the forests screeching and wailing, tearing at my hair and skin. Ancient trees cracked as though lightning-struck under the fire of my fury, the ground beneath my stamping feet opened up and valleys were formed. I dug deep down into the earth and screamed into the darkness, and the very heart of the world boiled.

I changed shape – wolf, heifer, eel – trying to find some form in which I could forget myself. Anything but a woman. Anything but my mother's daughter. It was only in the form of a flock of crows, my soul scattered into a hundred parts, that the pain waned.

It was in this form that I flew over the land and saw a new structure being built, a barrow being raised up to house the bodies of those lost in battle and allow their spirits to pass over into the world beyond; a land of beauty and light I knew of only in stories and believed to be a lie told to children. Great stones were piled up on top of each other and the bodies of our slain prepared. And yet my mother's body was unmoved, rotting, liquefying, her flesh being stripped off her bones by scavengers. Why should others be honoured while she was left to decay? Why should they pass over to whatever dream of a world lay beyond, while she passed only into memory? It could not be. I forced myself to return to human form, taking the shape of a woman, now fully grown, and pushed the anger deep down inside me so that I could trust myself to do as my mother had bid me – not to use my power on my people – and only then did I find my way back to the fort.

When I entered, the celebrations were underway; the Dagda was moving through the throng keeping everyone's cups full, Ogma stood on a table, reciting poetry of the great deeds of those gone. The men of the tribe lay about, comparing their wounds and exaggerating their deeds while the women sat and listened and cried for their lost sons and husbands. Nuada was not among them. Had his wound festered? Had he died along with the thousands of others? Would his body be placed within the barrow being built?

Spilt mead swilled with vomit on the floor of the hall; they had been at this for days. My stomach lurched. I almost unleashed everything on them, my own destruction be damned. But I felt a gentle hand on mine.

'Little sister,' Banba said softly, taking my hand in hers and stroking the talons back into place as my mother used to do. 'Though you are not so little now, I see. Where have you been?'

My sisters gathered around me, their gentle faces full of concern.

'We were worried about you,' Fódla said. 'Worried about what you might . . . do.'

'Do? What do you mean?' I shook Banba off and rubbed at where her fingers had left white marks on my skin.

'Mother was the only one who could cool that temper of yours,' Ériu said. 'And now she is . . .'

'Rotting in a field,' I said. 'While you flush your cheeks with mead. Why has she not been buried? Why has her body not been returned to her people?'

'Dian Cécht said . . .' Banba started, but her words shrivelled under my stare.

'What? What did that ulcerous old druid say?'

I felt a swell of rage build in me. Where had Dian Cécht been as my mother lay dying in the mud? Where had his exalted healing been then? Had he reserved it only for kings and warriors, while women and boys were left to die?

'That her death was an offering,' Ériu said, pulling her shoulders back as though proud, as though the sacrifice had been her own.

'Did you see the flowers?' Fódla said, her words slurred with the drink. 'So beautiful. And they say the ice that covered the land has melted into lakes because she gave up her life force. The land has come to life. It's what she would have wanted.'

I felt my lips harden into a beak, ready to peck out her tongue. What my mother would have wanted? What shit Fódla talked. What my mother would have wanted was to live a long and happy life and see her daughters become mothers and grandmothers. To see the home she had dreamt of for years become rich with life.

'Won't you come sit with us?' Ériu said. 'Come, tell us your tales of the battle. The men say you were mighty fearsome.'

'Ogma even said they would have lost without you, though don't expect him to say that to your face,' Fódla said.

'He's calling you our battle crow,' Ériu said, proud of me perhaps for the first time.

I looked over to where Ogma was standing, people of the tribe sitting by his feet as he wove his story, one hand waving, shaping the air around him, the other holding a horn cup that splashed mead on the floor. He glanced my way, perhaps feeling the sting of my stare, and raised his cup in my direction. As if that scrap of praise, that crumb of recognition, was enough for what I had done.

'Or if not tales from the battle,' Banba said, sensing my mood, 'come and share your stories of mother as we have been doing. Come, sing and cry as we have sung and cried these past days. We know how you are feeling.'

Banba's eyes were red and puffy, and pale tracks cut through the battle dust still on her face as it did on my other sisters'. They were offering to share their pain with me, and in sharing, to lessen it. And yet I wanted none of their kindness, none of their sympathy, for how could they feel what I felt? They had each other, I had only my vengeance.

'Where is Dian Cécht?' I said, turning my back on all three. 'I want to speak with him.'

'We haven't seen him for days. He and Nuada are held up in his workshop.'

I pushed my way through the gathering, desperate to be free of the noise, ignoring all who called my name.

'Come, eat,' the Dagda said. 'You look half-starved!'

I had no appetite for food.

'Come, listen,' Ogma said. 'I was just getting to the bit where you savaged ten men!'

I had no appetite for stories either.

Dian Cécht's workshop had been built at the edge of the fort. Walls made of stone and a roof of hardened reeds. A dried skin marked with a protective symbol covered the small doorway. I pushed it aside. It was dark and hot and no air moved inside save for ripples of steam coming from a pot cooking by the fire. I raised my hand to my nose to ward off the stench that emanated from it. I had revelled in the stink of death and decay, but whatever magic Dian Cécht was cooking up was unnatural.

34

Nuada was seated on a small stool, with Dian Cécht on his knees in front of him, slavering a thick unguent over the stump of his arm. The druid's grey-tinged lips moved in wordless spells. On the floor beside them lay an arm made of silver. The two men startled at my arrival.

Dian Cécht stayed on his knees, the ointment dripping from his hands on to the stone floor, while Nuada leapt to his feet. It was as if I had come across them in an act of lovemaking. The druid was dressed in folded white robes, the hem of which was black with grime from unknown sources. His hair and beard were white, but his teeth had turned brown and so he rarely smiled. He was small for one of our kind, slim, with long, nimble fingers that moved like spiders' legs and eyes as dark as guilt. Many a man and woman of the tribe owed their life to his administering, and yet we neither of us trusted each other. When I looked at him, I saw a future in which he destroyed a part of me, something I loved, but it was clouded in shadows as he tested his powers against mine.

He hated me, or feared me, though it amounted to the same thing. And in return I hated him. His magic came from potions and ointments. He had to cook up his spells in a pot, to dig around in the dirt for roots and rotting things and crush them under a full moon or on the first day of spring. They were fleeting, ephemeral. Whereas my power came from somewhere else. It flowed through and around me and could be accessed with a word. Words Dian Cécht would never know.

'What is it?' Dian Cécht snapped.

Nuada wrapped his cloak around himself. I saw then that Sreng's blow had damaged more than his arm. It had damaged his pride. Nuada who had taken so much sweet pleasure in his beautiful body, now hid it from sight. I saw a flash of a future with Nuada on the throne. Careful, cautious, so distracted with finding a cure for his arm that he would not care for his people.

'My mother,' I said.

'What about her?' Dian Cécht got to his feet, slowly, stiffly, as though his knees were pained. Did his own herbs not work on him?

'Why has her body not been moved to the barrow? Why have the rites not been spoken over her?'

'Her sacrifice was needed,' Dian Cécht said. 'Her soul is now part of the land. It will not pass over.'

A rush of furious protests caught in my throat like fish bones. I could not speak. My voice, my power, had deserted me.

'I . . . but . . .'

'But what?' Dian Cécht snapped.

'She was my mother.'

'Many mothers died,' he said, his mouth a cruel sneer. 'Why should yours be so different?'

I felt my talons press at the skin of my fingertips. Nuada stood and laid a hand on Dian Cécht's shoulder. His skin was damp with a glistening sweat. Even over the stench of the stewing herbs I could smell the stench of rot.

'I am sorry for your loss, Badb. But many died and not all can be honoured. I don't think there is a poet alive with the skill to remember every name of those we lost.'

I remembered everyone. Every name before and every name to come.

'I pray that we will never see such a battle again,' Nuada said.

What a fool he was. The battle of Mag Tuired was only the beginning.

'This is a place of healing,' Dian Cécht said, spittle stretching between his dry lips. 'Go. Go back to your corpse picking, Badb.'

He shooed me out of his workshop as though I was a sparrow pecking at crumbs.

I wanted to hurt them both, crush them to dust, and yet my mother's geas bound me tighter than any rope. I hissed and spun on my heel.

Nuada was weak. Afraid. If he stayed on the throne, our people would dwindle away to less than the Fir Bolg, to nothing. The only tale told about us would be of the battle on this day. But I saw a future for us, with stories told and long remembered. Someone else would need to take Nuada's place on the throne. One who could stir their bloodlust as the handmaidens stirred the Dagda's cauldron. One who could unsettle them and make their skin itch and bring me my revenge.

And so, over the next few days, I whispered to my crows who carried my secret to the air.

The land demands a new king.

The whispers were picked up by the women tending to the cows.

The land demands a new king.

And then in turn whispered it to their husbands, as they lay together at night.

The land demands a new king.

By the time the last stone had been placed on the barrow, the whole court was saying it. The land demands a new king. Another would have to take the throne.

Nuada tried to ignore the whispers. He called for the harpers to play and the poets to sing. But like a waking storm the whispers quickly became deafening. In those days, our kings ruled only for a short time, their kingship a cycle like any other. When the time came, they were expected to stand aside. And Nuada's time had come.

When the demands for Nuada to stand down could no longer be ignored, an assembly was called. The tribe gathered in the fort hall and a buzz of anticipation pulsed through all present. It had been some time since we'd had a new king.

Nuada sat on the throne, his one good hand a white-knuckled claw on the armrest, as a man might cling to a cliff edge. Then with a sigh, he let go.

He raised his hand. Silence descended.

'My family, my tribe,' he said. Even his voice was an echo of what it had once been. 'I have heard you. You deserve a strong king. A whole king.'

He tossed aside his cloak, revealing an arm cast of silver which had replaced the one Sreng had hacked from him. It was a thing of beauty. Nuada held it up and gazed at his own reflection in its burnished surface.

'My time has ended. Now, tell me, who should rule?'

Of the three brothers, only Ogma had yet to take the throne. And many thought it was his time.

'Ogma, our sweet-lipped champion,' Credne, our blacksmith, said. 'Take the throne.'

'Oh, no. My time is not come,' Ogma said. 'I prefer to be at the front of the battle poking my spear into my enemies, rather than at the back pointing at things.'

Before we had come to the land, the Dagda had been our king. And many wished for those times again.

'You, the Dagda, our great father,' Goibniu, our carpenter, said, 'the throne is yours by rights.'

'Oh, no,' the Dagda said. 'Not again. The Stone of Fál

doesn't sing my name. I still have too much eating, drinking and fucking to do to spend all my days measuring out grain.'

Who, who would take Nuada's place?

'I could rule,' I said, my voice barely a whisper.

The discussion continued around me. Who was strong enough? Wise enough? Who could recite the tales? Who would the Stone cry out for?

Me, I thought. Me! I could defeat every man here in battle, I could protect them from any threat as I should have protected my mother.

'I could rule,' I said, my voice low and cracked.

The women around me turned, assuming I was making a jest, but their faces grew pale when they saw the thin stick line of my mouth, my chin held high, though my hands were shaking at the thought of being seen.

I could stay with the women. I could stay quiet and soft and clever. Or I could take a step forward into the world of men. A world of noise and hardness and action. I felt fingers brush against mine; a woman's hand, trying to hold me back. I shook it off.

I stepped forward. 'I could rule.'

The talking ceased. The music stopped. All eyes were on me.

The silence stretched out from here to the battlefield where the bones of the children of Niet were being picked clean by my crows.

'A woman?' Ogma said, slapping his thighs. 'A woman! I'd rather my horse rule.'

They burst out laughing.

'Your horse would do a better job than you,' I snapped, my voice making dust fall from the bent sticks above our heads.

39

They covered their ears but didn't stop their laughter.

'You should not laugh!' I screeched and the stones around the fire cracked. But still they didn't stop.

'Hush, woman,' Nuada said, covering an ear with his one good hand and laughing along with them.

When my mother had hushed me, it was because she had wanted to keep me safe. When Nuada did it, it was to keep me small.

'Your shrieking served us well on the battlefield but now is the time for peace.'

Did he know that I was responsible for starting the whispers calling for him to give up the throne? I swallowed down the bile that rose in my mouth, pushed back the screech that pressed against my teeth and stared at Nuada. I could kill him, I could tear off his good arm and beat him about the head with it, I could tear out his heart and sink my nails into it. I moved towards him and felt myself pulled back, as though held in place by unseen hands. Nausea roiled in my stomach and my ears rang with piercing cries. I tried to push forwards but felt my skin burn as though reaching into a fire. It was the geas my mother had placed on me rising.

I stepped back, let my talons shrink once more beneath my skin. I could not hurt him. And yet, I did not need to. I took comfort in the future I saw ahead for him. Seven years lost in the obsession of regaining his arm, seven years before the throne would be his once more, but only for a season. That would be better punishment than death now.

I bowed to Nuada and kept my voice low. 'As you will it.'

One day, I would rule, I swore it. I would have to use skills I did not yet possess, I would have to plot and manipulate and kill my way to the seat of kings. I would have to think and act as a man does. My time would come, and then the tribe wouldn't laugh.

So, if they would not have me as their ruler today, then I would find them the king they deserved. If they thought they could have peace, I would find them a king who would stir them to battle.

I wove my way through the gathering. My sisters were watching the excitement, passing whispers and looks that said more than words.

As I pushed past them, Banba grabbed my wrist. 'Don't let the men anger you. They only do it because they fear you.'

She and I were the most alike. I believed that perhaps she even looked up to me, though I was the younger sister. She had told me she longed to join me on the battlefield with a spear in her hand, but she knew only spells, not battle feats. She and her triplet sisters were made to bring life, not death.

'You would make a fine leader, it's true,' Ériu said, tucking a strand of my hair behind my ear. 'You should have a son and teach him how to lead as I have done with Bres.'

'Or find yourself a husband and rule through him. That is what I shall do,' Fódla said. 'Once I find myself a worthy man.'

Banba laughed. 'Our Badb, tamed by a man. I'd rather no king than that.'

'But the land needs a king,' Ériu said, shocked by the idea of a land left to rule itself.

'The people could rule?' Fódla said.

They considered this for a moment as fleeting as a cloud passing across the sun and then laughed. The idea of it. A land ruled by its people. It would destroy itself.

Next to the triplets stood Brigid. Watching but saying nothing. She rubbed at her belly, and I saw a soft swell there.

41

She was pregnant, already bringing more life for the tribe. I stood behind her and laid my chin on her shoulder. She flinched at the strangeness of my touch, as I mostly kept my distance from her. Perhaps she thought I had come to seek her counsel, which she was always more than ready to give.

She leant her head against mine. 'Poor Badb, they are cruel to you. But you know only a man can rule.'

When had this become the way? Hadn't we once followed Danu, a goddess, not a king? Hadn't men and women once been equal? But as we settled the land, something shifted. As we built walls to defend us from attack, so the men appointed themselves the guardians of those walls, and the women were forced to hide behind them. What had been done in the name of protection, continued in the pursuit of dominance.

I felt power thrumming in Brigid. More powerful than me perhaps, and yet she never used it. She kept herself small and quiet. I hated her for it. I looked over at Bres, Brigid's husband, son of my sister Ériu. He was laughing with the men at cruel jokes poorly told. None ever dared joke at his expense, for his ego was too delicate and his blade too sharp. Now, there was a man who could be pushed to break any peace.

'How about your beloved Bres?' I whispered. 'Is he not strong? Is he not wise?'

'Oh, the strongest. Wise too, but . . .' Brigid looked down, a blush of shame on her pale cheeks, 'he is not fully of the tribe.'

'Even better,' I said. 'For the Fomorians will be mighty allies. What say you, Ériu?' I said, turning to my sister.

Her golden eyes lit up as she looked over at her son, drinking with the other young men of the tribe.

'Bres!' Ériu shouted, silencing the chatter. 'With Bres as

king, we can strengthen our relationship with the Fomorians. So should we ever need their help in driving the Fir Bolg further into the sea, they would answer our call.'

I admired her, for she was turning her shame into a strength. Bres's birth had made her a source of whispered gossip in the tribe. But should he become king, no one would dare tell the story of how she opened her legs for a Fomorian, our ancient enemy, whose name she didn't even know.

'Yes,' Brigid said, stepping forward, away from me. 'And the child I carry in my belly can be fostered to the Fomorians to deepen our bond with them.'

Yes, the shout went up. Bres as king. Bres. Bres. Bres!

Bres stepped forward. He wasn't as cunning as Ogma or as vital as the Dagda, and yet his beauty lit up the halls. He smiled at his name being cheered, as if it was only natural that everyone here should sing his praises. He threw back the mead in his cup and tossed the cup over his shoulder. It smashed on the floor behind him. 'All right then, I'll take the throne,' he said.

There was no resisting it now, but Nuada held on to the pretence that he was still in control. That his handing over of the throne was a choice, not his fate.

'Come then, Badb, give us your prophecy,' he said to me.

I looked into the future and saw what was to come. Words flowed into my mind and on to my tongue, though I had no control over them. *'A man born of two tribes will be the greatest king ever to sit on our throne.'*

Ériu and Brigid gasped in delight. Their boy: our greatest king.

I never lied to them. A man *would* come who was half Tuatha Dé and half Fomorian, who would bring light and joy to our people. But that man was not Bres.

'*Bres will turn champions into slaves,*' I said. '*He will build a fort that will take a thousand storms to tear down. Poets will sing of the hospitality of his hearth. He will unite our people.*'

I never lied to them. The champion he would enslave was our own Ogma, forced to spend every hour trudging back and forth gathering firewood for Bres's hearth. The fort would be built by the sweat and labour of the Dagda and it would almost kill him. The poets would sing of the hospitality of Bres's hearth, and the song would say how stingy it was. He would unite our people in their hatred of him. Bres would bring pain and punishment to the tribe, till they could take no more and they would rise up against him.

'Let us see what the Stone of Fál has to say,' Nuada said.

The Stone had been placed on top of the new barrow. The tribe proceeded out from the warmth of the hall, some carrying torches to light the way.

Banba slipped into place beside me in the procession. 'What games are you playing?' She narrowed her bright eyes.

'No games,' I said. 'I'm just telling what I see.'

We wound our way around the sloping paths of the barrow and came to stand in a circle before the Stone. It was bitterly cold and an icy wind clawed at our hair and clothing.

'Get it over with,' the Dagda said. 'I'm freezing my club off here.'

Bres stepped out of the circle and stood an arm's length from the Stone. The wind dropped. There was a heavy silence as we all waited. If the Stone did not sing his name, then he would have to die, for only a true king could touch the Stone and live. That was the way it had always been:

44

you either sacrificed your life in service to the tribe, or you sacrificed your blood to the land.

Bres tugged at the leather binding his feet. I saw his hands shaking. Perhaps he didn't believe himself so worthy after all. Barefoot now, he took a single step towards the Stone, flinching at the cold touch of the grass. He raised his foot and slowly, achingly slowly, placed it on the Stone.

Silence. I saw the Dagda's hand tighten on his club, ready to use it to crush Bres's skull. A sound like wind whistling through a cave started up. It grew louder and louder, spiralling around the hill, till it sounded like a woman crying out in ecstasy. 'Bres!' it called. 'Bres!'

We had our new king. For what does a stone know?

The Dagda lowered his club. Brigid ran forward to be at her husband's side. And all cheered and danced, spinning around and around the Stone.

'You weren't lying then?' Banba shouted, as she whirled past.

I never lied. I could have told them all what was to pass. But they didn't deserve to hear and they didn't have the wits to listen.

Bres would be the worst king ever to sit on the throne. And when they finally rose up against him, it would bring about a battle seven times more brutal, more bloody than the one we had already fought. And I would be ready.

I left them to their dancing while beneath their feet the bodies of our dead decayed.

'How so?'

'Dian Cécht crushed the boy's head with a rock.' He said it as if the punishment were nothing, that stoving your son's head in was no worse than giving him a strap across the backside.

Behind closed eyes I saw Miach's head smashed like an eggshell.

'Did Nuada avenge the boy who restored him?' I asked. 'Did his brother?'

'No, Cian ran for the hills and the old druid still lives. And is by the king's side as always.'

I spat. 'Nuada will not be king for much longer.'

The Dagda sat up, attentive and wary. 'You see Bres returning?'

I closed my eyes to see better. 'I see him returning and with an army of Fomorians behind him. Right now he is laying his case before the Fomorian king.'

'Then we'll overthrow him again,' the Dagda said, as if the last seven years of servitude had been nothing but a ball game where the teams take turns attacking and defending. 'When Bres was taken down, he cried like a baby. Even if he does go to the Fomorians they will laugh him out of their court. But, come, will you not lie down on the banks of the river with me and enjoy the sun on this day? War can wait.'

War could never wait. Hunger arose in me like heat in my groin. I licked my lips and tasted blood on the wind. The Fomorians were a greater foe than the Fir Bolg had been and they were on their way. I pushed the Dagda down and straddled him as the clouds unleashed the rain around us.

When we had finished our coupling, the sun fought through a break in the clouds and the little warmth felt good on my skin. The Dagda stood and re-tied his belt around his waist, which was thicker than it had been just moments before. With every minute, his vitality was returning to him.

'Will you come back with me to Tara?' he asked. 'There is a feast tonight to welcome Nuada back to the throne and my cauldron is already boiling.'

'If we are to defeat the Fomorians, we need a new king.'

'Well, it won't be me. And not you either,' he said, looking at me with one eye closed.

'No, not me. Not yet,' I said, looking into the distance of the time to come. 'But there is a man named Lugh. He will be a king who will put to shame all kings before him and all to come.'

'And where is this future king?'

'He is on his way to Nuada's court. As we should be.'

I stretched out my hands and called the birds to me. They took the loosened strands of my red hair in their beaks and ducked and wove around me till nine thick plaits lay around my shoulders once more. I picked up my smock, ragged and filthy, and with a shake it became a newly woven cloak of ruby red.

'Come,' I said, throwing the cloak around me. 'Let us go and welcome Lugh.'

6.

Bres, for all his meanness and cruelty, had done one thing right. Tara. A mighty fort perched on a high hill in the east, raised over the burnt bones of the people who had called this land theirs long before we had returned. The fort itself was protected by two circular walls of oak, each piece of timber the height of ten men and sharpened to a deadly point, with only a single way in or out that was guarded night and day. All forts built before were just shacks when compared to Tara. It truly was a home fit for a king. And a king was on his way.

When the Dagda and I arrived at Tara, eyes turned my way for I had not been seen at court for seven years and whispers passed from lip to lip. Where had I been? What had I been doing? And why had the Dagda brought me back?

'You look . . . well,' Ogma said, as I walked past him.

He always was a liar. I looked harder, sharper than before, as if I had brought some of my cave back in the angles of my face and the jutting of my bones. I saw my sisters near the front; they smiled and waved me to come and join them, though only Banba's smile seemed true. Ériu appeared to have lost some of her poise since her son had turned out to be a tyrant and Fódla was too distracted by the gathering to care too much about my appearance after such a long time.

I ignored them all and stood at the back, waiting for our new king to arrive.

They said that when Lugh arrived at Tara he had to nego-
tiate his way past the doorkeeper. They said the doorkeeper
asked, 'What skill do you have, for none enter the court of
Nuada without a skill?'

And so, Lugh replied, 'I am a blacksmith.'

'We already have the best smith the world has known
in the nimble-fingered Credne,' they said the doorkeeper
replied.

'I am a champion.'

'We already have a champion and that is Ogma.'

'I am a harper.'

'We already have a harper so skilled he can make dozy
men wake and the awake man sleep, and that is Abchan.'

'I am a physician.'

'We already have Dian Cécht.'

'I am a sorcerer.'

'Ach, sure, we already have loads of sorcerers. So many
I can't remember their names.'

And so they say it went till Lugh said, 'Right, well, ask
your king this. Does he have one man who possesses all of
these skills? If so, I won't step foot in his court.'

That had the doorkeeper stumped. He went and told
Nuada, who invited the youth in, for he had to see the one
with so many skills. Or that's how the story would go. Rubbish.

The truth is, the doorkeeper was already drunk from the
feasting and waved Lugh straight in. But Lugh didn't want
to shame him for it and so the story was told. But I have
no qualms with the shaming of men so I will tell the truth.
What the story did get right was that Lugh possessed all
those crafts he had promised. And more.

When he finally appeared, a hush descended on the gathering and I was quickly forgotten. Never had a youth so

beautiful been seen. Lugh glowed brighter than the sun which was setting over the high mountains in the west. His eyes were the colour of wet slate and his hair the colour of day-old blood. He was small, but walked as though he towered over all of us, as if it was his natural place to be above us. He had many of the qualities of the people of the tribe – the same glowing bronze skin and the lightness of movement – but he looked to have some of the Fomorian in him too. A thickness of limb and wideness of jaw. In many ways, he was a mirror of the traitorous Bres. But whereas Bres had been so smooth and perfect that he made your head spin to look at, Lugh had tiny flaws that made him easier on the eyes. His teeth were slightly too large, he smiled out of the side of his mouth, and if you looked very closely, you could see his skin was scarred by childhood pox. He glanced around the assembly, smiling and as at ease as if he was coming home to be greeted by old friends. He looked into the corners of the hall and saw me, fixed me with a slow, confident stare. I found my breath catch in my chest, as if I had been spied bathing naked by a stranger. Lugh's eyes passed over me, and I felt my skin vibrate as though it had been his hand that had brushed my flesh and not just his eyes.

Nuada leant forward on his throne and stroked his chin with his new hand. His silver arm was gone, and a smooth pink one now sat in its place. It bore none of the scars or toughness of his left arm and looked more like the arm of a child than of a king. The silver arm had suited him better, I thought.

'Who are you who comes uninvited to my court?'

'I am Lugh, son of Cian, grandson of Dian Cécht, fostered these eighteen years.'

Cian hadn't been seen at court since Dian Cécht had killed his brother, so was not there to deny this claim.

'Is that true, Dian Cécht?' Nuada asked his physician.

The hunched druid stepped forward. I thought of how he had crushed his son's head for shining brighter than his father. Had I been this youth, I would have kept my heritage a secret.

''Tis true the boy bears a resemblance to me,' Dian Cécht said.

This caused a ripple of low laughter in the assembly, for the youth could look no less like Dian Cécht had he four hooves and a curled tail. 'Tell me, who is your mother?'

'Ethniu – daughter of Balor.'

His announcement was greeted with a hiss. Balor was the champion of the Fomorians, a giant so feared that even his name could cause a ewe to lose its lamb. It was said that as a boy, Balor had looked into a toxic brew being made by the Fomorian druids and it caused a poisonous third eye to burst forth on his forehead. One glance from it would drain all life and energy from you. How could a creature so foul be the progenitor of the beautiful young man in front of us?

Dian Cécht whispered in Nuada's ear. A warning? A protest? Nuada waved the physician away and he skulked back into the shadows where he belonged.

'We've already been fooled by one shining half-breed, we won't be fooled again,' Nuada said.

'Ah, that I can understand.' Lugh's voice was like tree sap and I found myself drawing closer, wanting to hear it clearer. 'If it helps ease your fears, before I was born there was a prophecy that I would bring about the death of Balor. He had my mother locked away so that no man could touch her, but she, being a smart thing, found a way to, well . . .' He tilted his head and raised his eyebrows, suggestive and playful. Women around me giggled. 'She gave birth to three healthy boys,' he continued. 'But Balor, fearing the prophecy, had them wrapped in a cloak and sent off to a bottomless whirlpool to drown. I slipped out of the bundle and was later found on the sand chewing seaweed by your own Manannán mac Lir. He raised me as his own.'

We hadn't seen Manannán since we had first arrived and he had stayed in the sea. I had only caught glimpses of him dancing with his white horses in the breakwaters of the waves that crashed against the rocks in the west.

To show the proof of it, Lugh pulled a bound spear from across his shoulder and let the leather covering fall to the floor. We knew the spear as we knew our own limbs: it was the Spear of Striking which Manannán had been gifted by the druids of Goirias, one of the four treasures of the Tuatha Dé. Lugh spun it in his hand and it sang like birdsong. He slammed it to the floor, and the stone beneath cracked.

'As for my brothers,' Lugh continued. 'They were dropped into the abyss and for all I know, they are still falling. So, believe me, I have no love for Balor or any of his kind.'

Again, he caught my eye and I felt the shiver of recognition. He was like me, the last of a trio, now living for three.

Lugh's tale was met with rumbles of approval. Any prophecy that related to the death of one of our enemies was always welcome. But the tribe was still wary.

'Prove your worth to us, then,' Nuada said.

Lugh leant on his spear, scratched at his chin and chewed on the inside of his cheek. 'Well, I can prove my skill in wits by beating any one here in the game of fidchell.'

None knew what this game was. Lugh was later to teach me how to play, though the endless rules and tricks would infuriate me. I never mastered it and he would laugh at how I could win any battle but that one.

'If not wits, then strength,' Lugh said. 'Who is the strongest of you?'

'Oh, no,' the Dagda said as hands slapped at his shoulders, pushing him forward, for he was the strongest of the tribe. 'I'm too full for fighting. Besides, look at him. I'd crush him as soon as look at him.'

'Will none of you face me?'

'I'll take that bet, o lost, golden child,' Ogma said, stepping forward. He tossed the lamb's leg he had been eating aside and dabbed the grease from the edges of his mouth with a silk cloth. 'For I may not be as strong as my brother, but I am strong enough to beat you.'

Lugh only came up to his shoulder. Ogma could have crushed the boy and stripped his bones and used them to pick the lumps of lamb flesh from between his teeth.

'Choose a feat of strength and I will match it or forfeit my life,' Lugh said.

'Well, well, that is some bold talk for such a small boy,' Ogma said, patting the young man on the head so fiercely I was surprised he was not driven into the ground like a post. Had it been me patted like a stray dog, Ogma would be picking his teeth up off the floor. But this young man stood firm and let the slight roll off his strong shoulders.

'Come, young hero, come,' Ogma said. 'Seek glory and fame. But let it be said, after your death, you were the creator of this game.'

Lugh nodded his agreement of the rules.

Ogma licked his lips and looked around the hall. He

tested the weight of the throne, with Nuada still on it, which got the room laughing again, but it wasn't test enough. He picked up the Dagda's cauldron and tossed it in his hand but thought better of it when the Dagda made a small, warning twitch of his head. He placed it back and moved on. After more teeth-sucking and marching around the court, at last, he bent over and tugged a flagstone from the floor. It had taken twenty oxen to drag it in here. With a spin, Ogma flung the stone out the doors of the court. It landed fifty feet away with a thud that I felt in my belly.

Lugh looked out to where the flagstone was embedded deep in the earth, stretched his limbs as if waking from a long rest, and strode after it. The huddle of people in the court moved apart like a school of fish making way for a barracuda and gathered to watch in the doorway. Lugh picked up the flagstone as if he was picking up nothing heavier than a block of wood. With a flick of his wrist he threw it back through the doors and it landed perfectly in the hole it had come from, nearly taking off Dian Cécht's head as it passed.

Lugh walked back in, brushing the dirt from palms pink as a rabbit's nose. Ogma's glossy mouth hung slack, his eyes bulging. Never had he been beaten in a game before and here was a mere pup of a man putting him to shame. A tense hush settled. Ogma was not one who took losing well. And he was never, ever, lost for words.

'He's Balor's grandson indeed!' Ogma said, slapping the youth on his back and sending him sliding across the floor. 'If there is to be a battle between ourselves and the Fomorians, having this young man on our side will bring us a victory so glorious, even I could not do it justice in words.'

'I'm sure you'll give it a good try though,' Fódla said, a teasing tone to her voice.

She wasn't wrong. Not a single event befell us, that Ogma wouldn't write one of his bloody poems about.

Relief was like a song and soon everyone was laughing and reaching over themselves to slap the young man on the back, even though moments before they would have cheered Ogma on had the game gone the other way and he'd ripped Lugh's limbs from his body.

The Dagda kissed Lugh on both cheeks and welcomed him to the tribe. Dian Cécht wrapped his arm around the boy and welcomed him as his long-lost grandson. Watch your head around the old druid, I wanted to shout, so your brains don't end up smeared across the floor as your uncle's did.

I didn't dare touch Lugh, much as you would fear touching an open flame, so I stood at the back watching.

Nuada, too, did not join in with Lugh's welcome. Slowly, his silence became deafening. One by one, the people of the tribe pulled away from Lugh, as if they hadn't moments before been running their hands over his skin, marvelling at its smoothness.

Nuada waited till the noise died down. 'Well,' the king said, stroking his chin again with his fleshy new hand. 'He is strong. But is he skilled? Bring me a harp.'

The Dagda held up his hand. 'Wait, if he is truly as skilled as he says, then he needs a harp worthy of him. He can play mine.'

The Dagda's harp was one of his most beloved things. He would run his hands over its curves as if seducing a shy maiden. He played it before battle to soothe jumping hearts and make the men forget their fears. He played it after battle to mourn the lost and remember their names. He had even named the thing. Uaithne. But only the Dagda could get a song from its strings and he knew it.

The harp was sent for and handed over to Lugh. The Dagda bit on his lips, waiting for the fun to begin.

'I have never seen a harp so beautiful,' Lugh said, marvelling at the intricately carved oak. 'Did you carve this?' he asked of the Dagda.

'I did indeed.'

'Then you are a master and you must teach me.'

Lugh laid his long, lean fingers against the strings and we waited.

Ogma and the Dagda were nudging each other, already struggling to suppress their giggles at what a grand jape this was.

A single note ran out as pure as the first drop of rain after a drought, as sweet as the first honey of summer. Uaithne was singing for Lugh. The Dagda had never felt envy in his life – he'd had no need, for anything he had ever wanted he could make his own. And here was a young man, playing his beloved harp. The look on his face – delicious. I wished there were an artist gifted enough to capture it. He might as well have been watching a man fuck his wife.

Ogma looked from the Dagda to Lugh and back again and burst out laughing. Watching his brother also be outplayed was even more fun than throwing stones.

But as Lugh continued to play and the music swirled and danced in the halls, the Dagda softened too. Lugh might not have the Dagda's skill, but he had something else. Whereas the Dagda only played what he wanted to play, Lugh was able to sense what the assembly wanted of him and shifted the song accordingly. They called for soothing music and he played songs so calming the assembly slept. He played sad music and the assembly wept. He played happy music and they all danced and rejoiced. And I watched them all, knowing how and when each of them would die.

I saw Lugh's death too. Drowning in icy waters, his glistening skin turning blue, his pink lips gone black. I asked him later if he wanted to know when and how he would die. He laughed and said, 'Sure, stories don't die.' But they do. They die and they are forgotten and new stories take their place, just as kings follow kings.

After a while, Nuada sprang up off his throne. 'I had a prophetic dream,' he said. 'That a young man would come to us and he would overthrow the Fomorians. This is the man I dreamt of.'

There was silence. Nuada had spent a year undergoing agonies to grow his arm back, just so he could sit on the throne once more – and here he was, handing it over?

'You are the king I came to serve,' Lugh said. 'I could not take the throne from you.'

Nuada stepped closer and looked down on Lugh. 'Then take it for thirteen days, from Samhain till the Ivy Moon. By then, we will have crushed every Fomorian who dared look upon our cliffs. If, that is, the Stone will sing your name.'

Was this what Nuada was hoping for? That the Stone would remain silent and he could keep his throne?

Lugh was dragged outside and pushed towards the Stone of Fál, which had been carried with the tribe to Tara. Had anyone told him the cost should it not sing his name? Or was this another of their tests?

He stood, looking out at the impatient congregation, a nervous smile itching at the edges of his mouth. He'd come here to join forces with us, but had he imagined he would be handed the throne so easily? Had he known? I wondered again who this young man was and how powerful his magic must be to have all of us so enthralled.

He placed his foot on the Stone and at once it roared his name like a beast. The tribe joined in the roar, barking and howling like a pack of wolves. Lugh was our new king. Nuada stepped aside as Lugh returned to the hall and was given the throne. A golden torc was placed around his neck and the most beautiful slave girls of the tribe at his feet. My sisters eyed him hungrily, for each of them had secret desires to be queen of the tribe.

'Isn't he pretty?' Brigid had sidled up next to me.

I didn't answer.

'He will be in need of a wife,' she said.

I waited for her to suggest herself. After Bres's downfall, she had slipped his ring from her finger and reshaped herself as a virgin. 'Alas, I am already married to the land. But you might make a good queen?'

I looked around to see who she was talking to. Me? She couldn't mean me?

'What, and bear his children and sit at home keeping his bed warm while he goes off to war?' I spat.

'Plenty of wives go to war,' Brigid said.

She was right. Our tribe had many warrior women and plenty of them had married and borne children.

'I was not made to be a wife.'

I don't know if he heard my voice over the throng of the crowd, but he looked over at me once more. He smiled, head tilted, and raised a cup in my direction before drinking deeply. He licked the golden liquid from his lips and I found myself licking my own.

Brigid nudged me. 'You never know. You might like it.'

She winked as if she had suggested something filthy and wandered off to talk to our new king.

I would never be a wife. I could never let a man be my master. If I couldn't be ruler in my own right, I would be nothing. Or so I believed. Funny, the lies we tell ourselves. For I would be a wife and a mother in the time to come, though I didn't know it then. I would learn how to find the simplest pleasures in stroking the head of a sleeping child, of letting a man hold me as though I was the one who needed protecting. And I would know the pain that came from losing it all.

The feast went on and I left the court and walked out into the darkness. And yet, in my mind I saw Lugh's hands brushing against the carved oak of the Dagda's harp, and the wood became my own skin. The strings he plucked became the strands of my clothing, untied and falling to the ground.

I shuddered as if I could feel a cool breeze on my bare flesh and with my shudder I burst into a flock of crows, and flew away from the heat of the court and the heat of Lugh's gaze.

7.

The thirteen days Lugh was given the throne turned into a season. A season into two. Six months in which the chiefs of the tribe would gather in secret and strategize and talk. Six months with forges blazing, making more spearheads than there were fish in the sea, yet not a blow struck. Acres of oak forests were cut down to make spear shafts, which then lay in dampening piles like firewood. All the while, the Fomorians continued to emerge from their kingdom under the waves to raid our coast and take sacrifices for their goddess, Domnu. Crops died in the fields, cows went un-milked. Women were raped and their children taken for slaves. Indech, the Fomorian king, grew fat on his throne while our leaders did nothing but talk.

Lugh had little models of the warriors of both sides carved from wood and would move them around a table, as though he was playing one of his games, rather than weighing the cost of men's lives. Nuada, Ogma and, when he wasn't satiating his appetites, the Dagda, would attend to argue over what strategy to use and on more than one occasion, a little carved warrior would be thrown at a hot head. When their rage bubbled over and they slammed tables and screamed at each other, it was respected. Anger in a man was to be expected, encouraged even. Whereas anger in a woman was unwanted and unwelcome.

I had tried to keep my distance from Lugh, but I kept being drawn back to the court and back to him. I tried to tell myself it was because I wanted to be close to the strategizing, ready for war. But even I knew I was lying.

'What do you call this place?' he asked, pointing at a kidney-shaped scrap of land in the western sea on the map.

'We call it Árainn Mhór,' Ogma said.

'I would like to see it. It could be a good place for a fort, to guard against attacks from the west.'

'It would be reckless to cross this time of year,' Dian Cécht said. 'The waves are fierce. No boat would survive. You should wait till spring.'

'If no boat can withstand the crossing, then I'll swim,' Lugh said.

This was met with laughter from the men.

'Sure you will,' the Dagda said, slapping Lugh on the back. 'And I'll watch for your bones washed ashore.'

'You forget I spent my youth with Manannán mac Lir,' Lugh said. 'There's no wave that can stop me.'

This, it was agreed, was true.

'Will none of you come with me?' The men all looked at their feet or started examining their nails, none willing to risk drowning. 'Well, then, how about you?'

It took me a moment to realize he was addressing me. I met his eyes and felt my skin burn as though I had fallen asleep in the sun.

'I have heard tales of your boundless rage and that you can become any shape of your choosing. Are they true?' he asked.

On the battlefield I was without fear, but in Lugh's presence, my courage was like watered-down wine. 'They are.'

'Then come with me,' he said, taking my hand. 'We can rage and be reckless together.'

He was irresistible. And as soon as he set his will to have me, I was his.

I think he saw me as a challenge, as one might a wild horse calling out to be tamed. And tamed I was, of a sort. Standing near his light drove out the shadows that curled around my heart and his heat seemed to match the heat of my fury.

The journey to Árainn Mhór was the first of many we took. We would sneak off, far from Tara and the eyes of the tribe, and together we explored the edges of the land. We climbed her mountains and clambered through caves. Every new place we found, Lugh would stop and lay out his plans for it. On every hill he would one day build a fort, across every river he would build a dam.

One day we stood atop the highest mountain, looking out at the sea to the south. 'She's all mine,' he said.

And I think he meant the whole world.

Then he turned and smiled at me. A smile that made the ground tilt under my feet. 'All mine,' he said.

I felt myself hurtling towards him as though I had stepped off a cliff. I knew then why the women of the tribe called it falling in love.

When we returned from our explorations, he would map out the paths of the rivers and the lines of the cliffs and place his carved men on them, claiming it all for himself. And all the while, the Fomorians attacked our borders and took what they wanted for themselves.

Whispers about us crawled through the court, but most were laughed away. Why would Lugh, Lugh by the gods, who had his choice of every woman and man among the tribe, choose her? No, she is nothing but a pet to him, a tame crow that he feeds scraps to.

'Why don't you tell them?' I asked him once after he had crept into my bed at night when all others were sleeping.

'Because it's so much more fun this way!'

I tried to pull away from him, tried to escape his flame. And yet, when he would hold a hand up to silence the men around the table and ask me *my* opinion on what should be done about the Fomorian raids, my heart would flutter like a moth and I was burnt again. I only ever had one answer. Attack.

The men would roll their eyes and go back to moving their proxy warriors on their wooden boards. What did women know of strategy? What could they know of tactics? Their heads were too ruled by their emotions, their mood controlled by the moon. There were women warriors among the tribe, for sure, a few who were as good with a sword or spear as any men. And of course, there was me. None of the men would dare face me on a battlefield, though they would never say it. And yet none but Lugh wanted to hear what I thought.

Dian Cécht was always there, in the background, listening and watching like a spider in a web. He rarely said anything but would make his feelings known by sniffing loudly if ever I dared to speak. And yet when Lugh asked what he thought we should do, he had nothing to offer.

'I am a healer, not a warrior,' he would say, smiling thinly. 'I know my place.' And he would look at me and his smile would tighten.

'What's happening?' Ériu ambushed me one day as I left Lugh and the others, my ears ringing with hollow plans, frustration and impotence bubbling in me like gases in a bog. I had been avoiding the triplets, for in their voices and expressions I saw my mother and the pain washed over me afresh each time.

'A lot of talking,' I said, turning to find my way blocked by my other sisters.

'The Fomorians raided again last week and three women were taken. When will we have our revenge?' Banba asked.

'When the talking stops,' I answered.

'Lugh still hasn't chosen a wife?' Fódla asked. 'What?' she said, throwing her hair over her shoulder. 'It's as fair a question as any of yours.'

Ériu caught my eye, though I looked away. I knew that one day Lugh would take a wife and that it wouldn't be me.

Banba teased Fódla for being cock hungry.

Fódla slapped her belly. 'I'm hungry for everything.'

The sisters laughed and for a glimmering moment I let their warmth touch me, before recoiling from it as from hot iron.

'Be careful,' Ériu said, catching my arm as I turned to leave.

I laughed at her concern. 'There's no place for caution in battle.'

'I don't mean the Fomorians,' she said. 'I mean Lugh. Guard your heart as you guard your flank. Or he will steal it from you.'

I had always believed her liaison with the Fomorian prince was nothing but a foolish dalliance, but it was clear to me that he had cut her deeper than I had known. She was right to warn me about Lugh. Right, but too late.

Another six months passed and while I still savoured every moment I spent in Lugh's orbit, I sensed his fascination with me fading. The times between his visits to my bed grew longer with each day. But I found reasons to ignore the alien, twisting feeling in my stomach. It was only that I was anxious about the Fomorians' raids. Itching for the battle to start. So what if Lugh spent time with other women? We did not belong to each other. I could take other lovers too.

A year to the day I had met with the Dagda, the eve before Samhain, he and I met again on the banks of the same river. The summer had clung on long after its season, and the leaves were golden-tipped and just starting to fall. The harvest had been the richest I had known since our arrival; fruits hung heavy from branches still and were so full of juice it would run down your chin and hands. It was a time of abundance and restoration. A springtime in autumn. But it couldn't last for ever.

The Dagda was as bountiful as the land – plump and round – and he exuded all the many pleasures of the flesh. We lay down together on the sides of the mossy bank and took gratification in each other. Sinking into him was like biting down on a ripe pear, all softness and sweetness, and I took delight in it, as did he. Though I would be lying if I said my mind didn't wander to thoughts of Lugh, that I didn't think of his young, hard body even as I caressed the Dagda's soft one.

As we lay on the mossy grasses after our coupling, I asked the Dagda when the battle would begin.

'Soon enough.'

'What is Lugh waiting for?'

He shrugged. 'The weather to be right? The horses to be in the mood? Who knows?'

'I don't need an army. I could go now. I could strike down King Indech with my bare hands and end their tyranny.'

The Dagda's mouth hitched in a crooked grin. 'But what fun would that leave for the rest of us?'

Fun? Is that what battle was to these men? A game? No wonder they were happy to wait and wait, savouring the anticipation. But I had no stomach for games.

Blood-filled visions had been haunting my dreams as of late. And even when I closed my eyes during the day, I saw crimson. We had been playing for too long. The time for action had come.

'Enough,' I said, standing up.

I couldn't wait another week, another day, another moment. The time for planning was over.

'What are you up to?' the Dagda asked.

I gathered my crumpled dress and pulled my cloak around me once more. 'I'm going to start a war.'

I flew into the hall of Tara and found Lugh lazing on a pile of wolf furs, sucking the juices from a ripe plum. A young woman with deep brown eyes like a cow was wrapped around his legs. She gazed at me through long, flickering lashes. I felt my talons slide out under my skin.

Ogma sat opposite them, his fingers hovering over a carved figure of a king ready to make a move. Nuada lay, strumming a harp with his fleshy unfinished hand, while a slave girl fed him slices of apples dipped in honey. The other men of the tribe were sitting around, eating, talking, watching.

'Would you like to play?' Lugh asked me, his voice sweet as morning sleep. 'I've been teaching Buach here and she's very quick to learn. Aren't you?' He tapped her on the nose with his finger.

The woman giggled like a stupid child. I flipped the game board, scattering the little men to the ground where they lay broken, just as our enemies should be.

'Wake up!' I screeched.

The men covered their ears but I wouldn't be shamed by them, not after a full year of waiting.

'Get off your backsides and go to battle. You sit here planning and plotting while they laugh at us. You sleep while they grow fat on the meat of our cattle. Now is the time to make slaughter, smite bodies, burn their flesh, boil their bones down to make glue for our shields, make them cry out in agony as they have made our people cry. Crush, break, tear. With spears, swords or with your fucking teeth, I don't care what weapon, but take them up now and for fuck's sake, wake up!'

My face burned as if I had been slapped and tears itched at my eyes as though I had rubbed salt into them. I wiped the spittle from my mouth and tried to steady my breath.

Dian Cécht watched from the corners, his dark eyes narrowed.

Lugh bent down and picked up one of the pieces I had toppled in my rage. He held it up and twisted it in his fingers. It was the figure of a giant, with one huge eye, the lid held open by a golden ring. Balor. Lugh's own grandfather and our most feared enemy.

'What say you, Firgol? What have you seen?'

All the men in the hall looked to a young man sitting quietly in the corner. He wore the robes and face markings of a druid, though he had only a scattering of whiskers on his cheeks.

The young druid stood up and cleared his throat. 'Yes,' Firgol said, with a sigh heavier than his years warranted, 'battle will be realized.' He closed his eyes and a moment later, they snapped open, white, without the iris showing.

'*I see a fire wave of battle*,' he said, his voice cracked and growling as though coming from a beast's throat:

'Men felled like a forest.
Lugh shall revenge.
The great hero Ogma
Eager to break the phantom sea.
Warriors engaged in exacting tribute.
A plain of forts.
A milk territory where all men are free.
Nuada fierce-eyed surpassing the point of battle.'

He closed his eyes once more and when he opened them, they fixed on me, light blue and glittering with self-satisfaction. 'Battle,' he said, holding his arms out and making a small bow as though delivering the last line of an epic poem, 'will be realized.'

It was all of it horse shit. Ogma and Nuada both would die in this battle. There would be no milk lands where men were free. And yet, all the chiefs of the tribe were nodding now, listening to this pretence of prophecy, because it had come from a man.

Lugh threw the figure in the air and caught it in his fist. 'Let's get to battle then.'

There was a sudden bustle of activity. Food and drink were cleared from the tables and maps brought out. The serving girls were pushed away and the thralls called for. The Dagda arrived then, having finally caught up with me.

'Well, well,' he said, looking around at the rushing and sharpening of weapons. 'Whatever you said, it looks like it worked.'

Lugh clapped the Dagda on the shoulder. 'It's time!' He turned and pointed at Credne, our blacksmith. 'You! What powers do you bring?'

'That's easy,' Credne said. 'Any spear that snaps from its

shaft, or sword that breaks, I will give our warriors a new one. No spear point made by my hand will miss its cast. No body struck by it will be alive afterwards. The smith of the Fomorians can't do this. But I can.'

'And you,' Lugh said, spinning around to point at Dian Cécht. 'What power do you bring?'

'That's easy. Any man who is injured in battle, he will be whole in the battle the next day. No druid of the Fomorians can do this.'

'And you, Ogma, what power do you bring?'

Ogma stretched out his arms and neck, the tendons and sinews cracking and popping. 'That's easy,' he said. 'A third of the Fomorians I shall take on my own. I will bring swift death to their warriors and make widows of their women.'

'And you, mighty sorcerers, what do you bring?'

He turned to nine men who had the powers of magic and manipulation.

They spoke as one. 'The white soles of their feet will be seen after they are overthrown by our craft and their deaths will be a relief from their cowardice.'

'And you, the Dagda?'

The Dagda looked around at the expectant faces of the men. 'The power that you lot all boast of, I will actually do. Their bones will be like hailstones under the feet of horses as I crush them with my club.' He grabbed at his balls and shook them.

This brag was met with a cheering and heavy slapping of shoulders. Men.

'And you?' Lugh turned to me; the heat of his gaze made me feel as though my skin was bubbling like pigskin on a fire. 'What power will you bring?'

No one had ever asked me before. No one had ever seen me.

I struggled to find the words. 'I will strike. I will tear. Rip. Crush . . . I will break. I will . . . I will.' My rage built and built and there were no words to capture it. 'You really want to know what I can do?'

'I do.' He said it simply, genuinely.

'Then let me show you.'

I flew out of the fort and away to the south. I was a crane, a swift, a falcon, flying faster and faster till I came to the coast. The green below me turned black and then blue, till I was far out over the open waves. I dived down, deep beneath the waves as a salmon, a dolphin, a shark. And there I came to the coral caves of the Fomorians. I sought out their king and I found him sleeping.

8.

When I returned to Tara, the warriors of the tribe were still getting ready. As I strode in, holding two handfuls of flesh, they froze. Blood dripped to the ground beneath my feet, the *pit, pit, pit* of the drips the only sound.

I threw my trophies before Lugh. The men stared down at the bloody mess.

'Are they what I think they are?' Nuada asked, staring at the severed lumps.

'The more important question is not *what* they are,' Ogma said, 'but *whose* they are?'

'They are the balls of Indech. The king of the Fomorians,' I said, wiping my wet hands on my red cloak.

They all stared at me, mouths bobbing open and closed like landed trout.

'Well, that's one sure way to get their attention,' the Dagda said, laughing.

Lugh smiled. 'There's no turning back then. We will battle at dawn.'

'But you cannot fight,' Dian Cécht said to Lugh.

'What? Of course I will.'

'You're too precious. Your skills too great to be risked. You must stay here.'

This was met with much approval. Lugh had only been king for a year and the land had come to life. They didn't want to risk him in a battle, not if there were others who could die first.

'But what of the prophecy?' I asked.

'Yes,' Lugh said, pointing at me. 'She's right. The prophecy that I will kill Balor. What of that?'

Ogma slapped him on the shoulders. 'Don't you worry, little golden child. I'll bring you your grandfather's head.'

Despite his protests, it was agreed. Lugh would stay in the safety of the fort and the nine sorcerers were set to keep him out of the fighting.

'Will you stay with me?' he asked, as we went to leave.

The question baffled me. What could possibly keep me here when a battle awaited?

He scrunched up his face. 'I don't want to be bored while all the men are fighting.'

But he would have me here, doing what? Playing games? Feeding him honeyed apples? Fucking while the tribe died without me? Why would he even ask that of me? Who did he think I was?

He had other women for that.

'I'll keep an eye out for you on the battlefield,' I said, and left without another word.

Later that day the hosts mustered on Mag Tuired: the same Plain of Pillars where we had fought the Fir Bolg. The druids had thought it would bring us good luck to fight in the same place where we had once been victorious. But had they forgotten all those who had died there too?

Our warriors lined up on the edge of the plain. I could feel the fear coming off them like a stink. The Fomorian forces outnumbered ours and their strategy was stronger, too. We had been a skirmishing people, attack and withdraw, more used to fighting one on one than ranks of men at a time. They stood in tight formations and wore armour like none that had ever been seen before or since; layers of dark green scales like the skin of an ancient sea beast, and helmets that shimmered with a sheen like the inside of an oyster shell. They carried flint-sharp weapons tipped in poison from fish found deep in the oceans. I licked my lips. This would be the battle I had hungered for. This would be a battle worthy of me.

The horn sounded and the warriors charged, racing across the plain, and I soared over it all, screeching murder, turning blood to ice and bellies to liquid. The Fomorians didn't move. They simply raised their shields as we approached, creating a wall as solid as rock. We crashed into it and it was like throwing ourselves against a cliff face. With a deafening cry, they moved forward one step at a time, pushing us back and back.

So many of the tribe fell in that first attack that our blood became a river. As dusk fell at the end of the first day, the battle ceased and our wounded were dragged from the field. The Fomorians outmatched us in battle skill and in the numbers of their forces. But they could not match our magic.

Dian Cécht, whatever I thought of him, was the most powerful healer there had ever been. He and his daughter, Airmed, carried the wounded to the wells and spoke their words of healing over them, so that on the next morning, men who had spat their last blood were standing once more strong and ready to fight. Credne and his smiths had skills greater than the Fomorians could dream of. They worked throughout the night, smelting, metal striking, so that weapons that had been broken were mended and sharp and shields that had been shattered were restored.

On the dawn of the next day, as the Fomorians saw men they had known to be dead come running at them, holding weapons they had seen shattered, I saw the tendrils of fear wrap around their hearts. They had men. They had weapons. We had magic.

We learned later that they had sent Rúadán, the young son of Bres and Brigid, as a spy. Dressed as a stable hand, he had crept back to Tara and into the forge where he saw our carpenter, Goibniu, carving fifty spear shafts from a single tree trunk, our blacksmith, Credne, casting fifty spearheads at a time, and our whitesmith, Crón, sharpening each one with sand and her spit till it was sharp enough to slice a single strand of her grey hair in two. Rúadán touched the tip of one of the battle-ready spears and it pierced his flesh.

'You,' they said Goibniu cried out, seeing the boy sucking the blood from his finger. 'What are you doing?'

'I . . . I was sent to get a spear for Nuada.' Rúadán picked up the spear that had tasted his blood and held it in front of him.

Goibniu put aside his tools and approached the boy. Now, he knew that Nuada had a spear already, having carved it himself. He also knew that this boy was no more a stable hand than he was. His hands were too soft, his muscles too limp.

Rúadán panicked and struck out, pushing the spear into Goibniu's belly. There was no strength behind the thrust, but Crón had done her work well and the spear was sharp as grief. It went through Goibniu's stomach and clean out the other side. Goibniu looked down at the spear sticking out of him and Rúadán ran.

I was tearing the lungs out of a Fomorian spear hurler when I saw the boy run past me, heading for the Fomorian front line. He almost made it. But Goibniu pulled the spear clean out of his belly, hand over hand, spilling his innards to the ground, and hurled it after Rúadán. It pierced the boy through the back of the neck, severing his spine. He died before he hit the ground.

For a moment there was silence. The battle ceased. Brigid, who had been watching from a hill nearby, had seen her eight-year-old son running towards the Fomorians. She'd seen the blood-slicked spear cutting through the air. Had she been able to, she would have had it pierce her own heart. Had she been able to, she would have killed Bres before he'd ever taken her son with him.

She raced down the hillside, skidding on falling scree, and across the limbo between the two armies. A silence as heavy as snowfall descended on the hosts. None dared speak. None dared breathe. She gathered Rúadán in her arms and held him to her breast as though he was still a babe, as though she could feed the life back into him. But he was gone, and not even Dian Cécht could restore him. The water from her tears washed the blood from his body and the salt made the ground beneath them barren. She sang a song so bitter and sweet it broke the heart of all who heard it, words woven in praise of her beautiful, fallen boy. She sang of the deeds of his life, and she sang of the manner of his death. They say that keening had never been heard in the land before Brigid wept for her son, though thousands of women wailed for their boys that day.

Each day we battled. Each night, our wounded were dragged away and restored, so that slowly, the balance of numbers evened, and then tipped in our favour. And yet we still could not break their shield wall. It was like striking your head against a rock over and over.

Dark clouds covered the sun. An icy coldness sapped our strength while it only seemed to make them stronger.

'We can't last another day,' Ogma said, during a lull in the battle.

'We have to hold out,' Nuada said, wiping blood and sweat from his eyes.

'We could run,' a voice said, though I could not see who spoke the words.

'The first man to run will feel my talons in his back,' I snapped back.

A warbling, wailing cry was heard, like a crane calling for its young. We turned to see Lugh, standing one-legged atop one of the pillars. Light coruscated from him like a sunbeam caught in a diamond.

'Fight!' he cried, and his voice carried across the plain to each one of us and sounded as though he was standing next to us. 'Fight a slaughterous battle. A fierce battle. See how the sun breaks through the clouds – so will our forces break through their shield wall.'

The air was clear again, the skies blue. The men turned their faces to the sun and were renewed. We were ready. We had been fighting their battle. Now we were going to fight our way.

Spears slashed, shields crashed, swords whistled as they struck again and again. The warriors closed in on each other, sliding and falling on the slipperiness of the blood under their feet. If a warrior fell then, they were never to stand. Spear shafts were reddened, pushed through flesh and torn out to strike once more. Streams of blood ran over the bright skin of young warriors. A great many beautiful ones fell to ugly blows. It was a gory, brutal battle. But we were winning.

That was till Balor stepped on to the field. He was even bigger than the stories had said. Bigger than four of our men. Bigger even than the Dagda. In the middle of his mighty head was a single, closed eyelid and through the lid was a golden hoop, from which ran two ropes that fell over Balor's shoulders to where they were held by four young warriors. That eye, once opened, could destroy all it gazed upon. But he didn't need his eye to deal out deathly damage.

Nuada was the first to face him. He went to unsheathe the Sword Undefeated. Before he could raise it to strike, Balor grabbed him by the neck with one hand. With a sickening crunch like stepping on a twig in winter, Nuada's neck was snapped and he was thrown to the ground like a chicken bone sucked clean.

Ogma charged at Balor and was smacked aside, sent soaring away behind the Fomorians' shield wall where their warriors fell on him like maggots on rotting flesh.

Warrior after warrior stepped up and was crushed by Balor. I flew at him and was stamped beneath his feet and I lay in the mud half-dead, waiting for an end I had not seen.

'As big as you are, it's a small man who will kill you today.' That voice. As sweet as the sharpening of a sword, as the whistling of a spear through the air. Lugh was here.

'Ah, so the son of my seed has returned,' Balor said.

I found the strength within me to pull myself up out of the mud, to see Lugh, shining as bright as dawn on the winter's solstice.

'It was your cruelty that created me,' he said. 'You who had my brothers killed will now die three times for their deaths. My sword will be your destruction. My spear will drain you of your strength. My slingshot will smash your brains. Woe is he who stands against Lugh. Let the wolf packs of the Fomorians be washed away by the waves of my people.'

Lugh danced before his grandfather, leaping and flipping, performing battle feats the likes of which I had never seen.

'Open my eye!' Balor bellowed. 'So that I may look upon this chatty lad.'

The rope haulers pulled. The golden hoop lifted. The eyelid rose. Lugh closed his eyes and flung his sling, sending a stone slicing through the air. It struck Balor right in his eye. The blow was so fierce that it knocked the eye clear out of Balor's head, killing him instantly. The eye fell to the ground behind him, where it rolled around, casting its evil poison in the direction of the Fomorian forces. Half as many of them fell under the gaze of that dying eye as we had killed ourselves. They no longer had their fearsome champion. They were outnumbered at last. And yet, the war still hung in the balance.

The ragged remainders of our forces were on their knees. Broken men without hope. Without fire. My bones were broken, my flesh torn, and my muscles ached with a pain I had never known before. But I had power still. I reached for that space where the words lived, between thought and speech. I licked them on to the tip of my tongue like snowflakes from the sky, and then formed them into an incantation of stirring, of arising, of battle. I gathered words one by one and added them into the chant the way Dian Cécht added herbs to his cauldron; I wove them the way my sisters wove cloth. And when they were ready, I cast it out across the whole army.

'*Arise!*' I shouted, my voice sounding in every man's ear as though I were standing beside him.

'My kings, to battle.
Those who can strike, go seize your honour.
Those who speak battle spells, let your voices be heard.
Destroy their flesh, crush their bones.
The time will come for the singing of poems.
The time will come for the reciting of names.
Now, we must make one last, rushing assault.
Their wall shall be broken, their men taken for slaves.
I hear their screams,
I see their destruction bloom.
You will be reborn today in this red-wombed battle.
Men become warriors. Warriors become champions.
Arise now and send them to their dooms'!'

And arise they did.

The number of the dead outstripped that of the living. Blood became like a flood on the land, shattered bones fed the earth with their marrow. Then the last of their warriors threw his spear to the ground and fell to his knees. The battle was over. The land was ours still.

I looked over the churned earth: blood-soaked, shit-stained. Grass and wheat would soon grow green and gold, but for now all that rose out of the ground was bones. Severed limbs stuck in the soil, reaching out like branches.

Ogma lay, eyes open, blank and staring, the back of his skull crushed like a hollowed trunk. Nuada had been torn apart, his beloved fresh arm ripped from his body.

'Where is the Dagda?' I cried, looking for him among the dead. 'Where is he?'

'He went to get his harp back,' Credne said, coming to stand beside me. Even our smith had taken part in the last push, picking up weapons he had made for other men. 'A raiding party of Fomorians sneaked in during the battle and they stripped Tara clean.'

That bloody harp. I flew over the battlefield, sharp crow-eyes looking for the Dagda. A glint of the fading sun caught something gold. I found him, half-buried in the mud, surrounded by twenty dead Fomorians, clutching his beloved harp to his chest. His eyes stared ahead, blank, their twinkle snuffed out; his neck had been snapped. I laid my hand on his face, the bristle of his beard soft against my skin. I had thought him immortal. I had believed that, like his cauldron, he would go on giving for ever.

Those who were left standing dragged themselves home and soon the feasting began. And with the feasting, the stories.

'You should have seen me,' a warrior said. 'I took down three of the Fomorian bastards with my sword.'

'I killed ten,' another said, 'with a broken spear.'

'That's nothing,' said yet another. 'I tore the innards out of thirty of the beasts, with just my dagger.'

If you believed the tales, you'd have thought not one of us had died that day. But I looked out and saw only those missing. Ogma. Nuada. The Dagda. Our fathers, kings, my lover, gone. Brigid had turned her back on the tribe, cursing us all for her son's death, and had wandered into the wilderness to be alone with her grief. Of those I had arrived on the ships with, only my sisters, Credne, Crón and Dian Cécht had survived. I blamed Dian Cécht for not being able to bring them back. I hated him for the promise he made, that he could restore all who died. He had failed to mention it only worked as long as their heads were not cut from their necks or their spines crushed.

I wanted to feel something at the deaths of my brothers,

as I had felt at the death of my mother. I wanted to keen as the other women of the tribe did. Only an aching emptiness filled my heart and I could not find the words to sing for the depth of my loss.

'Come now, I want to hear tales of the battle,' Lugh said, his eyes glittering. Buach, his cow-eyed beauty, sat by his side, blinking up at him as though she were looking at the sun.

Lugh it seemed felt no sorrow at the death of our champions either. But whereas I was heavy and cold, he seemed to take joy in it all. As though the whole thing had been but a game.

'Your turn,' Lugh said, pointing his long, slim finger at me. 'Give us a story.'

'I have no stories of what happened here today,' I said.

'A poem then. Come now, I saw you, tearing off heads and ripping out innards. You struck fear into their hearts and poured courage into ours. You were magnificent.'

Words that would have once set my heart aglow now filled me with a shivering chill.

'I have no poems of what has been. Only of what is to come.'

I sensed my sisters tense for they knew my prophecies of old. But Lugh did not.

He leant back on his throne and stretched out his hand. 'Then tell us our future.'

'That I can do.'

The words flew out of me, through me, as though they were not mine. As though I was repeating an echo heard from far away.

'*I see peace.*
Our land, splendid beneath the bowl of bright skies.

Honeyed strength given to any who wish,
Sweet-mead worth the brewing.
The gifts of summer even in winter.
Here we will make strong places,
Spear-bristling forts that will stand till the end of time.
Here we will turn the earth and grow crops.
Here will our cattle grow fertile.
Every child, warrior strong.
Every cow, calf-fat.
Every dog, watch-dog fierce.
Every tree, spear-worthy.
Every stone, a solid foundation.
And everywhere birdsong as though a constant dawn.
Abundance in all things.
Peace for ever.'

A great cheering and stamping of feet went up.
'Wait, I see more,' I said.

They were happy now and wanted to hear it. They wanted to hear more of this honeyed peace and the calf-fat cows. But that was not what I saw. For after the time of bright abundance, I saw a time of darkness and famine.

'I see a world of turmoil.
A summer without flowers.
Cows without milk.
The sea fish-empty.
A land, hungry and barren.
Men, become cowards,
Women become whores.
Everyone a betrayer.
A deceiving time.

A dark time.
Till the end of all things.'

There was no cheering following these words. They stared, shocked and scared.

'Which one will it be then?' Fódla asked.

I closed my eyes and when I opened them I saw again the fort and my people in front of me, and not the horror that was to come. It was a jolt to see food on the table and fleshy faces staring at me, for all I had seen ahead was hunger and grieving and death.

'What?' I asked, for I had not heard my sister.

'Which future will it be?' Banba asked.

I looked at them, confused. Why didn't they understand? There would be peace, followed by war. There would be times of abundance, followed by famine. And back and forth for ever, till the end.

'Why, both, of course.'

My words sat heavy and uneasy like greasy food in a belly. They didn't want my words to be true. They wanted only the light.

'But how can both be true?' Buach asked.

'Oh, don't listen to her,' Lugh said. 'She's always much too serious.'

And while I felt my heart go cold, the tribe laughed, relieved to be able to get on with the drinking, eager to forget my vision.

When the time came, in years to come, for scribes to write my words down, many would leave out my second prophecy, wanting only to hold on to the good.

Lugh called for Uaithne and it was taken out of the Dagda's dead arms, the gold wood turned bronze from his blood. The music the harp played was so beautiful it lifted what weariness was left among the tribe. It healed them and made them whole. I understood then why the Dagda had given his life to get the harp back. You couldn't have your enemy possessing something so powerful as music like that. You couldn't let them have hope.

The night turned into day as the Tuatha Dé made a song of their mourning and I whispered the names of the dead to the darkness. The tribe might forget them, but I would not.

9.

When the feasting ended, Lugh set the tribe to work building the greatest tomb ever crafted, half a day's walk from Tara. It was to house the bodies of the Dagda, Ogma, Nuada and others who died. Great stones guarded the doorways, patterned with spirals to remind us that life is always in motion. We carved their names and lives on the stone in Ogham, thick, swift lines calling out to the years to come. They lived. They died. They were.

The tomb was positioned so that each year, the light of the solstice sun would cut a path down the passageway to light their way to the other world. I knew not what lay beyond. Maybe the tales of a land of light and life was just a story to ease our pain? Or maybe there was a world beyond this one? Either way, I believed I would never see my brothers again.

Lugh ruled for forty years. Forty years of peace and feasts and games that came and went in the blink of an eye. He had the horses put to racing for sport, rather than leading chariots, and spearheads melted down for jewellery. He turned the harvest into a season of celebration and gave it his name. He still loved his games, best of all the ones played slowly. He liked his opponents to think they were winning, right till the last move when he would strike and watch the smile slide from their face. They say he sent Bres a gift, just when the traitor believed he had escaped retribution: three hundred wooden cows filled with a deathly poison. Bres, unable to refuse hospitality he himself had never given, drank his fill and died screaming for his mother. Ériu closed her ears to his cries and did not weep over his body.

I had believed Lugh would be the finest king ever to rule, but in the end, he cared more for himself than for the land.

I spent less and less time at court, and more time in my cave. I missed the Dagda more with each Samhain that came and passed. I would still go to the river to wash each year, hoping that somehow he would find his way back to me.

'Have you heard?' Fódla said, racing up to me one day, her face flushed.

My other two sisters followed in her wake.

'Heard what?' I asked. Had the Fomorians returned? Another enemy? Were we in danger?

'Buach is fucking Cermait!'

Cermait was the Dagda's son, a man who was almost the match of his father. But I didn't understand why him bedding the beautiful Buach was such a cause of concern.

'You know, Buach. Yer one with the cow eyes.' Ériu waited for me to understand.

'Lugh's wife!' Fódla said.

Wife? I had thought Buach just another of Lugh's playthings. Despite knowing that I would never have been his wife, learning he had married stung like warm water on your hands on an icy day.

'Dian Cécht's only gone and told him about her affair, and now Lugh has said he is going to kill Cermait,' Ériu said.

'You have to stop him,' Banba said.

'Me?'

'You're the only one Lugh ever listened to.'

I laughed. 'Lugh only ever listens to himself.'

92

'Please,' Banba said. 'If Lugh hurts Cermait, his sons will retaliate. One of them, Mac Cuill, is my . . . my . . .'

She didn't need to explain. I had seen the way she looked at Mac Cuill, though I thought him weak and unimpressive.

'I will speak to Lugh.'

I found Lugh in the hall, alone and half-dressed. He had dismissed the men and sat, chin on his fist, scowling into the fire.

'Have you come to gloat?' he asked, as he heard me enter.

His words were slurred. Judging by the empty jugs in front of him, he had been attempting to drown his self-pity.

I kicked one of the jugs aside, sending it spinning across the floor. 'I've come to reason with you.'

'Reason!' He scoffed. 'You, of all people? You've never let reason guide you, only your passions. It's what drew me to you.' He closed one eye to look at me more clearly. 'What happened to you? What happened to your . . . your fire?'

How could I find the words to explain what the second battle of Mag Tuired had cost me? How losing the Dagda, Ogma and even Nuada had been too great a sacrifice, even for me.

'Forgive Cermait and Buach,' I said, changing the subject. 'Let them be happy together. You can find another woman.'

He sat back in his chair, muscled legs stretched out before him, his tunic open to the waist. 'But what if I only want one woman?'

'Then you're either a liar or a fool.'

He laughed. 'There's that fire.' He reached out his hand for mine. 'Stay with me.'

'You've asked me that before,' I said.

'But there is no battle to go to this time. Stay.'

I slipped my fingers into his hand, trying to ignore how

my skin turned to goose flesh under his touch. 'Will you promise me you will leave Cermait be?'

He kissed each of the tips of my fingers in turn. 'I promise.'

And so I stayed.

I heard a week later that Lugh crept into Cermait's hut at night and killed him without a word. He was a liar after all. And I was the fool.

Cermait's three sons, Mac Cécht, Mac Gréine and Mac Cuill, took swift revenge. I wasn't there when they came upon Lugh sleeping by the bank of a lake, speared him through the foot then drowned him, and took the throne for themselves.

When one of my sisters told me Lugh had been found, his once beautiful body now bloated and fish-feasted, I waited for the pain to come. I called to it, as you might call to lightning in a storm daring it to strike you, but I felt nothing. Just the cold after a fire has gone out.

The passage tomb was reopened, songs were sung, and Lugh's body placed alongside the bones of the Dagda, Ogma and Nuada.

'It will never be yours,' Dian Cécht called out to me, as I walked down the path leading away from the barrow after the stone was replaced. I felt as heavy as though I carried the barrow stones with me.

I turned to him. 'What do you mean, old man?'

'Cermait's sons will rule now. And after them, their sons and their sons after that. I will see to it that you never sit on the throne.'

'Kings for ever?' I asked, though I knew what his answer would be.

'For ever,' he said.

'We shall see.'

I left him, grumbling, cursing my name. My time as ruler would come, though he wouldn't be alive to see it.

As the tribe grew in number, they spread across the land, carving out portions for themselves. Forts were built to the north and south, forests cleared and put to farmland. Mines were sunk deep into the rich soil and metals extracted. Place after place was claimed and named for one of the tribe. And life went on.

One morning, I awoke to a biliousness that I couldn't ease. My breasts itched and my womb ached. I went to the river where the women bathed, hoping the cool waters would wash my ailments away. But before I could dip my toes in the water, a wave of nausea brought me to my knees. I was bent over by the riverside being sick when I heard my sisters come.

'Did you drink too much?' Ériu said.

'She can hold her drink,' Fódla said. 'It will have been the goat. I told you it tasted wrong. I feel sick myself.'

'You should see Dian Cécht,' Banba said, crouching beside me and pulling my hair back from my face.

I shrugged her off, not wanting anyone to see me in this pathetic state of weakness. I scooped up the fresh water and washed the vomit from my mouth. 'I'd rather drink my own sick.'

'Why do you hate Dian Cécht so much?' Ériu asked me. 'What has he ever done to you?'

Hated me since the day we landed here? Not saved our mother when he could have? Or perhaps I hated him because he smiled when he should frown and frowned when he should laugh? I didn't answer.

'Then go to his daughter, Airmed,' Banba said. 'She's almost as gifted as her father.'

'By the gods, don't let him hear that, or the poor girl will have her head smashed in like her brother's,' Fódla said, and they laughed as though the death of a son was nothing.

They finished their bathing and left me to my misery.

Later that day, I followed Airmed as she went on a morning walk out to the woods beyond the fort to gather herbs for her father. The sun beat down on my skin, making me want to burst out of it and fly high above where the air would be cooler, but I felt too heavy to become a bird. Instead, I became a she-wolf, stalking the woman through the trees.

Airmed wasn't a blinding beauty like many of the others of the tribe, but she had a way about her that was enticing and a voice that rivalled any. She sang as she walked, a light song I hadn't heard before. The words were a nonsense about barley, but the tune was as sweet as one the Dagda himself might have played. Perhaps he had taught it to her when she was just a girl?

Stopping by a bush of plants with yellow, disc-like flower heads, she bent down. 'There you are.'

She cut a fistful of the stems with a small knife and lay them in her basket, then plucked the head off one of the flowers, crushed the petals between her fingers and held them to her nose.

I crept closer. With my wolf senses, I could smell the scent from the flower: bitter and sweet at once.

'Tansy. It's good for migraines,' she said, turning to face me. 'If that's what ails you?'

I stood up, my long snout shortening, bent hind legs straightening, fur becoming hair once more. I had only said a few words to Airmed when she was a young girl, and now that she was a young woman, I didn't know what to say at all. Men, I knew how to talk to, if they let me talk at all. I spoke of battle and weapons. But women, I knew so little of their lives.

'Oh, dear. You look as green as they say my father did when we sailed here. What you need is . . .' She looked at the plants around us and spotted what she was after. A tall, purple plant, with a woody stem. She plucked it and walked over to me. 'Give us your arm.' She reached out for my wrist.

'What for?' I said, backing away.

She laughed, though it wasn't cruel. 'Our fearless battle crow, afraid of some lavender.' She hit me around the shoulder with the purple plant.

Reluctantly, I held out my arm for her. She tied the lavender around my wrist, weaving the stem back on itself to make a sturdy bracelet.

'There,' she said. 'Wear that for the rest of the day and it should keep the sickness at bay.'

I muttered my thanks.

'If you come by my workshop, I have stronger herbs that can help soothe an uneasy stomach.' She must have seen my hesitation, for she added, 'Don't worry, my father won't be there.'

She gave me a wink and returned to her task of seeking out plants and herbs. Before I walked away, she called out.

'Of course,' Airmed said, 'you could be pregnant.'

I laughed at the idea. But she was right.

Over the next six months, my belly swelled and became heavy as a life grew inside me. It felt as though my body wasn't mine any more, that it belonged to the tribe. My sisters cooed and fussed over my distended belly, stroking it, talking to it, excited to meet the baby. The others were less delighted, wary at what creature I might birth. I grew tired of the attention, and longed to change shape, to become an animal, a bird, a snake, anything but a human woman waddling around helpless. But I feared what changing shape would do to the baby inside me.

When I thought I could take it no more, when I was close to grabbing my spear and tearing open my flesh and pulling this thing out from inside me, the birthing began. Waters rushed from between my legs and a pain like none I had ever known erupted inside me. I thought I knew pain, for every time I changed shape, it broke my bones and tore my muscles. I had been crushed by Balor himself on the battlefield. But this was beyond that. This was an undoing. I cried out for help, and my sisters raced to my side. They half-carried, half-dragged me over to a small roundhouse at the rear of the fort, where the women all went to give birth. I had never been inside and the place terrified me. I had heard the screams coming from inside it, and not every woman who entered returned.

'It will be fine,' Ériu said, as I stopped on the threshold. 'Your body will know what to do.'

'And we will be with you,' Banba said.

I stepped inside. It was dark, with a single beam of light coming from a hole in the roof. Through this hole hung a thick strand of rope, with tight knots up and down its length. Below the rope was a bed of furs and straw. My sisters laid me down, just as another bolt of pain hit me like lightning.

In my pain and fear, I tried to escape by changing shape, but my sisters pinned me down, their strong arms holding me still.

'You can do this,' Banba said.

'I am scared,' I said. Words I had never spoken before.

She pushed my hair away from my face. 'Every woman is afraid. You are not alone.'

Fódla covered her ears as I screeched. 'Someone get her some herbs to soothe the pain, or her cries will kill us all.'

'Not Dian Cécht,' I cried.

'Don't be stupid,' Ériu said. 'What good is a man at a birthing?'

Airmed was sent for and came running in carrying a cloth bag. She had gathered and catalogued every herb in the land without her father knowing and kept the knowledge of them to herself. She stayed within the realm of women: herbs to soothe their monthly pains, roots to bring on their blood to wash their wombs of flesh that could have become a baby they did not want. Lotions to keep their skin soft and unguents to save their bones from creaking. She could cure headaches and heartaches and everything in between. And while she knew how to restore a fallen warrior as surely as I knew how to fell one, she dared not let her father know.

She knelt down next to me and pulled out a small brown jar. She put it to my lips.

'Drink. Poppy seed. It will help.'

I drank, hungrily, desperately, wanting anything to make the pain go away. The liquid was thick and sweet and burned my throat. After a while, a fogginess filled my mind and the pain eased: still there but it felt as though I was remembering it, dreaming it. I lost sense of time and place, floating away on a sea of silk.

I was given the rope to hang on to and told to hold myself up, while Ériu crouched between my legs. The pain

99

became me, and I the pain, each wave of it taking me deeper inside myself.

'Push,' my sisters shouted. And I heard the voice of every mother before me and every mother to come. *Push*. And I pushed.

Something slithered out of me and flopped on to the furs. Banba helped me lie down, while Airmed cut and tied the purple cord that connected me to this creature. Ériu picked the baby up and pushed her finger inside its mouth, as I had seen people do with newborn lambs. She held it by its feet and shook it, as you might shake the moths out of a cloth.

The child wailed, a screech so loud, so beautifully shrill, that it shook the dust from the roof.

My sisters all laughed, as the screaming child was put into my arms.

'He's her child, sure enough,' Fódla said.

He. A boy. A boy with slate-grey eyes and dark red hair, so dark it seemed black. A child who was perfect in every way. Except . . .

'What is that?' Airmed said, running a gentle hand over my son.

I looked down. Where his skin should have run smooth over the bone of his chest, there was a beating, pulsating swell of flesh.

'It's his heart,' Fódla said.

'No,' Airmed said, bending closer. 'Look. Not one heart. Three.'

Just as I had grown in my mother's womb with three sisters, so he had grown in my womb with three hearts. I held his body to mine, feeling the beat of them against my chest. I took it as a sign that he was born to love three times greater than any other child and I loved him a thousand times more than that.

I called him Meche. And as soon as he opened his eyes and looked at me, the storm within me quieted. I had no space in my body for anger, for every inch was taken up with love. Love and fear. Fear I had never known before or since. Fear that this child, who I loved more than I ever thought I had capacity to love, would be hurt. That he would be taken from me. And that I would be alone with nothing but my rage once more. A heart I thought was cold as stone burned within my chest, filling every inch of me with love.

Meche grew too quickly for my liking. If I had known the magic to keep him a baby for ever, I would have performed it. By summer he could walk and by the following autumn he was running everywhere. I followed close behind him, checking for stones that might graze his knees, bees that might sting his delicate flesh. I allowed no other child to play with him, for fear they would bruise him or taunt him. I dressed him in soft silks and rubbed protective herbs on his skin and spoke words of power over him as he slept. I gave him everything he wanted and more. I was his world and he was mine.

I built us a house within the ringed confines of Tara and filled it with soft furs, placed a warm fire in the centre and we were happy. At night, he would curl up in my arms and I would tell him the stories my mother had told me. Then in the morning, we would leave the fort and spend our days out exploring. He loved horses as much as I did and we would ride, my arms wrapped around his tiny body, him with his arms outstretched as if he could catch the wind.

He was curious about everything and wanted to look

under every stone and inside every cave. He babbled constantly, though he had yet to learn many words. And I would laugh as he pretended to hold conversations with frogs he had caught or try to sing like the crows that followed me everywhere. They loved him as much as I did. Their yellow eyes were always on the watch for any danger that could befall him.

The tribe, however, were wary of him. They saw the change he had caused in me as a distraction, or at worst, a kind of curse. They said my love for him had made me weak, when in truth, I had never felt stronger. They said he had been born without a father, that it was my will alone that conjured him. Or that he was the son of every man in the tribe at once. Only I knew the truth, but I wasn't telling, not because I didn't know, but because I didn't care. He was mine and mine alone.

The tribe knew about his three hearts but saw it as a warning rather than a blessing. That whatever he would grow up to do, he would do it threefold. If he became a warrior, he would kill three times as many as any before, be they friend or foe. If he became a sorcerer, he would have three times the power of any before and would be unstoppable. If he became a leader, he would rule three times as much land as any before, and his greed would be greater still. What would he become? What dent would the son of Badb, their battle crow, make on the land? Whispers surrounded him like a mist. But there was one whisper with barbs. That within his three hearts slept three coiled serpents.

It started as a silly taunt from the children of the tribe. They'd point at his chest and chant, 'Snakes, snakes, snakes.'

It was only his blood pumping through his veins. But they'd squeal and run away and tell their parents what they'd seen. And soon, it became a rumour, then the rumour became a story and the story became truth.

'That child should be destroyed,' I heard Dian Cécht say one day. 'The snakes slumber now, but when they awaken, they will consume all life in the land.'

Most people had the sense not to believe him, though many spat curses and made signs of protection if Meche and I walked past. I closed my ears to it all and refused to look further into the future than what the day ahead promised. I believed that if I loved him enough, I could stop any harm befalling him, and him doing any harm.

And so he grew. And I took joy in it. For the first time in my existence, I understood why women risked their lives to give birth to more children than they could feed and why the last word on many a warrior's lips as I watched the life drain from their eyes was their child's name. I focused only on the light in him: his laugh, the way he would hold my face in his podgy hands and look into my eyes.

He was as much at home in the world of men as he was in the world of women, running from Credne's forge, to learn the magic of metalwork from the old smith, to the huts where the women spun and wove sheep's wool. He would grab a hurling stick, though he barely had the strength to hold it, and chase after the older boys, then race after the girls to skip stones across the lake. His curiosity was insatiable, and there was not a rock within ten miles he had not looked under nor a cave he hadn't explored.

I chose not to see how he would overturn rocks and crush the ants he found there, or chase after rabbits and twist their necks in his hands. How he would catch salmon and watch them flap and flail on the shore, their gills gasping till they moved no more.

'If you're not going to kill it, throw it back in,' I said to him as he stood over a dying fish.

'Why?' he asked.

'Because there's no reason to let a creature suffer.'

'But why?' he asked again.

'We should only hurt those who hurt us.'

'You've killed men. Fódla told me. Did they suffer?'

I had no answer for him, for in truth they did suffer and many did not deserve it.

He looked down at the fish again. Its body curved like a smile as it twisted, gasping for breath. Meche stamped down on it, bones crunching under his foot. It went still and he smiled.

'There. It's dead now.'

There was an innate violence in him, but wasn't there in the heart of all men? It didn't mean the rumours about the slumbering snakes had any more truth than a drunken brag. And yet, the rumours grew as fast as he did. By the time he could ride on his own, everyone in the court turned their backs on him and hissed as he walked by. He was oblivious to it all; he cared for none but me and the horses we rode.

'Why don't you leave?' Ériu asked me one day. 'Take Meche away from Tara.'

'There are beautiful islands to the north, I have heard,' Banba said. 'You would be safe there.'

'And we would all be safe should the snakes awaken,' Fódla said.

I laughed at her gullibility. 'Snakes? Are you as stupid as the children? Don't you think I would know if there were snakes inside my son? Don't you think I would hear them hiss as I held him close to me at night?'

I led Meche away, dragging him by his hand. He cried,

wanting to stay with his aunts, for they had pockets full of fruit.

'We only want what is best for you and the boy,' Ériu called after me. 'And what is best for the tribe.'

My sisters were now queens, each of them married to one of the new kings, Mac Cuill, Mac Cécht and Mac Gréine, the three brothers who had killed Lugh. They were grandsons of the Dagda, though they had inherited none of his qualities. In truth, I struggled to tell the brothers apart, each of them as bland as oats left out in the rain. The three of them combined didn't make up one good king, not even if you wrapped them up in a single cloak. And yet, they were the rulers the people deserved. The tribe had become lazy after forty years of playing games rather than going to battle, taken to squabbling over the weight of corn and the teeth of horses.

My sisters tried to show their husbands how to lead, whether with kindness or fierceness, but above all fairness. But the men were convinced they were born to it and paid no heed to their wives' wise words. The kings and I were alike in this.

Part of me knew I should have listened to my sisters' warnings, just as their husbands should listen to their advice. I should have taken Meche and made a perfect little life for ourselves far away from everyone else. I should have even taken him with me to my cave where we could have slept, wrapped in each other's arms, till all who had ever heard the story of Meche and the snakes in his hearts were gone. And yet I refused to be driven out of the court by whispers. Not when I knew the true source of them. Dian Cécht.

I had not been there when Dian Cécht had killed his son Miach, though the image of it visited me again and again in my dreams. I saw Dian Cécht smashing his son's head against the cold flagstones of his workshop over and over till the young limbs stopped thrashing and his blood flowed like wine. I saw Dian Cécht standing over the body, the grey meat of Miach's brains on his hands. I saw his daughter, Airmed, weeping over the body of her twin brother as flowers and plants erupted out of his corpse. In my dreams, Miach's face changed and became Meche's. I would awake slicked in sweat and fired by hatred and would pull Meche into my arms. It was beyond my vast imagining how anyone who had held their child as I held mine could hurt so much as a hair on their head.

And yet, Dian Cécht was beloved by our tribe. He had brought people back from the dead with a touch of his staff. He had restored kings and healed warriors and there was no greater healer ever to walk the land. He had given Nuada his silver arm, what good it did him. He had stood behind Lugh, his grandson, as he had ruled, and now he whispered in the ears of our new kings. They forgave him his filicide and thought him wise. They thought him goodly.

But I do not forgive. And I do not forget. He could heal a thousand warriors and restore a thousand kings, but it wouldn't wash away the stain of killing his own child. He knew I saw the true him but knowing he couldn't hurt me directly, for my power outstripped his like a stallion to a mule, he took aim for my son.

One day, Meche and I left the tribe and rode out to a river called the Barrow, the Boiling River, with rapids that were said to kill a man if he didn't know the words to quieten them as I did.

'Teach me! Teach me!' Meche demanded, after I whispered the words to slow the river so that we could wade across.

I stirred up the waters again and whispered the words in his ear for him to try.

He tried to speak it, but his tongue could not form the sounds. The river rushed by loud as thunder.

'Why won't it work?' he asked, with tears in his eyes as though the water was taunting him.

'You have to keep practising, my little one.'

He tried again and again. I said the words and he said them back to me.

'Catch the words in your throat first and then spit them out,' I said.

He did as instructed. The waters responded as though they had heard the voice of their master and turned pond-still.

Meche threw himself into the waters and jumped up and down in pure joy. 'Teach me more!'

And so I did. I taught him the old words I could remember. How to calm a storm or cause a hurricane. How to tame a wild horse or soothe a birthing heifer. I kept the words to hurt and maim for myself. Maybe when he was older, I could teach him the words to turn the hearts of men to ice or how to make their blood boil. Maybe when I did not fear what he would do with them.

Meche had not inherited my powers of shapeshifting, but he delighted in how I could turn my strong, thick body into a slippery eel and swim between the rocks, or into a howling she-wolf and jump across the rapids with him on my back. He called out the names of beasts, both real and imagined, and I leapt into the air and landed on the soft damp grass in whatever form he had called out. Wild boar. Golden bull. Winged serpent. He clapped his hands and my heart beat in time. These transformations delighted him, yet the subtle contortions I made daily as his mother went unnoticed. Much of motherhood, I had come to learn, was a matter of shifting yourself to be what your child needed at any given moment. Warm and tender when they woke in the night crying, firm and still when they tested their limits. I had believed myself to be the only one of the tribe with the power to transform from one thing in a moment to another the next, but I learned that all mothers were shape-shifters of a sort.

After spending the morning by the riverbank, we dried ourselves in the sun. On our way back to the fort, Meche picked and threaded berries on to a hazel wand and his hands and lips were red with their juices. As we walked through the walls of the fort, he was sucking his fingers clean and laughing in delight at the messy juiciness of it all.

'See,' Dian Cécht said, as we approached. He pointed a gnarled, black-tipped finger at us. 'The child already feeds the snakes in his hearts on human flesh. He drinks blood, just as his mother has always done. The snakes slumber. But if we don't stop him now, they will awaken and consume all life on the land.'

Meche cried at all the shouting and dropped his berry wand. This made him cry more. He had some of my power in that wail – a shriek that made leaves quiver and fall from the trees and which sent a shiver of unease down people's spines.

I took him in my arms and hushed him. There would be more berries tomorrow, I promised him, winter was far away. As for the old druid, I simply smiled.

Come at me, that smile said. I have killed whole armies with my bare hands, I have torn the valour from kings and sunk my teeth into heroes. What do you think I could make of one as weak as you? He recoiled, holding his hand out as if warding off a curse and I took my son away. In my happiness, I was blind.

'Here,' Airmed said, handing Meche a flower once her father strode away.

She was one of few at the court who was immune to the poison her father was dripping into the minds of the tribe and she would stop and speak to us if we passed one another.

Meche sniffed at the flower and went to hand it to me, as he did with all those that he found.

'No,' Airmed said, laughing. 'Eat it. Its name is comfrey and it will make your bones strong and your breath as sweet as that face of yours.' She rubbed a thumb against his soft cheek.

I flinched as her hand stroked his face, the only other human ever to do so, and felt my talons itch beneath my skin. I'd had no need of them since Meche's birth, and they pushed through healed flesh ready to strike. But Meche giggled at her touch and I forced myself to be calm.

'He's a sweet boy,' Airmed said.

Meche became infatuated with Airmed after that. He gathered flowers and weeds on our wanderings and brought them to her to name. Meadowsweet, which soothed pain but was tough on the stomach. Gorse, to ward against fleas and lift the spirit of those who had given up hope. Elder, used for healing burns, but be careful not to sleep under an elder bush for you may not wake up.

He insisted on sitting next to her at the feasts. She bore his attentions with a warm heart and bounced him on her lap, which made him giggle with delight.

He drank joy out of every day, and with him, I learned to be happy. I understood then why my mother had wanted this for me. But I should have known it wouldn't last. It couldn't last.

10.

One day, word came to the court that a ship with red sails had been sighted off the coast. A magician called Íth, they said, had travelled from the south with a band of warriors and was on his way to meet with the ruler of the land.

We all gathered to see these strangers, for it had been half a century since any had landed on our shores. Mac Cécht and his two brothers began quarrelling about who should greet the strangers, each insisting that it should be them alone. When Íth and his men arrived the kings were still arguing.

These men from the southlands were so unlike each other in feature, I was surprised they were all of one tribe. The Tuatha Dé were all of the same colouring, with the same strong slim noses, sharp cheekbones and broad foreheads, and yet these men each looked as different from each other as we did from the Fomorians. Some had small noses, turned up as if sniffing the air, others had noses that were spread across their faces as though broken in battle. Some had skin the reddish brown of hawthorn wood, while others were as pink as a plucked hen. They were small compared to the men of our tribe, the height of one of our youngsters, and they were met with sniggers and jibes as they entered the court.

'Will your mammies be coming to take you home?'

'Why don't you come back when your balls have dropped, little men?'

Rough hands tightened on the hilts of sharp weapons, though they had the sense not to draw them.

Meche tugged on my skirts. 'Why are they so short and ugly?' he said.

'Because,' Ériu answered, for me, 'they live in small caves and if they grew any bigger they would crack their heads open when they stood up.'

Ugly they might be, but their clothing, brooches and weapons were decorated with beautiful patterns and carvings. Circles within circles and lines that swooped like waves unlike any made by our people. I saw Credne eyeing them hungrily. They wore no armour but had toughened leather tunics that would turn away even a hefty blow.

'What are those marks on their skin?' Meche asked, pointing at red and white lines that cut across their faces and limbs.

'Scars,' Airmed replied, 'from where wounds have festered. The poor creatures must not have healers where they come from. We should pity them.'

Pity would be unwise. For though small and scarred they might be, I saw strength in them, and more than that, I saw wisdom in their leader, Íth.

He was the oldest man I had ever seen, hair the colour of snow and skin that hung loose as heavy cloth. He had a man on either side of him helping him walk and eyes that were filled with fog. And yet, he saw clearly. Íth was welcomed to Tara, given the protection of hospitality and a seat at the table. Food was served and music played, and Íth was invited to tell us of his home.

He was not, he said, the king, but the brother of the king, a man called Mil, and as such, they called themselves the Sons of Mil. His people had wandered for centuries across different lands and had learned much and seen much.

'Though never,' he said, 'anything like what I see here today.'

All the while he spoke, the three kings kept up their squabbling. They fought over which was the best seat, tried to grab the best portion of the food before either of the others could take a bite.

'Why are you quarrelling?' Íth asked the brothers. 'Yours is the most beautiful land. Its soil is richer than any I have known. The weather neither too hot nor too cold. You have sweet honey and rivers filled with lazy salmon. Grain stores that would take a lifetime to empty. Your men are giants and your women bountiful. You have everything you need and yet you quarrel as though you were fighting over scraps. Make peace, brothers. Be grateful that this beautiful, lovely island will give you three times what any man could need and so can be shared among you three.'

Having passed judgement, Íth called for his men to help him leave the court so that he could begin his way back home. He had come in peace and left in peace. Yet his high praise for the land played on the three kings' minds. They put their quarrels aside and turned their ire on Íth.

'If he loves the land so much, he may want to take it for himself.'

'He will tell his people of our riches and gather an army to invade.'

'He can't be allowed to return to his homeland. He has to die.'

I laughed. Fools, the lot of them, so shamed by an old man that they were starting up trouble. 'Let him go home,' I said. 'If an army comes, then let it come.'

It had been too many years since I had unleashed my wings. Too many years of peace and I would welcome a war.

I could show Meche what it was to be a warrior, teach him the battle words and see him kill his first enemy. We could make sport of seeing these southerners off.

'Let them come and I will destroy them.'

'You?' Mac Cécht said, looking me up and down. 'And what good will you be? Or will you set your boy on them?'

Mac Cécht and his brothers had been just babes when the last battle was fought. They had never seen my talons or heard my true voice and if stories were still told of my thirst for war, they hadn't listened. They knew me only as the mother of a strange child.

'She is right,' Dian Cécht said. He had appointed himself the kings' advisor and sat on the left hand of each who ruled in turn. 'I have seen her unleash her fury in battle. If Íth and his men were to see her power, they wouldn't dare return.'

What was this? Dian Cécht and I had been quiet enemies from the moment we set foot on this land, him a man of healing, me a woman who had known only how to deal death. A lifetime of resentment and here he was singing my praises as the storytellers had once done.

'Her?' Mac Cuill said. He looked at my arms as thin as bone and my skirts that dragged through the dirt as I ran after Meche.

'She's a mother, not a warrior,' Mac Gréine said.

'Mothers can be warriors,' I said, Brigid's words flowing from my lips.

I wondered where she was now and if she had been here, could she have talked sense into these idiot kings?

'Go after them,' Dian Cécht said to me, ignoring the kings. 'Rain blood down on them as you once did our enemies. Strike fear into their hearts.'

I didn't know what his game was, and yet my need to prove myself to them was stronger than my wisdom. I wanted to show them who I really was, to make them choke on their sneers. I handed Meche to Airmed, bowed to the kings and scattered myself to the air with a sigh. I had forgotten how good it felt to unleash the darkness inside me, to stretch out and feel the edges of myself dissipate like mist.

Íth and his men were almost at their square-sailed boats when I swooped over their heads. I let forth a screech of old and their blood turned to ice in their veins. They threw themselves to the ground, calling out for whatever gods they worshipped, but their gods had not followed them across the sea and had no powers here. Only Íth remained standing, staring up at me with his pale eyes, his mouth open in wonder.

'What power,' he said. 'What fearsome power!'

I hovered above him, considering him with my yellow eyes. He was no threat to us, he was so small, so frail. Besides, he had been given the protection of the law of hospitality.

'Go,' I said my voice like a crack of thunder. 'Speak of what you have seen and know this land is guarded.'

I had delivered my message and he would take it back with him. He turned, his weak body moving quickly, eyes still on me so he didn't see the outstretched tip of a blade, held in the hand of Mac Gréine.

Íth staggered back, blood pumping through the sieve of his hands when another blade struck him in the back. Mac Cuill withdrew his knife and punched it in again. Íth was dead before he hit the ground. Mac Cuill and Mac Gréine then turned on Íth's men. Those who weren't fast enough to make it to the boats fell to the kings' blades. Of the one hundred and fifty who landed with Íth only twelve escaped, carrying with them their tale that monsters and oath-breakers lived in this land.

'You fools,' I said, coming to stand before Mac Cuill and Mac Gréine as a woman once more. 'What have you done? He was no harm to us.'

'Who are you to question a king?' Mac Cuill said, wiping the blood of Íth's men from his face.

'You're no king,' I said.

I flew back home. I was going to do what I should have done the day Meche was born; leave the tribe and take him with me somewhere safe, somewhere free of foolish men.

I half-ran, half-flew to my home and tore the leather off the doorway. On the floor lay Airmed, in a deep sleep. Her body was curled around a gap, as if she had wrapped herself around a small object. Or a child.

I kicked her in the ribs. 'Where is Meche?'

She stirred but her eyes didn't open. I bent over and shook her shoulders, my talons sliding out from under my skin and digging into her flesh. It was then I smelled a spicy sweetness on her breath. Elder. She had been drugged. I dropped her to the ground, her body limp as a landed fish, and flew out the door.

'Where is my son?' I cried and the people of the tribe pressed their hands against their ears. 'Where is he?'

None would meet my eye. I was used to them turning away from me, but this was different. This was not fear or disgust. This was shame.

'Meche!' I cried and it cracked the earth beneath my feet.

'Badb, what is it?' Banba asked, running towards me, my other sisters close behind.

'I can't find Meche!'

A look passed between them as they spoke to each other without words.

'Tell me!'

Ériu spoke, though her voice cracked. 'I saw him with Dian Cécht. We didn't think . . .'

I didn't wait for her to finish. I scattered myself to the sky as a hundred crows and searched the land, looking for his beautiful dark head asleep in a mossy grove, his pale white skin, running with the horses. There was no sign of my boy. Perhaps he had returned to the river where we had spent the perfect day. The fear that had clutched my heart sank deep into my belly. If he had gone to the river alone, he could have drowned in the rapids. His tiny body could have been dashed against the rocks. I almost fled. I almost flew up into the clouds and allowed myself to dissolve, rather than face that fear. But if there was even a breath of life in him still, he could be saved. I would bow to Dian Cécht and kiss his gangrenous toes if it meant he would heal my son. I gathered myself there, at the banks of the river, and looked into the still, slow waters. Waters that had the day before roiled like the ocean in winter. A river that had been impassable without my magic to silence it, was now gentle and still and inviting. Floating on the mirror surface was a dark, oily residue. I stared at my own face in the reflection as I dipped my hand into the water, pale and twisted. My fingers came out black and smelling of burnt flesh. I saw a lock of hair floating on the surface. Dark red hair, so dark it seemed black.

My boy is dead. My boy is dead. My boy is dead. It pounded over and over in my ears in place of the sound of my heart which had stopped beating. My reason for living was gone. My only joy, stolen. Never again would we ride, him wrapped safe in my arms. I would never feel his kisses or hear his sweet laughter. I would never know the man he would become or the life we would have.

'You should be grateful.' It was Dian Cécht with Mac Cécht beside him. 'You were never fit to be a mother.'

I could hardly hear him for the rushing in my ears. I was falling, hurtling through an abyss of darkness and pain and rage. I wanted it to swallow me up so that the pain would stop. Pain that felt as though someone had punched through my chest and ripped my heart from it. I had to look down and check that I had not done that very thing with my own hands. But my skin was untouched, my heart still beating beneath it. A scream built up inside me, pressing against my ribcage. They had thought it was Meche who would end all life on this land, but it was me. I would kill them all and if that meant I would be undone, I would welcome it.

Dian Cécht was right. I was made to bring death, not life. If I couldn't be a mother, I would be a destroyer.

'It was I who did the deed,' Mac Cécht said proudly. 'I slew your monstrous child and threw his hearts into the flames and his ashes into the river.'

But I knew from his black smile who had guided the king's hand.

'And tell me, Dian Cécht,' I said, turning to the old druid, 'did you find the hungry snakes you were looking for?'

Nothing. Silence. There had never been snakes coiled in his hearts. Only a man's fear. Dian Cécht saw how my love for Meche stilled my rage and how that stillness had made me dangerous. A wild, angry woman is so easy to ignore. To laugh at. To hush. A woman who has mastered her rage, learned not to fear the power that stems from it, that is terrifying to little men like Dian Cécht. In taking Meche from me, he had hoped to undo me, to unleash the fury once more and let it tear me apart. He had wanted to return me to the wild, howling, hopping-mad creature that was so useful in battle and so useless in life.

The hurricane screech that swirled within me stopped. Passed as all storms do. This was what they wanted. They wanted me to destroy myself. I wouldn't give them the satisfaction. I wouldn't give it to any of them. I would no longer be their Badb, their shrieking battle crow. I would be something else. Something even more dangerous.

I looked at the calm river. Angry waters that had been named Barrow were on that day called Berba, for the stillness that came after the ashes of Meche's flesh were thrown into the rapids. Silent water. Just as Meche's death had stilled the waters, it could still the rage in me. Instead of making me wild, I became steady. Instead of rage boiling my blood it turned it to ice. And I was all the more terrifying for it. Instead of a forest fire, I was a snow-covered mountain, a moment away from avalanche.

I couldn't turn my power against the Dian Cécht without dying, for he was of the tribe and my mother's binding words stayed my hand. But I could bring about his destruction another way. I wouldn't just kill him, I would see to it that he experienced the eternity of agony I did before his death. I would bring down on him thrice what he had done to me. Everything he loved, I would destroy. And the thing he loved most of all was himself. I would strip him of his power, make him weak and useless and see his own medicines used against him. And only then would I permit him to die.

As for Mac Cécht, he wasn't a fit king. Neither were his brothers. Petty, weak men so easily manipulated. They would learn what the revenge of a powerful woman looked like. I wouldn't just take the throne from them, I would see that none of their blood ever ruled again. The whole of the tribe would pay for this. There wasn't a man or woman among them who was fit to rule. And so I would take the land from them, force them into exile, till they became nothing but whispered memories. One of theirs had taken my son from me. I would take everything from them. And it would begin that day.

I flew into the air once more and only then allowed myself to cry out for my son. A hundred beaks cawing his name. Every crow across the land picked up my call.

Meche. Meche. Meche.

I I.

The ships carrying what remained of Íth's men had made it beyond the eighth wave when I caught up with them. They were desperate, twelve men doing the work of a hundred. The oars floundered in the crashing waves and they struggled to stay clear of the jagged rocks.

I landed on the mast of one of their sails and called down to them.

'Sons of Mil,' I said, my voice calmer, colder, than I had ever known it. 'You have been dealt a great wrong on this day. Promises were shattered. Trust betrayed. This is an island of traitors. Go, gather your men and when you return, I will not stand in the way of your revenge.'

I called for a wave and sent them on their way home.

It wasn't long before the Sons of Mil were spotted on the horizon once again. A thousand ships, each holding one hundred and fifty men. The Tuatha Dé might be stronger and have the gift of magic, but they were desperately outnumbered.

'Strike them down before they can set foot on the soil,' Mac Gréine said to me. He was panicked, for he knew he had broken one of our oldest laws, the law of hospitality, and retribution was less than half a day's sail away.

'But I am only a mother, not a warrior,' I said.

'You swore to protect us,' Mac Cuill said, clutching at my arm.

'I swore to protect the land,' I said. 'I never said anything about *you*.'

I wrenched his hand from my flesh, squeezing his fingers tighter and tighter till I heard the gentle popping of bones. Pain shot through me like lightning, as I tested the limits of my geas. But it was worth it to see his face.

They were an honourable lot, these Milesians. When they landed and found the three kings unprepared for battle, they made a deal. They would, they said, retreat back into the waters, a distance of nine waves beyond, and if we could prevent them from landing again, they would turn their boats around and return home. But if they could disembark, then they would take the land by force.

Dian Cécht told the three kings to take the deal, convinced that he and his druids could stir up enough magic to keep these weakling invaders at bay. But he had not counted on my aiding them.

The Tuatha Dé were no longer worthy of the land. Íth's praise of her beauty had sounded hollow to their ears because they had started to take her for granted. They had been so busy counting their barley stooks and grain stacks, they had stopped seeing the bounty of the acorn forests that lay scattered across the hilltops. They cared more about their ale stores than the sweet rivers that flowed all year round. They carved deep into her flesh and pulled out gold and silver and copper, and cared more for that than they did her limestone or clay. They had neglected the land and she in turn would neglect them.

Or perhaps that's how I wanted to see it? When it was in truth me who turned my back on them? Either way, it was just. I had the power to bestow sovereignty and the power to withdraw it. The Tuatha Dé had lost before the battle had even begun.

I flew above the treacherous storms, summoned by our druids to hide the land from the invaders. Although *perhaps* I flapped my wings a little harder than needed and *perhaps* vortices were formed at the tips of my feathers clearing a path through the darkness so that the Sons of Mil could bring their boats closer to shore. Perhaps.

They were led by a warrior poet called Amergin, a man with skin the colour of tanned leather and eyes that glinted like emeralds. He climbed to the top of his boat's mast and called out for safe passage, not to a god of his people, or to one of ours, but to the land herself.

'I invoke the land of Ireland,' he shouted into the winds, naming our country and claiming her.

He called out to Ireland, to its fruit-strewn mountains and hilltop wells, to its waterfalls and deep pools. He called out to the clinging bogs and craggy mountains, the mossy stones and rolling hills. 'Lofty Ireland darkly sung,' he said. 'I invoke the land of Ireland.'

And she must have heard him all right, for a wave picked his boat up and placed it safely on the gravel shore. As soon as Amergin placed his right foot on the sand, he became a part of the land and she became part of him, just as I had done. Although instead of drawing in her pain, he drew in her power.

'*I am the wind on the sea,*' he said, his clear voice carrying
     over the quieting storm.
'*I am a wave on the land,*
I am the roar of the sea,
I am the stag with seven tines,
I am a spear that roars for blood,
I am a salmon in a pool,

I am the god who puts a fire in your head.
Who but I can tell the ages of the moon,
The mysteries of the tomb?'

I liked this Amergin. Though in fairness he was a little too pleased with himself.

I took no part in the battle as they threw first words and then spears at each other. I took up no weapon as Mac Cuill and then Mac Gréine were slaughtered, their bodies hurled off cliffs, as the invaders pushed ever inland towards Tara.

Maybe I could have shrieked fear into the hearts of these marauders and sent them fleeing back into the sea, their guts running down their legs. *Maybe* I could have stopped the slaughter. But I had only begun to taste the wines of my revenge and I wouldn't stop till I was drunk on it.

Men and women I had once called family died screaming and I did nothing. Children no older than Meche ran screeching from burning huts, their skin bubbling, and I did nothing. I turned away from the dying of my people, just as they had turned away as Mac Cécht dragged my child to the waters and cut out his hearts.

I watched, in the shape of a she-wolf, as Dian Cécht was pushed to the floor and his skull cracked on the same flagstones where his son's had. The Sons of Mil grabbed vial after vial from his shelves and poured them down his throat till his skin turned black and blood pooled from his eyes. They left him drowning in his own potions, his body convulsing in agony.

I padded towards him, becoming a woman once more. Crouching over him, I stared into his eyes as the light dimmed.

'I will see to it that your body is never found,' I said. 'That no rites are spoken over your bones. You will never pass over to the other lands.'

He tried to speak, to curse me one last time, but only bubbles of blood formed on his lips. I kept my promise. As soon as the light in his eyes was gone, I tore his body to shreds, burned the parts and scattered the ashes to the wind.

It was an easy victory for the Sons of Mil. Mac Cécht, the last king alive, though barely, called for a truce, acting as if it wasn't a surrender.

He hid his wounds under a golden cloak and tried to look strong when he made them an offer.

'You have fought well,' he said, through shards of missing teeth. 'We will allow you to keep half of the land, the rest is for us.'

It was the very same offer we made the Fir Bolg when we first landed. But these Sons of Mil were cleverer than the Men of Bags.

Amergin smiled. 'Then we claim the half of the land that is above. And you may have the half that is below.'

You had to admire the pure bloody cheek of it. Taking the land for themselves and exiling us to the mounds and caves below. What could the Tuatha Dé do but accept? The tribe had been devastated. Scarcely a man of warrior age was left alive. My sisters had survived, through cunning or through some other craft, I didn't know, though I was glad of it. They had taken no part in Meche's murder. Airmed lived too and tended to the sick of the Tuatha Dé and the Sons of Mil alike, rubbing her herbs into wounds that healed under moonlight.

My sister Ériu accepted their offer, for Mac Cécht had not a breath left in his body, and the tribe were given seven days to leave the land.

I returned to the river where my son's ashes flowed. The water, cold as heartbreak, danced between the dark rocks, slick with moss, and brown trout snapped at dragonflies.

'Have you no deals to make?' said a voice rough as granite.

Amergin had followed me to the river. He was less beautiful now that I saw him up close, his features bore no symmetry and in truth his chin was weaker than I thought when I'd seen him calling to the land, the wind buffeting his hair.

'I have nothing of me to give,' I said. 'I no longer have even a name.'

'Then let me make you a deal.'

I looked down at him. He came barely up to my elbow. What deal could he make me?

'Stay,' he said. 'Be my bride, my queen. And as payment, I give you a new name. The Morrigan.'

Great queen.

Power. The thing I had once hungered for could be mine. Was it really as simple as that? Oh, what I would do as queen. I would see this land become mighty and rich and none would dare to invade again. It would flourish under my rule as never before.

'And I would be your equal? Would we rule together?'

He hesitated. 'Well, I would be king, so . . .'

So . . . no. I would sit by his side, as my sisters had sat beside their kings, and my thoughts, my hopes for the land, would have to be filtered through him, like water through silt.

'Find yourself another bride,' I said.

If I couldn't have it all, I wanted none of it. And though I refused his deal, I kept the name he gave me. The Morrigan.

12.

All things pass.

With every summer a winter. With every day a night. Or so the poets like to say.

The time of the Tuatha Dé in the land now known as Ireland had passed. We arrived by water and so we were to leave by water, though there were no mighty ships to carry us away and we bore no glorious treasures. Only what we could carry on our backs or load on to our honey-horses and red-eared cattle. We left only our names tied to the land to mark that we had once ruled there. We left only our stories.

As we packed and prepared, there was much griping and kicking of stones. Angry discussions about raising an army and taking on the Sons of Mil once more. Plans of sending our best warriors to sneak in at night and cut off the heads of Amergin and his brothers.

'And where is this army?' Ériu asked, looking around at the bedraggled few that remained. 'Where are our warriors? Gone. It is time for us to go too.'

Banba glanced across at me. There was a warrior amid the tribe still. I could, should I wish it, drive the Sons of Mil back to the sea, I could visit them in their nightmares and tear their hearts from their chests and their valour from their groins, as I had with the Fomorians and the Fir Bolg. It was only because I took no part in the battle that we had lost. But when I battled the Fomorians, I had believed the tribe worthy of winning. Worthy of ruling. And then they had betrayed me.

Banba opened her mouth as if to speak and I shook my head. I was no more going to fight for the tribe now than one of our cows. Our time had passed.

'But where are we to go?' Airmed asked. 'They took claim to all the land above.' Her eyes were red with the lack of sleep as she had spent days and night searching for her father. But not a scrap of Dian Cécht could be found.

'Then we will find somewhere below,' Ériu said.

'We should at least tear down Tara,' Fódla said. 'They shouldn't have somewhere so beautiful to rest their stinking feet,' she spat.

'Let it stand,' Ériu said. 'A reminder of our craft. A reminder of how beautiful we once were. Come, my family. We're lucky to have our lives. Let us go in peace for I am weary of war.'

'That's all well and good for you to say,' Crón said. Her grey hair was now completely white, and nimble fingers that had once sharpened spears to deadly points were swollen at the knuckles. But her back was straight as ever and her eyes as keen. 'I saw you parleying with their poet, flicking your hair and making your deals. Is it true you promised to name the land after you so long as you left without a fight?'

This had been the rumour swirling around Tara, for Ériu had been seen talking to Amergin, though none had had the courage to say it to her. She was still queen after all.

'I made a deal to save what few of us there were left,' Ériu said. 'I would have given them my voice, my sight, my body, anything they asked for if it meant saving my people. My name was the least of the trades I was willing to make.'

Banba laughed. 'Sure, I made the same deal. Amergin said they would name the land after me.'

'Me too,' Fódla said. 'Though I had been expecting he would extract a more . . . bodily price.'

'You'd been hoping for it, you glorious little slut,' Banba said, pinching her sister's cheek playfully.

'If I had to open my legs to that beautiful poet to save us, well, I was prepared to be the hero we all needed.'

My sisters' teasing shifted the mood, their light laughter driving away the heaviness that hung over us like a winter mist.

'Do you have space for one more?'

We turned to see Brigid. We had not seen her in almost fifty years, not since she had keened over the broken body of her son. She wore a cloak of green silk lined with a thick grey wool, though it had seen better days. Moths had eaten the silk and the wool had felted. Like my sisters and I, she had not aged.

She was met with warm hugs, tears of joy and endless questions. Where had she been? What had she been doing? Why had she stayed away so long?

'After the death of my son, my pain was too great, my hatred for you all too vast,' she said. 'It took all these years for my tears to stop flowing and for my heart to heal.'

I knew her pain. I knew her hatred. Though I did not have a heart that was capable of healing. Mine was broken like a stone, and like a stone it would remain broken.

She took my hand in hers and brought it to her lips. 'I heard about Meche,' she said.

None had dared speak his name since they had killed him. None but the crows. Hearing it now in her soft, light voice brought him back to me for a moment and I loved her more than I had ever done.

'I am so sorry. I heard he was a beautiful boy,' she said. 'I wish I had met him.'

'He would have liked you,' I said. For it was true. He would have brought her flowers and begged her to sing in her beautiful voice, something I had never been able to do for him.

With a last squeeze of my hand, she turned back to the tribe.

'I bring word from Manannán mac Lir,' Brigid said.

'He still lives?' I asked.

I'd not heard from Manannán in a hundred years. I had thought he must have dwindled away, becoming one with the waves.

'He not only lives, but he thrives. He has found a place where the tribe will be happy. Where they will be safe.'

Manannán was used to taking in strays and fosterlings, as he had taken in Lugh. And now, it seemed, he was to take in what remained of the Tuatha Dé.

'I am here to guide you there,' Brigid said.

And so it was that on the final day of the year, the tribe gathered up their belongings, harnessed their beasts and made their way east.

'Where, exactly, are we going?' It was Firgol, the druid so beloved of Lugh when he was a young man. Now he was old and his sea-blue eyes were the colour of milk.

'Below,' Brigid said.

'Below? What does that mean?' Fódla said. 'Into the dark?'

She spoke the fear they all carried. The Tuatha Dé were, after all, beings of light. How long could they survive in the dark?

'Trust me,' Brigid said. 'All will be well.'

130

After three days' hard travel, we came to the same coast we had arrived at those many, many years before. A cloud of mist covered the waters and in it, I saw my family as they had been then. Dancing in the waves, laughing and singing. Home. Home, they had said. But we had a home no more.

Manannán emerged out of the mist. His hair had turned the colour of sea foam and his skin was mottled like aged bronze. And yet he looked so like our lost kings, the Dagda, Nuada and Ogma, that looking at him made my heart ache for them. What I wouldn't have given to see the Dagda one more time. To lie with him on the bank of our river under the sun. To talk strategy with Nuada even if he didn't listen. I'd even put up with one of Ogma's endless poems, if I could see his face once more. But they were gone. Nothing left of them but memories.

'Come, my family,' Manannán said as the refugees approached. 'And be happy, for the land where you are going to is more beautiful than you could believe.'

'Is it not dark and cold?' Fódla asked.

Manannán laughed, and his laughter was like the cry of a gull. 'No, it is a land of light and warmth. A golden place. Leave the Sons of Mil to this land. Leave them to their cycle of birth and death, of famine and feast, for in the new land we shall not age, we shall not grow hungry. Never again shall we have to battle to survive, for it is a land of peace, for ever.'

'Is it this the place you foresaw?' Ériu asked me.

The two futures I had seen after the battle with the Fomorians, one of peace, one of strife. Had it been divided so simply as this? Above darkness and below light.

'Perhaps,' I said.

The muttering turned into excited chattering. The heavy sadness they had carried with them from Tara lifted.

'The others are waiting,' Manannán said.

'Who?' Fódla asked.

'The Dagda, Ogma and Nuada have already found their way here through the barrow pathways. And my beautiful foster son, Lugh, has come home too.'

The small gathering cheered and hugged each other. The stories about the other lands had been true after all.

'My son?' I asked, unable to say his name. My hands shook and I felt something strange and foreign swirl in my belly. Something I had not felt since our days on the boats. Hope.

It vanished as quickly as it had come. Manannán shook his head. No more needed to be said. Meche had not been buried, words had not been spoken for him. He was lost to me for ever. I had no more curses left for Dian Cécht. But at least I knew that my son was not the only one who would never see the other lands.

'Well, come on then!' Banba said, impatient with the heavy mood. 'Why are we waiting?'

Brigid swung her cloak off her shoulders and flung it out with a flick of her wrists. The mist that hung over the water cleared, as if waving away steam from a boiling pot. The waves were still as polished stone, and each member of the Tuatha Dé saw their reflection in its surface.

Manannán pointed beneath the waters to a shadow of a cave. 'Through that cave you will find yourself on the sandy shores of the land of promise. All you have to do is dive in.'

The tribe jostled with each other. Who would go first? Who would be the first to set up our new home?

Crón pulled up her skirts around her bony knees and waded into the water.

'It's not cold!' she said, smiling back at us.

When the water was around her waist, she dived down, as agile as a trout, and vanished through the cave.

'Who's next?' Manannán said.

'Shouldn't someone stay?' Ériu asked. 'To make sure they can't follow us.'

'I will shroud the water paths in mist,' Manannán said.

'Will that be enough?' Fódla asked.

'What of the caves? The bogs? There are other ways to cross over,' Banba said.

'I will stay,' I said.

They had been expecting it, I think. Or hoping for it at least. What use was there for a being of war in a land of peace? What use was there for one who could see death, in a place where there was none? For though I longed to see my brothers again, I had never been like them, not truly. I would not be welcome in their land of promise.

'Are you sure?' Banba asked. Always the kind one.

'I took no part in the battle with the Sons of Mil and so am not bound by their conditions. I will stay. Manannán can guard the waterways between this land and where you go. And I will guard the dark places.'

Manannán nodded. 'This is for the good.'

'I will stay, too.'

A light, female voice spoke clear. I hardly believed it could be Brigid.

Just as my announcement was met with silent acceptance, so Brigid's was met with loud protest.

'No,' they said. 'You can't stay.'

They needed her. She was one of them. Please, they

said, please come with us. They cried and tugged on her arms. Why? What was she doing? A land of abundance and plenty, it was what she was made for.

'I love this land,' she said. 'I love the changing seasons, watching the crops grow. My gift is to heal, and what use is there in a place where there are no wounds? I will stay.'

'Then we shall return,' Ériu said. 'Every year, on the night of Samhain, we will come riding out, astride our beasts, and for one night the land will belong to us. And we will dance again with our sisters under the moon.'

She rested her palm against my cheek and took Brigid's hand. Banba and Fódla joined and we all five embraced. I watched as they dived under the waters, setting the mirror surface rippling. After some time, the water was still again and the Tuatha Dé were gone. Only Brigid and I remained.

She picked her cloak up from the ground and threw it back around her, the rough grey lining now facing outwards, the shimmering green against her skin.

We eyed each other, she and I. I had never liked her much, but I loved her then.

'I'll be seeing you then, little bride,' I said.

'And I'll be seeing you . . . crow.'

We embraced and walked away.

13.

Kings arose and fell. The land changed. The oak forests were cut down to make hill forts, stones were hacked from mountains to make tombs. And I waited in the depths of the earth, guarding the pathways as I had promised.

There was no day or night in that place. No time. The Sons of Mil settled and tended the land and had more sons. They would send their fledgling warriors to meet me in the darkness. They would crawl on their bellies over the slick stones as if returning to the womb, but instead of pain they were met with fear. They waited in a dark blacker than any night they had known, till they could hear the rush of blood in their ears and their hearts beating in their chests. Some would bite back their cries and shed silent, unheard tears. Others would roar into my cave, which swallowed all sound. If I found them worthy, I would gift them with furious nightmares and visions of battle and glimpses of their futures. It was a test of their becoming a man. Not all passed.

Those who did, returned to their tribes changed. Angry and afraid. I didn't teach them how to be men, down there in the dark. But I did teach them how to bury their fear, to hide it and never speak of it. For that is what they believed it meant to be a man. For before they could commit violence to others, they must perform this violence to themselves. I set a fire in the soul of every boy who came to me. One small battle at a time, feeding my hunger, like licking at the water that ran down the walls of the cave. It was enough to keep me alive. Just enough.

In my limbo, I dreamt of all that could have been. I dreamt of battle. I dreamt of death. I saw fragments of the future. A battle that would shape the land. A battle so glorious I would awake covered in a hot sweat at the thought of it. I hungered for it.

The Tuatha Dé had not accepted me as their ruler and it had cost them everything. The Sons of Mil had offered me a place on the throne, but only as consort. But perhaps, if I couldn't have power as a goddess, I could have it as a mortal? From what I had gleaned from the boys sent to me in the darkness, the Milesian kingship was passed from father to son. I was a shapeshifter. If I could become a wolf, a heifer, a crow, I could become a man. In becoming it, I could destroy it. Men's hold on the land was like iron, and if I had to break each of their bony fingers to make them give it up, I would do it. All I needed was to find myself a king to become my father.

I would have to leave this body behind, to be born again in a new one. I had often wandered the land in my dreams, so would this be any different? Merely a dream that would last a human lifetime?

Shifting my shape always came with pain, though I had become accustomed to it over the years. A cracking of bones and tearing of tendons. But simply leaving my body behind, slipping off my skin as you might a silk cloak, there was no pain, no sensation of any kind. I became a being of pure thought, of pure spirit, and drifted up into the air, floating like a dandelion seed caught on a breeze.

Far below me I saw the whole of the land, rough edges like a calfskin lain out to dry. I had seen the maps Lugh had made when planning his battles. How wrong they had been. They had not captured her curving arms, reaching out into the sea as if calling to travellers from the west. I sailed like a cloud through blue skies, over mountains, cliffs, lakes, forests. I saw humans cutting and carving into the land, chopping down trees, hacking chunks of slate, forcing the rivers to take new paths. What a savagery man performed on the earth.

The wind took me north, to the province of Ulaid. Singing caught on the currents drew me closer, calling me back to life. A wedding was being celebrated. Between Áed Rúad, the High King of Ireland, and his new wife, Líadan. The tables were heavy with food, though I could not smell or taste it. The fires burned bright, though I could not feel their heat. I could see and hear, but as though sensing it all through water.

The drinking and dancing slowed and soon, the guests snored in corners or sang slurred songs, their heads in their arms, and Áed led Líadan to their bridal bed to consummate the marriage. I hung in the corner of the room, like smoke from the fire, and watched.

They were both barely old enough for the act that was expected. His hair as red as the fire that crackled in the hearth; hers, black as the coal the fire left behind. They sat, in their underclothes, side by side. His hand quaked as it reached out for hers, and a shiver passed through her as their flesh touched for the first time.

'You don't have to,' he said, 'if you don't want to. We can wait, no one needs to know.'

She laced her fingers through his. 'It's all right, my husband. My mother told me what to expect if I am to bear you a son.'

'I don't want to hurt you,' he said.

'Everything worth having comes with pain.'

She drew him into her. And I followed soon after.

I settled there, for a while, in the floating liquid nothingness of her womb, which reminded me of those dreamlike days on the ships. Time lost meaning, with no night or days to count. I heard the murmuring of life through the veil of her skin, which became eyelid thin as I grew in size and strength. She would sing to me when I was restless and run her hands over her belly, causing dappled shadows like looking at the sun with your eyes closed. For the first time since my arrival, I felt at peace. But the time came when I could feel the bones of her ribs pressing against mine every time she took a breath, her lungs pushing down on my back. I remembered the day Meche was born, the desperation I felt to have him out of me, and now I felt that same desperation. I could be contained no more. I stretched out, ready to be born.

I thought I would be born fresh, my mind a blank stone to be carved on, helpless as any human child, but all my memories, all my powers, were still mine. It was only my body that was now bound by human frailties and the passing of time. It felt strange. Contained. Crushed. Almost like when Ogma would wrap me in one of his hugs and I would push to break free. Or when I had tried to wear the shoes Goibniu had made for me. Not painful, but unpleasant.

I had also thought I would be born a male, an heir destined to rule, for I had never truly felt at ease within the world of women. But as I glanced down at my soft, pink flesh, I saw I had been born female. Was there, then, some essential part of me that I could not undo?

'Well, how about that,' I said, a goddess's voice from a babe's mouth.

The midwife, who had been washing blood from my face, dropped me to the floor, her hands flying to her chest as though trying to keep her heart from bursting out. She sank to her knees before folding up, dead. Humans, it seemed, were afraid of me from the first.

I tried to move my head, but it was too heavy for my weak spine to hold. I swivelled my eyes and saw the woman who had birthed me. She lay on the pile of rugs and furs, in a pool of dark blood and shit, her belly still swollen, her limbs hanging loose. Her eyes were empty of life, her skin already going cold. Though she had carried me, protected me within the liquid safety of her womb, she was not my mother and I felt little more than disappointment at her death. Whether she had died from the shock of having given birth to an unnatural child, or had been too young to go through the agonies of childbirth, I did not know. All I knew was that I was lying on a cold floor and that if I stood any chance of being picked up and cared for, I was going to have to hide my nature. I almost abandoned the whole idea right then. Almost abandoned the soft, pink body to its fate and returned to my strong, unbreakable one still waiting in the liminal space between this world and other. But that's when Áed entered the chamber.

He had grown a little since I had last seen him sitting alongside his new wife on the night of their wedding. His shoulders were broader, his arms thicker, though his beard was still a little patchy in places. He ran at first to his wife, gathering her up, calling her name. When he realized she was gone, he howled in agony, a noise I'd never heard a man make. It was like a beast. I knew that pain. I felt it when Meche was taken from me, an ocean of agony that I wished would kill me so I could feel what Meche had felt and death could be one last thing that we could share. I still feel it now when I remember how it was to hold him in my arms, to breathe in the scent of his skin.

I cried out, making as soft a gurgling as I could. Áed came then to me and picked me up in his strong hands. I have been looked at in many ways. In fear, anger, awe, confusion, lust, even amusement. But never in love. Not even Meche ever looked at me the way Áed did. Not even my mother. Áed looked at me as if I was the sun that warmed the earth and the moon that moved the tides. As if I were more precious than gold, more fragile than a snowflake. Love. It was intoxicating. And so I stayed.

'I will call you Macha,' he said. 'For the beautiful plain that surrounds our land.' And Macha I was called.

Áed was cousin to Díthorba and Cimbáeth, the three of them grandsons to Airgetmar, once High King of Ireland. As was the way at the time, they ruled in rotation, taking the throne for seven years each before handing on to the next. I was born at the end of Áed's first rotation, as he passed power to Díthorba.

For the first fourteen years of my life, I lived mostly among the women of the court – nursemaids given the care of me, other mothers and wives – and their children. At times, the sound of a baby crying, or child laughing, would remind me of my Meche and it was like a jagged knife twisting in my heart. I did not recoil from it but sought out the pain as you might draw a blade across your own skin, just to feel alive. I was afraid I would forget him: the colour of his eyes, the smell of his hair. Each punch of pain kept him with me.

I felt that I knew the women, too. Their voices or the way the light caught their hair would remind me of my sisters, and a gnawing loneliness would twist in my belly. When I lived among them, I had pulled away from the women of my tribe – my sisters, Brigid, Airmed, even my mother – when all they had wanted to offer me was their kindness. Now that I longed to connect with these human women, to make up for what I had lost, they were the ones to turn from me, afraid or wary. And they were right to be fearful. I still had to learn how to temper my voice for I sounded like no human child and knew that if they heard it, it would terrify them. And so I kept silent and I watched. I got used to the wearing of shoes, though I would tear them off whenever there were no eyes on me, which was rarely. I learned how to weave rather than fight, to smile when I wanted to scream. And I watched.

Their lives seemed to be an endless cycle of work. My people had seen to it that the land was bountiful beyond measure. Animals grazed ready for the picking, fish filled the rivers, plants grew with ease. These mortals could have spent their every waking hour doing nothing but sitting by flowing waters, eating fruit and singing, and yet they worked. Squeezing more and more out of the soil. More crops. More cattle. More gold. As though the land owed them something.

The women bore the heavier share of the work. They worked like bees. Constant, never ending. It was they who kept the court running, weaving cloth and making clothes, preparing food and milking the cows. They joined the men in building walls and advising on strategy but left them to their storytelling and carousing. They were weaker of body, but stronger of will. And yet they had to work twice as hard to earn their place in the court.

The women lived a secret life measured by the moon.

And they had learned much of Airmed's skill with herbs, which they passed between themselves. Herbs to help a woman bear a child. Flowers to rid her of one she did not want. They traded stories as they worked. Warnings of who could be trusted and who should be watched. Gossip of who was sleeping with whom, and who had lied about what. They talked endlessly about sex. Which men of the court they would lie with given the chance. The size of the men's members: some small like withered slugs, some so huge as to be a danger. And the laughter, oh, how they laughed; even when they should be crying they found reason to laugh. Where men lived big, these women lived deep, wide, filling their days. I loved them all, even if they didn't love me.

Many were wary of me as a young girl and would leave rooms as soon as I walked in. I knew too much, they said, heard too much. I could read the ogham runes scratched on stones and blocks of wood before I was three years old and count all the cattle in the field before that. They said my eyes held too many secrets but most of all, they were scared that I never spoke. They blamed me for my mother's death and didn't understand why Áed was so adoring of me.

They all wanted to know when Áed would take another wife and have a son. Who would follow in his place in the rotation of kings if he didn't have an heir? They said he had loved the woman who birthed me from his own childhood, but that love in marriages was as much use as it was for goats.

'I'd bear him a son,' one of the women said. She had only a few teeth left in her head and her long hair was grey. 'If my womb wasn't already as withered as an old mushroom!'

'I can't wait for when my womb withers,' said another, who was pregnant with her tenth child.

'Stop your ceaseless rutting then,' a third replied, tutting at her.

'It's not my fault my cunt is a hungry thing!'

They howled and moved on to talking about other matters, and I sat in the corner and listened.

What would I do if Áed was to take another wife and have children? Would that dim the light that shone in his eyes when he looked at me? I had seen other men of the court cast aside women, children, friends, when a new love came into their lives. I had felt the sting when Lugh had done the same to me.

It didn't matter, because though Áed might be like other men, I was not like other women. I could see to it that he would never leave me, never love any other more than me. I dug deep inside myself for the old words I had not spoken in years. Words of binding and blindness. I crept into his bedchamber at night and whispered them into his ears. A spell to ensure that Áed showed no interest in any of the women of the court, and instead poured all of his attention on me. Causing men to desire a woman is a simple enough enchantment. Causing them *not* to desire anyone is another thing. My first spell failed, the words drifting away like a cobweb. I tried again the next night, going deeper into myself, and this time it worked. Would his natural love have been enough without my spell? I would never know. He was bound to me till death.

When he wasn't hunting or drinking, he kept me by his side and taught me everything he knew, which was little. I smiled and pretended it was the first I had heard of battle strategies, or court politics, or how to guarantee your bulls covered the right cows. We developed a language, spoken with hands not tongue, and were each other's world. By

143

the time Áed's second rotation as king came about, I was his scribe, marking everything that was said and done as he presided over the allocation of grain and the gathering of taxes. Many wanted to know when I would be married off to strengthen Áed's power or stave off cattle raids.

'She is too young to be married,' he would say to any who asked. 'I will not lose her as I lost my own dear wife.'

'She is two years older than Líadan was when you were married, my king,' one of Áed's advisors complained.

'And look at her, she's as strong as a carthorse,' another said. 'It's time she was wed.'

'I will say when it's time!' Áed shouted back. And the matter was settled, for though I believe he sensed the reason in their words, his heart would not let him act on it. A heart that was bound by my magic.

It pleased me to stay with him, watching and soaking up life as a human, and I tried not to care whether he truly loved me or if it was my magic that held him in thrall.

While the poets told stories to entertain the court of grand, mighty deeds, I learned that the things which meant the most to the humans were so small, so mundane, that had I not been watching, I might have missed their significance. The growing and harvesting of seeds. The soft strength of good leather, cured in just the right way. The feel of rain after a hot day. The tiny, stolen moments between chores, when you could be silent and feel the rumble of the earth beneath your body. Sleep after a long day and awaken to a bright morning. Love. Between friends, families and lovers. These small magics they had in excess. And yet they were unsatisfied, always wanting more.

There were battles, squabbles really. Cattle raids and disagreements over land. I had to fight to keep my heart from pounding when I heard the clash of metal on metal, to stop my eyes from shining when the men came back, wounded and dying.

After one such battle, I was helping Áed strip himself of armour and tending to his bruises, though there were few. The raid had been a swift one. Áed had led his men across the border to Tír Eoghain, lands ruled by a chieftain named Lugaid Laigdech, and had killed him and his wife in their beds, leaving only a baby boy alive.

'He had become too powerful,' Áed said, as if he needed to explain himself to me.

I moved my hands in gestures that only he and I understood, my fingers dancing. *I wish I could have been there.*

He hissed as I pressed herbs into a cut on his arm. Then stopped my hand before I laid bandages over the wound. 'Would you like to watch a battle one day, my child?'

Not watch battle. Fight.

He took my chin between his thumb and finger and smiled at me. 'What need have I for sons when I have you?'

Will I lead when you are gone?

He kissed me on my forehead. 'If I could will it, you'd lead now. But it's not the way of things.'

I stuck my tongue out to express my displeasure and he laughed, before wincing at the pain. I finished tending to his wounds and left him to sleep.

The way of things. *Pfff.* I would bend the way to my will.

By the time I had lived through sixteen winters in this body, I saw how while the women of the court still kept away, the men of the court drew close. Won't you come riding with us, Macha? Won't you come and hear us tell our tales? Their eyes shone the way the Dagda's had when I met him at the river. And yet I had no interest in taking any of them to my bed. Sometimes, when one of them was overly insistent, with me or with another woman of the court, I would lure him away with a flash of my eyes. When he was found the next morning, bones crushed, blood soaking the straw of his chamber, I was nowhere near. Must have been a wolf, they would say. Must have been a monster.

I was growing weary of having no voice, and yet I could not trust it yet. At nights, I would sneak out of my chambers and go deep into the woods. I would scream and scream till my throat was wonderfully raw. And then I would practise speaking, to the deer and wolves. To the foxes and mice. It did not fill them with terror. Slowly, I was learning to find my voice. But I still could not trust it.

Díthorba and Cimbáeth, the two men who ruled in turn with my father, came to the court often to share food and their apparent wisdom with Áed, and he always had the best wines brought out for them and the plumpest cattle slaughtered for the feasts. The three of them loved each other as brothers, and squabbled and fought and laughed and joked as brothers do. Cimbáeth I liked. He was quick to laugh and slow to anger. Under his portion of rule, the land did well. He focused his energies on the growing and harvesting of crops, and was often seen walking through fields, rubbing soil between his fingers before bringing it to his lips, to declare it fertile or in need of rotation. His hands were calloused from the wielding of scythes, not swords. He loved discovering new strands of vegetation and had flowers planted around the court. The women of the land loved him most of all, as he was less likely to send their sons and husbands and lovers on unnecessary raids. Even though I was now considered a woman, he still brought me fruits and nuts, just as he had when I was a little girl, and loved producing them from behind my ears to make me smile. He was kind and he was gentle and he spoke to me, not as a child, but as an equal, as though he saw something of my true being.

Díthorba I did not like. His temper was too easily raised by the smallest of things: a serving girl spilling wine on his tunic would be beaten, a horse that refused to pull a chariot would be whipped. Under his reign, the land suffered. Men went on stupid raids and fewer of them came back each time. The land went untended and the barley shrivelled in the fields. He demanded everything and gave nothing. When his seven years were over, the people sighed and singing started up again.

Áed was a wonderful father, but a middling king. He had neither Cimbáeth's curiosity nor Díthorba's ire. He listened to the advice he was given by the seers and followed it blindly, good or bad. He presided over squabbles between neighbours and generally came to fair resolutions. He raided other kings when they were getting too powerful but used clever strategies that resulted in more of them ending up dead than us. He upped the tax, but he put it into cattle and mostly he was respected if not loved. His greatest gift was that of storytelling. He had a great wit and loved the play of words. When the mood took him to tell a story, he could have the court transfixed as he wove tales about the gods that had gone before. One night, when his brothers had come to be fed and entertained, he told a story I had only heard once before. From the Dagda himself.

It was a tale about the day before the battle with the Fomorians, when the Dagda had been sent to talk to them. The story I heard was that the Fomorians kept filling the

Dagda's bowl and the laws of hospitality bound him to finish every last spoonful before he could at last leave, full and waddling. Over the years, it seemed the story had grown.

'And so the sneaky Fomorians,' Áed said, a glint of mischief in his eyes, 'threw the ol' Dagda into a pit, filled to the brim with porridge and said to him, "Eat your way out of that or you will be put to death!" Now, the Dagda had the appetite of a god, so he wasn't worried. He called out for a spoon and got to work. He ate and he ate. And just as he got to the bottom of the pit, the Fomorian bastards would pour more porridge in. And so he ate some more. At last, when there wasn't an oat left in the whole Fomorian court, they could do nothing but let the Dagda go. He climbed out of the pit, his belly huge. Even bigger than Cimbáeth's here,' Áed said, slapping his cousin's stomach, 'if you can imagine such a thing. And he waddled away, his belly dragging on the ground.'

Áed did a fine impersonation of the Dagda, waddling around the hall, and he had the whole court slapping their legs and howling in laugher. I had to bite my lips to keep myself from laughing out loud with them.

'Oh, yes, the Fomorians laughed too,' Áed said, wagging his fingers at the audience. 'But the joke was on them, sure it was. Because all the time, the Dagda had merely been stalling so that the forces of the Tuatha Dé Danann could prepare for war. And the next time the Dagda faced the Fomorians, they were defeated!'

Cheers and clapping met the end of his tale.

'Give us a poem,' one of the court cried.

'Yes, a poem!'

'How about the Morrigan's prophecies!' Cimbáeth said,

gazing down at his food. And though he didn't look in my direction, I felt somehow as though he were watching me.

'Oh, no,' Áed said, waving the request away. 'Too long. Too messy. I will stick to stories instead. Let another recite that.'

A woman poet took up the challenge, reciting the words of predictions I had made for my people those many years before. It was believed that we were living through the fertile times, as foretold in my first prophesy. As for my second, none cared much about it, for they believed they would be well dead before it happened. And even as the poet spoke the words of my dreaded warning, the gathering grew bored and returned to their drinking before the recitation had ended.

On the last night of Áed's second rotation as king, he and his two cousins gathered for a feast. It was Cimbáeth's turn to rule next and so the atmosphere was one of optimism. The harpists played dancing music and there was much laughter. There was also tension, however, between the three kings. They sat around the table, jaws clenched and hands twitching. When they spoke to each other, it was with short, curt phrases. What, I wondered, had caused the friction between the cousins?

When Díthorba's eyes met mine I knew. He looked at me as he did the leg of lamb in front of him – as something to be devoured.

So, I signed to my father, when most of the guests were asleep and he was moments away from collapsing himself. *Díthorba wants to marry me?*

Áed blinked his red-shot eyes and tried to see me clearly. 'How did you know?'

I shrugged. Wasn't it obvious, he wanted even more

power for his line? And if he and I were to have a son, he wouldn't have to share power. Only Cimbáeth's heirs would stand in the way, and Cimbáeth showed no interest in taking a wife.

He looked at me like I was meat.

Áed made a snorting noise, as he struggled to kick off his boots.

You said no?

He waved my question away. 'He has all the women of the land to pick from. I can't have him taking my best advisor away from me.'

Whether there was any truth in this, or whether it was simply because he didn't want Díthorba holding that much power, I wasn't sure. But I was grateful. The idea of Díthorba as my husband made my stomach roil. And yet, marrying a king would give me the power I craved.

I'd rather Cimbáeth, if I had to marry any of them.

Áed pinched my cheek and looked at me with one eye closed. 'He'd sooner marry a field than my little plain.' He laughed at his wordplay and fell asleep, with one boot still on.

Cimbáeth ruled for the next seven years and the crops grew. Díthorba ruled for the seven after that, and they died again. Just as winter follows summer. Díthorba made his offer of marriage a few more times to my father, and each time he was dismissed.

'She's a hag now, anyway,' Díthorba said, the third time he made the offer, spitting at the dirt by my feet. 'No one will have her.'

A hag? I was a woman in my third decade, and yet I had hardly aged. I was in my full power and beautiful. A hag! What a fool he was.

By Áed's third rotation, his body was still strong but his mind grew ever more feeble. He would send the men on stupid raids for starved cattle. He increased the grain tax in summer but forgot to increase the rationing during winter. He stopped listening to the seers and instead listened to his own mind, which was more confused each day. With each month that passed, more young men died for nothing and the stores remained bare. The stones of the fort were starting to crack around us yet he refused to make repairs.

I did not know if it was my magic that had caused his mind to unravel or simply the wearing of age. But I knew that he could not carry on as king.

'By the time Áed's rotation is done,' I heard a washer-woman say, 'there won't be any of us left to rule!'

The next morning, as he readied himself for a meeting with the other chieftains, I went to him. I brought him oat bread and honey, which I knew to be his favourite, and sat by his right side.

Father, I signed to him. *Let me handle the dealings with the chieftains today. You look tired.*

I laid my hand on his forehead, as though checking for heat there. It was cold and dry as always.

He pushed my hand aside and his eyes, which had always shone for me, were now dark with suspicion and fear.

'No!' He threw the honey and bread to the floor. 'You have to stay away from them. They want to take you away from me! I have to keep you safe. Only I can keep you safe!'

Perhaps all men tried to control the things they loved in the name of protection. But by safe he meant quiet and unseen, and I had been silent for too long.

14.

On the first day of Samhain, I went to my father and gave him the crook of my elbow.

'Morning, Macha, daughter of mine. And where are you taking me on this fair day?' His anger from the night before was forgotten.

I smiled and led him down the back stairs and out of the court, via a path only the servant girls knew. I led him out of the walls around the fort and into the forest.

After an hour's walking, he stopped. 'I'm tired, Macha, how much longer?'

I pointed ahead of me at the winding path cutting through the trees, indicating that it was not much longer.

We left the forest and started to make our way up a hillside.

'My feet are weary, Macha, how much further?'

I pointed ahead of me to the top of the hill. We were close.

I led him down the other side of the hill. Each step caused him pain, but I led him further and further away. Finally, as the sun was reaching its zenith, we arrived at a waterfall. The trees were golden brown, sunlight breaking through the gaps left by autumn. The water cascaded down the rocks, like hair falling down a woman's back.

My father sighed at the beauty of it.

I smiled at him. *Now then, wasn't this worth the walk?*

'What is this place?' he asked. 'Why have I never seen it before? Why have you never taken me here?'

I shrugged, as if to say, How is it my fault that you rarely leave the confines of the court? He ruled a whole land, and only saw a portion of it.

I bent down and undid his boots and helped him towards the edge of the pool. Weakly, with more and more of his weight borne by me, he stepped into the water.

'Oooh, it's cold,' he said with a giggle. And there he was. My father. Full of joy and light. Eyes shining only for me.

I tucked my skirts up and we waded deeper and deeper into the water, till it was up around our knees, our waists, our chests.

'I haven't swum since I was a boy,' Áed said, letting the water take the weight that his bones could no longer bear.

He floated on his back, arms paddling like eels, smiling up at the rainbows dancing in the spray. I laid my hand on his forehead, smooth of worry for the first time in years. And I pushed him under the rippling water.

He struggled for a while, legs thrashing, nails clawing at my arm, and his efforts stirred up the water, till it was raging rapids. But I stood firm and soon he was still. I let him be sucked towards the falls which now thundered like horses' hooves and returned to the court, my skirts drying as I walked.

I sneaked back in the way I had gone out. No one had seen me leave with Áed or return alone. I slipped into the flow of life at court like a salmon slipping into a shoal.

His body wasn't found for three days. Washerwomen found him and dragged his corpse to shore. They didn't recognize him at first. The force of the waterfall had stripped him of his gold-edged cloak and the eels had feasted on his flesh. It was only the gold torc about his neck that was identifiable as belonging to the High King of Ireland. I wept along with the wailing woman paid coin to howl at his death. He was buried along with his favourite horses and swords by his side. Gold was laid at his head and feet, and grain and wine was placed by his hands, should he need a bite to eat when he got wherever he was going.

Díthorba and Cimbáeth sent word that they would arrive at court within the week, eager to lay their claim. Had Áed had a son, the kingship would have gone to him. As it was, there was only me. When Díthorba and Cimbáeth arrived, I was already seated on the throne.

Díthorba's face, red from the long journey, grew redder still when he saw me. Cimbáeth tilted his head and looked at me, as he might a new species of plant he had discovered. They were both as old and worn as Áed had been, though they retained their wits.

'What,' howled Díthorba, as he strode towards the throne, 'are you doing?'

'Taking what is rightfully mine,' I said.

Díthorba froze. The whole court gasped. None had heard me speak since the day I was born. They had thought me stupid or cursed. It had taken me over thirty years before I could speak without causing fear. Now that I had found my voice again, I was going to use it.

'I claim the throne as Áed's heir.'

'That's impossible,' Díthorba bellowed, angry as always.

'That's highly unusual,' Cimbáeth said, curious as ever.

'Just because something has not been done, does not mean it cannot be done. I will rotate my rule every seven years, as per the original agreement. And when your time comes, I will share it with your eldest sons. And so it shall pass.'

'A woman cannot rule!'

I clenched my teeth. I had heard this before and it was as bitter to me now as it had been when Ogma declared it. If they couldn't see wisdom, then they would see strength.

'Then I challenge you to battle, five days from now. Defeat me, and I will stand down. You and Cimbáeth can squabble between yourselves and the land can swing from ripe to ruin for a thousand years. But should I win, I take the throne.'

Díthorba laughed, as my tribe had done when I said I should rule them. I could feel my blood rise, hissing and bubbling under my skin.

'I will defeat you. And what's more,' Díthorba said, 'I will marry you, and put babies in your belly to remind you of a woman's true purpose.'

The thought of his sweating body crushing mine chilled the heat of my blood and the food I had eaten that day churned in my stomach.

'I would rather choke.'

'You can choke on my cock,' he said, grabbing his member. Some of the court laughed at this, but any who were looking at me had the sense to hold their tongues. 'In five days then, woman.' And he left.

I might have a frail human body that could be broken, but I had magic and power he could never imagine. He had no idea what he was going up against.

Áed's court was in confusion as they waited for the battle. Their loyalty was to Áed their king, not his strange, watchful, silent daughter. And yet I had begun to reveal my true power to them. They sensed the prophecy in my words, they felt the thrum of my magic weave about the court. I spoke and they obeyed.

For five days, I prepared. I had my women collect the

herbs and flowers Airmed had said had power: gorse for protection from misfortune, primrose the bringer of good fortune, and blackthorn, the keeper of dark secrets. I bathed in them and I spoke the words of old that would toughen my skin and strengthen my arms. Armour was prepared for me, two mares chosen to lead my chariot, and an oak cut down to make me a shield. I decided to carry my father's bronze-red spear, despite the protestations of the smith. 'I could make you a sword of iron!'

He showed me then a lump of what I took to be rock. But when he rubbed at it with his calloused thumb, a grey metal shone within. This metal reminded me of Sreng's spear, forged from a fallen star. I reached out to touch it and it bit me. I pulled my hand away, glowering at the smith. Was this some jest he was playing? He was as confused as I was annoyed. I tried again, but as soon as my skin touched the iron, it burned as if I was touching a hot coal from the fire.

Iron was to be my enemy. The enemy of all of my kind.

'I will carry my father's red spear,' I said, not wanting him to see this weakness in me.

I was dressed and my armour strapped on. It was nothing compared to the weapons and adornments I had worn as one of the Tuatha Dé, but I was only going up against a man, not an army. I wove my hair into nine thick strands and painted my eyebrows and face with red clay.

'How do I look?' I asked one of the handmaidens who had been aiding me. A girl my father had taken for a slave on one of his raids, who I had set free upon his death. I had set all of the slave girls free, though most had chosen to stay, having forgotten where they had ever come from.

'Fearsome, my queen,' she said.

'Perfect.'

I walked out as the sun was rising, and I looked as glorious and as terrifying as any human woman had ever looked. A whisper went through the court. A goddess. She's a goddess.

The more they called me goddess, the more I got to like it. It had a nice ring to it after all. Without my summoning, a crow took it upon itself to land on my spear and cawed loudly at the gathering.

Not just any goddess, you bloody fools! the crow seemed to say. *She is the Morrigan.*

I called for my chariot and charioteer and they were brought forth. The horses were jumpy, but I laid my forehead against their noses and whispered calming words in their ears. We rode to the spot where the battle was to take place. Díthorba was late, of course. A petty insult. He was also drunk. I could almost smell the ale off him across the clearing. Had he been drinking his courage, I wondered, or was he so confident in his victory that it hadn't occurred to him to cease his carousing the night before? It didn't matter to me. The morning sun reflected off my bronze armour and shield boss and he had to raise a hand to protect his squinting eyes. He had brought his three young sons with him, who were as handsome as he was old and haggard. Three little kinglings in waiting, each more hungry for power than the next. I wouldn't put it past any of them to stab their father in the back and take his throne for themselves. They would have to get in line. Díthorba and I had a score to settle.

I considered him. Red-faced and puffing. I could rip out his lungs and strangle him with them. I could dig my nails deep into his chest and squash his heart like a ripe fruit. I could bite into his throat and drink his blood like wine.

With a word, I could have every beast of the field and air turn against him and trample him underfoot. There were so many slow and beautiful ways he could die.

'Come then, hag.'

Hag. That word again. Why was it that being old was the worst thing they could think of for a woman? I looked around at the women who had come to watch, those who were past their childbearing years, and all I saw were sharp eyes that sparkled with wisdom and strength that ran deep beneath their loose skin. These women had survived. They'd outlived husbands and some had outlived sons. While Díthorba would not live to see another day.

'Let's get this over with for I have—' He didn't have time to finish before my spear pierced him through his mouth. Life flickered in his eyes just long enough for him to realize he hadn't had the last word. He died, choking on my spear.

His sons cried out. Nightmare. Phantom. Screech owl. Night hag. They called me all the names, old and new. They looked more like children having a tantrum than warriors ready for battle. Their armour was too large for them, chafing at virgin, pink skin. Their weapons, too large for their soft hands, the blades untested and not a notch out of them. I saw fear in their eyes and smelt shit in their breeches. This was their father's battle – it had been his arrogance, his greed that had got him killed and now they would follow him. I don't know if it was a great tiredness for the stupidity of man or pity for them that overtook me, but I had no more desire to see their heads on my spear than I did their bodies in my bed. Crushing them would be like crushing the skull of a puppy. What challenge was that for a goddess? This was not the power I had become a human to taste. It was sour and my stomach turned at the thought of their deaths. And yet they would have to be defeated for me to hold on to power.

I closed my eyes and breathed in. A great sucking wind swirled around me, sending my hair dancing and the dirt by my feet spiralling. And then I screeched. Screeched as I had when I faced the Fir Bolg and the Fomorians. A sound that hadn't been heard in the land in a hundred years. It shook the ground and turned the fire in Díthorba's sons' bellies to ice. It sucked the leaves from the trees and drained the strength from their limbs. They dropped their weapons, cried like the children they were and fled, away from the battlefield where their father's body lay, and far into the wilderness. They would return. But when they did, then I would deal with them as the men they would become.

My great victory was declared and songs were sung and poetry composed to the Great Queen Macha – the only woman in the list of the High Kings of Ireland.

I spent the next weeks surveying my lands. What my father had let go to ruin over the past years, I restored. The people he had ignored, I listened to. They were afraid of me at first, tales travelling ahead of me, faster even than I could ride in my fastest chariot. I was a sorceress. I was a demon. I would eat their babies as I had eaten my own, for how else could they explain how I had none?

But the tales that were being told in the wake after each of my visits changed shape. Instead of eating babies, my touch turned a barren womb fertile. Instead of bringing drought, I brought fertility. I wasn't a sorceress, I was a goddess. With each village and fort I visited, I won the respect of the people. The land returned to life and I began to feel powerful again.

A month after I had taken the throne, Cimbáeth came.

'Come to face me in battle, Cimbáeth?' I asked as he entered the court. He was an old man, and there would be no glory in crushing him.

He held his hands up. 'Oh, I'm cleverer than that, Macha. Or is it the Morrigan they're calling you these days?'

I shrugged; either name would do.

'No, I'm here to make you an offer,' he said.

'I'm listening.'

'You were always good at listening.'

I permitted myself a smile. I had always liked Cimbáeth. 'Go on then.'

'I propose that instead of us rotating power every seven years, we simply rule together. As husband and wife.' He could see that this was distasteful to me and added quickly, 'Husband and wife in name only. I have no interest in bedding you and I understand you take little interest in it yourself. And as I already have a son, I have no need of an heir.'

'I didn't know that.' My father had always said Cimbáeth seemed to have no interest in bedding the women of the court.

'He's a sweet boy, and his mother a simple fisherwoman. I try to keep them both out of politics. But when I die, my rule should pass to him. So, you see, I have no need of an heir. I propose an alignment, like the ant and the aphid.'

'And am I the aphid being milked or the ant doing the milking?'

He tilted his head to the side. 'It's hard to watch your back when you're also watching your front.'

It was a wise suggestion from a kind man. I agreed and the contracts were drawn up and the festivities arranged. We were married within the week, and Cimbáeth shared

my throne, though not my bed. We made a good partnership. He tempered my frustrations, and I gave direction
to his daydreams. For seven years we ruled and the land
was happy. The population grew till the fort was packed
to bursting.

After some time, I heard rumbling that the sons of
Díthorba were gathering strength in the south of the land.
They were spreading stories about me. That I was cursed.
A leper. That any who set eyes on me wouldn't live to see
the next day. I had killed my own mother, they said, bedded
my own father, and my hunger knew no limits. They drew
men to them, as their stories grew in strength. It was only
a matter of time before they raided my lands, next year, if
not before this year was out. I decided that instead of waiting for their attacks I would seek them out.

I told only Cimbáeth of my plans to travel south and
find the three sons. I dressed in plain robes of linen, called
for my oldest chariot and set forth. The business of ruling
had tired me, and I was itching for a little fun.

I came upon Díthorba's eldest son in a forest clearing,
eating his breakfast. I could kill him with a word, but where
would be the play in that? I could seduce him with a look,
but again, I wanted more of a challenge. Hag they had
called me. Then a hag I would become.

I unwound my hair, and let it turn grey and ragged. I
transformed my robes into rags of flax cloth. My smooth,
pink skin, I made wrinkled and grey. I looked at my reflection in a pool. Still not enough. I summoned lumps to grow
across my face and arms, ulcers to burst on my hands and
feet. I twisted my limbs till I was a hunchback leper. I was
as hideous as they had described me.

I stepped forward into the clearing and called out to

the man. 'Son of Díthorba. Will you not pass the time with me?'

'Get out of my way, hag.'

I blew air towards him, a kiss of breath from a goddess. He made it three steps before the scent reached him. Like honey to a bee, he was drawn in. As revolted as he was by my physical form, he couldn't contain his arousal. 'Who are you, lady?'

'I am but an old leper, begging for scraps. Will you share your bread with me?'

'I will share more than my bread. Come, I must have you.' He loosed the belt around his waist and his breeches fell around his ankles. He waddled towards me, arms outstretched and member erect. I ran my hand carefully against his cheek and he shivered at my touch.

'Your hands are like silk,' he said.

I ran my hand down his strong arm, feeling the curve of muscles there.

'Your touch is like fire,' he moaned.

I ran my hand over his chest, my clawed fingers dancing through his chest hair. And then, with a push, I knocked him to the ground. There was a moment when he still believed we were about to make love, but then I grabbed his arm and flipped him over, pushing his face into the dirt. While he struggled against me, I tore his belt from his breeches and tied his hands and feet, like a pig ready for slaughter. The more he struggled, the tighter his binds became. I crouched down next to him and whispered in his ear. 'Not so revolted by a hag after all.'

His eyes glinted with recognition. And he began shouting and bellowing for aid. But there was none. I dragged his trussed body into a thicket of brambles and I moved on.

I came across Díthorba's second son washing himself in a stream, his clothing in a pile by the riverbed. Seducing the eldest son had been too easy. I made myself even more hideous, adding boils, pulling out my front teeth and yanking out chunks of hair. I stepped out into the clearing.

'Son of Díthorba,' I said. 'May I come and bathe with you?'

'Be gone, hag!' he replied. 'I will not have your foulness pollute this water.'

I ignored him and stripped off my rags and stepped into the river. As soon as my toe was submerged, the second son took a shuddering breath, as if breathing in the sweetest scent.

'Lady, come to me. Let me wash your hair, kiss your feet. Let me worship you.'

I waded through the water till I stood in front of him. He was more beautiful than his elder brother. His skin even softer, his muscles tighter. I ran my hand against his cheek.

'Your skin is softer than seal fur,' he said.

I ran my fingers down his neck, tracing the contours of his tendons.

'Your touch is like ice.'

Before he knew what was happening, I knocked him down and grabbed a handful of reeds from the river and used them to bind his hands and legs like a lamb ready for the spit. I pulled him to the shore and crouched over him.

'Not so revolted by a hag after all.'

I dragged him, spitting and shouting, to the same place I had hidden his brother and moved on.

I came across Díthorba's youngest son asleep in the branches of an oak tree. He was the most beautiful of them all, with a strong jaw, wide eyes and brown hair that danced around his face in sweet curls. For a moment I was tempted to shake off my hag form and take my pleasure with the young man. And yet he had stood next to his brothers while they'd spat insults at me. He'd spread rumours, pouring poison into the ears of my people. He had to pay. I made myself even more crooked, twisted one of my feet till it faced behind me, pulled out more of my teeth and my hair and rotted the fingers from one hand. I coughed, and he opened his eyes.

'Son of Díthorba,' I said, 'may I come and rest with you a while?'

He swung his legs off the branch and stood up. 'Mother,' he said, addressing me in the polite form, 'come, rest your bones, for it looks as though you have had a long journey.'

His gentility tested my resolve. I sat in the crook of the tree and watched him as he watched me.

'Thank you, son,' I said.

His eyes traced the lines of my body, crooked and malformed though it was. He licked his lips. 'I have never lain with a woman.'

His breath grew heavy and his arousal quickened. He closed the space between us.

'But I would lie with you now.'

The sparkling light in his eyes darkened. He leapt on me, pushing his face into mine, pinning my arms to my side with his hands. But his strength was no match for mine. I pushed him away, tore a vine from the tree and wrapped him up, like a fly in a spider's web.

'You were so close to escaping my wrath,' I said, looking down at him. 'And then you showed your true nature.'

He knew me then. 'Please, please, forgive me. I did not know it was you.'

'And should that make it better? That you would treat a helpless crone worse than you would a queen?'

I dragged him to where his brothers were waiting. I shook off my hag form and called my horse and chariot to me. I tied all three of them to the axle of my chariot and dragged them back to my fort.

When I threw them on the floor before the throne, there were gasps followed quickly by jeers. *Kill them. Rip out their intestines. Put their heads on spears.*

My mouth watered at the thought of sinking my teeth into their flesh, of flaying their skin. But I had a better idea.

'I will put their strength to work,' I said. 'They will build the greatest fort in the province.'

I pulled a map of our land on to the table and took a brooch from my cloak. I used the pin to scratch a circle, marking the boundaries of a fort one hundred and fifty feet wide. The three sons were dragged away and made to work night and day till their backs were broken and my fort was built. I named it Emain Macha. The Brooch of Macha.

Cimbáeth and I moved there, ruling as one till he died of a plague which took many of the men, including his sweet son. I nursed him as he died, sores peeling back his skin to expose dark, rotting flesh beneath.

'This is no way to die,' I had said to him, as he coughed up blood like clay.

'A man is not measured by his death,' he said, each word a blade in his lungs. 'But by how he has lived.'

'Tell that to the poets,' I said. But he was already gone.

I ruled alone for the seven years after that. It was lonely and it was exhausting. Carrying the weight of their hopes, their prayers, was as crippling as Ogma and his firewood. There was never enough of me to give. I would answer one demand and a hundred more would come. I would make one decision at dawn and have a thousand more to make before sunset. Before taking the throne, I was invisible. A watcher in the shadows. Now I was seen, standing in full light, and it was blinding.

The people sensed my tiredness and the fragile belief they had in me was fading. They called me *cailleach*, witch, and wondered when I would follow my father and husband into death. I could feel the land herself turning away from me. Our last harvest had been a poor one and the cattle had lost more calves than they delivered. I wondered what had become of the Stone of Fál, the last treasure of the Tuatha Dé. And if I found it, if I laid my foot on it, would it cry my name?

One morning, I was awoken to warning bells. I dressed and went to find the source of the commotion.

'Invaders, my queen,' one of my guards said, pointing to a group moving in the distance.

It was a raiding party of twenty warriors. As they drew closer, I recognized their weapons and clothing as belonging to men from Tír Eoghain, the land that had once been ruled by Lugaid Laigdech before Aéd had taken it for his own. I knew the cause of this raid and the name of the man who led them. Rechtaid Rígderg, son of Lugaid Laigdech, come at last for his revenge.

'Let us go out to meet them,' one of my warriors said. 'I will take fifty men and crush them before they are an arrow's distance from Emain Macha.'

'No,' I said. 'Let me go. Alone.'

There was much protest, but they had long learned they could not set themselves against my will.

It had been many years since I had strapped on my

armour and ridden out for war, and my fingers struggled at the buckles. I called for my chariot and rode out to meet Rígderg.

'Come at last,' I said as Rígderg and his men stopped in front of me.

He was nothing impressive. Short and stocky with thin strands of brown hair that blew like cobwebs in the wind. His sword was newly forged and its sharp edge glinted in the early-morning sun. Had he ever used it? I wondered. Had he ever killed anyone?

I could have defeated him, as easily as I had any of the men who had come to test me. I could have seduced him as easily as I had Díthorba's sons. But I was so tired. I had wanted power, but I learned that ruling was not about power, it was about compromise. And with each concession I had shrunk some of myself, slicing pieces of myself away to fit in the box I had built for myself.

I stepped out of my chariot and closed the distance between us. I peeled off my armour and lay my shield on the ground. I lifted my chin, giving him easy access to my throat. As Rígderg hacked my head from my neck, I smiled. When my spear dropped from my limp hand, it felt as though I had laid down the weight of a mountain.

15.

I returned to my old body waiting deep beneath the earth. I stretched, my bones coming to life once more. This body was weaker than I remembered and bore some signs of age: my breasts sagged, my skin was mottled like moss on a stone. Yet being back in my old skin, feeling the blood of the Tuatha Dé rush through my veins once more, I felt stronger than I had as a human. As I moved, I sensed power returning to me.

I ran my dry tongue over sharp teeth. Hunger gnawed at my belly and thirst clawed at my throat. The cave had begun to crumble, the entrance blocked by fallen rocks. The humans no longer sent their boys into the darkness, for their goddess had not been there to greet them. The pathway to the otherworld was safe. And I was without purpose.

Who was I? If not a warrior, if not a queen, if not a goddess? Was I nothing?

I drank cool, sweet water and slaughtered a deer for fresh meat, and yet I hungered still. It was different from the bloodlust that had consumed me in the past. I laid my hand over my chest and felt the ache beneath. The same ache that dogged my final days as Macha. Loneliness.

I missed Aéd as he had been when he was young and his eyes shone with love for me. I missed Cimbáeth and his curiosity about the world. And for the first time since they had left, I missed my family.

Oh, how I longed to hear my sisters' soft chatter, to feel

the Dagda's strong arms around me. And Lugh, shining, golden, fickle Lugh, would he even remember me?

The tribe had kept the promise they made and each year, on the night before Samhain, Lugh, the Dagda and my sisters would ride out of my cave on their glowing white horses, the rest of the tribe behind them. Snarling beasts followed in their wake, sniffing the grounds for mortal blood and for a night the land belonged to the Tuatha Dé again. When the dawn came, they would return to the lands of summer and sunlight. Sometimes they would take a human back with them. A giggling babe that had caught their fancy or a beautiful young woman or man they could not resist.

In the early years, I returned to Cruachan and waited. When they came riding out, I called out to them, but they, caught up in the frenzy of the wild ride, neither heard nor saw me. And so I stopped going for it was too painful.

But if they were able to pass over, then surely so was I?

It became so clear. My time in the lands above was done. I was no longer needed to guard the pathways, for there were none left who knew they even existed. I could at last join my family as I should have done those many years before.

I washed, brushed out my hair and felt a lightness come over me as I turned not towards the sky, but to the earth. I walked deeper than I ever had before into the darkness of my cave, crawling on my belly across wet stones and through slick mud. I swam through cold waters that seemed never to end. Just as I had not a breath left in my lungs, I came at last to the shores of the other lands.

I lay, panting, on sand as soft as milled oats. My strength returned to me and I stood blinking in golden sunlight that shone like a meadow at harvest, though I felt no heat on my skin. The mud that had coated me was gone, and I was clean as though I had just bathed. Ahead of me, I saw a shimmering meadow of flowers and ferns of all kinds swaying in a gentle breeze. The trees hung heavy with fruit and the hills rolled and fell, covered in soft green mossy grass. A river ran through it, like melted silver, and bright salmon leapt in the shimmering waters. A bank of swans came to settle on the river, honking their arrival. In the distance I saw herds of horses running freely with no fences to contain them and crystal-white cattle, heads bowed as they grazed on soft grass. None kept watch, for there were no wolves to prey on them, no snakes to bite them. I caught glimpses of children out of the corners of my eyes and heard their laughter, though when I turned to look at them, they had vanished into the air.

I walked forward and as I was about to step foot on the grass of the meadow, I felt myself being held back by invisible arms. The image of the meadow rippled and twisted, as though I had been looking at a reflection in a still lake that someone had thrown a stone into. I held my hand up and felt for the boundary between where I stood and the beautiful land beyond. I felt heat and a thrum of power buzzing against my hand. I pushed against it, hit it, screeched at it, but the more I fought against it, the harder the barrier became so that it was like trying to walk through stone.

I saw then, walking across the meadow, my sisters: Ériu, Fódla and Banba. They were gathering flowers and dancing through the long grasses, then stopped to dip their small feet in the waters of the river. They were unchanged. Still as young as the day they had passed over.

'Sisters,' I cried out. 'Beloved sisters!'

They did not hear me. They danced and laughed while I fell to my knees on the soft sands and hung my head.

'You're not welcome in Tír na nÓg.'

I looked up. It was Lugh, wading through the shallow waters behind me, carrying an oyster the size of his hand. I had almost forgotten just how truly beautiful he was. His lips were like rowan berries, his eyes like bluebells and his eyelashes were as dark as an unquenched blade. He looked at me and smiled, but it was a smile that held none of the warmth it once had.

'And why not?' I asked.

There was a time when I had lost myself in his beauty. When I had sat playing games with him, watching him while he watched the board. I would lose, just to see him smile. And then he had tired of me, just as he tired of all games.

He peeled open the shell and held it to his red lips. He sucked the sweet flesh of the oyster into his mouth and swallowed.

'You broke your geas,' he said, throwing the shell into the waves.

I had only one geas placed on me. The dying binding of my mother never to use my power to hurt the tribe. And I had not broken it. I told him so.

He walked around me in a slow circle, taking in the wrinkles around my eyes, the marble lines running up my calves, before stopping in front of me.

'You killed Dian Cécht.'

I shook my head. 'The Sons of Mil killed him. He was dying of the poisons they had forced down his throat before I even laid a finger on him.'

'Ah, but you watched.' He wagged a finger at me, as though I was a child being scolded for stealing fruit. 'And then you tore his body apart so that he could not receive an honourable burial. So he could not join us here.'

I looked again to the meadow where my sisters were lying in the soft grasses, bathing in the heat of a sun I could not feel.

'He deserved no less for what he did to . . .' I couldn't bring myself to say my son's name. Even after all this time, the pain was like a pierced lung.

'That may be so. But nonetheless, you're not welcome here. Sorry, I don't make the rules.'

'Since when?' I asked. For Lugh had always set the rules of any game we had played before.

He smiled, as though I had caught him cheating at fid-chell. 'Maybe when you die it will be different. Oooh, perhaps I should kill you?' Lugh said, looking up, as if waiting for an answer in the sky. It was blue passing into deep purple without a single cloud. 'Dian Cécht was my grandfather after all. It would be just.'

Lugh had been the most famed warrior of the Tuatha Dé; he had killed Balor, but he had never tested his powers against mine. 'You could try,' I said.

My talons pushed against the calloused tips of my fingers. It had been decades since they had pierced my flesh, but I knew they would still be sharp.

Lugh laughed. 'You know, I don't know who would win. Isn't that fun?'

'Battle was always a sport to you,' I said.

'And to you it was . . .' He tilted his head as he gazed at me, trying to find the right word.

I answered for him. 'Everything.'

'Yes, so it was.'

He sat on the soft sandy shores and patted the ground beside him. I walked further away, pacing back and forth before the veil that blocked my way forward.

'What great battles have you fought recently?' he asked. 'Oh, come, you must tell me every detail. How I long to hear new stories. I have heard all of Ogma's tales a thousand times and I am so bored!'

The truth was that I had not been in a battle since Lugh and I last fought side by side. There had been skirmishes, I had killed men, but I had not had a battle of old.

He must have seen the answer in my expression. 'Shame. You were always so magnificent on the battlefield. After all, it's what you were made for.'

I closed my eyes and saw myself as I had once been. A spear-hopping creature of fury. Leading armies against enemies. He was right, I had been magnificent. But that version of me felt long gone. As though I had lost her somewhere in the darkness of my cave, as the fury bled out of me and into the nightmares of the boys who had come to be made men.

'Oh, well, I must be going.' Lugh stood, brushing the golden sands from his hand. 'It's been good seeing you, Badb. Or Macha or whatever you call yourself now. I will send your love to your sisters and to the others.'

He walked away into the meadow where I could not follow, the air around him glistening like morning mist, and didn't so much as look back.

16.

I returned the way I had come, back through the cold waters. As I swam, I cursed myself for attempting the journey. Even if the way had not been blocked for me, what would I have done? Sat in the sunshine next to my sisters as they laughed? Joined Ogma in his tales? I was not needed there. I had never been needed there.

The darkness of my cave seemed even blacker after the brightness of the other lands, and though it felt as if I had only been away for a matter of hours, my birds told me that decades had passed. I ate a little, drank a little, and tried to sleep. I dreamt. And in my dream I saw two great bulls in battle. One white. One brown. Each more beautiful than any creature to have ever walked the earth. In their battle they carved up the land. Where their horns gouged into the soil, valleys were made. Where their hooves struck at rock, mountains were formed. Flesh was flung and blood sprayed and the land was cleaved in two. Before I could understand the meaning of this vision, I was awoken by a soft nose, nuzzling against my skin.

I opened my eyes to see the huge brown eyes of a beast staring at me. It mooed sorrowfully. Was this one of the bulls from my dream made real? How had it found its way here, into the gloom of my dwelling? Had I called to it in my dream? I ran my hand over its skin, soft and smooth as rabbit's fur, and down its hindquarters, feeling the thickness of the muscle under soft skin. I felt then a round, heavy belly and udders, full of milk. A cow, not a bull. And one near to birthing. I knew then the cause of sorrow, for her udders were fit to burst.

I squatted and grabbed hold of the teats. Milk sprayed out in fast jets on to the ground, from where it ran deep into the darkness. It must have been days since she had been milked.

'There,' I said when I had finished, 'is that better?' She pushed her forehead into my hand and I scratched her between the eyes. 'Come, let's get you home.'

I was about to lead her out of the cave when I heard a shouting. An angry howling like a wolf in pain. I told the cow to stay and went to find the source of this noise.

'Who is howling and disturbing me so?' I said, walking out into the sunshine.

At first, I thought it was a man, for the figure was tall, with broad shoulders and thighs thick and muscled. But as my eyes adjusted to the light, I saw it was a woman. She had hair the colour of bark and skin nut brown from time in the sun. She held a spear in a strong hand and shook it at me.

'I am Odras, wife of Buchet, and I have come to reclaim my cow, you . . . you cunning raven-caller.' She waved her spear in my direction. 'Give it back to me or I'll take it from your dead hands.'

I looked back over my shoulder. I had intended to find where the cow had come from, but now I was in a mind to keep her for myself.

'You would forfeit your life for a cow?' I asked, amused by her furious spitting. She might look like a warrior, but she hissed like a kitten.

'Not just any cow. My husband's most prized heifer,' Odras said.

'Then why has he not come to reclaim her for himself?'

She stumbled over her words, her flushed face paling a little.

'He doesn't know it's gone?' I said, understanding a little of her desperation.

'I fell asleep and she got away. When I awoke, I raced after her, but it was too late. Your cave had swallowed her up. Please, I have already failed to give him a child. I don't know what he will do if he learns that I have lost his beloved cow.'

'If your husband would strike a wife as loyal as you over a lost cow, then you should be shaking that twig at him, not me.'

'Oh, no, he would never strike me. He has never raised a hand against me. He is a good man and a good husband.'

'Then what?' I asked. What could any man do that would make a woman as strong as this quake so?

She took in a jagged breath. 'He may leave me.'

I laughed. How ridiculous this woman was. 'Then let him,' I said. 'Look at you, you could be the equal of any man and yet you stand here wailing because you want nothing more out of life than to be a loyal wife?'

'I would sacrifice everything for him, for that is what it means to be a good wife. Please, please.' She fell to her knees, sobbing, bubbles popping from her nose. 'I love him. He is my whole life. I can't live without him.'

Her begging turned my stomach. Her tears made bile rise in my throat. She was strong, and yet she had kept herself small. She belonged on a battlefield, hacking heads from necks. Stories should be told about her bravery, her brilliance, and yet the only tale that would be told about her was what a good, loyal wife she was.

Let her cry, I thought. Let her be nothing but tears

177

flowing for ever from here to the sea. I spoke words over her, and she was unmade. A pathetic, sobbing woman one heartbeat, a wild, rushing river the next. It was a kindness. Better be a powerful, torrid river than a weak woman. Better be anything but that.

I led the cow out of the cave and she drank deeply from the water that had once been her mistress. In the days that came, the cow gave birth to a beautiful brown bull that I helped into the world. I held him in my arms for a moment, slick with fluids, and stared into his brown eyes. I saw in them death and destruction to come.

I kept the bull and his mother, hidden from the eyes of humans by a magical mist where time slowed. I slept by the river and my dreams became Odras's dreams. Instead of battle, I dreamt of the warm touch of a man's hand; instead of power, I dreamt of a child crawling under blankets at night to be comforted. Small joys that I had once had. What if I could shrink like that? Would it shrink my aching loneliness too? If instead of a goddess, instead of a ruler, I could become just a woman, a wife and even a mother? Hadn't I been happy when I had been with Meche? Hadn't I been needed?

It would be so simple. I knew what it was to be a human woman, I could become one again. But instead of reaching for power, I would seek contentment, just as my mother had once wanted for me. I could take on the form of Odras and return to her beloved husband and be welcomed into his life. But no. I would always know it was my magic that bound him, as it had once bound Aéd. I needed to know if I was capable of being loved without any of my power.

I listened to the prayers of men caught on the winds and for the first time in my existence, I answered one.

17.

Across the Ulaid border to the north was a man named Crunden. He was a good man. Not a brave one or a wise one, but I had no need of either bravery or wisdom. I had more than enough of that myself. Crunden was a farmer of cattle and a father of children who had lost their mother.

I had heard his prayers on the wind: 'Please, gods, send me a good woman.'

I was not a good woman. Neither good nor woman. But I could change my shape at will, so why not my nature? I could become a wife and mother and live a life small enough to feel full, shrink myself down to the size of a house and a man and children and feel some edges to me. Maybe that would heal my aching heart?

I left the cow and her baby hidden from eyes and time and went north. The land had changed since I had last gone walking. The five provinces had now become five kingdoms, each ruled by a different king. Connacht, in the west, where I had made my home in Cruachan; Mide in the north-east, where Tara stood still; Mumhain in the south, from where the Sons of Mil first came; Laigin in the south-east, the largest of the provinces; and Ulaid in the north, where I had lived and died as Queen Macha.

Winter had crept over the land. The trees were bare as crow-picked skeletons. The grass in patchy tufts buried under mud. The wild animals of the land had to break the ice that covered their drinking spots with their dry noses, before setting grey tongues to work licking at nothing but dirt. Wolves, deer, foxes all put aside their cycle of hunter and hunted to drink at the same sorry spots. It was too cold to rain even, the water turned to shards of ice before they hit the ground.

I travelled further north, staying to the river ways, till I crossed into Ulaid, now ruled by a young king called Conchobar mac Ness, and found my way to Crunden's land. I wove through his small cattle herd, brushing my hand against their hides; they were thick and plump still, despite the harshness of winter. Their hay was well stocked and the water butts filled. If a man cared this much for his cows, what fine care he would take of a wife. I tried to remember what Odras had looked like and modelled myself on a version of her. Shook out my nine tresses and replaced them with a single brown braid. Turned my cape of feathers into skirts of rough wool and tried not to mind the itching. Being a wife meant making sacrifices, isn't that what Odras had said?

There was no one there when I let myself in to Crunden's home: a crannog with a gentle sloping roof built on reclaimed marshland. The fire in the hearth was starting to splutter, and so I hitched up my skirts and got to my knees to tend to it. I breathed on the embers and they caught, flames dancing once more, and I thought of Brigid for the first time in many years and how she had the skill to coax any spark into a fire. The warmth felt good against my cold, damp cheeks. I had felt the heat of the great fires that kept the Dagda's cauldron bubbling. The flames of a battlefield set to light. The fires of Emain Macha kept ever burning. But I had never felt the simple warmth of a hearth. This was more like sunlight on your face in the summer. More like a kiss. I added more logs to the fire, thinking of Ogma and his servitude. How he had been forced to carry fire-wood for Bres, the weight of it bending his back. Would it be such a bad thing, to have such a simple purpose? To do nothing with your days but feed a fire?

I had watched the women of this land as Macha, listened to them, and channelled what I'd seen and heard. I thought of Odras and wives like her and pushed myself into the shape of them. I got to my feet, bare on the cold flagstones, and set to work. Cleaning, tidying. I found grain and dried meat in the store cupboard, and a small patch of herbs and vegetables growing outside: nothing like the stores of Emain Macha, but enough for a humble meal. I began cooking in a small iron pot over the fire I had brought to life. Such simple acts. I didn't know where I had learned them.

The house was warm, the floor was swept and the food nearly ready when Crunden and his children came home. There were three children. A girl, a boy and a babe, held in the girl's arms. Neither of the two toddling children came up higher than my hip. I didn't know the age of humans, but they can't have seen more than five winters. The babe was hardly off the breast. They were scruffy, dirty-faced and their clothes looked tattered at the edges. But they were strong. Like the cattle outside, Crunden had kept them well fed. He himself, however, looked lean, his legs slim, his collarbones jutting through his skin.

He had been too busy stamping the mud from his shoes and fixing the leathers that draped over the doorway to keep out the wind to notice me at first.

'Oooh, it's warm—' he said, as he turned around.

His hand shot to a small club that hung at his hip, ready

to defend his family from invasion. But as his sunken eyes took me in, looking me up and down, he softened and shook his head in wonder at what was before him.

'Who?'

'Come, husband,' I said, my voice soft and tempered. 'Come, warm yourself by the fire. And the little ones, oh, look at the state of you all. Come, I'll have you all fixed up in no time.'

The children came at once, drawn in by my honeyed voice. Crunden, however, stood frozen in the doorway. 'Husband?' he said at last. 'But you are a goddess.'

I had not hidden my true form well enough.

As I approached him, I realized he was not as tall as the form I had taken. I shifted myself with each slow step, shrinking myself so that by the time we stood close, I was looking up at him. Men, I understood, wanted to feel stronger than their wives.

'Yes, husband. I am your wife now. I will take care of you. But there is one condition.'

His eyes drank me in, running over my hair, my wide hips, my strong arms. 'Anything.'

'It is but a simple condition, nothing at all.'

'I would do any task for you, name it. I would climb to the top of Slieve Donard and bring you back ice-cold waters to quench your thirst. I would go into the lands below and steal apples from the trees of Tír na nÓg. I would risk the wrath of King Conchobar himself to bring you food from his table.' He was a talker, this one. A dreamer. It was a wonder he hadn't talked the legs off his cattle and the ears off his children.

I stopped his chatter with a finger to his lip. 'You must tell no one that I am a goddess. That is my one condition.

As long as you keep your silence, I will stay here and care for you and your children and we shall be content.'

He laughed at that. 'Is that all? I had expected you to ask for a handful of my flesh or the colour of my eyes, which I would have given to you willingly and more.'

'We are agreed then.' I clapped my hands together, and a peel of thunder rolled as the pact was made. 'Now, sit, sit. You look as though you could eat a mangy horse through a bramble hedge.'

He sat, the children too, and I fussed about them, feeding them, cleaning them, cooing over them.

One of them looked up at me with their big, wide eyes. 'Are you our mother now?'

My instinct was to screech. To recoil from the need in those eyes. To run and run and run. I had been wanted before, by my beloved Meche, by my dear father, Áed, but never needed in this raw, clinging way. It disgusted me and enticed me.

I pushed down the repulsion and smiled. 'Yes, child, I'm your mother now.'

I turned then to Crunden, the man I had chosen from all men of the land because his need had been the greatest and his nature the softest. A good man and a good husband. A man who loved easily and who, I believed, loved me from that very moment. But could I love him? Could I love this soft, gentle human? Could I allow him to have mastery over me, knowing I could crush him in a moment? He had none of the Dagda's power, none of Lugh's light, and I had been unable to truly love them, so why would he be any different? Perhaps love took time, like ice melting. Or perhaps being loved would be enough?

'And what should I call you, fearsome queen?' Crunden asked.

I thought of the name Áed had given me. It had served me well enough as a human and might serve me again. 'You may call me Macha.'

So it was that my life as a wife began.

18.

As Crunden's cheeks plumped out and the children sprouted up, I grew smaller and smaller, as if I was giving some of my life to them. I spent my days cleaning, cooking, listening to the children play and sing. I set traps for rabbits and skinned them for the pot. Helped Crunden milk the cows and bring calves into the world and learned the use of the plough. My nights, I spent in Crunden's bed, as he took a husband's payment: pleasant enough, if always over too quickly and never concerned with my satisfaction.

But dusk I spent alone, running with the king's horses.

Conchobar wintered his horses on a plain that bordered Crunden's lands. A herd numbering one hundred times one hundred and every one of them strong and beautiful. I had few dealings with the king. He had become king when he was just seven years old, so Crunden told me, his mother trading her hand in marriage to King Fergus for her son's place on the throne. It had been a deal that was only meant to last for a year. But Conchobar's mother was a better leader than many and her whispers in her son's ears had made the people of Ulaid love him. So when the year was up, they decided to keep him. Fergus stepped aside, smiling, making alliances with the new king, but all the time he was watching for his chance to make the throne his own once more. Conchobar ruled for seven years, with his mother's good guidance, but when she died his true nature showed through. He was not, in truth, the ruler they had believed him to be. He was prone to fits of pique, his ego easily bruised. But as long as everyone around him kept low, their eyes averted and their praise to the rafters, he served them well. He assembled a group of warriors and named them the Red Branch, after their practice of displaying the severed heads of their enemies on tree branches. They were believed to be the most brutal, the most fearsome, in all of the land, and took to raiding the borders knowing that the other provinces would be too afraid of them to extract revenge. Aside from his Red Branch warriors, the only other thing that earned him praise of the poets was his horses. And on that matter, the poets spoke true.

I would slip off my heavy shoes and join them on their evening run. My feet so swift they hardly touched the earth. I would run with the horses, the thundering of their hooves an echo of the beating of my heart, till I outran them all. Only then, in those brief moments, did I feel free. When the sun set and the horses dropped their noses to graze, I would put my heavy shoes back on and return to Crunden's hearth.

One evening, after I had been with Crunden for a year, I found him waiting for me on my return, his eyes wide, his manhood hard.

I smiled as I approached him, amused at how easy it was to impress human men. 'What is it, my husband?'

'By all the gods, woman, you are a wonder. You alone in the whole of Ireland can outrun the king's horses and here you are, not a bead of sweat or a flush in your face. It has been a year that you have tended to my hearth and attended my bed and I sometimes forget your true nature. How did I get so lucky to call a goddess my wife?'

I had chosen him because he was a good man. It sounded

simple, but it was rare in this world. He was kind and he was gentle and I found that I liked to make him happy.

I took his hand and laid it on my belly. 'More than just a wife, I am soon to be a mother.'

I'd felt the swirl of life in my belly twice since being with him, but I had taken the herbs taught to me by Airmed and after washed in the river and let my blood flow, not yet ready to bear him children. The pain of losing Meche was still too vast, too strangling. But at last, I decided I might risk motherhood again. Risk the pain of loving.

When I had carried Meche, I had been eager for his birth, desperate to fully own my body again. But now, I enjoyed being pregnant. I liked how my body changed shape not because of my will, but because of the will of the twins within me. I knew it was twins as I could feel their fluttering hearts like moths in my womb, their whispers like voices heard in another room. I liked how Crunden fussed over me, rubbing my feet while he sang our babies songs and wove them long tales. His only demand on me during that time was that I take my bed rest and give up my running with the horses for fear that I might shake the babes free. I ached for the freedom of the run but I agreed. One more small sacrifice.

I knew I was fit enough and strong enough to keep working till the end, but I permitted it. It entertained me to play at being a weak woman. I ate anything I could get my hands on and slept till noon and let the children run wild and it was all encouraged. It was a luxurious laziness. So unlike when I had retreated before.

Around the time I was due to give birth, King Conchobar sent word that Crunden was to attend a feast to celebrate his betrothal to a young woman called Medb, the daughter of King Eochu Feidlech of Connacht. I pitied this Medb. I had seen whipping scars on some of his horses of late; a man who would beat a horse so viciously would be sure to beat a wife.

Conchobar was always throwing feasts so that his people could raise their cups to his name and sing songs of his greatness. I admired the poets of his court weaving such rich cloth from such weak threads. Crunden had never before been summoned to the feast.

'Why now?' I asked. 'Why does he ask you to go now?'

'It's been a full year since I showed my face at court, I supposed he's wanting to check I'm still alive.' Crunden laughed it away but something cold and heavy turned in my chest.

'Don't let him go, Mother,' one of my unborn children whispered.

'Nothing good will come of this,' sighed the other.

Not yet born and they'd inherited their mother's gift for prophecy.

I asked Crunden not to go, but he brushed me off. I begged with him. Attempted to seduce him. But he was set.

'Hush, woman,' he said. 'My king calls and the summoning of a king is worth seventy times the fussing of a wife.'

'Or the warning of a goddess?'

'Ah, but you're no longer a goddess, are you? You're my pretty Macha.' He stroked my cheek with his calloused hand. 'Now hush.' And he left.

Crunden's children watched me, huddled in fear, as I paced the floors waiting for his return. I could turn into a flock of crows and go and spy on him. I could whisper to the spiders in the rafters and the beetles in the wood and have them report back. I could become a great wolf and tear everyone at the feast to shreds. But for the babies inside me, I remained.

When heavy footsteps crunched on the stones outside the door, I knew it wasn't Crunden come home. I opened the door to two of Conchobar's Red Branch warriors.

'And what do you think you're doing coming here with your swords out at this time of night?'

They hesitated, seeing me pregnant or seeing me fearsome, I don't know. But it was only a flicker of a moment before they chose their orders to their king over their own wits.

One of them laid hands on my right arm. 'You're to come with us, wife of Crunden,' he said.

'Why?'

The other took my left arm. 'To prove your husband a liar and watch him die.'

I'd come to care for Crunden in my way, and it sounded as though the fool had got himself into trouble and needed me. I told Crunden's children not to worry, that their father would be home soon, and allowed myself to be taken.

They bound my wrists and bundled me on to the back of a chariot and we set off into the night. The two guards didn't speak to me on the journey and so when we passed through the wooden walls of Emain Macha, I still had no idea what I was about to walk into, only that blood lay ahead of me.

'Don't go in, Mother,' one of my twins said.

'Shake off their bonds and run,' the other warned.

It would be no more than wiping a cobweb from my hands to loosen their rough ropes; I could tear these men's heads off and add them to my staff. But Crunden was inside and he needed me.

189

The heat and noise of Conchobar's halls hit me like a punch as I was brought inside. Fires were blazing, all were singing and shouting. The Red Branch warriors were deep in their cups and I watched as the serving women kept filling and filling, hoping that the men might pass out rather than drag them to their beds. The platters were empty, the feast almost at its end, which is always when things turn dangerous. When the men get bored of the entertainment put on and start looking to make entertainment of their own.

I had never seen them before, but I recognized some of the men from the tales Crunden had told me about the court. The hard-eyed Fergus, the fretful druid Cathbad, and King Conchobar himself, who looked to be part wild boar. Some said that Cathbad was Conchobar's true father, the old king's daughter having taken him to her bed to fulfil a prophecy, though I could see no similarities in their looks or manners. Cathbad was slim and narrow-faced, and fidgeted endlessly as though at any moment an enemy might burst through the doors and attack them all. While Conchobar was broad, and had a thick, large forehead. He lay on his throne, legs tossed over the side, as though he had not a single care to trouble that large brow of his. Behind him stood a woman dressed in white, with silver chains hung around her neck. She shared Conchobar's wide forehead, though her face narrowed to a sharp point, like an upturned teardrop, and had large, bird-like eyes that scanned the crowd. Her mouth was pursed tight, as though she was forcing herself not to speak. Deichtre, Conchobar's sister and charioteer, she must be. Crunden said she had been a wild girl, running off with her friends without giving a word to the king. If that had ever been true, those days were long gone, for the woman before me was as trapped as any slave.

On the steps below the throne sat my husband, and never a sorrier thing had I seen. They'd bound him as they had me. I strode forward, refusing to bow before the king as I approached, and a slow silence settled over the assembly.

'I'm here for my husband,' I said. I hardly recognized my own voice. I had spoken in courts before. The gods themselves had asked me for counsel. I had ruled in this very court as Queen Macha. But it had been some time since I'd had eyes on me and there was a waver in my voice as if I did not believe I deserved to be here. As though in trying so hard to be a wife, I had forgotten how to be a goddess.

When I spoke, Conchobar pulled himself upright. I could see the reason he took offence so easily. He was short. As short as one of Crunden's children back on the farm. His throne was raised on a plinth and he'd stacked animal furs on the seat. I even believed I saw a thicker heel on his boots.

'You're here because I called you here, woman.'

'And why is that?' Crunden refused to meet my eye. What had the man done?

'Your husband has made an outrageous boast and we have brought you here to see the truth of it.'

'What boast is that?'

'A strange one indeed. For now I lay eyes on you, I see that he could have made many a boast. When the men bragged of the beauty of their wives, he kept silent, when it is clear you are more beautiful than any woman in court. When they crowed of their wives' loyalty, he kept silent, when it is clear you are more loyal than any. When the men boasted of the fullness of their wives' breasts he kept silent, when it's clear yours are fuller than any.' The court laughed weakly.

'You compare women as though we were cattle,' I said. 'I'm not surprised my husband stayed silent.'

'But when it came to talk of horses –' Conchobar stood up from his throne and walked to the edge of the plinth – 'your husband's tongue would not cease its wagging. It is known that I have the finest horses in the whole of Ireland, is that not true?'

'They are beautiful creatures, to be sure.'

'Nothing in the land is swifter than they, is that true?'

At last, Crunden looked at me and I knew then what his boast must have been. That his wife could outrun the king's horses. I stayed silent.

'Nothing in the land is swifter than they, is that true?' Conchobar repeated, his voice raised and the flush in his cheek deepening.

My silence was infuriating him. But I was caught. If I said that was true, I would be calling my husband a liar and he would be put to death. But if I said there was one thing in Ireland that could outrun his horses, he would put that to the test and me with two babies about to be born. Caught like an eel in a trap, not able to move either forward or backward. Crunden, you fool.

'Speak, woman! Your husband says there is one swifter. Is this true?'

'My husband is no liar,' I said at last, my voice taking on some of its old pitch. Birds were unsettled from the rafters. Rats retreated into their holes. The beasts that lived at the edges of the court knew what was coming. The men, however, didn't.

There was a moment's silence before the laughter. Great

peals of it. What entertainment this must be for them, between the harpists and the farting jesters. Many didn't even know why they were laughing; they hadn't been following the events of the evening and were simply laughing because those around them were.

'You're telling us,' Conchobar said, 'that *you* can outrun my horses?'

I nodded.

'Well, then –' Conchobar sat back on his throne, the smile on his face faltering – 'I guess we shall have to see this wonder for ourselves.'

I had killed kings before. I could kill this one. But that would mean abandoning Crunden.

'It's not too late,' whispered my unborn child. 'You can still escape.'

'Don't you know you're a goddess?' said my other child. 'Leave Crunden, he is not worthy of you.'

That was true enough. He was sobbing, snot running down into his beard. How had I ever shrunk myself for this pathetic creature? And yet I didn't want to see him die. I believed I could still save us all.

'My lord,' I said, forcing myself to keep my voice level and respectful. 'Give me just a few days, for the birthing of my children is nearly upon me. Then, I will run for you.'

'I will not wait,' Conchobar said, spittle flying from his wet mouth. 'The Lughnasa races begin tomorrow, and my sister, the finest charioteer in the land, will lead the first race and we will see if what your husband says is true.'

'Come, brother,' said the woman next to him, with a forced laugh, as though this were all a joke. 'You cannot deny a pregnant woman her bed rest. The races can surely wait.' She ran a hand over her own belly, and I saw the gentle curve of a woman newly with child.

'Do not forget who is king here, Deichtre,' Conchobar snapped. 'I will not be told what to do. If you won't lead my chariot, then I will do it myself.' He turned again to me. 'You will run tomorrow, or your husband will die.'

As dawn rose on the first day of Lughnasa, the harvest festival Lugh had claimed for himself, I was taken to the grazing grounds outside Emain Macha. The sun turned the plains of the kingdom gold. The horses drank dew from the grass, peaceful and watchful, not knowing the part they were to play in the curse that was to come. The men of the court roused themselves, weary with drink and lack of sleep. Some mumbled that this should wait till after I had given birth, but none dared say it to the king. Only Conchobar's eyes shone. How keen he was to be proved right, how eager to see me crushed. He had a restless, itchy energy, as if my threat to him had burrowed under his skin like a rash, like a poison. Deichtre, Conchobar's sister, stood behind him, her shoulders back, her mouth a thin line. A red swelling marked her slim face. It would soon be an angry bruise. Had that been Conchobar's work, punishment for speaking against him? She shook her head at the whole sorry mess and returned to the fort, unable to watch the race.

Conchobar had his chariot brought to him and harnessed to his two finest horses. They complained when they sensed his hands on the reins, for it was clear he did not know how to command them, and he whipped them to obedience. I was to run on foot with the herd. Seven horses were selected and all of us were herded behind a rope of hemp. The horses snorted, whinnied and dug at the soil with their hooves, annoyed at this impingement on their freedom. I walked barefoot through the grass, the wetness of the morning dew gathering at the hem of my skirt. I could feel the pulse of the earth beneath the soles of my feet and a stirring in me began. They dared to question my strength, my powers? They would see just what the Morrigan was capable of. I walked through the horses, laying my hands on their strong necks, whispering words of soothing. The children in my belly were quiet; they had given their last warnings and I had ignored them.

'When the sun hits the standing stone,' Conchobar shouted, 'the race will begin.'

We all waited for the sun to make its journey. Just as the light crested the tip of the standing stone, I thought I saw a figure in the distance, shimmering in the golden dawn.

Conchobar yelled at his horses and his chariot thundered away. When I looked back, the figure was gone. The horses ran and I ran with them. I was one of them, my heartbeat in rhythm with the pounding of their hooves, my breath bellowing like their snorts. For a moment, I forgot Conchobar and his mocking, Crunden and his stupidity. I forgot everything but the feeling of power in my limbs. I could undo myself and become one of the horses: turn my clenched fists to hooves, my fleshy arms to muscled legs. My screech could become a whinny. But the babes in my belly, what would become of them? Would they be born foals? Would they become twisted in the transformation? Some small part of me held on to them and I kept my human form. But I still ran and ran and in the running I was free. A pounding, dirt-flying, sweat-smelling freedom.

I overtook first Conchobar's chariot and then the rest of the herd. Conchobar's fierce complaints were nothing but wind in my ears. I was ahead by a nose, by a leg, by a full length. The finishing line was the standing stone ahead, its shadow a chasm in the earth. I leapt across it and laughed. I had won.

Conchobar jumped off his chariot and shouted for the horses to be killed at once. He stormed back to his Red Branch warriors, spitting and cursing my name, leaving me and the horses behind. There was nothing he could do to me now: I had won his race and my husband had been proven true. Crunden would be set free.

I had been left alone with the horses and for a moment, I was happy, gleeful. I listened for the voices of my children, hoping their fears were gone. There was only silence.

The pain came like an undoing. Deep in my belly, a yawning, rending, deep pain. I had never experienced agony like it. It came in waves that crashed over me, a pounding, a pummelling. Each time I believed that I could experience no pain worse, and each time it grew till there was nothing left of me, only the pain. I had watched men and women die in agony, and nothing could have been worse than this. When I had given birth to Meche, I had had my sisters with me, and Airmed's herbs to ease my pain. Here, my only birthing companions were the horses, the only balm my hatred of Conchobar and my husband. The muscles inside me twisted harder and harder, as though every ounce of pain was being wrung from me. It felt as if someone had reached inside me and was pulling at my womb. The more I tried to fight it, the worse it became, like trying to fight a crashing wave. I could no longer hear my children; I no longer felt their legs kicking at my insides. They were dead and I surely would follow. At last, accepting that the birthing of my twins would be my end, I surrendered to the pain and pushed them out of me. A boy and a girl, they lay in a tangle of grey flesh, slippery, boneless and cold.

One of the horses, a mare, lowered her head to lick at their noses, as she would one of her own foals. I was too exhausted to lift a limb and reach out to them. My babies were gone. And I was empty once more, pain folding in on pain. A great rushing void that could swallow the whole world.

Then came the rage. The biting, rending, shredding rage I had buried deep within me for fear of it consuming me. Let it, I thought, let it burn through me and leave nothing in its path like a purging fire. Let me unravel and leave nothing but that fury. I screamed and my scream became a storm, tearing across the land, ripping trees from the earth and toppling standing stones. I scattered myself as far as I ever had, every atom of me tossed and thrown in the howling winds, hoping to dissolve, to be no more.

Like a storm, it passed and I remained. Weak, broken, but alive. Not whole, never again whole, but alive. The fury burned in me like acid. I would not carry this alone. I looked over at the men who had done this to me as they crawled out of the holes in which they had hidden from the storm. Crunden sobbed, pathetic and weak.

He fell to his knees. 'Forgive me, my love. Forgive me. Forgive me.'

What good were his tears now? He should have died, rather than let Conchobar and the men of Ulaid do this to me. How could I have cared for a worm like him? I would punish him. I would punish them all. I would cause them such pain they wouldn't know themselves. I would curse them for what they had done to me.

In all the time I had been with Crunden, I hadn't used my

magic. I had kept my voice soft and gentle. It had been so long since I had spoken the old language of my people I had almost forgotten the shape of the words that had power to shift and move the world. I reached for them then, felt them set a fire in my head, and spat them out at Conchobar and the men of the Red Branch.

'Cowards,' I shouted, using my true voice once again, and they shook seeing me for the goddess I was. 'Pathetic men. Your pride makes you weak. Weaker even than a woman in childbirth. I curse you now. When the time comes that you most need your strength, it will desert you. When you are under attack, you shall be helpless. For nine days and nights, every fighting man of Ulaid will endure the pains that I did today, that every mother has endured, the pains of childbirth. Your screams shall go unheard, your agony will be unrelenting, and you will remember what you did on this day.'

With not even a glance at Crunden or his cruel king, I gathered up my dead babies, leapt over the crowd and vanished into the morning mists.

I named my children Fir and Fial – True and Humble – for had their father been those things, I would never have lost them. I held them to my breast, kissed their foreheads, rocked them in my arms, calling out to my people to bring them back to me. But my cries, my voice, went unheard. I laid them to rest, digging their graves with my own hands and speaking the old words over their bones. Would they pass over to the other lands? Or would they join Meche in the abyss of nothingness? I did not know. But I knew that, either way, I would never see my babies again.

I had tried to be what they expected of a woman. I had become a wife and a mother. I had kept myself small and silent and still that was not enough for them. They had taken it all from me because they couldn't bear knowing a woman was greater than them. Even that flicker of my power seen in the outrunning of their precious horses was too much – they wanted it all for themselves.

I returned to Crunden's home one last time. To set it ablaze. I watched from a nearby hilltop as he ran out, screeching, his body a living column of fire until it was nothing but ash. I spared his children, for what had they done but be born to a weak and perfidious father? They called out for me, called out for the woman who they had called mother, but I closed my ears to their cries.

Conchobar tried to forget me, and yet the new fort he built on his land still bore my name, Emain Macha – not the Brooch of Macha, as it had been once, but Macha's Twins. Named not after a powerful queen, but for a wronged woman. You can guess which of the versions the poets love to tell most. The one which ends with me covered in blood, weeping for my dead children. Poets are in love with women's pain. They love nothing more than a story that sees women on their bellies, drowning in their tears. But if there was anything I knew it was how to turn anguish into anger and anger into action. I set myself against Conchobar and his men. I would lick their pain from my fingertips like honey, sucking one delicious agony after the other. There would be no peace for the men of Ulaid.

19.

I crawled on my knees (oh, how the poets would have loved that) back to Cruachan and my cave between the worlds. And as I waited I dreamt of the bulls again. A battle more bloody than any I had ever known as the bulls tore the land apart. In my dreaming, I saw a woman standing over the battle. At first, I thought it was myself I was seeing. But then I saw her face: heart-shaped and beautiful. A hunger I recognized set her eyes alight and blood-spray covered her golden armour. I saw Conchobar on his knees in the mud before her, cursing her name.

I awoke with a thirst the like of which I had not known in years, and wondered had I been cursed as King Eochaid had once been. I licked at the damp walls of my cave, but it did nothing to satisfy. I knew this yearning of old, the yearning for battle, for revenge. I had not finished with King Conchobar and the men of Ulaid.

I could kill Conchobar. But that would be too easy. I wanted to make him suffer, as he had made me suffer. I wanted to strip everything he loved from him, as he had stripped all that I loved from me. And this woman, this warrior, I knew she was to be the cause of much pain for Conchobar, a spear splinter in his belly, festering and foul. A slow and painful cancerous poison. I had to find her.

I emerged from the darkness and called to my birds, asking where I could find her. They told me seven years had passed as I had slept and that a new king was to be crowned in Laigin. There was to be an óenach in Tara, a gathering under truce for all the kings of the five provinces to meet and forge their allegiances while measuring up this new king. She would be there. I dressed in my darkest robes and travelled west.

I hadn't stepped foot in Tara since the Sons of Mil drove my people out. It had grown, tripling in size, as they built new ring forts and wrapped fences and ditches around the mounds my people had built, claiming it for themselves. Some of the forts were set aside to house the dead, a place for their bones to rest. Others for stores for food or weapons or for feasting. They had carved up the land on the approach to the hill, creating two deep ditches that ran in straight parallel lines, long enough for two hundred men to lie head to toe. On each side they had raised a wooden fence, so tall it hurt your neck craning to look up to the top of it. A route plunging straight into the soft, round heart of Tara. No guessing what they were thinking of when they built this. It led all the way to the largest of their new forts, where it was said the banquet would be taking place that night.

In the form of a plain and poor brewster, I walked the long procession alongside hundreds of others. It was raining hard, but that wouldn't dampen their excitement. All were eager for the feasting, fucking and fighting that was promised following the coronation of a new king. At the end, a mound had been raised up out of the ground and on top of it stood a round building, with a sharp, sloping roof. The sound of chatter inside was louder than a war drum. Hundreds of people were crammed in under the roof, drinking and eating and giving praise to their kings. The light from scores of candles dripped sticky wax and gave off the stink of sheep's fat. It was hot as a midsummer's day thanks to heat from a roaring fire, over which hung iron pots and turning spits of pig and sheep. Next to the fire was a long table where sat the kings of Ireland, with Conchobar at the centre.

Conchobar. My insides twisted at the sight of him. I smelt again the fresh turf and horse sweat, felt the tearing in my belly of my babies pushing to be born; I licked my lips and tasted their deaths. When I looked at my hands, I saw the dirt under my fingernails still fresh from digging their graves. All because of this man. My hatred for him was like bog wood, hard and twisted. I almost struck him down then, but his death wouldn't be enough to satisfy. I wanted to see him ruined. I wanted him on his knees as I had been. If he died, there would be no battle and no vengeance.

Conchobar laughed, his voice cutting through my visions, and my hands were clean once more. I smelt only the smoke of the fire and the stink of life around me. Since I had last seen him, he had cut his curly dark hair and grown a beard, to hide his weak chin no doubt. He stroked it as if he was thinking important thoughts. His were the richest robes, his gold the heaviest. Next to him was Fergus, the man who had once been king, whispering in his ear, the pair of them cosy as courting lovers. They positioned their bodies as though not a part of the gathering, but as though above it. Next at the table was Éogan mac Durthact, a low king who ruled over Fernmag, a scrap of land on the contested border between Mide and Ulaid. He was a loud, brutish man with a nose that grew like a fungus on his red face. His enmity for Conchobar was well known, though he could no more be trusted than a patch of blue sky in spring, for his loyalties switched fast and often. Sitting beside him was Mesgegra, the young King of Laigin, who itched at the new fur robes around his neck and eyed the others with justified wariness.

There were women at the table, wives of the kings, who smiled through tight lips as their menfolk talked around them, and nodded at whatever nonsense they were spouting. But one woman shone out above all others: the woman I had been searching for. She was dressed in the many-coloured robes of royalty and held herself not as a wife, but as a queen, a ruler in her own right. She sat facing away from the others, staring into the fire as though wishing for the night to be over. When she turned to see the cause of Conchobar's laugh, I saw she was younger than she had been in my dreams. In my vision, she had been dressed in shimmering armour, a powerful warrior in her prime. But the woman I saw here was not long out of her girlhood, eighteen, twenty perhaps, though she had the same strong jaw, which clenched as the men around her laughed over bawdy tales, and bright eyes that didn't miss a thing. She wore her hair loose about her shoulders, with only a small circle of gold around her head.

'What is that woman's name?' I asked a passing serving girl.

'Why, that's Queen Medb,' she replied.

'Conchobar's bride?' I remembered the name as the woman who had been betrothed to Conchobar. Could the woman I had come to find be the wife of my enemy?

The serving girl snorted, as if mocking my stupidity. 'Not any more. She left him and now she's married to Tinni mac Conri. After her father died, she needed a husband to sit beside her as she took the Connacht throne, and it wasn't going to be Conchobar!'

A young, pale man sat next to Medb, his hand possessively

grasping hers when it wasn't used for shovelling food in his mouth. She would smile at him every now and then, laugh at a joke he made. Appeasing his ego. But it seemed clear to me that she was the one with the power.

Medb held a baby in her arms, who could have been no more than a week or so old, and fed him from a calfskin. Not her own child, I sensed. And yet she held him to her as if she feared someone would rip him from her arms. When she looked at him, there was a mix of love and terror. A look I knew well. There was another child, a boy perhaps six or seven years old, pulling at her skirts. She seemed to love this child too, thumbing his cheeks and planting a kiss on his head, before calling for a handmaiden to take him away. He was dark-haired with a big mouth and weak chin. There could be no doubt who his father was.

I watched Medb, but mostly I watched Conchobar watching her. They had once been married and now sat a table apart, her hand being kissed by another. His hatred for her radiated off him like steam off a horse's back on a cold day. It was a mirror of mine for him and I loved her instantly and as fiercely as if she had been one of my kin.

I wasn't the only one to notice the way he stared at her, as if he could flay her skin with his eyes. Three women were huddled together near me talking over their mead.

'Would you look at Conchobar giving dagger eyes to herself. And all she did was leave him after a year,' said one.

'You daft bitch, that's not the cause of his fury. Didn't you hear? She killed his new wife, Eithne, her own sister, and tore that babe there from her belly before the body was cold. That's what Conchobar's men are saying anyway,' said another, her voice a little slurred with drink.

'The men of Ulaid are talking out of their arse then and

so are you,' a third woman said, her voice husky with age. 'I was there, I saw it with my own eyes. Eithne died in child-birth. Two whole days she was at it before she took her last breath and Medb saved the child. Sliced Eithne's belly open and pulled the baby out, wailing all the while with the grief of her sister's death. She kept the child alive with the warmth of her own body.'

There was a collective '*Ahhhh*' from the other two women. They had heard many stories and this one fitted best.

'Sure, Eithne was too young to be bedded. Conchobar should have known to wait a year at least before putting a baby in her,' the first to speak said.

'He likes 'em young. You heard about the child he's kept somewhere. Felimid, the Harper's girl? Aims to marry her when she's old enough,' the second said.

'Wasn't she the one Cathbad made the prophecy about?'

I leant closer, trying to pick out their words over the thrum of noise, sipping at a drink that had been pushed into my hands.

'That's yer one. Said she would become the most beautiful woman in the world.'

I shook my head. A prophecy condemning a woman to beauty never ends well.

'No wonder Conchobar wants her then. But maybe he'll learn and leave it till the girl has had a few moons before giving her a baby.'

'What happened to Cathbad?' one of the women asked. 'He never used to leave Conchobar out of his sight. I liked him. He smelt nice.'

'He stormed off after Conchobar ignored the other half of his prophecy.'

'Which was?'

'That rivers of blood would flow for the fighting over this girl and it would split the Red Branch in two.'

I choked on the mouthful of weak mead I had taken into my mouth. The three women turned to see what had caused the noise. One wiped my spittle from her face with disgust.

'Will you watch yourself, woman?'

I muttered my apologies and they returned to their chatter.

'Cathbad said if Conchobar had any sense he'd have killed the baby as soon as she drew breath,' the middle of the women said.

There are always two sides to a prophecy. And always one side that people want to hear and the other they close their ears to. I foresaw no great battle over this baby girl they spoke of, though I did see much violence and much sorrow.

'But of course, Conchobar ignored him. So Cathbad cursed Conchobar that the Mac Nessa line would end with himself and last I heard he was living up a tree.'

'Conchobar's head is too full of ambition to leave any room for sense. He's a vicious one. Takes what he wants when he wants it. It's a wonder Medb was able to walk away from him without finding a knife in her back on her way out the door,' the eldest one said.

'So, where's this child then?'

'Leabharcham was set to look after her. Took her somewhere far away, I heard.'

'Leabharcham the poet?'

'That's yer one.'

'Sure, what would she know about looking after a baby? She never had one herself.'

'I'd wondered where she'd gone to. She always had the best gossip.'

A man holding a large jug shoved past me, filling cups as he went. I had to step away to avoid being forced to drink his vinegary wine. No longer able to hear the women's talk, I returned my attention to the table of kings.

Medb stood. 'I'll put him to his bed and be back,' she said to her husband, kissing him on the top of his head as you would a child. She pushed past the kings and queens and didn't even look in Conchobar's direction, yet she shivered as his eyes raked across her skin like claws.

A song or two were sung before Conchobar stood and waved towards the doors. 'Taking a piss,' he said.

Fergus called for the harpers to play louder, the drummers play harder. I did not know then that it was to drown out Medb's cries. Or that Conchobar had planned this revenge. I never thought that a king, who had his pick of the finest women of the land, would have need to force any woman to bend to his will.

Not long later, when Conchobar came staggering back into the feasting hall, rubbing at four angry marks of broken nails dragged down his cheeks, I knew what had been done. Everyone there knew and yet none moved. Even Medb's new husband did nothing but sit and stare into his cup of cold mead which he held with two hands, knuckles white. Conchobar smiled at the men around the table, a satisfied grin. He wore the scratches, the proof of his actions, like a battle scar. My stomach turned as he took his seat again and began to eat. How could he have done what he did and still have an appetite?

I cursed myself. What good was it to see men's deaths if I couldn't see their cruelties? What good my power if not to stop men like Conchobar? I had awoken because I had foreseen Medb – mighty, powerful, magnificent – leading an army against Conchobar, but I had failed to see what price she would have to pay for that power.

I looked at him through one eye and took a measly comfort in the future I saw for him. With his mind slowly rotting like an apple, drooling and senseless, until the day when his head burst open. No glorious warrior's death for him. I wouldn't allow it. He would die old and shitting himself, an obsession with an imagined enemy tormenting him till the end, and his people would sigh with relief when at last they were lifted of his burden. It wouldn't be enough to punish him for what he had done to Medb, for what he had done to me, but it would be something.

20.

The sky was star-pricked and there was no moon to see by as I left the banqueting hall, but my eyes were keen enough. A man was retching on the ground, his hand propped up against one of the vast pillars of the procession pathway. He was dressed in the manner of a Connacht warrior, in a deep blue cloak with his hair shaved at the sides. Fluff covered his chin and lip. Not yet a man then, though trying to drink like one.

'Where can I find your queen?'

He wiped the vomit from his mouth with the back of his hand and pointed towards a round, wickerwork hut on the edge of the enclosure.

'Don't tell her,' he shouted after me. 'Don't tell her I did nothing.'

I hissed at him and he doubled over again to vomit, this time throwing up his own guts and bone. He looked in horror at the putrescence that had come out of him before falling dead.

The hazel branches of the dwelling were still green and the lime plaster shone bright white in the gloom. Like the scattering of buildings around the edges of the fort, it had been newly built for the óenach. I knelt before the small doorway and crawled through, my head bowed. Any un-welcome visitor attempting to enter a homestead would be met by a cold blade or heavy cudgel resting against the back of their heads. How then had Conchobar entered in safety? Had Medb trusted him? Believed herself safe from his violence? Perhaps she believed a king would have more honour?

I found her, knees pulled into her chest, face pressed into the dirt floor, the low fire flickering out. She groaned, like a cow in early labour or a horse dying; a low, guttural, primal sound of anguish.

I suppose I should have felt pity, compassion, but in truth it angered me to see her like that. Vulnerable, weak. Where was the haughty warrior of my vision?

'Rise,' I said, hoping with a word I could transform her. She curled in tighter, as if my word was another slap. The baby gurgled in his cot. Had he slept through her screaming? Did it remind him of the screaming of his mother as he entered the world? Is that why men are born so able to stomach women's pain?

'Rise,' I said again.

With this one word, I had forced dying heroes to their feet, I had driven weary armies to victory, but it wasn't enough to stir Medb. I reached into her heart as I had done with warriors throughout the years. I expected to find fear, anger, something familiar that I could take hold of and crush, but I was hit by a wave of emotion, the like of which I had never known. A swirling, ugly, gnawing, fungal thing that was spreading through her like venom. I had sensed some of this in Odras, the woman I had transformed into a river. But in Medb this feeling was all-consuming. And at last, I knew its name. Shame.

She felt shame. At what *he* had done.

I sat on the reed-covered floor, stunned. The shame should be all his. The pain should be all his. She bore no responsibility for what had happened to her beyond being born a woman. Was this in the heart of all mortal women? Were they born with it as they said my boy Meche had been born with snakes? And like those imagined snakes, would their collective shame grow and consume them? How many women carried this inside themselves and for why? How many women took the actions of men and made it their responsibility? I had spent so long trying to see the world through the eyes of men, trying to think like them and act like them, hold power like them, that I realized I did not understand the hearts of women.

I may not understand it, but that didn't mean I had to accept it. What use was shame? It was a shrinking shadow of an emotion. No, I refused to let that sit with her for a moment more. I would take it from her and leave fury in its wake. Grounding myself and readying my mind, I reached inside her heart once more. I knew words that could inspire greatness in the hearts of men. I could transform fear to bravery. I reached out with my hands, talons shifting under my skin, and I clawed the air, twisting and shaping it as I was twisting and shaping that thing inside her. I sent tendrils of magic through her body, mycelium-like fingers seeking out that darkness that was eating her, and with a tug, I wrenched it out as I had once wrenched out lungs and intestines. I looked at the oily, gangrenous substance that slicked my hands and with a breath, it caught fire and burned like bog gas.

I laid my hand on her shoulder. She flinched at my touch, her eyes wild and white like a horse ready to bolt. They focused on me and I saw the iron-hardness of them. *Yes*, I thought, there is my warrior queen.

'Rise,' I said once more, softer this time. Not a command, but a hope. With both hands on her shoulders, I pulled her up off the floor. 'It is done.'

I ran a hand over her hair, as I remembered my mother had done when I was in one of my wild moments. Medb allowed the tears to come then, tears which she had not let him see, hot, soothing tears. I had once believed a weeping woman the worst thing a creature could be; I had unmade a woman whole for daring to weep before me. But now I understood the healing power of tears. Salt water, like the sea, washing away the filth left by the tide.

After a time, Medb brushed the tears away and properly looked at me.

'I know you,' she said, her brow furrowing.

'We have never met.'

Medb pushed her hair out of her face and stepped closer, looking at me as though trying to make out a shape through the fog. Realization flared in her eyes like a fire blossoming to life.

She smiled, cunning, cautious. 'Oh, but I have seen you. In the corner of my eye when I have watched men die. At times when I dreamt of war. My people raise monuments to you, they pray to you for strength before battle. Why are you hiding?'

I stood back. It had been many years since I had truly been seen. In all the time I had been living among mortals, I had tried to look as one of them: small and fragile. Even as I had spat my curse on the men of Ulaid, I had done it in the form of a weak, human woman. Did I even remember the goddess I had once been? I let my rough tunic fall to the floor and pulled the shawl from my head. My hair turned from a muddy brown to the golden red of bronze, my face which was round and soft became hard as granite and I allowed myself to grow, till my shoulders were pressed against the roof and my head bowed against the timbers.

'My goddess,' she said, gazing up at me, her eyes wide and glittering. 'My great queen.'

I smiled. Amergin, the first son of Mil to rule this land, had called me that once, but he had wanted to claim my power for himself. This woman before me, she simply marvelled in it.

'Your homes are not built for the likes of me,' I said, pulling a strand of straw from the thatch out of my hair.

This made her laugh. 'Then make yourself a little shorter,' she said. 'Shorter, but not smaller.'

I retained my form – strong, broad, powerful – just now I wouldn't have to bow indoors.

'What are you doing here?' she asked. 'What is one of *your* people doing here?'

'I have business to settle with Conchobar.'

'That beast.' She spat and began to pace back and forth. 'That is the last time I feel his stinking breath on my face. That is the last time he lays a hand on me.' She looked to me, knowing something of my powers of prophecy. 'Is it the last time?'

'It is.'

She brushed her skirts down and straightened the gold band she wore around her head. It had been a gift from her mother on her wedding day. A gift from a queen for a queen. It had once belonged to one of my people, left behind and then passed down through generations of mothers. My sisters may even have worn it. It was a little tarnished and bent, but still held some power.

'Never again will any man dominate me. Any man I allow into my bed will be my equal in all things. Not a single ring of gold shall they have above me. Never again shall a man have power over me.' She spoke these words as a spell, a binding promise to herself and the world. 'And as for Conchobar – I will kill him.' She bent down over a bundle of cloth and pulled out a short dagger. It glinted in the light from the dying fire. 'Tonight. As he sleeps and snores, I will plunge this into him, just as he plunged himself into me. I will cut his manhood off and feed it to him.' She stared at her warped reflection in the burnished blade.

'You could do that,' I said. 'And his men would hunt you down. They'd tear you apart.'

'It would be worth it.'

'It is not his fate to die this day. Or for many days to come.'

Medb spun around, lips pulled back over teeth that were stained with blood from where she had bitten her tongue as he forced himself on her, ready to attack, anything to challenge my prophecy. I saw then a little of the woman from my dream vision and I smiled.

'No.' She stamped her foot on the reed floor. The babe stirred from the sound and she lowered her voice again. Even in the heat of her anger, her thoughts were of the child. 'No. I want my revenge now. Now. I cannot wait years, while Conchobar swans around, filling his belly with food, taking any woman that it pleases him to.'

'He won't be the first man to live a long life while all around him suffer.'

She stared at the ground, while her fists clenched and unclenched. 'Tell me at least, if I do not kill him, it will be a man of Connacht who does?'

I closed my eyes and looked forward to Conchobar's death. Confused, flickering images danced across my mind. A brain scooped out and kept as a trophy, flung at Conchobar's head, where it would lodge for seven years before finally bursting like a pus-filled sore. I opened my eyes and tried to make sense of the images.

'He will die by the hand of a Connacht man, but it will be a Laigin king that will end his life.'

She threw her hands into the air. 'Gah! Why do you gods have to speak in such riddles? You know how infuriating it is, don't you?'

Medb sat down on a wooden stool, newly carved and covered in sheepskin. She winced at the pain. Her rage had made her forget her injuries for a moment.

'Tell me, how do I die?'

She wouldn't believe it even if I told her. That the child who lay sleeping, the one she had saved by pulling him out of her dying sister's belly, would bring about her death.

'It will be many years from now and you will still be beautiful.'

This seemed to appease her. 'I would have liked to have killed him.'

'You will not kill him,' I said. 'But you will defeat him.'

She smiled. 'Tell me.'

I spoke then, in my voice of prophecy. It was weak at first, from lack of use, but grew stronger with every word.

'I see you golden
A champion unparalleled.
The armies of Ireland united
Against a vast herd.
The men of Ulaid stricken
A curse no man can bear.
The Red Branch broken
Scarlet gushes of blood
Conchobar on his knees

217

His valour gone.
And your name sung throughout the ages.
Medb, warrior queen of Ireland.'

The light from the fire danced in her eyes and she saw it too. The leader she could become. She looked down at her hands. At the space between them, thinking of the gap between the queen she was now and the one I told her she would be. 'For that, I will need more power. More wealth. More—'

We heard a shouting. A clanging of blade on blade.

Medb tilted her head as if listening to the twittering of a bird in the distance.

'What is that?'

I closed my eyes, and borrowed the eyes of a crow, perched on the roof of the hall. I saw men standing facing each other, weapons drawn.

'Your husband has finally found his courage at the bottom of a cup. He has challenged Conchobar to a fight.'

Medb shook her head. 'Sweet, foolish Tinni, Conchobar will crush him.'

'You could stop him,' I said. 'You could save Tinni.'

She turned to me slowly, her eyes like flint. 'Just as Tinni could have stopped Conchobar tonight? Just as he could have saved me?' Her mouth tightened, her chin sharp as a spearhead. 'If I am to become queen of all of Ireland then I will need a stronger husband.'

She looked to me, as if to give her permission. I was struck again by how young she looked. Years away from the queen she would be.

'I did not see Tinni mac Conri by your side on the battle-field,' I said.

She nodded. A deed done.

I borrowed again the eyes of the watching crow and saw Tinni, his head crushed and misshapen, blood dripping from Conchobar's knuckles. He hadn't even given him the honour of dying by a blade. Another stone on the barrow of reasons for Medb to hate Conchobar, though ridding her of Tinni may have been the only kindness the man had ever done her.

'Tinni was a gentle man, but gentle men do not lead armies,' Medb said, as if repeating something she had been told. Tinni was still warm, his blood only just flowing on to the ground, and yet she had placed him in the past.

She began to pace around the hut, walking in a full circle one way and then back the other. 'I'll need the other kings on my side. And some of Conchobar's men too, some will need to turn against him. That shouldn't be hard with all the evil he does every day.'

The animal cloth covering the doorway twitched and a tangle of curls pushed its way through. One of Medb's handmaidens. Clumsy, she clambered into the dwelling and remained on her hands and knees.

'Oh, my queen. My poor, precious queen. Tinni mac Conri, your husband, is dead.' She kept her head bowed.

Medb nodded. 'So it is.'

The woman waited, as if expecting more from Medb. As if expecting anything. Wasn't a wife meant to mourn her husband? Wail over his body? Compose the laments for his life? There were no tears from Medb. No tearing of her hair. If there was to be a keen for Tinni, it wouldn't come from Medb.

'Is there anything I can do to ease your pain?' the hand-maiden asked, a probing hope in her voice that Medb felt any pain at all.

'Fetch me water,' Medb said. 'And new clothes.' She ripped her tunic from her body and threw it to the handmaiden.

This handmaiden looked at the bloodstains on the cloth. I knew this woman. I had heard her prayers for revenge, whispered in the dark of night. She had been taken in a raid when she was a young girl by King Eochu, Medb's father. The raid, as most raids were, had been over cattle, but Eochu had taken a handful of slaves back with him. She knew only too well what Medb had gone through that night. Did it please her, to know the daughter of the man who stole her had suffered as she had done? I know if I had been that slave girl, I would have taken balm in it. But then, if I had been that slave girl, Eochu and all his family would have burned for what they had done.

'As you wish, my queen.'

The handmaiden left and Medb sat down again, wrapping a wool blanket around her body.

'What should I call you?' she asked me. 'Or will the Morrigan suffice?'

I thought of all the names I had been called in the past. For my new purpose, I would need a new name.

'Nemain,' I said. The enemy. 'Call me Nemain.'

'Well, Nemain,' she said. 'Where do we begin?'

I sat by the fire and gazed into the flames, looking for the future there. 'What does Conchobar love most?' I asked. If we knew what he cared for, we could begin to strip it from him.

'Other than himself?' Medb said. 'Gold, cattle, the usual.'

'Then we will take his finest bulls and ten times our weight in gold. What else?'

'Fergus, perhaps, his only friend?'

220

'Good. We will make Fergus despise him as he has never despised a man before. What else?'

'The Red Branch, his mighty warriors.' Her eyes lit up as an idea came to her. 'The girl!'

'What girl?' I asked.

'The one with the prophecy. Deirdre. We take her from him, and it will break the Red Branch – and in doing that, it will break him.' A smile itched at her mouth. A smile of victory.

'Then,' I said, 'we start with Deirdre.'

21.

I found Deirdre and Leabharcham, the woman who had been given care of her, living in the woodlands at the bottom of a valley deep in the heart of the land. It was a wise choice for a place to hide; protected on two sides by jagged, black rocks, to the rear by a thick pine forest, and ahead a deep blue lake. They'd see or hear anyone coming for miles. It had been a long winter and snow still covered the ground in places. The wolves were hungry for the frozen earth cracked like twigs snapping under their paws, alerting any prey of their presence. I could hear their howling as I flew over the valley, icy winds dragging at my black feathers.

I might not have seen the dwelling, had it not been for the grey trail of smoke, as the roof was also covered in snow. The fort – if it could even be called that, for it was more hut than homestead – had a small patch of wild flowers and a single cow who had seen better days. I flew down and perched on the gnarled branch of an ancient yew tree.

A young girl emerged from the house in a cloud of heat steam. She was indeed beautiful, with deep grey eyes and high, sharp cheekbones. She moved light and swift, as though she might take flight at any moment. She had something of my people about her and for a moment, she reminded me of Brigid. I'd heard she was around here somewhere, carving a life among these people, never letting them know who she truly was.

'Close the covers over, girl, you'll let all the heat out,' a sharp voice from within the dwelling rang out.

'But it's such a beautiful day,' Deirdre replied.

She was one of those types, then. Who sighed at the beauty of a rose or who watched the clouds sail by in the sky and wished she had wings.

I closed one of my yellow crow eyes and looked for her death. Even I shuddered at the sight of that beautiful face broken, at those sparkling eyes dulled. Brains smashed against rocks. Not a pretty death.

'Come out here, Leabharcham, and give me one of your poems,' Deirdre said, and even her voice was like song.

Grumbling, Leabharcham appeared. She was wrapped in a patchwork of furs and her face was lined with the privilege of age. Her hair was grey and she kept it cut short, hacked off with a knife if I was any judge. For what need does a woman have for long hair when hiding in a place like this?

'Poetry is best told by the fire, not out in the cold.'

'Nonsense,' Deirdre said, grabbing the old woman by her hand and dragging her out to stand beside her. 'There,' she said, stretching her arms out as if trying to coax the whole snow-covered landscape into them. 'Isn't it beautiful?'

Leabharcham took a deep breath and let it out again; a cloud dancing up to the sky to make more clouds. 'Yes,' she agreed. 'Yes, it is.'

'Give us a poem then,' Deirdre said, squatting down, elbows propped on her knees and fist under her chin.

Leabharcham drank in the view for a moment, then cleared her voice.

'In winter
Soft silence as the land sleeps
The trees heavy-headed with snow
Where the birds make icy nests, still singing.

Spring will come
And colour burst forth once more.
But for now, silence.
Soft silence. As the land sleeps.'

I'd never heard a poem like it. The poetry I had heard had all been in the service of retelling the great deeds of kings or in prophecy. This gentle little poem was in service of nothing more than this moment. It gave me shivers and I ruffled my feathers to be rid of it.

'Perfect,' Deirdre said with a sigh. 'You always find just the right words.'

The old woman sat down on a log next to her foster child, though it took her some effort. 'I don't find the words, they find me.'

The two sat in silence, watching the snow fall like blossoms in spring. Something in me wanted to pierce the beauty of this place, as a reminder that life is not all sweet poems and singing birds. I saw a dead mouse and I hopped down and got to work, pecking at its entrails, splashing blood on to the white snow.

'Conchobar may visit again, when the snows are cleared,' Leabharcham said.

Deirdre's face crumpled in disgust. 'Why won't he just leave me alone? His breath stinks of a pigsty.'

'You shouldn't say that about your future husband,' Leabharcham said.

'But I don't want to marry him.'

Leabharcham looked at the floor. 'I know, child, but you don't have any choice.'

'Why? Why can a woman not have a choice as men do?'

'And if you had a choice, who would you marry? You've never even met another man other than Conchobar. How do you not know he's the most handsome of the lot?'

'Because if there is this much beauty in nature, there must be beauty in men. I would marry a man . . .' She looked about her for inspiration and her eyes set on me. 'I would marry a man with hair as black as the wing of that crow. With skin as white as the snow. And cheeks as red as the blood spilt.'

I cawed with irritation. I had hoped that seeing the spilt entrails of this mouse would be a shock to the girl, that pain and death was everywhere, but she even saw the beauty in that.

'Does such a man as that exist?' she asked Leabharcham.

The old woman sucked at what was left of her teeth. 'Well, it does sound somewhat like Naoise.'

Deirdre closed her eyes and caressed her neck as though imagining his hands on her skin. 'Oh, even his name is beautiful. You must let me see him. You must.' She took the old woman's hands in hers and placed them to her face.

Leabharcham tried to resist. She was loyal to Conchobar and she'd been given a duty. And yet she'd raised this girl from a babe as if she were her own.

Perhaps. Perhaps this was how I would make the first cut. If Conchobar had his mind set on marrying Deirdre, how angry would he be if another man got to her first? The juicy parts of the mouse finished, I chuckled to myself. Oh, how his hot head would burn then and in his anger, he would show his true self.

How might a man worthy of Deirdre, a better man than Conchobar in every way, happen upon this secluded valley? I looked at the old lady, my yellow eyes burning into her pale blue ones. She would have to do it. She would have to bring them here by cunning. She knew cunning well enough, or else she wouldn't have survived Conchobar's court till her age. She just needed a little push.

I looked deeper into her past, looking for the bruise I could dig my thumb into. There, a memory of her, the same age as this girl now, desperately in love with a young man who died in one of Conchobar's stupid raids. I called up to the winds and they danced through the leaves, whispering his name. You were young once, Leabharcham, you knew true love and the gentle touch of a kind man, and Conchobar took it from you. Think what he will do to this girl. Even if it is fated for him to be hers, let her know happiness first. Let Conchobar not be the only man to have touched her.

I saw the old woman's will melt like the ice dripping from the trees. 'There may be a way I could arrange for you to see him. See him, mind. That is all.'

'Oh, I love you.' Deirdre covered the woman's liver-spotted hands in kisses.

'Give over, child.'

Later that day, Leabharcham wrapped herself up in her cloak and took her staff and headed out of the valley. I stayed with Deirdre, watching her.

With Leabharcham gone, the girl's face changed. The soft brow devoid of worry became etched with lines. The glittering light in her eyes darkened. No longer was she in love with beauty: she was focused. She paced back and forth, chewing on the side of her thumb hard enough to make it bleed.

'I can't marry Conchobar,' she muttered to herself, spitting over her shoulder on to the ground after speaking his name. 'You hear me,' she shouted, her voice echoing around the valley and setting the birds flowing. 'I would rather die.'

Many a woman has made this claim and then surprised herself at what she could live with. But I believed Deirdre. She had a power to her: had she been raised in the court, she would have been trained to be a sorceress, taught the right words to manipulate man and matter. Out here, in this lonely valley, she had nothing but her will. But it was strong.

Leabharcham returned as the sun was setting and Deirdre put her smile back on.

'Well? Did you see Naoise? Did you tell him to come?'

'Let me warm my bones first, child,' Leabharcham said. 'You'd better not have let the fire go out with your daydreaming.'

Deirdre bit down on the bottom of her lip. 'Oops!'

Leabharcham shook her grey head and the two went back inside.

Why was Deirdre playing the helpless fool? She had no more daydreamt when Leabharcham was gone than she had wrestled giants. She'd been planning and trying to think her way out of the trap Conchobar had set for her. Perhaps being thought weak was her power?

I flew to the thatched roof of the house and became a black mouse and sniffled my way through the hay so I could watch them.

Deirdre got the fire going again and set a pot of stew boiling. Leabharcham untied her cloak and unbound the wrappings around her feet and took the best seat by the fire. Deirdre sat before her and took the old woman's gnarled foot into her lap and rubbed at it.

'Well?' Deirdre said again.

'I saw him.'

'And is he beautiful?'

'He is.'

'And did you tell him to come?'

'He is one of the Red Branch warriors, loyal to Conchobar. I couldn't just tell him to pop by for a visit.'

'Then what did you do?'

'I got chatting with him and his brothers and I happened to move the conversation on to hunting and how I knew of a valley, not a few hours' ride, where there were wily boars and lightning-fast deer and only the greatest hunters would be able to catch them.'

Deirdre laughed, revealing a little too much of her own cunning. 'And being men, of course, they thought themselves the greatest hunters in the land?'

Leabharcham smiled. 'They'll be here within the week.'

'I will be ready.'

'Don't get your hopes up, my little one.' Leabharcham took the girl's face in her hands.

'You don't think he'll want me?'

'Oh, he will want you, I have no doubt about that. He will want you more than he has ever wanted any woman. But he will not want to carry the shame of betraying his king.'

'Then I will make him.' That was not the petulant stamp of a spoilt child. It was prophecy. Oh, what she might have been had Conchobar not smuggled her away here. Perhaps it had not been her beauty he had wanted to possess, but her power?

Deirdre caught herself and went soft again. She curled up at Leabharcham's feet and laid her head in her lap.

'Tell me the story again,' she said.

Leabharcham ran her fingers through the girl's hair. 'Which one? I have told you many stories.'

'The one about how I screamed when in my mother's womb and it was heard for miles around.'

'I don't know why you like that story so much.'

Deirdre looked up at the woman. 'Because it was the last time that anyone truly heard me.'

Leabharcham wove her tale and the fire dimmed and I was cosy and warm in the nest of hay above them and so we three women of power slept.

It was three days before Naoise and his brothers came thundering towards the valley. Deirdre had kept herself distracted from the waiting by gathering herbs to bathe her skin and hair. I guided her hand a touch, directing her to the more powerful plants and flowers Airmed had taught me. Hawthorn for beauty, meadowsweet to soothe, rowan for protection. When she had finished her ablutions, she glowed.

'Where are they?' she asked Leabharcham.

We could hear them crashing and slashing their way through the woods and had there truly been any game worth hunting, it would have been long gone.

'Perhaps they are lost.'

I went to give them a hand. Transforming into a white deer, I raced in the direction of the three brothers.

'There!' one of them shouted, finally seeing me.

I ran and they gave chase. I wove between the tall pine trees, branches jutting out at neck height ready to kill a man who was not careful. I leapt the prickly gorse bushes that clung to the ground, ready to scratch and bite at unwary legs. I drew the brothers closer and closer to Deirdre's clearing. When they were just feet away, I turned into a crow again and flew back to my perch to watch.

The brothers slowed their horses to a trot as they saw movement beyond the trees.

'Welcome, warriors of the Red Branch,' Deirdre said, her voice cracking a little with nerves. 'Come, you must be hungry, we have food on the fire.'

Deirdre caught Leabharcham's eye and smiled. 'He is just as handsome as I imagined,' she whispered.

The three brothers dismounted. They were all transfixed by Deirdre's beauty. Naoise couldn't take his eyes off her. She laid it on a bit thick, truth be told. She had him with just her smile, she didn't need quite so much wiggling of hips. But it was honey to a fly.

'Tell us your name, fair maiden,' Naoise said.

'My name means sorrow to all who hear it, so call me sorrow.'

'I can't imagine any word that could cross your lips could make us sad.'

He wasn't that clever, this one. The name Deirdre meant sorrow, after all.

'But when I tell you, you will run away and that will make me sad.'

'We are warriors of the Red Branch,' the middle brother said. 'We run from nothing. And certainly not a woman's name.'

'Hang on there,' the elder brother said, a little wiser than the others. 'Why would we run?'

'Because I belong to another, though it would be my

heart's greatest joy to belong to you, Naoise.' She fluttered her eyes at the boy and his cheeks burned hotter than the fire.

'Me?'

'Tell us your name, girl,' the elder brother demanded. 'As your guest, you cannot refuse my request.'

Damn, she muttered under her breath. 'My name is Deirdre.'

Her name landed between them like a horseshoe on a stone floor.

'Oh, shit,' the elder brother said.

'Well, this food has been lovely,' the middle brother said, 'but we had best be on our way now.'

Naoise's will was weakest. He took the girl's hand in his and raised it to his lips. 'And now, I may die happy, knowing I have kissed the hand of the most beautiful woman in the land.'

'You can kiss a lot more than my hand if you get me out of this place,' Deirdre said, wrapping her hand around his.

'But you belong to Conchobar,' Naoise said, backing away from her.

'Belong? Am I a milk cow? To be bought and sold?'

The men shared a look that said, *well, yes.*

'We must go,' Naoise said, trying to extract his hand from her grip, but she held fast.

'Are you rejecting me?' she said.

'For all it breaks my heart, I am,' said Naoise.

'No,' she said.

Faster than a snake, she grabbed his two ears. 'You fear the shame if you take me, but I tell you this. Leave me here and the sounds of mockery will ring in these ears for ever. The man who could have made the most beautiful woman in the world his bride but walked away, what a fool.'

She wasn't pitching her voice quite right.

'Leave me alone, woman,' Naoise said, trying to shake her off.

'Try again,' Leabharcham urged.

Deirdre breathed in, steadying herself, and I added a little of my voice to hers.

'You will take me,' she said, binding him.

'I will take you,' he said.

That a girl.

'Hang on,' the elder brother said. 'We can't be stealing Conchobar's child bride from under his nose. He'll have our skins.'

'Then we run, far from here,' Naoise said, his eyes still glowing from Deirdre's power.

'North,' his brother said. 'We can go to Alba.'

'Then let us go,' Deirdre said, grabbing a small sack of all her possessions that she had already packed.

She kissed Leabharcham goodbye and they were gone within the hour.

'What say you, the Morrigan?' Leabharcham said, looking up at me. 'Will she be happy?'

I should have known those eyes could have seen through me. I took on woman form and sat beside her and looked into the future that lay ahead.

'She will be happier than any woman has ever been.'

Leabharcham smiled.

'For seven years,' I said.

'Ah. And then?'

'She will be more sorrowful than any woman has ever been.'

Leabharcham nodded. 'At least she will have tasted happiness before Conchobar takes it from her.'

233

'Is that better?' I asked. 'To know what you are missing?'

Leabharcham sucked on her gums. 'I don't know, but it is life.'

Ever the poet.

So I left Leabharcham as Deirdre and her new husband and his brothers rode north for freedom. Could I have saved Deirdre? Could she and Naoise have lived happily for the rest of her days? Perhaps. But this is not that kind of story.

22.

While I was away, Medb had been busy. She had returned to her throne in Connacht and within days of burying Tinni mac Conri, had married a man called Ailill mac Máta, a simple but strong man who had once been chief of her body-guard, and one of her favourite night-time companions.

When I returned, I found her sitting on the throne, her new husband on her left-hand side, already pregnant with his daughter. She introduced me to her court as a fedlem, a prophet poetess, and placed me on her right-hand side. I watched Medb rule and marvelled at how easily it came to her. She was a ruler like no other. She made no pretence at being anything but a woman and wielded her beauty as others wielded iron. When I had ruled in Ulaid, lifetimes before, I had remained a virgin, believing that sharing my bed with a man would mean giving up my power. Medb laughed at such a notion.

'Sex is a weapon, my beloved Nemain. Sometimes the only one a woman has to hand.'

She did not shy away when men desired her and would use the promise of a night with her as easily as the promise of a hundred cattle or her weight in gold when negotiating with kings. She would extract a binding oath of fealty from men at the height of their pleasure and leave their beds before they awoke. She was named after the honeyed drink of mead, and men in her presence were as heady and foolish as any who had drunk deeply of it.

The men of Connacht adored her, and intoxicated by her beauty would run into battle at a word. The women, though often jealous, felt safe under her rule, for she extracted a heavy blood price from any who laid a hand on a woman and made it known that those who crossed her borders for such a purpose would not make it back to their homelands alive. Her people loved her. But they feared her too, for her fury could be as hot as her lust, and it rose as quickly. I imagined what my mother would say had she seen Medb in one of her rages, smashing bowls and tearing down the silk tapestries that covered her walls. She would have advised her to be gentle, speak softly, but Medb would only have laughed at that and told her she'd speak how she liked. No one could tell Medb what to do. Not even me.

'Will you teach me how to fight?' she said one day, as we watched the men in training while she nursed her new-born girl.

Ailill mac Máta was teaching the men the proper use of a spear. His muscles shifted under his skin, slick with sweat as he thrust the spear forward and back, forward and back. His technique was good, but his aim was poor.

'I thought you said sex was your weapon,' I said.

'Can't a woman have more than one?'

I didn't answer, assuming this was another of her fancies that would pass as soon as something else caught her attention.

'If you won't teach me,' she said, 'I'll get Scáthach to do it.'

Scáthach. The shadowy one. A woman after my own heart. I had heard the stories about how she was one of the greatest warriors in the world, so great that kings from all across Ireland sent their sons to train with her on her island fortress in Alba.

'A fine plan. I've heard she's a good teacher.'

Medb punched me on the arm. 'Come on,' she said. 'I don't want to go all the way to Alba to learn from her, when I have you, the goddess of battle herself, right here. I've heard the stories, you know? How you could dance across spear tips and would rip men's lungs out. I bet Scáthach can't do that.'

I considered Medb. Her long, slim arms and soft hands. She had never held anything heavier than a dagger. If she was going to learn how to fight, we had work to do.

'Maybe we'll start with a sword, and we can get to the spear hopping later.'

Rather than practise as the men did with a multitude of weapons, we stuck to just one. The sword. I had the smith make one from bronze, for it was lighter than iron and would not burn my skin when I was instructing her. Medb was a quick learner, and unafraid of the pain that comes with training. After each session, she marvelled at the bruises that covered her skin in something close to pride.

'I've only received bruises dealt unfairly by the hands of men. Earning them yourself is almost pleasant.'

We trained in secret in the morning, while during the rest of the day we looked for more ways to vex Conchobar and take the throne of Ulaid for Medb. Any peace he brokered, we worked to undo. Any promises he made, we pushed him to break. If it seemed that accords were being forged, we stirred up enmity. We thwarted him in every small way we could, slowly eating away at his peace, without any man knowing it was us behind it.

I was there on the day the news of Deirdre's escape was delivered, for I had wanted to see his reaction for myself. It was everything we could have hoped for. Conchobar had taken his impotent rage out on the messenger, ripping his tongue from his throat and leaving him to choke on his own blood.

'Find me the girl!' he had roared, the messenger's blood freckling his face. 'Find her so that I can show her what happens to any who dare to stand against me. Bring her to me, so that I can destroy her.'

I could see discomfort stirring in the hearts of some of the men. Deirdre was just a girl and their king he might be, but they knew what Conchobar did to girls. The Red Branch was cracking and I took delight in it.

At nights, I would fly to Emain Macha and whisper into Conchobar's ear and his dreams would be of the laughter of women and the scorn of men. I flew to Fernmag, a scrap of land on the Ulaid border, where Éogan mac Durthact played at being king. As he slept, with half an eye open, I whispered into his ear gifting him dreams of Conchobar plotting against him. At last, when the dreams of betrayal haunted their waking thoughts, both kings called their men and went to battle.

It was a petty but pleasingly brutal skirmish, in which Éogan had narrowly claimed victory. After the last of his warriors had headed for home, their howls of triumph fading into the darkness, I walked the scarred battlefield, breathing in the echo of the fight. Many had died and many still lay dying. I picked the flesh off ribcages, dug my beak into eye sockets and feasted. I wriggled my bare toes in the bloody earth, the way a child might their feet in sand. I smelt the metal of blood and swords and licked my lips.

In my wanderings, I came across an arm sticking out of a pile of bodies, like a sapling fighting its way to the sun. I bent, lips curled back, ready to dig my teeth into the gangrenous flesh. The hand moved. With a shove of my foot, I rolled bodies away to reveal the man beneath. His face was caked in blood and dirt and he was buried up to his chest in black sucking mud and dead men. His shoulder had been cleaved down to the collarbone, but he was alive. Barely. He moaned and groaned like a cow giving birth.

Defeated men shouldn't survive battles. They should win or they should die.

'Help me,' he cried.

I hitched up my skirts and squatted. I could help him. I could end his torment. With a flick of a finger, I could knock his head from his shoulders and send it flying. I saw a gold torc around his neck, bloody but shining. A king then, but which one?

I wiped mud from his face and saw that it was Conchobar. He looked old beyond his years, skin wrinkled and face puffy, as though the bitterness that flooded through his veins had poisoned him.

'You!' he said, his eyes widening in recognition. It had been years since we had last come face to face, but he knew me still as the woman who had cursed him.

'Me,' I said.

He wasn't destined to die that day, but that didn't mean I couldn't see to it that he suffered. I put my foot on his face and pushed him down deeper into the mud. He screamed out in pain and I drank it in like wine.

It was then I heard a name being called, a high-pitched cry caught on the wind. A woman, perhaps, his woman? I leapt up into the air to see who had come to my feast.

It was a boy. His arms like twigs, his legs like sticks. He couldn't have seen more than eight winters. He stood at the edge of the black battlefield, holding nothing but a hurling stick as a weapon, calling out the name of his king.

'Conchobar? Where are you?'

My heart twisted in my chest, for was he not the image of my Meche grown? I had often imagined the life my son would have lived, dreamt of his deeds, the woman he would marry, the battles he would win, the stories that would be told about him. I dreamt it all so vividly that I would awaken and gasp that he wasn't still with me. And it seemed that he was here once more. The same wild curls, the same rosy cheeks against bone-pale skin. Even his mouth was the mouth I had seen laugh a thousand times. It took all my strength not to run to him and wrap him up in my arms: my boy returned to me at last.

'Conchobar! My king, where are you?' he called again.

'I am here, Sétanta,' cried the dying king, spitting mud and blood. 'I am here!'

The boy, Sétanta, headed towards the sound of Conchobar's voice. And as he drew closer, I saw differences between this boy and mine. Whereas Meche would have been light of foot, Sétanta tramped down the earth with each step as if angry with it. Meche's hair had been deep ebony red, but this boy's hair was the colour of autumn acorns. When I looked into his eyes, I saw none of Meche's endless, unlimited curiosity. I saw nothing but ambition and arrogance and the dream of my child walking, breathing, living again, vanished like heat vapour on a dry track.

And yet I still felt a magnetic pull to the boy I could not explain. Sétanta was not my child, and yet he was so alike to Meche in appearance. And so alike to me in his character. He carried my rage, my hunger, my desire to shape the world. Attributes that are dangerous enough when buried deep in the mountainous heart of a goddess, but terrible when pulsing in the fragile heart of a mortal. I saw then a halo around the boy. A hero light. He had a destiny, good or bad, it would be great. And I would be a part of it.

It was dark, a pitch blackness that meant he couldn't see his hand in front of his face, and yet he walked. Mud sucked at his feet, he tripped over the broken bones of his dead kinsmen, and yet he walked. Sétanta seemed to be without fear. I wanted to test the limit of his courage, to teach him the meaning of fear, just as I had when the Sons of Mil sent their boys to me in the darkness.

My crows cawed and dived at him, scratching his skin, and yet he walked, his only guide the voice of a dying king. Beside me, two men lay choking on their last breaths. One had half his head missing, the other had been cleaved in two at the waist. I did not have the skills to bring the dead back to life, but I could delay their deaths for a while. I spoke the words and kissed their lips, breathing some borrowed breath into their lungs. They coughed, spluttered and marvelled at being alive. I pointed them in the direction of Sétanta. The man with the legs pulled himself to his feet and carried what remained of his brother on his back, wading forward in the direction I compelled them.

I looked up at the sky, black as one of my wings. A person could only fear what they could see, and if he could see nothing, he would fear nothing. With a breath, I blew the clouds away from the moon, so the horrors of the battlefield were bathed in a silver light.

The whole time he was walking, Sétanta talked, chatting away as if he was going for a stroll on a warm spring morning. He talked about the affairs of the court, how his training with the boy troop of the Emain Macha was going, and how there wasn't a boy among the troop who could beat him. Every now and then, he would stop and call out again to Conchobar, then get his bearings and move on. He was but fifty feet from his king when my revenant warriors stepped in his way.

'Help me, child,' the man on his feet said. 'I have dragged what is left of my brother across the battlefield, but I can't carry him any longer. Carry him for me.'

'Help me,' the half-body groaned.

The boy looked at the man on his feet, head smashed like an eggshell; he looked at the body over the man's back, intestines trailing on the ground.

'Get out of my way,' he said, waving his hurling stick at the revenant. 'You're already dead and the sooner you lie down and accept it, the better it will be for all of us.'

'Carry him for just a little while,' the dying man said.

'I will not. I can only carry one man out of here and it won't be one who has no business walking or talking.'

'Here then,' and with that, the man hurled the torso from his back at the boy.

It took Sétanta off his feet and knocked his stick from his hand. He thrashed and squealed under the weight. Teeth snapped at the boy's throat, but he held them off, his arms shaking with the effort of it. Fingers clawed at his cheeks, but he pushed back. Weakness now flowed into him and with it fear. Just a trickle, like squeezing wine from a single grape. His first taste of it and it was sweet to me.

Tears flowed down his cheeks, cutting a path through the dirt and blood. This ghoul would defeat him and his king would die and he would never become a hero, all because he was too afraid to fight.

'Call yourself a warrior?' I said, my voice a mocking

242

whisper in his ear, and a rumble of thunder that shook the battlefield. 'Overthrown by phantoms! Killed by a half a man!' I laughed, my laugh a hiss in his face and a bolt of lightning. 'You don't have the stuff warriors are made of. You might as well die here in the mud along with your king.'

Even cowards could be brought to their feet by the words of satirists and this boy was no coward. The mocking had the desired effect. His weeping turned to a howling. His weak arms filled with the strength of rage. He pushed the body off him, throwing it all the way back to Fernmag, and snatched his hurling stick back up. As the other wraith came at him, he swung his stick and knocked what remained of the man's head clear across the field. The body collapsed to the ground, a pile of dead flesh at last.

I watched as Sétanta's shoulders rose and fell with each gasping breath he took. The rage of my taunting had blown away the fear, just as I had the clouds from the moon. Yet as he stood there, muscles feeling the strain, spit and blood on his face, the fear crept back in again.

'Conchobar!' he cried out, and this time there was a quake in his voice. 'Where are you?'

A pathetic groaning was his answer. The boy set his path by the sound and moved on.

He came at last to his king, up to his shoulders in the mud and bodies of the men he had brought to this battle to die. The boy clambered down and got to work, pulling and pushing.

'Sétanta,' Conchobar said, his voice weak and weary. 'You shouldn't have come. Why, a man twice your age would have died of fright.'

'Nothing scares me, Uncle, you know that.'

Uncle. No, it couldn't be. What cruel fate was this: to

send me a child so like my own, and for him to be the blood of my enemy.

At last, Conchobar was free and the boy dragged him on to his back and the crows followed him home.

23.

The years passed and my vengeance hardened with each turn of the wheel. Some wounds healed, others festered. Conchobar hunted for Deirdre but could not find her and the slight ate away at him. The boy, Sétanta, grew, performing mighty deeds. And I watched him, knowing one day we would meet again.

Medb had her son and nephew, both fathered by Conchobar, fostered to kings, forging allegiances. If she was glad to see the sons of Conchobar go, she did not show it. Medb and Ailill's child grew up beautiful but dull. She was named Finnabair, White Ghost, for the paleness of her skin, and Medb struggled to love her as much as she had hoped. Medb built a great fort on a hill in Cruachan, not far from the cave I still called home, wrapping walls around standing stones and raising the land up so she could see for miles around.

She and I grew closer with each passing year. I'd had sisters and lovers, handmaidens and husbands. But never in my many lifetimes had I had a friend. It had started in anger, forged by a shared hatred, but it became something more than that. I was the only person she truly trusted, and she was the only person who didn't fear me. We would share our woes and in sharing them, they lost their sting. We laughed together, cried together. But mostly, we planned Conchobar's punishment.

The promise of my curse hung heavy over the lives of

Conchobar's men. They knew that if Ulaid was attacked, when their need was most dire, their strength would desert them and they would be struck by the agony of birth. But for it to befall them, we needed to attack.

'The army won't follow me unless Ailill agrees to the raid,' Medb said, one evening as we scoured our plans. Maps and battle charts were strewn across the table, I'd even borrowed from Lugh and had little men carved to represent the five provinces of Ireland: Connacht, Mumhain, Mide, Laigin and Ulaid. Medb's daughter, Finnabair, lay asleep under the table, her knuckles stinging from the raps Medb had dealt her every time she had tried to take one of the wooden figures to play with. Medb wouldn't have minded had Finnabair wanted to play war, but she had only wanted to rock them like babies.

'You're nearly a woman, Finnabair,' Medb had snapped at her. 'Soon it will be time for you to be having real babies, not playing with toys.'

Medb knocked the wooden figures aside and laid her forehead on the table, banging it slowly in a steady pounding rhythm, like the sound of a distant war drum. We were so close now. The hatred towards Conchobar had grown in the hearts of the other kingdoms like a weed. All it would take was one last push to bring him to his knees. All knew that Medb was the true power in Connacht, but she still needed her husband's support if she was going to attack.

'Then you'll have to force his hand,' I said.

'I've tried. He says he hates Conchobar as much as I do, but he won't risk breaking the peace.'

Peace. I spat. There was no peace in the land. Conchobar carried out raids with impunity every year, sending his Red Branch warriors to take women, cattle and land. But none

246

dared stand against him alone. We needed a reason, a spark that could become a fire.

Every time I closed my eyes, I saw the bulls fighting, white horns dipped in blood, black hooves crushing bone. I had believed them a symbol for the battle to come, but what if I had been missing something all along?

I thought of my beautiful bull with the dark brown hide, birthed from the cow I had stolen from Odras. He was still grazing on my lands, safe from harm and time. It was the kind of bull men would go to war over.

The next day was Samhain. I returned to my cave and readied my chariot as if I was to go to war, but I had only one horse lead it. I wrapped a deep red cloak about my shoulders, and let it drag behind me as I rode out of my cave, the beautiful Brown Bull driven before me. His coat was the colour of an autumn conker and his horns were as white as pearls. He was the size of a ship that could carry forty men.

'And where are you off to looking so mighty fine? For don't we have an appointment on this day?'

I turned to see the Dagda. Alive and vital as the day we first arrived. Not an extra line marked his face and there wasn't a white hair to be seen in his beard, though he was a little thicker around the belly. He'd no doubt been eating his fill from his cauldron and singing his songs along with the rest of the Tuatha Dé in the land of the young. He was no less huge than he had been, his smile no less broad. The sight of him lifted my weary heart like the sun burning through morning mist.

'I waited for you for the first fifty Samhains,' I said, not wanting him to see what joy his presence had brought me. 'The hundred and fifty after that, I had better things to be doing.'

'Has it been that long?'

'It's felt longer.'

We stared at each other, eyes drinking the other in, the long years falling away between us.

'Lugh said you came to visit.'

I snorted. 'Did he now? Well, that was a hundred years ago.'

'Get away. To me it was only a day. You should have called for me, I would have seen you across. He was only messing with you.'

I cursed Lugh. How had I not seen he was playing another of his games? But maybe he had done me a kindness. 'I don't belong there anyway.'

'What do you mean?' the Dagda said, slapping me on the shoulder. I had forgotten how strong he was. 'Of course you do! We are your tribe.'

I tried to find the words to explain, but they danced away from me. How could I explain that I was tied to this place? My tribe might not need me, the descendants of the Sons of Mil might not want me, but the land herself, she needed me and I needed her. Her wave-crashed rocks and smooth, mossy stones, her raging waterfalls and gurgling bog pools, her lush, mist-covered valleys and deep, end-lessly deep lakes. She was mine. Always mine. She was as wild as I was, as untameable.

'I belong here. The other lands are too . . . peaceful.'

This amused him, though he did not laugh. 'Too peace-ful, hey?'

He smiled at me and I felt my resolve melting and my lust rising. He always had that effect on me. But I had a job to do.

'I can't pass the time with you today, for I am on my way somewhere.'

'And where might that be?'

'To start a war,' I answered.

He clapped his hands together and thunder rolled in the distance in response. 'Fun. Can I help?'

I considered him. 'You can drive my bull.'

His smile widened still. Another might take offence at being slighted so. But the Dagda seemed entertained by the idea of the most powerful of gods taking on the most menial of roles.

'I shall be your drover!' He picked up a hazel twig from the ground and with a shake of his wrist, it became a forked staff.

'And you will keep your mouth shut. This is my story, not yours.'

'But—'

I glared at him with one eye closed. He nodded, giving me a small bow. 'I shall speak not a word and my name will be kept secret.'

We set forth north, the Dagda driving the bull beside me. We travelled overland, though the Dagda complained that it would have been faster if we took the pathways of the land beneath, but it had been some time since I had gone wandering.

It was a beautiful day of light showers and rainbows, and I could tell it was taking every ounce of his considerable strength not to give a constant commentary on every place we passed, telling me how it got its name. As if I didn't already know.

'How much further?' the Dagda asked.

'Only a few miles more. Across the border into Ulaid and then to Cooley, where a cattle lord named Daire mac Fiachna keeps his herds. And there I will leave the bull.'

The Brown Bull bellowed at the idea of being taken so far away from the lush grasses of his home.

'The beast doesn't look happy being driven by you.'

I turned to see a young man standing in the road, fists thrust deep into his hips. He was fifteen, sixteen at most, hardly old enough to have hair on his cheeks or on his balls, but a soft fluff rested on his upper lip. Light auburn hair fell in messy curls over his forehead. It was him. The boy, Sétanta, whom I had seen on the battlefield, now nearly a man. He was still as beautiful as he had been then, though he tried to look fierce and terrifying as he stared at the Dagda. A boy standing up to a god.

'And what business is it of yours?' I asked. 'This bull doesn't belong to you.'

'All the cattle of Ulaid are my business.' He stepped forward and ran his hand against the bull's neck and pressed his nose into the nook of its giant forehead. The bull snorted happily at his touch.

'The business of this bull is too great for you, boy,' I said.

'Why is a woman doing the answering, when it's the man I'm questioning?' he said.

I laughed, thinking him insolent, innocent. I admired his bravery.

His young face twisted in rage at my laughter as if no one had ever dared to laugh at him before.

'He's got balls,' the Dagda said, in our language. 'I'll give him that.'

'What are you saying?' the boy demanded, his voice cracking.

'Though by the sound of his voice, they've yet to drop,' the Dagda said.

'Answer me!' The boy threw his spear at my chariot.

Before it struck, I hopped into the air, dancing on the spear as it flew beneath me. Spinning, I cast off my cloak and skin and became a crow.

The boy stared up at me, mouth hung open, as I perched on a branch and gazed at him. I saw the fear in his eyes then, for he knew who I was, the tales of the Morrigan had not been forgotten in Ulaid. 'If I had known it was you . . .'

'Too late,' I said. 'As soon as you cast your weapon you sealed your fate.'

He tried to laugh. 'You can't hurt me. Your people rule the underworld – mine rule the land as far as can be seen.'

'Oh, I can and I will hurt you,' I said. 'For I will bring about a battle the likes of which you cannot dream of. I will rain down vengeance on your precious land.'

He curled his hands into fists, and his face became a twisted snarl. 'Then I'll fight in this battle of yours for I am destined to become the greatest warrior of the age. So, do whatever you want, you shapeshifting crone. Come at me as an eel to drown me and I'll crush your ribs. Come at me as a wolf and I'll drive my spear in your eye. Come at me as a cow, leading a herd of cows to trample me, and I will break your legs.'

I laughed again and his face wrinkled in disgust as though no one had ever laughed at him before.

'We shall see,' I said.

I nodded to the Dagda to carry on. We left Sétanta spitting after us and led the Brown Bull to Cooley where we left it grazing amid the herds of Daire mac Fiachna.

'I can't convince you to come back with me?' the Dagda said, as we stood by the banks of a deep lake. A pathway to the land below.

I shook my head.

'Shame.' The Dagda waded into the lake. 'Be seeing you then.'

'Perhaps,' I said, believing this was the last time I would see him.

'Watch out for that boy,' he said, as waters were around his waist. 'Whoever he is, he has a story ahead.'

The Dagda saw it too then. The glow that marked out those destined for greatness.

'He might be fated to be a hero,' I said. 'But I am a goddess. He stands no chance against me.'

If only I had known.

24.

A month later, and the whole land knew of the Brown Bull of Cooley and of its magnificence. Medb was ready to set her trap.

One night, I watched from the shadows as she and Ailill lay side by side, the sweat from their lovemaking slick on their skin.

'Isn't it wonderful that we are equal in all things?' she said.

And he, all post-coital stupid and overly pleased with himself in general, replied, 'True, you are lucky to have me as a husband.'

'Lucky?' Medb said. 'Why is it me who is the lucky one and not you?'

'Well, aren't you better off now than the day I first took you?'

'What are you on about, man?' She sat up, covering her breasts with a sheet. 'My fortune is greater than yours.'

'Give over,' Ailill said. 'There's no one who has greater treasures and wealth than I have.'

Even in the dark, I saw her smile. 'Prove it.'

And so the counting began. Every scrap they owned was laid out and measured. Every bracelet and torc. Every cloak and fur. Every weapon. Every warrior. Every bite of bread. They found that they were equal in every aspect. In gold, cloth, grain, retinue.

'See,' Medb said, delighted with herself. 'We are equal in all things.'

'Never has any man or woman been more equal,' I said, adding bait to the snare.

Ailill tightened his eyes at me. He never much liked me, and yet he knew he could never be rid of me. Wherever Medb went, I was close behind.

'Ah, but you are forgetting my greatest treasure.' Ailill grinned, as though he had already won this game.

'And what is that?' I asked.

Ailill smiled. 'My beautiful white bull.'

'Medb has herds of her own and bulls as fine and fertile as any in the country,' I said.

'But none are as fine or as fertile as mine,' Ailill said.

'Let me be the judge. Let me see this bull of yours,' Medb said, as if she was only faintly interested.

As cocky as a boy leading his first woman to his bed, Ailill led us to his herds.

'There,' he said, pointing to the heart of them. He had no need to point the bull out. He had named it Finnbhennach. White-horned. And it was clear to see why. Finnbhennach's horns shone like the moon and were tipped in gold. He was as tall as three men at the shoulder and as long as a barrow. Gold and chains ran from his ears to his flaring nostrils. He turned, each step shaking the earth beneath his hooves.

'You're right, Ailill,' Medb said, 'I have no match for this beast. And until I do, I cannot lie with you, for I have sworn an oath that I would never lie with a man who placed himself above me.'

Ailill saw then the mistake he had made. His face went pale. He had a choice: win this game or lose his husband's privileges with Medb. He chose to lose. 'Then I give Finnbhennach to you as a gift.'

'No,' she said. 'That cannot stand. I will have my own bull.'

'But my love, there is none!'

'There is one,' I said. 'The Brown Bull of Cooley.'

Medb and I tried to hide our smiles. 'Then I must have it,' she said.

Ailill shook his pretty head. 'I know of this bull. They say it is so huge, that thirty of the boy troop of Emain Macha can stand on his back from shoulders to haunch. A beast so fertile he can cover one hundred heifers a day. But he belongs to one of Conchobar's men, a man named Daire. He won't give him up.'

'You let me see about that,' Medb said, patting Ailill on the cheek.

She sent word to Daire in Cooley, to ask if he would part with the Brown Bull. She offered him all kinds of treasures, including a night in bed with her. A month later, a messenger returned with Daire's answer.

'Daire agrees that you may have the Brown Bull for a year and a day. And he looks forward to receiving his payment.'

Ailill was pleased, knowing that for the year she possessed it, they would be equals again and he would have access once more to her bedchamber, though he was less pleased by the payment she was offering. Medb sent her men to collect the Brown Bull and I went with them, riding in the pocket of one of the men in the form of a mouse, to see what trouble I could stir.

Daire welcomed the Connacht men, giving them bed and food for the night. But he also gave them drink. A lot of drink. And as they reached the end of their cups their usually tight lips loosened and their usually sharp wits were dulled. They started griping with Daire's men, bragging about the wealth of their queen and how it outstripped that of Daire and even King Conchobar himself.

'If she is so wealthy, then why did she come begging to our master for the lend of his bull?' one of Daire's men asked. 'If she is so wealthy, why did she not offer him more gold, rather than the warmth of her thighs?'

'Maybe she's still hungering for Ulaid's cock?' another of Daire's men said, grabbing his balls.

Daire's men laughed. The Connacht men put down their cups.

'She will never sleep with a pig like Daire,' I whispered in the ear of one of Medb's men. 'And she will keep the Brown Bull for her own.'

'Queen Medb would rather sleep with a pig than your lord, though she'd have trouble telling them apart,' the man said, repeating my words as if he thought them his own. 'And once she has the bull, she won't be giving it back.'

The men got to shouting, hurling insults at each other.

'What is the cause of these squabbles?' Daire shouted, silencing the noise. 'I would have peace in my home.'

'These Connacht dogs say that Medb plans to keep the Brown Bull for herself.'

Daire's already red face went redder still. 'How dare you. Get out. Out! Medb will never have the Brown Bull. And you can tell her what to do with her gold and her thighs!'

What a fool he was to make an agreement and then break it. What a fool he was to reject Medb. It became a symbol of all the promises the men of the Red Branch had broken. A sign that Conchobar's men couldn't be trusted. They thought themselves better than the rest of the men of Ireland, their cattle better and their women more beautiful.

'Let us see about that,' the men of Ireland said. 'Let us see how they fare when we march across their borders and take the Brown Bull and whatever else we fancy.'

It was all talk. Brave words by stupid men. Just the thing needed to start a war.

25.

Medb sent her finest storytellers to the southern provinces to spread word of Daire's betrayal. She had, they said, been promised the Brown Bull in good faith by Daire, and when she refused the advances of the sweaty, pox-ridden cow-herd he broke his word and refused her the bull. She was, they said, going to take what was owed her and they were invited to join her in the raid. In payment, they would have their equal share of the wealth they stripped from the land. As a sweetener to the deal she also, secretly, offered each of the kings her own daughter, Finnabair, as prize. If taking that swaggering bastard Conchobar down wasn't honey enough, marrying Finnabair would add to their own power. And once they'd taken down Ulaid, they could turn to the other provinces and soon enough be the sole ruler of the whole land. What king could resist such a call? Each of the provinces answered, and as summer moved to autumn, the four armies assembled at Medb's fort in Cruachan.

The men of Mumhain wore cloaks of light blue and gold, each pinned in place with a brooch at their shoulder. They wore their hair short and carried broad iron spears atop slender shafts. The men of Laigin wore purple cloaks and hooded tunics that fell to their feet. Their hair was smooth and cut to their shoulders and they carried round shields with jagged, blade-sharp edges and heavy spears as thick as pillars. The men of Mide wore green cloaks speckled with threads of gold and dark tunics that came to their knees; they carried full-length shields and short, stabbing swords. While the men of Connacht, who stood ready to greet the others, wore cloaks woven of deep blue, each thrown over one shoulder, with a black raptor stitched on the back. Their hair was shaven at the sides, and ran long over the nape of the neck, and they carried spear shafts made from carved bog wood, tipped with long silver blades.

Many of the men knew each other of old, whether from meeting at gatherings or facing each other in skirmishes. The men of Mumhain bore scars inflicted by the shields of Laigin, while the men of Laigin had reason to fear the black spears of Mide. And all had reason to be wary of the warriors of Connacht. It was an uneasy peace. The men eyed each other up, checking out their strength, their weapons. They threw insults about the way the others wore their hair or the last time they had washed.

From her fort on the hill Medb watched them gather. Nearby forests had been ravaged to make her wooden ramparts, each pole sharpened and ready for the head of an enemy. Inside, she had gilded everything she could with burnished bronze, and lit fires in every corner, so the place shone like a setting sun.

She chewed on the inside of her cheek and stroked a red squirrel that was curled about her neck. A month before, she had rescued the squirrel from a boy who had been using it for slingshot practice. She'd had the boy whipped and nursed the squirrel back to health, some said feeding it milk from her own breasts. It chirruped in her ear, as though giving her counsel.

'Well?' I said.

'Well what?'

'Aren't you going to speak to them? Stir their spirits and raise their battle lust?'

'Every one of them who has left a love or friend behind will be cursing me,' she said.

'Then let them curse you. Let them hate you, if they must, but make them follow you.'

She had the women dress her in her most dazzling gown and had her heaviest gold draped around her shoulders. Her blonde hair was intricately woven to create a crown upon her head. Her lips were ruby with Parthian red, her eyebrows blackened with pitch and she wore a blue cloak, speckled with gold thread that was clasped at the shoulder with a simple gold pin. Her armour, though as strong as any worn by any of her warriors, curved around her body, so that none who laid eyes on her could mistake her for a man. Finally, she went down to meet the hosts. I may be the goddess, but on that day, it was Medb who looked like one.

I became a small blackbird and perched myself on her left shoulder, so I could whisper in her ear. Her squirrel twitched its nose at me, but I silenced it with a snap of my beak.

'Greetings, sons of Ireland,' she said, her voice a little weak, a little unsure.

I shaped the words in my mind, the old words for strength, for hearing, and I wrapped them around her throat.

'Sons of Ireland,' she said again.

Good. Stronger. She had them now.

'We stand here, shoulder to shoulder with men and women from tribes we may once have called our enemy, but who we can now call friends, united against the tyranny of Conchobar and the Red Branch. I see the mightiest warriors this land has ever known before me, and I take strength in their skills and courage. But I also see the ghosts of all of those who have died by Conchobar's command standing with us. They cannot take their revenge. But we can. What man among us has not lost a brother, a father, a son, to Conchobar's cruelty? What woman here has not felt the unwelcome touch of Conchobar or his men? I say, no more. Let him fear, as we once feared. Let him tremble, as we once trembled. We go for the Brown Bull, for what riches we can strip from the land, but we will return with more than just what we can carry in our hands. We will return with a new-found courage in our hearts. We raid, not for spoils, but for justice.'

It was a good speech. Even the poets gave her that. Spears were clashed against shields, feet stamped on the ground. They were ready for war.

And yet the druids, waiting for their auspicious signs, wouldn't let the armies leave for two full weeks. Two weeks in which the grain stores of Cruachan dwindled and the mead was increasingly watered down to make it stretch. The men took to fighting among themselves, old grudges deepening, new ones forming.

'What is taking so long?' I said, as restless for this to begin as any of the warriors.

'The druids say we have to wait,' Medb said.

'The druids always say that. Till they don't.'

'You'd have me ignore them? March off under a black sign?'

'No, but I'd suggest that it was as much in their interests to get this thing started before there's nothing left to eat or drink in your halls but horse piss and dust.'

Funnily enough, the next day the druids saw an eagle flapping, or a snake eating its young, or a hare fucking or whatever it was they thought was the sign they needed and, at last, the hosts were given the word to set off north.

We rode through pine forests, birds flying at the sound of our approach, hacking down trees that stood in our path so that we were sticky with resin. We waded through peat bogs that sucked at our ankles and left our clothes stinking of musk, soil and sulphur.

We came to a stream that marked the border between Connacht and Ulaid and began to wade across. As soon as the first Connacht warrior set foot on Ulaid soil, a great wailing filled the air. The voices of thousands of men screeching in agony.

'Hear that!' Medb shouted, spinning in circles, her arms outstretched, as though the cries of anguish were music to dance to. 'That is Macha's curse, bringing the men of Ulaid to their knees.'

Medb's warriors covered their ears, trying to block out the noise. Never before had a man made that sound, for no man had ever suffered the pains of childbirth. And now every man of Ulaid made it as one.

Medb laughed at the fear of her warriors. 'Were you so afraid when your wives cried out like that? Your sisters? Every mother knows that pain and now our enemies know it too!' She took my hands in hers. 'You truly are the Morrigan.'

'Did you doubt it?'

'Never!'

I lifted my head to listen to the cries of the men. It was sweet as birdsong to me. Suddenly, I felt reality crack, opening up a space between the present and the future. I looked down at my feet. The cold, clear water of the river turned thick and red. A waking vision.

'*I see it crimson. I see it red,*' I said, the words flowing out of me.

'What?' Medb said.

'*I see it crimson. I see it red,*' I said again, staring at Medb and seeing her standing in a river of blood. The vision was clear. We were walking into a bloodbath.

Ailill and the men beside Medb looked to her, fear glittering in their eyes.

'The blood will be theirs,' Medb said. 'Can't you hear their cries? That is your curse.'

I shook my head, trying to shake away the images that burned into my eyes. Words that were not mine, that came as if from the earth, poured out of me.

'*I see a battle,*
A golden man with blood on his hands
And a hero-halo round his head.
The host coloured crimson by his hand.
He towers on the battlefield.
In breastplate and red cloak
Holding death-dealing spear
The warped man deals death.
I see him moving to the fray.
Take warning, watch him well.
Whole hosts he will destroy.
Thousands will yield their heads
Because of him.
The forge hound.
Cúchulainn of Mureteimne
The hound of Culann.'

26.

The vision passed and I came back to myself.

'Who is this Cúchulainn?' Medb asked me when I had recovered.

'I don't know,' I said.

'How can you not know? You're the one who said his name.' Medb was frustrated by my prophecy, but not as frustrated as I was.

'I don't know where the words came from,' I said. They were like a flock of birds flying through me and I just caught at the feathers of them.

'Who here has heard of this Cúchulainn?' Ailill shouted to the assembly.

A voice called out from among the group, though I could not see the face of who spoke. 'He is the greatest fighter of the boy troop of Emain Macha.'

I knew of the boy troop. Children trained in the fighting arts by Conchobar's Red Branch warriors. Ulaid had trained their young men in arms for generations past. But ever since I had laid my curse on them, Conchobar insisted the families of his province send their boys to Emain Macha to be schooled as a last line of defence.

'A boy?' Medb laughed. 'A single child against all the men of Ireland? No wonder you see red. It is his blood you see.'

A boy would be free from my curse, for I had only promised pain to the men. But Medb was right: how much trouble could one child really cause?

The voice spoke again. 'More than just any boy.' A young man stepped forward, wearing the dress of a Connacht warrior. He had a slim face and slender limbs and wasn't more than a boy himself. 'Cúchulainn has trained in every weapon and is the greatest warrior in Ulaid. If he has come to stand against us, we should be afraid.'

Medb looked down at the man from her chariot. 'I thought the men of Connacht were made of sterner stuff.'

With that, she drove her chariot forward, towards the north, ignoring the young man's warning. But I could not ignore it. Every time I closed my eyes I saw that river of blood, and a youth, golden and glorious, like the gods of old.

We pushed deeper into Ulaid territory and from every hut and hostel, every farm and fort, we heard the screams of agony from the men, struck down by my curse. Just as they needed strength, they had none. The women and their children watched us march by, arms folded across their chests. We left them unharmed for we had no business with the women of Ulaid.

After a day's march we set up camp next to a river. As the sun set, Medb strode through the camp, talking to the men, trying to make them love her. Behind her, she paraded Finnabair, her daughter, showing her off to the warriors. Whereas Medb was tall and strong, Finnabair was small and frail as a bird, her skin the colour of the inside of an eggshell. Whereas Medb slept with any man she chose, Finnabair was still a virgin. And it was her virginity that Medb used as a lure. For what man wouldn't want to be the first to claim that delicate creature as his own?

I followed the two women, a figure cloaked in red. While the men stared at Medb and Finnabair with hunger and longing, they dared not look at me for fear I would make their eyes explode out of their head or their guts spill out of their arses. Stories that the Morrigan walked among them had spread throughout the hosts. Men bowed their heads as I strode past, and I left whispers in my tread.

Sometimes, when I tired of being a walking phantom, I would ride on Medb's shoulder as a blackbird, though that squirrel of hers would bark at me. She stopped to talk with the men: about the weather, the food, their loved ones back home. And all the time Medb was scanning their eyes for the truth. Were they loyal? Would they follow her when the time came? Two conversations taking place at once. One in words, the other in looks.

She stopped by a gathering of Mide men. A man was entertaining his fellow warriors with a bawdy tale but as we came close, he stopped mid-sentence.

'Oh, please,' Finnabair said. 'Don't stop.'

The man stood up. 'I don't think it's a tale suitable for the ears of queens, my lady,' he said, his pale cheeks flushing around a thick beard.

'You'd be surprised what these ears have heard,' Medb said, giving him a glittering, seductive smile. She stroked the squirrel around her neck, running her fingers through its fur. And yet the warrior's eyes remained on hers. They did not roam up and down her body as a man's typically did. They did not appraise her as they might a cow ready for breeding. He looked at her as he might another man. As he might a king.

'Tell me your name,' she said.

'Calatin, my queen.'

'Do you have everything you need, Calatin?' Medb asked.

'We do. The ground is soft. The company fine. And your mead is the best in the country.'

The other Mide men raised their cups in agreement to this.

'I am glad to hear it. And if there is anything you need . . .' Medb left it hanging. An invitation.

'All we need is for the raid to start so we can get it done and go back home to our families.' Calatin's hand wandered to a bracelet of willow and wool around his wrist. It thrummed with magic.

'Did your love give you that?' Finnabair said with a sigh, her eyes as keen as my own.

Finnabair was obsessed with love. She spent her days dreaming of it, singing songs about it. Didn't she know the daughter of a queen could never hope for love?

'My wife gave it to me.' Calatin held up his wrist. 'She made it to protect me from the blades of my enemies.'

And to keep your heart loyal, I thought, scenting the herbs used in the binding. Yarrow for love. Thyme for loyalty.

'She must love you dearly,' Finnabair said. Perhaps she hoped to bind a man to her in the same way.

'She must be a powerful druid,' Medb said, pushing her daughter aside to admire the neat and careful work of the binding.

'She is. And a warrior too. Truth be told, she would have been of more use to you in this battle than I will be. But she is pregnant. Twins, the midwives say.'

For a stabbing moment, I remembered holding the grey bodies of my own twins in my arms. Slippery as fish.

'Triplets more like,' one of the Mide men said.

'He's put a whole litter in her, if her belly is any sign,' another said.

'Then she must rest,' Medb said. 'And I hope to meet her when this is all over.'

266

'She would like that, my queen. She told me, should I meet you, I was to—'

We never found out what his wife had told him to say. There was a thud, like a stone hitting mud, and Calatin went still. On one side of his head, a small dark hole. On the other, a bursting of flesh, skin peeling like the petals of a blood rose. He fell to his knees, face down into the dirt.

One of his friends jumped up to see what had happened. There was a whistling sound, as a breeze blowing through a tree, and that man fell too.

'Magic,' one cried. 'Death coming on wings.'

But I sensed no magic.

A third, then a fourth, fell to the invisible attacker. Something landed on the ground by my feet. I bent to pick it up. A stone, wet with blood and sticky with brain. There was no magic, just a man with a sling. But whoever he was, he could see in the dark and had the aim of an eagle.

'Down,' I shouted.

The men threw themselves to the ground, pressing their faces into the mud. Finnabair gasped, put her hand to her lips and fainted. At least she was safely down.

Medb looked to the stone in my hand. I had told her that she would die by a slingshot, hurled by one who had once loved her. Had her time come? Was one of her lovers out in the darkness casting death at her? She lifted her neck, straightened her back. If she was to die she wasn't going to do it grovelling on the ground like a pig snuffling for food.

I heard it that time, the stone cutting through the air. The aim was true, right for Medb's head. No, I thought, it can't end now, not like this. I screamed at her to move.

Reacting to my cry, her squirrel, her beloved pet, circled her neck and moved to sit on her head, to get a better view of the threat. With a wet thud, the stone pierced the creature's skull and it landed on the ground, dead.

Medb threw herself after the squirrel and scooped up the small body. It was still, not a breath of life left in its tiny lungs, its head a cracked walnut. She pressed it to her body, the blood from its crushed skull dripping down between her breasts and rocked it back and forth, sobbing.

'Cúchulainn,' someone shouted out. I recognized the voice as the young Connacht man who had spoken on the road. 'This is the work of Cúchulainn.'

'Find him,' Medb screamed at me. 'Find me this Cúchulainn!'

I launched myself into the air, flying in the direction from where the shots had come. I found him hiding in a copse of trees on a hilltop overlooking the camp, slingshot in his hand, staring down at the lights of the campfires.

His pale skin was touched with sunburn and he smiled with teeth white as pearls. He couldn't have seen more than sixteen summers, yet his shoulders were broad as any grown man and his thighs thicker than many. Muscles, carved from training, strained against his leather tunic and his hands were rough with callouses from working with weapons. Lights danced in his eyes, like stars on a clear night, and a glow of hero light pulsed from his skull. How had I not seen it? How had I not stopped him? For the boy who was knocking the heads off of Medb's men as if he were knocking apples from a tree, the young warrior with a deadly aim, was none other than Sétanta. The same child I had mocked into bravery on the battlefield, the spitting young man I had met on the road.

He let off another slingshot and howled in triumph like a wolf as one more of the warriors of Ireland met their end. He had to be stopped. I breathed in, ready to screech. I would boil his eyes in his head, turn his guts to liquid, he would die screaming.

My cry caught in my throat. Pain shot through me as though I had swallowed a hot coal. I could not hurt this boy, any more than I could have hurt my own Meche. Spilling his blood would be like spilling my own. He was protected by more than just his armour. He had the mark of destiny on him. He would bring glory to his people and sorrow to his enemies in equal measure. I could not see his death, for the hero light that surrounded him blinded me to his future. But I knew with an unshakeable, unexplainable certainty that I would be there when he died, though it would not be by my hand.

If I could not hurt him, then I would cause him to run screaming home to his mother. I appeared before him and howled, hoping to strike fear into his heart, but it was only the men of Ireland who shook at my shriek. Below, they ran in confusion, some throwing themselves on their own spears to escape the terrible sound.

The boy dropped his slingshot and staggered away from me, but soon gathered himself. His face crumpled as he snarled, teeth bared, eyes wild. I think I had never seen anything quite so beautiful, so familiar – his face was like a mirror. He howled again, like a wounded beast, trying to strike fear into me. Me?

'You don't scare me,' he said, standing once more. He meant it too. Hardened warriors, kings and gods themselves feared me. But not him. If I couldn't scare him, then, I would shame him.

'Coward,' I hissed. 'You strike in the dark. Where is your honour?'

He snatched up a spear that had been propped against a tree and leapt at me, landing on my shoulders, the cold iron tip of his spear pointed at the crown of my skull. I never could stand the touch of cold iron.

'I am no coward. You take that back. I am Cúchulainn! Warrior of Ulaid! Destined to be the greatest warrior there has ever been and that means I won't be dying today. So scream all you like, hag. You can't hurt me.'

I threw him off me and he spun in the air, landing on the ground like a cat. He had mastered the battle feats with ability far beyond his years. Not since the time of Lugh had I seen such skill. The blood of my people must surely flow through his veins.

And there it was, the reason I could not act against this boy. Why, even a thought of hurting him caused me pain. How had I not seen it? He must be a child of one of the Tuatha Dé. And that meant he was right, no matter what he did. I was powerless against him.

27.

Poets don't only tell the past, they also weave the future. The knowledge that your life will become a story is powerful enough to turn tides of war. And Cúchulainn knew his story. He knew, in his bones, that he would survive this raid, which made him brave beyond measure and sowed fear in the hearts of any who tried to stand against him.

Those who were slain that night were buried, and those who lived slept restless and wary.

'Did you kill him?' Medb demanded to know when I returned to the camp at dawn.

I shook my head. 'He is a child of the Tuatha Dé.'

Medb knew of my mother's dying words and of how they had bound me. She hid her fear well though.

'If he's just a boy, then he will be easily dealt with.'

'Not just any boy. He is the nephew of Conchobar.'

'Sétanta?' Medb said, and the red flush in her cheeks paled. 'I knew him as a toddler. He would use my dogs for target practice. He must be crushed.' She turned to face her assembled forces. 'Who among you will kill this dog that snaps at us? Who will prove their worth to me?'

The men grumbled and looked down at their feet. None of them wanted to kill a boy, for where was the honour in that?

'I will!' A young man pushed his way to the front of the gathering.

'Fráech!' Finnabair gasped and ran to him.

'Who is this?' Medb asked.

'I am Fráech mac Idaith,' the man said, turning his face so that it caught the beams of the morning sun.

Fráech was broad and muscled, with a strong chin and slim nose. White teeth shone like bleached bones as he smiled.

'He is my love,' Finnabair said, pulling her slim shoulders back and raising her pointed chin before her mother. 'The man I long to marry.'

'Is that so?'

So there was more to sweet, silent Finnabair than we had thought. The girl had kept a secret from even me.

'Queen Medb,' Fráech said, falling to one knee. 'Let me kill this hound and in return, I ask only that you let Finnabair and I marry, for I love her more than life itself.'

'Oh, Mother,' Finnabair said. 'Please, please let him.'

Medb looked the young man up and down, taking in his dark hair woven with gold threads, the gold rings that glistened on his fingers and the dark kohl that he smudged around his eyes. She had been hoping for a more political match than this painted kingling. But if he was willing to rid her of the hound of Culann, then her daughter would be a price worth paying.

'Go then. Kill Cúchulainn, and Finnabair will be yours.'

Finnabair and Fráech kissed, a clumsy, messy kiss. At last, Fráech pulled himself away and strode off to the fight, Finnabair blowing kisses after him. They truly believed that their love was strong enough to protect him against Cúchulainn.

He lasted five minutes.

Cúchulainn dragged Fráech into a river and held his face beneath the waters till he breathed no more.

After that, none of Medb's warriors wanted to stand

against Cúchulainn. They said it was because he was only a boy, not even a beard on his face. But they knew in their hearts it was because they feared him. Feared his fate. A lone boy against a thousand of Ireland's greatest warriors. A story like that has power.

'What are we to do?' Ailill asked, as we gathered in the tent, hiding from Cúchulainn's stones which were flying again. 'He is killing our men one by one.'

'We must make a truce, so that he will stand aside,' Medb said.

Ailill laughed and Medb's jaw clenched at the slight. She did not like to be laughed at.

'And why would he make such an agreement, when he has the advantage?' Ailill asked.

'We will give him Finnabair.'

Finnabair didn't even look up from her weaving, as if being thrown like a scrap of meat to feed a rabid dog was all that she expected for herself. That she was being promised to Cúchulainn – the one who had killed her true love Fráech just that morning – seemed not to sicken her. Her hands were steady as she worked. Had it been me, I would have gone to kill the boy myself.

'No,' Ailill said with an iron in his voice I had never heard before. 'She has already been promised to Nad Crantail and Lárine mac Nóis. They are good men and either would make a good ruler. But I will not see my daughter offered to this monster of Ulaid.'

Finnabair had been offered to so many men at this point, including the seven kings of Mumhain, that if they all came to claim her, there wouldn't be a scrap of the girl left.

'*Our* daughter,' Medb said, stepping forward so her face was a breath away from Ailill's.

'I am not afraid,' Finnabair said suddenly, putting down her weaving at last. 'If my marriage to Cúchulainn can stop the killing, then I am willing.'

It was agreed then. Medb sent three women to make the truce, for she knew that if she sent any man, Cúchulainn would kill them before they got within shouting distance. Word returned later that night that Cúchulainn had accepted, but only if Finnabair was brought to him by her own father.

'I shall go and ready myself,' Finnabair said, standing.

How could this meek child be the daughter of Medb? She had none of her mother's fire. None of her rage. I wanted to shake her.

'You're just going to go then?' I asked, following her out of Medb's tent. 'Hand yourself over like a pig for a feast?'

She turned and when I looked into her eyes I felt as cold as if I had dived into a lake in winter. There was no life in those eyes. She might as well be dead already.

'I will do my duty.'

'Others in your situation have refused,' I said.

She laughed, as if I were teasing her. 'Like who?'

I tried to think of any. There was only one. 'Deirdre.'

Finnabair sighed. 'Didn't you hear what happened to Deirdre?'

I had not.

'Conchobar sent his men to hunt her and Naoise down. When they were found, he had every man she loved killed in front of her eyes, before dragging her back to him. For the last year, he has bedded her nightly,' Finnabair said. 'And when he couldn't break her, he asked, who did she most hate in the world after himself and she said Éogan mac Durthacht, the man who had killed her beloved Naoise. So, Conchobar was going to give Deirdre to Éogan to do

274

with as he willed for a year. Like "a ewe between two rams", he said.'

I swallowed. I had known there was misery ahead in Deirdre's life, but I had not counted on the depths of Conchobar's cruelty.

'She threw herself off the chariot on the road to Éogan's fort, dashing her head against a rock,' Finnabair said, a dreamy quality to her voice, as if she could imagine no more beautiful a thing than to have your brains smashed out. 'Mother is pleased by the whole affair.'

'Why?'

'Because Conchobar's most loyal friend is on his way to join our forces, so disgusted was he with the way the king treated Deirdre.'

Conchobar's beloved Fergus turned against his king. The Red Branch split. Just as we had planned it. And all it cost was the life and love of a girl.

'The poets are pleased too,' Finnabair said. 'They are already saying Deirdre will be the most beloved woman there ever was.'

Poets. The lot of them should be rounded up and forced to walk into a bog.

'Are she and I so different?' Finnabair said, running her plait through her fingers. 'I had a man I loved and who was killed in the most brutal way. I am now being offered up to his murderer. Why will her name be remembered and mine forgotten?' Still that blank, dead-eye stare, as if she had retreated deep inside herself.

'Because she fought her fate,' I said.

With a little nudge from me, I thought, because I wanted to be a splinter in Conchobar's side. I wanted him to suffer. I was more interested in his pain than hers.

'You think I should fight mine?' Finnabair asked, meeting my eyes. I saw nothing but blankness in them. 'You think I should find some handsome warrior among the men here and ask him to run away with me?' She looked around at the men of the camp as they tended to their fires and sharpened their weapons. 'And tell me, which one of them would choose happiness with me above power? Who would rather a simple wife than a queen-to-be?'

She wasn't as dull to the manoeuvres of politics as I had credited. 'You could just run away with yourself.'

She paused at this. 'I wouldn't know how to be alone.'

'You'd learn. And you might even find a man out there who only wants a woman to be by his side while he milks his cows and sows his seeds, a man who has no care for power. But you won't find them here.'

As she was thinking on this, Medb found us.

'Sweet daughter,' Medb said, tracing the side of Finnabair's face with the back of her hand. 'Go and ready yourself. We're sending you up to Cúchulainn at dawn. You'll ride with Amadán.'

'The fool?' Finnabair said, the first sign of fear in her wavering voice. 'Won't my father come with me?'

'We cannot risk our king. We're sending the fool up with you in your father's stead, dressed in a likeness of the king, with his crown and cloak. If he stands far enough back and sends you ahead, Cúchulainn won't know the difference. But you will be safe, I promise you.'

'As you will it, Mother,' Finnabair said, and returned to her tent to wait for her fate.

'You can't let him have Finnabair,' I said. 'You know what he will do to her.'

'I have no intention of letting him so much as touch a

hair on her head. We just need to get close enough to him to strike.'

'And you send a fool to do a warrior's job?' I asked.

'Amadán is more than a fool. He is the best man in all of Ireland with the sling. Let's see how the hound of Cullan likes having his own stones flung back at him.'

Dawn rose, pink and purple like a bruise on a young bride's cheek, and with it the spirits of the camp. Cúchulainn had not killed any of the host that night. The relief put them in good humour, and many a joke was made about how the boy had taken his rest that night to save his strength for his wedding night with Finnabair.

The girl was ridden out of the camp on a chariot, her hair bound in two tresses that fell between the sharp wings of her back. She was as pale as a warrior before their first battle, though someone had smeared beetle red on her cheeks and lips. Next to her rode Amadán, a short man with a copper crown perched crooked on his head and Ailill's cloak wrapped around his shoulders. It swamped him, and he had to scoop it up in great folds not to trip over it. More used to leaping and dancing, Amadán fought to stay steady and calm, but his hands shook under the cloak where they held his sling and bag of stones.

Medb watched the sorry retinue go, chewing on the side of her thumb. Ailill refused to be a part of it.

'No good will come of this plan,' he said.

For the first time, I agreed with him.

An hour later, a shouting started up in the camp, spreading from man to man. Angry and sorrowful. I pushed to the front to see the cause of the disturbance. Finnabair walked back through the walls. Her long hair was hacked short to the shoulders, what was left of her tunic scarcely covering her frail body, revealing ribs that were those of a calf in winter, as though it had been weeks since she had eaten. She could barely carry her own weight. She stumbled, and a Connacht warrior ran forth and caught her. I recognized him as the one who had answered Medb on the road to Ulaid. He picked her up as if she were a bundle of wheat and carried her towards her mother.

'Finnabair!' Medb cried, and I had never heard so much fear in her voice. She ran her hands over her daughter's face and arms, her chest and legs, checking for any wounds. When she found her daughter unhurt, she stepped aside.

'Bring her inside,' Medb said, leading the man towards her tent.

The man lay Finnabair on a pile of furs on the floor and as he moved to leave, Finnabair reached out with a thin hand and grabbed his. 'Please,' she said. 'Don't go.'

The man gazed softly down at her, as a father might gaze at their child in a cradle.

'What happened?' Ailill said, sitting on the other side of his daughter and stroking her short hair.

Finnabair struggled to sit up and called for water. The warrior picked up a cup and handed it to the girl, but instead of taking it from him, she brought her lips to it and drank as he held the cup.

At last, she spoke. 'He knew. From one hundred feet. He knew it wasn't you, Father.'

Of course he'd known.

'I told you,' Ailill said, shaking his head. 'I bloody told you.'

Medb's jaw clenched but she refused to look at Ailill. 'What then?' she asked.

'He cried treachery, betrayal, and all kinds of curses against us. Then he picked up a standing stone, as large as you, and flung it far across the plain. Before Amadán could load his sling, the stone struck him clear through his belly, piercing him to the ground. I've never seen a man die before.' She stared off into the distance.

'And what of you?' Medb asked. 'What did he do to you?' Her fists clenched white.

'He threw a great stone at me too. But it missed me, by just this much.' She held her shaking hands up, less than a foot apart. 'It passed through my robe instead, pinning me. And then he approached me, looked me up and down and said he wouldn't have me anyway. Cut my hair off with his spear.' She brushed its ragged ends. 'My hair . . .'

'And then?' I said, my mouth dry as stone.

Finnabair blinked, as though waking from a dream. 'Then he walked away and I tore myself free.'

'He didn't . . . hurt you?' Medb asked, looking at her daughter.

'No.'

I'd never heard a sweeter word. I felt the relief of it wash over Medb. She fell into a chair, her shaking hands reaching for a jug of wine.

'She's lucky to be alive,' Ailill said, staring at his wife.

'It wasn't luck,' the warrior who had carried Finnabair into the tent said. 'Cúchulainn doesn't miss. Had he wanted her dead, she would have been crushed by the stone.'

'What's your name, warrior?' Medb asked.

'Ferdiad of the Fir Domnann.'

'And you know Cúchulainn?'

'I trained with him.'

I looked at his slim arms and legs. They did not look like

the limbs of a warrior, though his muscles beneath his skin were tight and taut as ropes.

'Then tell me,' Medb said. 'Is there any that can stand against him?'

'Perhaps,' he answered. 'Loch, son of Mofemis, might be skilled enough.' He didn't sound sure.

'Yes,' Ailill said. 'Loch is a mighty warrior.'

Medb considered this. 'Good. Send for Loch.' She drank from her cup, draining the red liquid in one go.

'I will go with him,' I said.

'Why?' Medb asked, choking a little on her mouthful of wine.

'I will fight Cúchulainn alongside him.'

It had been leading to this; from the moment I first laid eyes on him, it was inevitable.

She grabbed my hand. 'But you can't kill him, not without dying yourself. There has to be another way.'

'I can't kill him,' I said. 'But I will weaken him. That way, Loch may stand a chance of killing the hound.'

28.

When did this stop being my story? you might wonder. Had I bound myself to Cúchulainn by promising I would be the guardian of his death? Or had it been on the battlefield, when I filled the heart of a child with fear to fire his courage, that my fate became entwined with his? His story had a magnetic force that pulled mine off track. But I knew it wouldn't last. He might be a hero, but he was mortal and the deal he made for greatness was to die young. It would only be a matter of time.

In the morning, I dressed in a cloak of every colour, shook the grey out of my hair so it shone like fox fur and went to meet with the hound of Culann.

He sat by a river, eating blackberries plucked from a bush out of season. It was late autumn, and the berries should be as bitter as broken promises, but they looked as sweet and juicy as though it was summer.

'Another princess come to offer herself to me?' he said, as I approached. 'Don't you know it's not for a woman's backside I have come to fight?'

His voice had deepened a little since we had met on the road, and it no longer jumped up and down in pitch, though he still grew no hair on his face. In the sunlight, I could see the colours of his hair, red and brown and golden all at once. It was coiled in three perfect knots at the nape of his neck, with a bundle of curls that fell about his forehead. He had dressed in a tight-fitting red robe, gathered with a brooch of silvered bronze, and underneath he wore a striped jacket made of silk and adorned with every kind of embroidery and braiding. She must have loved him, whoever had made that for him.

'I have come to bring about your death,' I said.

'Ha! Good luck with that. I've told you already, I know my fate.' He threw a handful of berries into the air and caught them in his mouth. Red juice dripped down his chin and he wiped it away with the back of his hand.

He was right to be so nonchalant. My ancient promise not to harm my people still held.

'Today, perhaps, but know this, boy, your death will be my making and I will stand over your rotting corpse.'

'And will you cry for me, old woman?' He ran a hand through his hair, pushing curls out of his eyes.

'No, I will laugh.'

'Laugh all you like, for my name will ring throughout the ages as the greatest warrior ever known.'

I gazed at him with one eye closed. 'You let me see about that. Poets may sing your praises, artists paint your likeness, but I am unending and have seen to the furthest edges of time. I will have the last word.'

He paled, knowing my words to have the ring of prophecy to them. But whatever fear I had stirred in him passed as quickly as a cloud over the sun.

'Ah, well, if I'm not going to die today, then I won't worry about it.'

He was infuriating and yet his bravery was captivating. I had never known a creature like him.

'Be gone with you. I have a true warrior to fight.' He looked over my shoulder to where Loch was riding towards us in a chariot led by two palomino mares.

Loch was as heavy as a bear with thick fingers that wrapped around his spear so tightly the whites of his knuckles shone through like pearls around a woman's neck. He was as slow as a bear too, and yet I'd heard he was one of Medb's most skilled warriors, and that he knew all the battle feats. He wore light armour, the better to move swiftly, and his hair had been freshly shaved; the blood from a small nick trickled behind his ear.

Cúchulainn didn't look impressed. 'Seriously?' he said. 'You think *he* stands a chance of bringing my death?'

'You may not die today, young pup,' I said. 'But you will bleed.'

With that, I leapt into the air and dived into the waters as a dark eel, slippery and cunning.

Loch and he measured each other up, meeting first with words and then with weapons, though Loch did more grunting than speaking. They started the fight with light spears, spinning and striking. Loch was better than I had expected; he struck fast and clean and knocked Cúchulainn off his chariot and into the river.

Cúchulainn stood and shook the water from his eyes. As he stepped forward, I struck as an eel, wrapping my long, strong body around his ankles, tighter and tighter, hearing the grinding of his bones against each other, and he fell crashing into the icy water. The pain I caused him I felt triplefold, cutting through me like daggers. This was the cost of testing the limits of my geas, and yet I held tight. While he struggled to loosen my hold, Loch leapt and slashed him across the chest. The outrage of the pain overtook Cúchulainn and he tore his legs apart, bursting through my slippery grip. He leapt straight into the air, his body undulating like a salmon, before slamming down in the water, his heel crushing my eel ribs. I slipped away as the battle continued.

Loch and Cúchulainn swapped their spears for swords and traded blow after blow while I became a she-wolf, grey-furred, sharp-toothed and hungry. I launched myself at him and sank my teeth into his arm, tearing flesh from his bones and spraying blood, though it felt as if I was wrenching my own arm off. While we both howled in pain, Loch punched his sword through Cúchulainn's stomach. Enraged, Cúchulainn flung me off and took aim with his sling, knocking out one of my eyes with his shot. Yelping, I skulked away and the battle continued.

Loch and he threw aside their swords and picked up their heavy staffs, moving back and forth, equally matched, equally fierce. Loch swung his staff and struck Cúchulainn about the thigh with a bone-cracking blow. As Cúchulainn fell to his knee, I took on one last form, a white, red-eared heifer, with a herd of the same behind me. We charged at Cúchulainn, trampling him into the ground. Each touch of my hooves against his skin was as a rock crushing my bones. As I passed, he struck me with his staff, breaking my leg.

Cúchulainn was weak, bleeding from his chest, stomach and groin, his ankles crushed and the flesh hanging off his arms. Loch hesitated. And Cúchulainn reached for a many-pronged spear I had not seen him use before. It whistled as it cut through the air, a sound as sweet as birdsong. With a wet thud, it plunged into Loch's chest. Loch looked at it with surprise, as if wondering how such a thing of beauty might have sprouted from himself, before toppling to the ground.

Cúchulainn sliced Loch's head off, just for good measure, and howled like a beast. His rage was beautiful to behold. It twisted his young features and made them monstrous. I don't know which of us was more wounded; Cúchulainn or myself? He had taken out my eye, crushed my ribs and broken my leg and because I had broken my geas in harming him, I could not heal myself. The only one who could heal me was the boy himself.

Cúchulainn crawled away, crying in pain like the boy child he was, calling out about why no warrior of Ulaid came to help him, how he was all alone and dying. While he had fought like a man, as he lay bawling on the ground, he looked more like a baby.

Weak though I was, I approached him again, now in the form of an old woman, bent-backed, club-footed and one-eyed, leading a cow that was heavy with milk.

Cúchulainn called out to me. 'Wait, Mother, give us a drink of milk. Please, for as well as dying of my wounds here, I am dying of thirst.'

I milked the cow into a cup and handed it to him.

'Bless you,' he said and he glugged it down.

With his blessing, my ribs were healed.

He drained the cup and handed it back, asking for yet more. The milk, being from one of my cows, slowed the flow of his wounds. I milked the cow again and handed the cup to him once more.

'Bless you,' he said again, as the milk knitted his bones.

And with his blessing, my leg was healed.

A third and final time, he finished the cup and asked for another drink. I milked the cow and handed it to him. He drank, and his wounds were healed.

'Bless you,' and with his final blessing my eye was restored.

'And there was you saying you'd give me no help,' I said, throwing off my grey cloak and grey hair.

He threw the cup to the floor and roared. 'You!'

He was as quick to anger as I was, and I felt again that pull of connection between us.

'Some warrior of Ulaid you are,' I said. 'Going around healing your enemy.'

He threw his spear at me and I snatched it out of the air. It was not like any spear I had ever seen. It was made from bone, but not from the bone of a creature that walked the land – a sea monster had given its life for that spear. It was covered in spikes up and down its length, and if it entered a man's belly, the retrieving of it would shred his flesh. It was a spear designed not for fighting, but for killing. I knew that spear, I had heard tales of the men it had killed and it didn't belong to any boy from this land. It was the Gáe Bulg, the Spear of Death.

'Where did you get this weapon?' I asked him.

He darted forward, fast as a cat's paw, and snatched the spear from me. He spun it in his hands, grinning wildly. It whistled as it sliced through the air and left trails of oily rainbow colours in the darkness. 'I won it.'

'You lie,' I said. 'You're a coward and a liar.'

He threw the spear at me again. The jagged barbs cut through the air like a sea creature through the depths. I hopped high into the air, dancing along the spear's shaft as easily as walking along a sturdy tree branch, before rupturing into a pack of crows.

Each one of my birds dived at him, and he threw himself to the ground, covering his head. I pecked at his hair, his flesh, but I knew I could do him no real harm. I re-formed and stood over him, one bare foot at his throat. 'Tell me,' I compelled him. 'Who gave you that spear?'

Bound by my magic to speak only truth, he told me. 'It belonged to Scáthach.'

Scáthach the warrior woman from Alba.

'Not possible. She would never have given up that spear.'

A smile crept across his face as a worm over a corpse. His youthful beauty scarred by an ugly darkness. 'I took it from her, didn't I?'

He snatched the spear back up and ran away, laughing.

29.

Scáthach was said to be the greatest warrior since the time of the Tuatha Dé. How had this boy taken the finest weapon ever made by mortals from her? I had to know. She lived in Dún Scáith, a fort built high on a mountain on an island shrouded in mist. It was the furthest I had travelled since I crossed the seas with my people many lifetimes before, and the further I got from my land, the weaker I found myself. By the time I set foot on the shores of her island, I had only a glimmer of my powers left.

It was another full day's travel up hills and across vales. The land was the colour of a day-old bruise and there was magic in the very air. I passed standing stones which must have been placed by giants; and waterfalls, in which danced spirits, older even than I was. I paid my respects and travelled on. The land seemed to rise ever upward, so that my muscles ached with the climbing, and just when I thought I could climb no more it would fall away, steep as a cliff's end. Everything was sharp and spiked; even the purple flowers that covered the land bit me when I tried to pick them.

At last, I reached Scáthach's stronghold. A jagged fort of stone and iron sitting on a rocky outcrop, it looked born from the land itself as if a mighty sorcerer had commanded the walls to build themselves out of the rocks. Waves crashed around its base, hissing like snakes. It was shrouded in a magic darkness and had I been a mortal woman, I wouldn't have been able to penetrate it. I pushed through the protection, feeling the magic tingle against my skin. Between the land and her fortress, there was a gap of twenty feet, and below it the angry waves and barbed rocks. I had heard that Scáthach put all who came here to tests. This was the first.

Had I had all my powers, it would have been nothing. I would have flown across as an eagle, screeching at the waves for daring to hiss at me. But I would have to do this without them. I wrapped my skirts up around me, cursing them for their weight, and I leapt. It was not a graceful landing. The wind was taken out of me and my chin scuffed on the black rocks. I almost thought I heard a mocking laugh over the sound of the waves, but it was just a gull.

'You can shut your gob,' I said.

The next test was a sheer wall, slippery with moss and sea salt. I dug my nails into the cracks between the stones and climbed up and over, falling in a lump on the other side in a bed of scratchy sea thrift. Even if Cúchulainn passed these tests on his way here, how had he escaped with the Gáe Bulg in his hand?

I'd never had a colder welcome at a fort. I climbed a narrow, winding staircase that would only permit one person at a time to pass, and came to a square courtyard. Sand covered the floor and as I walked across, I kicked something white ahead of me. A pearl? A shell? I picked it up and rolled it around in my hand. A tooth. I was standing, then, on the famed training grounds of Scáthach, where the greatest warriors had their teeth knocked out of their heads.

At last, I came to the doors of Dún Scáith. Guarding the way was a young woman, barely out of girlhood. She had long, dark hair, plaited and bound in gold threads, a helm covering the top of her face and leather armour moulded to her sinewy body. What I could see of her face was lean and angular – strong jaw and cheekbones. She wasn't what the poets would call beautiful, though any man would want her for the strong sons she would surely bear them. She wore a thick silver torc around her neck and twisting metal bands ran up her arms. She held a spear which was not unlike the Gáe Bulg; carved from a single white bone as tall as she was. As she moved it to block my passing, I saw how her fingers bulged at the knuckles and bent at unnatural angles, as if they had been broken and set badly. And yet she had moved as fast as a viper's strike.

'Name yourself,' she said, her words spoken as if through a mouthful of gravel, the accent of these parts.

'A warrior,' I said, giving up only a portion of myself.

'We have enough warriors here.'

'A sorceress then.'

She scoffed, a dry, chuckling rasp. 'Warrior and sorceress, is it? Don't get many of them about. Don't have much need for them, either.'

'Let her enter, Uathach!' a voice shouted from inside.

The young woman, Uathach, swore but lowered her spear and stepped aside.

It took my eyes a moment to adjust to the darkness of Scáthach's halls. The fashion of her home was different to our round forts. It had square walls and high windows and was colder inside than out. No fire flickered in the hearth and no animal furs covered the walls, though I could see the black stains from where a fire once burned and the ragged scraps from where cloths had once hung. It was as if someone had tried to make this place as hostile as possible.

At the far end was a large wooden throne made of twisted branches that coiled around each other like a nest of snakes. On the throne sat a woman, the great warrior Scáthach. She had one strong leg crossed over the other, an arm slung over the back of her throne. It was a studied image of nonchalance which I didn't believe for a moment. She looked rigid with discomfort. Like Uathach, the door-keeper, she too was clad in armour, though the leather of hers was softer, more creased, more tested. Like Uathach, she wore a torc, though hers was made of gold. And like Uathach, her features were sharp like carved stone. Mother and daughter, for sure.

A two-handed sword was propped against the throne. I'd rarely seen a sword so large, the metal alone would have cost a herd of cattle, and the craft that had gone into its making thrice that amount. It was just within reaching distance, so she could snatch it up and bring it swinging down on the head of any unwelcome intruders before they made it to the end of the hall. A second woman stood behind the throne, keen eyes watching me move. She was almost the twin of the woman on the throne – the same colouring, the same lean, etched muscles, earned from years of training. She wore no armour, for she was nursing a baby on her breast, though her tunic and skirts were those of a warrior: prac-tical and unlikely to tangle about your feet. She too had a torc around her neck, though hers had the greenish tint of bronze. This would be Aífe, Scáthach's sister and herself a mighty warrior. I had heard that the sisters were enemies, set against each other. And yet, here they were together under the same cold roof.

Uathach followed me in, staying so close I could feel her breath on the nape of my neck. There were other women watching from deep in the shadows, sharp eyes ready to cut me, drawn lips ready to curse me. All ages, all shapes and sizes they were. But all had a harshness to them, as if carved from the rock upon which this fortress stood. And all were silent as snowfall.

I had heard tales of Dún Scáith, of how it rang with the sound of blades clashing night and day as she trained the sons of the greatest warriors in the north of the world. And yet, apart from the baby, there were no males here.

'What brings you to my island, Nicneven?'

The name Nemain said in her tongue. She had heard of me then?

'I have come to know how you allowed the Gáe Bulg to be taken by Cúchulainn?'

That name drew a hissing and drawing of breath. I looked at the faces of the women, snarled in anger like a pack of lionesses ready to pounce.

'You will not speak that name in these halls,' Scáthach said, sitting upright on her throne. 'You will not speak it!' She wrapped her hand around the pommel of her blade and charged at me. She swung her sword and I readied myself for the blow, but she stopped, the tip of the blade nestled in the nook between my collarbones.

'I gave that boy everything,' she said. 'I trained him, taught him, loved him. I even offered him the hand of my Uathach when she came of age, without having to pay the bride price. And he repaid me by stealing my most precious weapon and attacking my daughter.'

I felt another sharp point in my back. Uathach's blade aimed at my heart.

'He took the Gáe Bulg,' Uathach said, dragging her spear across my body as she came to stand before me. 'Just as he tried to take what he wanted from me. I fought him,' she said, her body shaking with suppressed rage. 'I fought him so hard he broke each of my fingers and when my friend came, hearing my cries of pain, the boy killed him and then ran.'

Why was I surprised? Why did my heart feel as though it was shrinking, hardening into stone? Cúchulainn was Conchobar's nephew, after all. He had been told the world would be his, that he would be adored by all. I had wanted him to be worthy of the stories and glory. I had wanted him to be a hero. But he was a monster.

'He took what he wanted from me, too.' The woman with the babe at her breast stepped forward. 'Though I was the only one he also gave something to.'

I knew the look in her shining eyes. I had seen it on the face of Medb. An acid shame and disgust eating away.

'I saw him running, the Gáe Bulg in his hand,' Aífe said, taking her breast from the babe's mouth and covering herself. 'And I tried to stop him. I shattered his sword and had mine pressed against his breast. But he used trickery. Lies. He told me my beloved horses, the things I love most in the world, had fallen over the cliff. As I turned to see the truth of this, he struck me from behind with a rock. I awoke with his blade at my throat. He gave me a choice. Give him the warmth of my thighs or die. I chose not to die.'

Whatever feelings I had for Cúchulainn, whatever hold he'd had on me that I had not been able to explain, were extinguished like a flame. I wished him dead; more than that, I wished him never born.

I had played a part in awakening the hero in him, but I would also play a part in his undoing. It might be that he could not be killed. That he was, as he had bragged, protected by prophecy. But death was only one way to defeat a man.

'Know this,' I said. 'I will set myself against him. I will see to his destruction.'

Scáthach turned and sat once more on her throne, her daughter moving to stand on her right, Aífe on her left.

'And what makes you think you will succeed where we have failed?' Scáthach asked.

Fair. For I stood in their cold, dark hall with only a glimmer of my skills.

'You know my name? You have heard my stories?' I asked.

They nodded. They knew them.

'Then you know that I never lie. I will be your vengeance.'

This seemed to appease Scáthach's women. I saw a hunger for retribution in their eyes that I knew well. They would have imagined every kind of punishment for Cúchulainn. In their dreams they would have seen his skin torn from his muscles, his balls ripped from his loins, his bones broken, teeth smashed, eyes gouged. There was no limit to the pain they wished for him.

'But tell me, does he have a weakness? A way to hurt him?'

They considered this, whispering among themselves.

'There is one man who could hurt him,' Scáthach said at last. 'A man I trained beside him who was his equal in skill. His skin is like horn and they say he cannot be killed by a man's hand.'

I imagined a giant, a monster like Balor, who would make the ground quake with every step.

'Give me his name.' I would search the earth till I found him and I would set him in Cúchulainn's path.

'His name is Ferdiad.'

'Ferdiad?' I said, remembering the man with light brown

295

hair and plain, soft features who had tended to Finnabair like a nursemaid. It couldn't be. That gentle creature couldn't be the one who could defeat Cúchulainn.

'He and Ferdiad were like brothers, perhaps even more. They were matched in every martial feat, but unmatched in manner.'

'How so?'

'Where the hound is cunning and cruel, Ferdiad is clever and kind,' Uathach said.

'Where the hound will use any trickery to win, Ferdiad is honourable,' Aífe said.

I had yet to see a champion who was kind and honourable. That sort of thing got you killed.

'You may struggle to persuade him to stand against his friend, though,' Scáthach said. 'He loves the boy.'

'I shall see,' I said. 'And in case you are right and Ferdiad is too soft-hearted to fight his friend . . . The boy.' I pointed my finger at the child who was now sleeping, milk drunk, in Aífe's arms.

'What of him?' Aífe asked, holding him tighter to her chest.

'Train him. Train him harder than you have ever trained a boy before. And in seven years' time, send him back to his father.' It was a prophecy, a curse. 'I promise you this, he will destroy Cúchulainn.'

The three women looked to the sleeping child, the hint of smiles on their faces.

I didn't lie. What I foretold would happen, just not in the way they hoped.

'Send my best wishes to Ferdiad,' Uathach said. 'He was always kind.'

'Too kind,' Aífe said. 'He won't stand a chance. Not against the son of a god. It's all just sport to Cúchulainn.'

My skin went cold. It had been so obvious. I had known he must have the blood of my tribe in his veins, but had not stopped to consider who his father must be. How had I not seen it the moment I laid eyes on him? Had I not seen the same light that surrounded him in another? I knew at last who his father was. A god who loved games.

Lugh.

30.

The winds that fought me as I travelled home were as icy and brutal as my anger. I had thought Lugh had lost interest in the world of men. And yet here he was, meddling in my vengeance.

I was too weak to fly all the way home, the winds too strong. So I called up rocks from beneath the sea and walked the final steps between Alba and Ireland. As soon as I stepped foot on the soil, I was returned to myself, my powers flooding back into my limbs. I was tied to this land and it to me.

'Lugh,' I shouted to the air, my voice ringing with its shriek of old.

There was no answer but the lapping of waves and the crying of gulls. I crouched down and laid my hand on the earth, calling out to the spaces below where my people feasted and played while time itself lost meaning.

I reached inside myself. 'Lugh!' I shouted again. My voice shook the ground, the waters of the sea bubbled as though in a cauldron, it echoed through every cave and crack in the earth.

'No need to shout.'

I turned to see him sitting atop a rock, examining the beds of his nails. The winds dropped and the sun came out as if it was pleased to look upon his face once more. He was as beautiful as ever. Too beautiful.

He had once been my great, golden hope for abundance

on the land, and yet he, like all men I had seen lead, had let the power go to his head and the indulgence go to his heart. He'd died over a woman, who, like the land, had chosen another.

'What the fuck are you playing at?' I screeched.

He was taken aback for a moment. The women of the Tuatha Dé were mostly gentle and slow to speak. Perhaps he'd forgotten who I was.

'I have no idea what you mean.'

'You always liked playing games, so let me join in. This whelp you have fathered – what are you playing at?'

He slid down off his rock and came to stand by me. 'Oh, you've met my little puppy Sétanta? How is he?'

'He goes by the name of the hound now. The hound of Cullan. And rightfully so. He is a dog. A liar. A thief. And a defiler of women.'

'But strong and cunning and undefeatable in battle,' said Lugh. 'I would have thought you, of all people, would love him for that.'

Acid rose in my throat, for he was right. I had loved Cúchulainn for who I believed him to be. I had loved his rage and his battle skills and his appetites.

I spat. 'There are men who are his equal.'

'Oh, no, there aren't, you see. I've seen to it. He is quick as a deer. As cunning as one of your crows.'

'This land is mine now. Its people mine to protect. And I warn you, Lugh, if this boy gets in my way—'

He cut me off with a laugh. 'Oh, he will. He will. I have made sure of it. We have been watching what you're up to here. With your cow-breeding and queen-making. You were told to stay and guard the boundaries between our world and this one, not to interfere.'

'I *chose* to stay. Just as I choose who rules this land,' I said with a stamp of my foot that cracked the earth. Being in Lugh's presence undid me, returned me to the jittering, hopping-mad creature I had once been.

'But a woman?'

'I ruled as a woman.'

'Oh, yes, we saw. Sweet Queen Macha. Killed her own father to take the throne but even that she had to share with her husband. Her name will go down in the roll of High Kings. Well done.' He clapped his hands together in slow, mocking applause. 'But Queen Medb,' he continued. 'If she wins this battle, her thirst for power will be as unquenchable as your vengeance. She will not stop till she rules all of this land.'

'And I will help her.'

He wagged his finger at me. 'You cannot take part in the battles of mortals. It would be unfair.'

'Since when did you care about fairness?'

He tutted. 'It's the only thing I care about. Which is why I will stay out of the fighting.'

It's easy to be bothered about balance when you're the one holding the scales. He might mind about fairness, but I did not. 'You asked me once to stay out of a battle and I give you the same answer today as I did then. Go fuck yourself. This is my war and I will fight if I choose.'

He laughed at my profanity. 'This will lead to no good, just you see. Power must be shared. It is the only way.'

'Shared between men, you mean.'

He shrugged, as if my argument was too weak to bother with. 'Either way, this isn't about power. Not really. It is about punishment.'

'A just punishment,' I spat.

For the agony they had caused me. For Medb. For Deirdre. For Aífe. For all women who dared to say no.

'If you say so,' Lugh said, looking again at his perfectly stained nails.

'I do say so. So, tell me, how will you stop Medb taking over the north, when I have cursed all the men of Ulaid to be stricken with the pains of childbirth? Pains no man can endure.'

'Ah, yes, nicely played, that one.' He was so smug I wanted to take the rock he leant against and use it to crush his skull. 'But Cúchulainn is not yet a man.'

'Yes. Don't you think I know this? Stop your game-playing. What are you getting at?'

'Cúchulainn is not the only boy in Ulaid who can fight.' He put an elegant finger to his pursed lips. 'So enjoy your little game of fidchell. But don't forget that it was I who taught you how to play.'

He clapped his hands together and vanished.

I stamped my feet again and roared, threw myself on the ground and pounded great fists full of the earth. I tore my hair loose from its tresses and pulled chunks out. The rage roiled in my blood as it had the day I had set foot on these lands, swirling, monstrous, inextinguishable. I tore ancient yews out of the ground and knocked the tops off mountains with them. I kicked stones the size of men and sent them flying across the land, where they thudded into the earth standing upright. I hadn't thrown a tantrum in nearly a hundred years. I felt a bit better.

He was playing with me. Toying with me. Trying to get into my head. I wouldn't let him. I stood and smoothed down my crumpled cloak, gathered up the rage and pushed it back down inside me, a cold diamond of wrath. So what if Lugh's boy could stand alone against the four armies? So what if I couldn't hurt him? There were other ways to break him, as easily as he had broken Uathach's fingers. I had promised her and her mother as much. Time might have no meaning for my brothers and sisters in their home in the land of the ever young. But as I had stood guard over the years, watching each season come and go, I had learned something they had not. Patience.

I had believed this raid was about sovereignty, but Lugh had seen true enough. It was about punishment. I had set myself against Conchobar for what he had done to Medb and me; now I set myself against his nephew Cúchulainn for what he had done to Aífe. I would destroy them both in the name of all wronged women. Their bodies might survive this battle, but I would see to it that their spirits did not. They would see all they loved die before them and because of them. And after the battle, I would make the years they had ahead long and worthless. They would not sleep a single night without seeing me in their dreams. They would live but live in fear knowing I was coming for them.

Let Lugh test his power against mine. Let the god of light and love crash against the goddess of death and darkness and see which was stronger. If he'd placed his boy between us in this game of tug, then wolflike I would tear him from his grasp.

No swift death for Cúchulainn. No glorious death in battle. He would die slowly and broken; I would watch and when he breathed his last, I would be there.

31.

'There is a man who stands a chance of killing him.'

I flew into Medb's tent, my heart still pounding, my hair as wild as a gorse bush.

Medb was sitting, head huddled, with a man while Ailill busied himself drawing battle plans. The man was new to the camp though I had seen him before.

She jumped to her feet. 'What happened? Where have you been? I thought . . .' There was a slight quiver in her voice. It was not anger that tightened her throat, but relief. Had she thought I had abandoned her?

'I have been to see Scáthach. This boy, this beast, we have to defeat him.'

'Come, sit, tell me everything.' Medb pushed Ailill from his chair to give it to me and clicked her fingers at Finnabair to get me a drink. I finished the bitter wine in one gulp and reached my cup out for more.

I told Medb what I had learned about Cúchulainn.

'I am sorry,' she said when I had finished.

'Sorry? Why?'

'Because I know that, despite yourself, you had affection for the boy.' That was the problem with having friends. They sometimes knew you better than you knew yourself. She held her hand up to silence my protestations. 'He is of your blood, the last in the line of the mighty Tuatha Dé, there is no shame in it.'

Shame. What a stupid, useless emotion. Anger could set

a fire in a man's belly. Hate could move mountains. But shame did nothing but eat away at the heart like worms.

'Come,' she said, slapping me on the arm, trying to snap me out of my wallowing. 'Tell me the name of this fierce and mighty warrior who can stand against Cúchulainn.'

'Ferdiad.'

She paused a moment and then laughed. 'Ferdiad? The skinny thing who Finnabair was making eyes at?'

'What word of Ferdiad?' Finnabair said, suddenly waking up. 'Has he asked after me?'

Medb rolled her eyes. 'Apparently, he's the only man who can defeat our tormentor.'

'No, please, no.' Finnabair grabbed Medb's hands and held them to her lips. 'Please don't send Ferdiad against him. He's my one true love.'

Had not Fráech been her one true love a matter of days before? This girl's heart changed as quickly as the weather in spring. She thought only a man could save her, grabbing on to each one who passed as though clutching at a log in a river.

Medb slipped her hands free of her daughter's and turned her back on her.

'Who is Ferdiad?' It was the man Medb had been talking to when I arrived. He had been listening to our talk, but I could sense his frustration at not being at the heart of the conversation. He stood behind Medb and wrapped an arm around her, as if trying to take possession of her.

'Let me introduce you to our latest recruit,' Medb said. 'And no better man do we have among our host. This is Fergus mac Róich. And Fergus, this is—'

'You need no introduction, my lady,' he said, bowing low, though he kept his eyes on my face. I had last seen Fergus

306

that night in Tara, sitting beside Conchobar laughing and singing with his king. He was bigger than I remembered, though he wore loose clothing, as if trying to hide his muscled bulk. He was handsome, in a solid, carved-wood kind of way, and he wore the creases and wrinkles of his face well. Grey kissed the hair at his temples and in his red beard. He smiled, though it did not go to his eyes, which were the colour of fresh iron. He had once been King of Ulaid, though Conchobar had robbed him of it. And now, he had turned sides and was ready to stand against his kinsmen. He was not a man to be trusted.

'You were Conchobar's man?' I asked, gesturing for him to stand up.

'I was, this is true. I was loyal to him in all things. I would have followed him further still had he not shamed me by breaking his word.'

'What word did he break?' I asked.

Fergus took a deep breath, as if bored of telling this story. 'After many years sending men searching for Deirdre, Conchobar at last found her. Married and happy with Naoise, living a simple life on a barren island in Alba. Conchobar swore to me that he had forgiven her, and forgiven Naoise, and sent me to bring them home to Ireland. I gave Deirdre, Naoise and his brothers sanctuary in my home. I gave them my word that they would be safe. But one day when I was out hunting—'

'Conchobar sent Éogan mac Durthacht to kill all the men and had Deirdre dragged back to him in Emain Macha,' Medb said, almost gleefully, as though the murder of innocent men and the pain of a young woman brought her joy. Even I had never delighted in the deaths of those who had not deserved it.

'Every last one of the men killed,' Fergus said. 'He broke his word and turned me into a liar.'

I should have known it wasn't for Deirdre's honour that Fergus had turned sides, but for his own.

'I told you Conchobar wasn't worthy of you,' Medb said. 'After what he did to me and my sister.'

Fergus took her hand and kissed the back of it. 'I should have listened, my queen.'

I saw the dark of Medb's eyes flare in response to being called 'my queen' by this man. She licked her lips in anticipation. If they weren't already bedding each other, it wouldn't be long.

'So when are you going to go and fight Cúchulainn?' Ailill asked, standing by Medb and taking her hand from Fergus's grasp.

'Oh, no,' Fergus said, stepping back from the couple. 'I can't fight him. I practically raised him. No, I am here to fight Conchobar and reclaim my throne, not fight boys.'

'He's no boy,' Ailill said. 'He's a beast. He's killed three hundred of my men already.'

'Our men,' Medb said, reminding her husband of his place.

'I am sorry for that,' Fergus said. 'But I will not fight him.'

'Are you afraid?' Ailill asked.

Fergus laughed. 'Of course I am! And so would you be had you seen the warp spasm on him.' He saw that we didn't know what he was talking about. 'When a fierce rage overtakes him, he becomes a hideous, unstoppable thing. When it took Cúchulainn for the first time, the only way we could stop him destroying the whole of Emain Macha was for the women to bare their breasts at him. When he looked away in embarrassment, we grabbed him and dunked him into a vat of ice-cold water which exploded in steam like a sword being plunged into water from the forge.' He drank from his cup as though putting out a fire of his own. 'No man stands a chance.'

'But you must try,' Medb purred. 'Only you have the strength to defeat him.' She ran her hands over his biceps. 'You have the wits to outthink him.' She truly had no shame.

'Please,' Finnabair said, taking Fergus's heavy hand in her tiny one. 'Don't let her send my beloved Ferdiad against him.'

Fergus's resolve seemed to soften as he gazed down at Medb and her daughter. 'I will speak with Cúchulainn,' he said. 'See if I can persuade him to stand aside.'

He strapped on his scabbard, though I saw it had no sword inside, threw his cloak around his shoulders and stepped out into the cool darkness.

He returned an hour later. The only man sent to Cúchulainn who had returned alive.

'Is he dead?' Medb said, leaping to her feet as Fergus ducked his head to step inside her tent.

'Is Ferdiad saved?' Finnabair asked.

'Cúchulainn lives.' Fergus grabbed a cup of wine from a table and poured it down his throat.

'Then how are you still alive?' Medb looked at Fergus in a mix of wonder and mistrust.

'I asked him to yield and he yielded. I told you – the boy sees me as a father,' Fergus said.

What deal had this man made to survive against Cúchulainn? What promises had been sworn?

'So will he stand aside? Will he allow me to take the Brown Bull?' Medb asked.

I had almost forgotten that all of this death and pain had been in the name of a cattle raid.

Fergus drained his cup and grabbed another. 'He will not.'

Medb threw her hands in the air. 'Then what was the point in speaking to him?'

'You'd rather I died?' Fergus asked.

'I wouldn't have minded it,' Ailill said, though none but I heard him.

Medb and Fergus started shouting at each other. Finnabair started wailing, tugging at the strands of her cropped hair, bemoaning the inevitable death of her newly beloved.

'Enough,' Medb snapped. 'Send for Ferdiad!'

The young man was brought to Medb's tent. He stood before us, head bowed, slim hands hanging by his sides. He was only a few years older than Cúchulainn himself and looked as though a bad winter would see him off. I saw no hero light around him and he carried no unstoppable weapon. Could he truly be the only one who could defeat the hound?

'You trained under Scáthach?' Medb asked.

'I did.'

'She said you were Cúchulainn's equal,' I said. 'Brothers almost.'

Ferdiad sighed, as if this praise was a weight he did not wish to carry. 'We were well matched, it's true.'

'And were you there when he broke Uathach's fingers?' I asked. 'When he tricked Aífe into surrender?'

Ferdiad looked down at his feet. 'I was not, or else I would have stopped him.'

This seemed to please Medb. She smiled, a wolf's smile. 'Then you must fight him. Don't you see, he is a beast. You are the only man who can defeat him. And as reward, you will have my daughter here. See how she has already fallen in love with you.'

Ferdiad looked down at the delicate Finnabair. I saw no lust in his eyes, no temptation. Only pity.

'I am a warrior of Connacht,' Ferdiad said. 'But Cúchulainn is my friend.'

'Then you must choose,' Medb said. 'Your people or your friend.'

I could see Ferdiad's torment, caught between his love for Cúchulainn and hatred for what he had done. He sighed and came to his decision. 'I will fight him. Tomorrow, I will fight him. And damn us both.'

As soon as Ferdiad left, the rowing started up again. I left them to it, sick of it all. I fed on the beauty of bloody battles, not the cat scratches of squabbles.

'You don't have to fight him,' I said, catching up with Ferdiad. 'Every man has a choice.'

He looked up at the inky darkness of the star-pricked sky, no clouds to show him his future. 'The men of the camp say you know when every man will die. Tell me, what do you see?'

I closed my eyes and looked into his future. It was not good.

'You will not die by Cúchulainn's hand,' I said.

'Why don't I believe you?'

Because you have more sense than any for a hundred miles around, me included, I wanted to say. Instead, I said, 'I never lie.'

He walked off in the direction of a tent where the men would gather to drink and sing through the night.

'Will you not rest before the fight?' I called after him.

'No. I'm off to get drunk.'

32.

He was true to his word. Ferdiad drank through the night and right till the dawn, so he was huffing the stink of drink the next morning. He had his charioteer bring him cushions and skins for the floor of his chariot so he might sleep some of it off on the ride up to meet Cúchulainn. I flew overhead, watching but knowing what was to come.

Of all the battles fought in that cattle raid, the most beloved of the poets was the one between Cúchulainn and Ferdiad. For what is more noble and glorious than two brothers tearing strips off each other? They met on either side of a ford in their chariots and it was said they greeted each other as brothers, which is to say they traded insults.

I sat on top of the stone that had crushed Amadán the fool, and watched as my birds picked what was left of his flesh from his bones.

'I'm sorry to have to kill you today,' Cúchulainn said.

'Kill me? Sure, when we trained together under Scáthach, weren't you my squire, cleaning my spear and making my bed?'

'True, and your bed needed making anew each morning because you kept pissing in it out of fear every time we were to fight.'

'Let's get this over with, shall we?' Ferdiad said.

And so they fought, hacking and leaping and wounding each other, but neither seemed to want to deal the killing blow. The holes in them were so big that had a bird been flying by, it could have flown clean through their wounds and carried away their guts.

When dusk crept towards them, Cúchulainn suggested they break off for the night. And then they put down their arms, kissed each other, and shared food and tales by the fire, tending to each other's wounds as gently as a mother to their child. They slept curled up around each other, like dogs in a den. And I believed they were more than brothers to each other.

But when the sun rose, they went at it again, first with the insults and then with the swords. And just when either had the other on the ground, he would pull back and allow him to get to his feet. The wounds that had healed the night before opened and the blood that poured from them made their grips slippery. Hack after hack. Blow after blow. Till again, on the second day, the sun started to set and both warriors were still standing. Just. So for another night, they laid down their arms and spent the evening together, reminiscing of old times and enjoying each other's company. Soft rain fell and they slept till the dawn.

On the third day, Ferdiad woke with a dark cloud of a mood over him.

'What is it?' Cúchulainn asked, as he buckled up his armour.

'One of us will die today.'

'You know it will be you. You should never have come – you should never have listened to Medb. Finnabair is a fine woman and all, but a man should never choose a woman over his friend.'

'I'm not doing this for Finnabair, you fucking idiot,' Ferdiad said, truly angry for perhaps the first time.

'Then why, brother? Why set yourself against me?' Cúchulainn asked.

'If you don't know, then I won't be the one to tell you.'

Never was there a more beautiful duel than the one on the ford that day. The two greatest warriors in the land, showing their true skills at last. Both perfectly matched, as though one was a mirror of the other, they showed off their training in performing feats that had never been seen before that day or since. They howled like beasts as they struck blow for blow, each of them hurling down strikes from early morning's gloaming till the sun rose and turned their skin red. They were wild with vexation, raging at each other, for neither could gain the upper hand, their love turned at last to hate out of sheer frustration.

In a desperate move, Cúchulainn leapt on to Ferdiad's shield and tried to strike at him from above. Ferdiad flung the shield away with Cúchulainn on it, sending him crashing into the waters.

Cúchulainn lay on his back, gasping for air.

'Are you going to lie there?' Ferdiad shouted, hoping to shame him into rising. 'Sure that was nothing. A shake as gentle as a mother rocking her child. Would you have me tell the men of Ulaid how you died on your back, with your breeches wet?' He picked his shield up once more and waited.

Cúchulainn dragged himself to his feet and with the speed of the wind he leapt again on to Ferdiad's shield. And again, Ferdiad shook him off and threw him back into the waters.

It was then Cúchulainn began to change. His limbs twisted like an ancient tree, his bones cracked inside his skin, his eyes bulged, his jaws extended like a snake's, the hair of his head stood up like spikes strong enough to skewer apples, and blood poured from his eyes. It was the warp spasm, just as Fergus had described. He was hideous to behold. He was glorious.

His body swelled and he seemed to grow till he towered over Ferdiad, blocking out the sun. He raised his clasped fists, ready to hammer them down on Ferdiad's head, but Ferdiad struck first. He pushed his sword clean through Cúchulainn's breast. The warp spasm flickered out as quickly as it had come. Cúchulainn staggered back, with each step returning to his true shape. He fell once more, into the river. The blood from his wounds turned the water red and Cúchulainn didn't move. A kingfisher skimmed along the surface, plucking scraps of his flesh from the water.

'It's true then,' Cúchulainn said, his voice weak, sobs shaking his chest. 'You cannot be killed by a man's hand.'

'I didn't want to do this, Sétanta,' Ferdiad said. 'But you had to be stopped.'

Ferdiad looked down at his hands, at the sword covered in his friend's blood. He closed his eyes, trying to find the strength to do what he knew needed to be done.

Cúchulainn rolled on to his belly and dragged himself over to his spear – the dreaded Gáe Bolg. He placed it in the fork of his toes, and sent it soaring, putting the full strength of his legs behind it. It punched into Ferdiad's chest, straight through his heart. I had not lied. Ferdiad had not been killed by a man's hand.

'You cheating little . . .' Ferdiad said, before he fell.

The poets say Cúchulainn sobbed and lamented, that he held Ferdiad's body in his arms and cursed Medb for sending him to fight. They say he laid kisses upon his brow and stayed with him till nightfall. But did they also say how he stripped him of his gold jewellery and weapons? How he cut open Ferdiad's body to make sure he got his precious spear back? How he left his mutilated corpse for the animals to feed on?

Not so much.

'All was play, all was sport, till came Ferdiad to the ford.'

That's what they said Cúchulainn said. As though the deaths of all of the others he had massacred had been just a game.

Warriors are remembered for their cruelty. Their most brutal deeds become righteous when woven into legend, songs sung for them and statues built, always with a sword raised and a chin lifted, even if they'd had no chin to speak of in life. While the soft, gentle acts of kind hearts are lost, vanishing like morning mist. Ferdiad would be remembered for his death, not his life. He would be remembered for his horn-like skin and battle feats, for how he could strike faster, harder and truer. But his life would be forgotten. No one would recite poems for how he brought hot soup to his sick mother or gathered wild flowers for his sister. No one would sing about how his laughter sounded like water dancing over stones. He would be remembered as a corpse in the arms of a hero and nothing more. But I would remember him how he was before he came to the ford. I would remember the man, not the hero.

33.

Cúchulainn had not slept for eight days and nights. His body was broken. Fated or not, he wouldn't survive another night. I watched over him, for I had promised I would be the guard of his death.

The sky was of the deepest blue, scattered with stars and not a cloud to dull their shine. Cúchulainn lay on the cold, hard ground, his tears flowing with his blood. I saw again the boy he had been when I had first met him on the scarred battle-field. Afraid, alone, trying to be brave. In that meeting, I had shamed him into action with a taunt that had saved Conchobar. Had I kept my tongue, Conchobar would have died in the mud and there would have been no need for the raid.

'And where would the fun have been in that?'

I looked down from my perch to see a young warrior dressed in a cloak of every colour leaning against the tree, crunching on an apple. He must have brought it with him from the otherworld, for the apple harvest was over.

'Lugh,' I said, hopping down to stand beside him in the form of a woman. 'Back again?'

'I can't let my son die on this night.'

'And what happened to staying out of the battle?'

He finished his apple and sucked the juice from his fingers. 'I said I won't fight. But nothing was said about healing his wounds.' He threw the apple core over his shoulder where it instantly became a tree bursting with fruit and began walking up the hill towards Cúchulainn.

I followed, as a bat, flitting across the night, my ears keen enough to catch every word.

Cúchulainn struggled to his feet as Lugh approached. 'Name yourself!' he shouted, though his voice was weak and the effort of speaking set him coughing.

'You can call me Ildánach,' Lugh said. The Skilled One. The show-off.

Cúchulainn looked at Lugh, at his shimmering perfection. 'You're not from these parts, are you?' Cúchulainn fell down to one knee, and no matter how hard he tried he couldn't pull himself to standing. He gave up and leant against a rock.

'I am one of the Tuatha Dé. As are you. For my blood flows through your body. Though I see most of it is flowing out of your body right now, my son.'

Cúchulainn laughed and it became a wet cough. He spat blood on to the ground. 'You're no older than I am. Besides, I know my father. Súaltam mac Róich, he carved me my first spear, made me my first sling, and sent me to be fostered with Conchobar so I could become even greater.'

Lugh sat beside him. 'So you thought you got it all from him, then?'

'Got what from him?'

Lugh squeezed Cúchulainn's arm. 'Your powers. Your strength.'

'I don't feel all that strong now as it goes.'

It was true. His hero light was fading.

'Sleep,' Lugh said. 'You will feel better in the morning.'

'I cannot. For who else will guard the borders from Queen Medb and her lot?'

He looked over at me, now perched on a tree as a crow. Oh, that rage. If I could drink from it.

'Sleep.'

'Promise me you won't leave Ulaid undefended.'

'I promise. I will see that the province is protected. Sleep.'

The word was a summoning. Cúchulainn slid to the ground and sank into a deep, bog-like sleep, like sinking into the grave.

Lugh gently stroked his son's head, twisting the bronze strands around his fingers. When Cúchulainn was deep in his dreaming, Lugh placed herbs in his wounds and spoke healing words. I watched as the gaping holes in Cúchulainn's body closed up, the bruises turned purple then green. I hopped closer to see. I had never had the gift of healing wounds. Only of dealing them.

'Did Dian Cécht teach you the use of those herbs?' I said, remembering how the old healer had restored dead men after battle and yet killed his own son. And my son, too.

Lugh shook his head. 'His daughter, Airmed.'

Sweet Airmed, who Meche had followed around picking flowers for her stores. She had been soft and gentle and gifted beyond measure, and yet none remembered her name. I had hardly done.

'How is she?'

'Well. She and your sisters have become a force to be reckoned with. They send their best, by the way. Ériu tells you to be careful. Fódla tells you to be cunning. And Banba tells you to do whatever the hell you like, and not to forget that you're a goddess.'

I couldn't help but smile. My sisters. My beautiful sisters. Missing them was like an ache.

Lugh stood back and looked at his work. Any sign of Cúchulainn's wounds was gone, leaving only a silvery trail of scars like snail tracks across his skin. He snored like the boy he was and muttered in his deep sleep. There would be no waking him now.

'You lied,' I said. 'You'll no more guard Ulaid in his place than you'll dance a jig.'

'I don't know. I have been known to dance a jig or two.' Lugh grinned.

How had I once thought that smile charming, that face pleasing? Now all I wanted to do was punch it.

'Then the raid is over,' I said. 'Medb has won.' The words felt like ash in my mouth. I had achieved the thing I had worked all these years for, and yet my victory felt empty, as if something precious had been stolen from me.

'Not so fast.'

Lugh nodded towards where the sun was rising. A line of figures, shadowed by the sun behind them, was approaching. One hundred and fifty at least and each carried a heavy weapon over his shoulder.

'The warriors of Ulaid have arisen at last?'

'Not the men,' Lugh said, with a smile.

As the host approached, I saw what he meant. They weren't warriors. They were boys. The famed boy troop of Emain Macha carrying their hurling sticks, come to stand as their friend and leader slept.

'It will be a slaughter.'

Lugh shrugged. 'Die now, or die later, what difference does it make?'

With a wobbling, cracking yell from voices not yet broken, the boys charged.

34.

The poets said that the boys put up a mighty fight, that they killed fifty men for each of them.

Poets lie. The boys died quickly and they died easily. Even I turned away from the bloodshed. But I heard their cries. Gurgling screams through blood-filled lungs. They called out for their mothers, desperate and afraid. They cursed their fathers for sleeping while they died in agony. They had thought it all sport till the blades of the men of Ireland met their soft, summer skin.

It took longer than it should have, the men of Ireland having no true ardour to see the boys die. But die they did. Bones not yet grown, snapped like twigs. Arms not strong enough to hold a sword, ripped from shoulders. Beardless heads hacked from slim necks.

When at last it had ended, I walked the battlefield, finishing off any of the boys left bleeding and wounded, the only kindness I could offer them now.

I found Medb, standing at the edge of the battlefield, Fergus by her side. Ailill was behind them, crouched over and retching at the smell of blood and spilt bowels.

Medb was pale, her teeth clenching so hard I heard them crack. Was it worth it? I wanted to ask. If this is what vengeance looks like, was it worth it? I knew what it was never to be satiated, that there was no amount of blood that would quench the thirst. But I was a goddess. Surely for a human this would be enough?

I had foreseen crimson and red and now it had come to pass. So much death that even my stomach turned. I had set this into motion, like a stone rolling down a hillside gathering speed, and it would crush all beneath it. Medb and I so blinded by our thirst for vengeance we hadn't thought of the cost.

'Come on,' Medb said. 'Let's get this damned bull.'

Medb called for her chariot, and rode across into Ulaid, across the bones of the boys, her hair flying out behind her. Ailill followed after on foot, stopping every few steps to retch again.

Only Fergus remained. His face was speckled with blood. He must have taken part in this massacre and not simply watched.

'So the men of Ireland were unwilling to fight one boy, but they massacred one hundred and fifty without a thought?' I said.

'Because no one will remember the names of these boys,' Fergus said, wiping the blood of a child from his spear tip with a silk cloth. 'But they will never forget the name of Cúchulainn.'

But I will remember their names. I do.

Cathal. Éibhear. Abban.

Naomhán. Tadhg. Mánús.

Fiach. Odhran. Connell.

Ruadhán. Ailbhe. Eanna.

Aodh. Dónal. Breandán.

Oisín. Cian. Lorcan.

And on and on. I committed every name to my long, long memory.

The Brown Bull didn't run when Medb caught up with him. Perhaps he was as weary of it all as I was. He bowed his head and allowed them to strip him of his adornments. The delicate gold links that hung, jangling, from his horns were replaced with a heavy iron chain that wrapped around his head. The garland of sweet-smelling flowers was torn from his neck and in its place hung more iron chains. He was so weighed down by iron he couldn't lift his head.

As they led the Brown Bull south, one lone Ulaid warrior stepped forward, blocking Medb's way. He was barely a man, his youth must have freed him from the pains before the others, though he still looked pale and weak, his skin sweating and his limbs heavy. Rochad mac Faithemain, one of the most beautiful men in Ulaid. His hand shook as he stood in Medb's path, trying to find the courage not to run.

Medb took pity on him and made an offer. 'Wait till all the men of Ulaid have arisen, and then fight.'

In return, she offered him what she had offered all of the warriors. Her own daughter.

He accepted with a nod and stood aside as Medb rode away with the bull while Finnabair stayed behind with Rochad. I paused a moment with them.

'You can say no,' I said. 'I can take you away. Your mother never need know.'

Finnabair dipped her chin and looked up at me through lashes that had been darkened with soot. 'At least he is handsome.'

And so it was. Rochad took Finnabair to his bed. Two beautiful young fools together. And afterwards she returned to Medb and he returned to Ulaid to wait for the armies to awaken.

When the seven kings of Mumhain heard that Finnabair's virginity had been taken by a man of Ulaid, they turned on Ailill.

'That girl was promised to me, along with fifty hostages, to get me to join this raid,' the first king said.

'She was offered to me,' the second king said. 'And a herd of one hundred cattle.'

'And to me,' the third said. 'Along with her weight in gold.'

When all seven of the kings realized they had each been offered the girl, they drew their blades and the men of Connacht drew theirs. Two hundred died fighting each other. Those left living spat curses at Medb and many abandoned the raid.

When Finnabair heard of how many men had died in her name, she wandered off into the mountains, sat down and simply faded away. A more beautiful death than dashing your head against a rock, I suppose. And she had been right, few poets would tell her tragic story and though they called the place where she fell Finnabair Sléibe, Finnabair's Mountain, only a handful would remember why.

I flew back to Cúchulainn for I had promised I would be the guard of his death. And yet his death did not come. Lugh's magic had done its work and the boy awoke from his blessed sleep, healed and strong once more. He jumped to his feet and gambolled around like a newborn lamb, marvelling in how his bones were fixed, how the fist-sized holes in his flesh were knitted and smooth.

He spied me on a tree branch. 'What did I tell you?' he shouted up. 'I am not fated to die in this raid.'

'It's not over yet,' I said. 'There is still time. And while you have slept, the battle has gone on without you.'

He sniffed. Caught a familiar scent on the air: a tang of metal, of blood.

'What have you done?' he said.

He leapt on his chariot and followed his nose. I flew after him. When he arrived at the plain where the slaughter of the boy troop had taken place, he found nothing but mud and blood and the bones of his playmates. In the distance, he saw a trail of men heading south, moving like rats from a burning barn; Medb's invading army heading back home with the Brown Bull.

Was it sweet, to see the pain he had dealt being paid back to him threefold? To see his whole homeland violated by the heavy tread of the invading armies just as he had violated women? To see hundreds of his brothers slaughtered, just as he had slaughtered Ferdiad with trickery? Was it delicious? Was it everything I had wanted?

I had believed it would be, but now all I felt was empty as though the rage that had kept my heart beating in my chest was gone. Perhaps it had flowed out of my blood and into Cúchulainn's?

I watched, perched on the ribcage of one of the dead boys, as Cúchulainn's body began to shake. His bones twisted inside his skin, cracking and splintering. The sinews of his head stood out like ropes. One eye sank back inside his head while the other burst out and hung down his face. The hair of his head stood up like thorns on a rose bush, he screamed and fire burst from his mouth. His grief was uncontainable. Monstrous. Beautiful. If it had taken the waters of Emain Macha to cool his rage before, only a bath of blood would do so now.

Cúchulainn raced after Medb's army as it moved further south and attacked their unsuspecting flanks. A whirling, frenzied blur of blades and fury. For every one of the boy troop they had killed, he took down three. For every drop of blood they had spilt, he extracted a pint. By the end of the day, bodies were piled up as high as a wall. None could stand against him. None would dare.

As the night came to an end, Medb's forces were in panicked disarray. Someone, anyone, had to stop the boy.

'I will go to him,' Fergus said. 'We made a pledge that should we meet on the battlefield, we wouldn't harm each other. He will be bound by that.'

Fergus stripped off his armour, laid down his weapons, and walked toward the howling beast that was Cúchulainn, naked arms outstretched. 'Cúchulainn, my boy, you have done enough. And did we not promise we would not fight?'

Cúchulainn stared at Fergus as though he did not know him. And slowly, as though awakening from a dream, he stopped. The binding of the pledge they had made held Cúchulainn's hand. His eye sucked back into his skull, his bones slotted back into place and he was his old self once more.

Tears flowed down his face and he fell to his knees. The wounds Lugh had healed were open and bleeding once more. He was alone, just a boy, with the remainder of Medb's army ahead of him, not even his rage to protect him now. He had had enough. The death of Ferdiad. The death of his boy-troop playmates. He was broken. For nine days he had fought the armies of Ireland alone. But for nothing. The Brown Bull, the cause of all of this death, had been taken. The armies of Ireland had won. Cúchulainn bent his head, ready for death to take him.

A single, bright horn sounded from atop a hill in the distance. A great, grey cloud hung in the air, pouring down the hill like mist in the early morning.

I flew above the plain to see that the grey mist was the breath of horses and men, and the dust of the earth as marching feet descended on the plain. The forces of King Conchobar, the warriors of the Red Branch, risen at last and come to fight.

35.

Dark and steady the men of Ulaid came, bringing dread and terror. The clash of their swords on shields sounded like thunder and Medb's men quaked from the vibrations. I circled above, screeching as Conchobar led his forces down the hill, like a swarm of ants come for honey.

I returned to Medb and found her, Ailill and Fergus frozen, staring at the horde marching down the hill towards them, come for their revenge.

'How many are there?' Medb asked.

'Hundreds, maybe thousands,' Fergus answered.

Medb stared wide-eyed at line after line of warriors descending. It was the first time I had seen her unsure of herself since the night we met. She looked from the host of Ulaid getting closer with every beat of their drum to her men. So many had died already for her wrath, when would the scales be balanced?

Our eyes met and I saw then that she was done. That she was sick with it all. At last, we had found the limits of her vengeance.

'Go,' I said. 'Call the retreat. I will stand in their way.'

She nodded, grateful. But before she could sound the horn, Ailill spoke. 'We will wait,' he said, lifting his chin and trying to look like the leader he wasn't. 'We still outnumber them.'

I looked out at the ragged remains of the armies of the four provinces of Ireland, held together by a tattered dream long turned nightmare. Four thousand were left standing. Barely.

'It's not their numbers that scare me,' Fergus said. 'You'll not find any in the whole of Ireland, or in the whole west of the world, who can endure the men of Ulaid in their fury and in their rage.'

Medb swore and I saw the reason for it. Conchobar, leading the forces, had come into sight. Proud as ever, though pale and more slender than he had been. The nine cursed days confined to his sickbed had robbed him of some of his vitality. I took pleasure in that. I hoped he'd remembered the pain of the woman he'd forced to race for his sport as he lay sweating and tortured. The poets later said the men of Ulaid had awoken from the curse and charged into battle stark naked, wearing nothing but their weapons. But judging by the state of Conchobar's appearance, he'd not rushed to the plain and had taken the time to bathe and dress. He'd even had his eyebrows painted and hair curled; it fell in dark ringlets to his shoulders and smelt of violets, though it couldn't hide the stink of his breath. His beard was forked and bound in gold and he was dressed in a purple pleated tunic, wrapped around his shoulders and fastened at his chest with a brooch of red gold. Slung across his back, he had a long, gold-hilted sword that was as tall as a man. In one hand he carried a shield engraved with golden animals, in the other he held the slender shaft of a broad grey spear made for stabbing. He smiled with a look of triumphant terror.

Behind him came the warriors of the Red Branch, each of them more fearsome than the last. They carried scalp-edged, death-dealing shields and long spears, thick as palace torches, though they looked ready to tear us apart with nothing but their teeth. They surrounded Cúchulainn, pulling him to his feet, and marched on. He hung like a slaughtered pig in their hands. Life drained out of him with every step.

The drums stopped. The marching ceased. Conchobar held up his hand, giving the symbol for a truce.

'What are you going to do?' I asked Medb.

'What else is there to be done?' she said.

She walked forward, and Ailill and Fergus followed behind. I walked after them, a hooded crone, silent and watching. Medb, like Conchobar, had taken the time to dress, but while he looked tired and gaunt, she was fresh and rosy-cheeked as though come from weapons practice. Her golden hair was bound in two braids, thick as the gold torc around her neck. She wore armour with golden birds on the spaulders, and had a bronze sword with a woman's grip on her back. I'd taught her to fight and she was the equal of any of the men standing here. But only I knew her well enough to see the weariness in her eyes.

She stopped before Conchobar. Cúchulainn stood beside him, propped up by two men, holding on to a spear with slippery, broken fingers, to stop himself from falling.

'Come at last, Conchobar?' Medb said. 'You look as if you've been dead these past weeks.'

'You thought you could raid my land and slip away unnoticed like a thief in the dark, Ailill?' Conchobar said, pointedly ignoring Medb as if he hadn't had to turn away from the sun reflecting off her gold, as if she wasn't the most glorious woman he had ever laid eyes on. 'Though I am not surprised. Had you any honour, you would have waited till the curse had lifted.'

'A curse you brought on your men, Conchobar, thanks to your stupidity and cruelty,' Medb said. 'Only a fool would fail to take advantage.'

Conchobar looked around as if trying to discern where the noise had come from, as if Medb's voice had been a

333

strange bird call overhead. 'My nephew, a single Ulaid boy, held your united armies at bay,' he said, rubbing the back of his hand against Cúchulainn's bruised cheek.

Cúchulainn tried to smile, tried to speak, but only blood bubbled at his lips.

Conchobar turned again to Ailill. 'How do you think you will fare against the men of Ulaid, now that the Red Branch has arisen?'

'What's left of it,' Medb said, twisting the barb. She glanced at Fergus who stood by her side. His jaw crunched and cracked as he bit down his anger at facing Conchobar. He'd sworn that the next time he laid eyes on the king he would kill him for breaking his promise. But the rules of a truce held his hand.

'I heard you've lost your sword, Fergus,' Conchobar said. 'Tell me, did you give it to a whore in payment?'

Fergus laughed, bitter and dry. 'You've never met a woman that you didn't treat as a whore,' Fergus spat. 'But the only payment you've ever given is in punches. Tell me, how did it feel to know Deirdre would rather die than suffer you one more day? Did it stir your loins to see her body broken, thrown against the rocks, or does it only excite you when it's you who hands out the beatings?'

Conchobar sucked at his teeth. 'You think Deirdre had it tough? Wait till I am finished with Medb. I made her my bitch once, and I will do so again.'

Medb flinched and for a moment I saw her as she was when we first met, folded in on herself, afraid and ashamed. I laid my hand on her back and whispered in her ear so that none but she could hear me.

'Never again.'

She pulled her shoulders back, lifted her chin and looked

334

Conchobar straight in the eye. She was the taller, and she looked down on him, a smile more unsettling, more mocking than any words.

Fergus didn't have her power. He resorted to spitting threats. 'Just you wait till I have my sword in my hand,' he said. 'I'll send your men's heads flying thicker than hailstones. I'll send their necks buzzing like bees on a fine day.'

'We'll see. A truce till sunrise,' Conchobar said, looking again only at Ailill. 'While we make camp and tend to Cúchulainn's wounds.'

Cúchulainn struggled to lift his head. 'I will fight with you,' he said, though I had to strain to hear him speak.

'You have done enough,' Conchobar said. 'It is the men's turn now.'

It was agreed and they retreated to their tents. Cúchulainn was carried away by four men, the blood dripping from his body. He had undone the work of Lugh's magic and was close to death once more, though he cried the whole time for them to let him stay. It was said they had to strap him down to keep him still long enough for the healers to tend to him.

Medb waited in her tent and sharpened her sword, over and over, the grinding of metal on stone like teeth on bones.

'It will be blunt by the time the day is over,' I said.

'I have others.'

'Will it be enough?' I asked. 'If you kill every last one of them, will it be enough?'

She threw her sword to the ground and stood, facing me. She was pale, a greenish pallor to her rosy skin. 'How could you ask me that? You!'

'I am vengeance, Medb. I am fury. It is all that I know and all that I am. I am the bitterness that lives in the heart

335

of every wronged person. I am retribution served swift and reprisal served slow. My heart sings when blood flows, my mouth waters at the crushing of bones. It is the only time I know peace. I was made for this. I have fought against it, tried to become what others wanted of me, but I cannot escape my nature. Whereas others of my kind were made to see that crops grow and cattle fatten, to bring love and life to this land, I was made for this. But you, Medb, my friend, my only friend, were not.'

Her face hardened, her chin walnut-wrinkled. 'Tell me then, what was I made for?'

'To rule.'

She shook her head. 'No, Nemain, that is what you wanted. I only wanted to see Conchobar broken.'

I had believed that Medb and I shared the same heart, the same mind. I had thought that she wanted to be Queen of all of Ireland. But she had only wanted retribution.

'Vengeance? At what cost?' I asked.

Thousands of men had died thus far and thousands more would die tomorrow.

'At any cost,' she said.

She was like stone. How I loved her for it.

'Well, then, I guess we fight.'

She picked up her sword again and set to work with the whetting stone. 'Do we stand any chance?'

I looked down at her. How could someone be so strong and so frail at the same time? We had started this war together and we would end it together. 'I will be with you,' I said.

'You will fight? As you did when you fought for your tribe?' She looked up at me with the same glittering eyes as the night we had first met. Eyes filled with hope for something more than a life of pain and submission.

'I will fight.'

She reached out and squeezed my hand. 'Then if I finally get to see you in all your fearsome glory, this will have been worthwhile.'

As the sun sank behind the mountains, I walked out and stood on the ground between the two camps and threw back my hood, revealing myself in my true form. In the half-light, I looked into the future and spoke of what I saw.

'Crows gnaw necks
Blood bursts
In the fierce fray
Flesh is hacked
Blades in bodies
Battle blindness
War is waged
Man tramples man
Hail, Ulaid!
Woe, men of Ireland
Woe, Ulaid
Hail, men of Ireland!'

Each side chose to hear what they wanted. Chose to see my words as a sign that the battle would be theirs and theirs alone. But there would be no winners, only war.

36.

The battle began in the dark, all the better to hide the men's fear. Medb, Ailill and Fergus stood at the front of the line.

'You'll be wanting this then,' Ailill said, handing Fergus his sword.

'Where . . . How . . .?'

'I took it from you,' Ailill said. 'You left it propped up against a tree when you were fucking my wife. I had meant to kill you with it myself. But . . .' He shrugged.

Fergus threw down his spear and took his sword in both hands and spun it through the air. It sang like a shepherd's whistle calling his flock home.

'If you're done comparing the size of your swords,' Medb said, 'shall we?'

The men of Ireland, led by a queen, charged. And I burst into a shrieking murder of crows, diving at the forces of Ulaid. It had been three hundred years since I had last been in a true battle, three hundred years since I had fought the Fomorians. What had come as easy as breathing then, when I was still young and wild, was a struggle to me on that day. Each drag of my talons through skin felt as though I was weighed down with chains. Each bite of my teeth into flesh was like chewing on leather. I had once had the power to turn the hearts of men to ice or to make their blood boil. I had once been able to whip an army into a frenzy with a word, awaken a god to battle or make a hero shit his breeches. My power, like my vengeance, had once been as unquenchable as a forest fire. But on that day, it was I who was burnt. And yet what little power remained in me was still five times that of a man. I crushed bones, spilt guts, and the men ran screaming from me.

One man froze before me, his bones quaking. I knew him. Éogan mac Durthacht. The man who had killed Deirdre's love, Naoise. The man whom Deirdre had killed herself rather than be given to.

He was short with stubby arms and a nose that had been broken and not set properly. His face was covered in sores that oozed pus. He may have once been handsome, but it was as though the evil of his spirit had seeped through his skin.

'This is for Deirdre,' I said.

I plunged my hand into his stomach and pulled out a handful of guts. They fell to the ground like a catch of eels. He would die slowly and painfully. It wasn't enough to make up for the pain he had caused. Nothing would be enough.

Ailill shouted instructions from the rear, as though he were still on the training grounds of Cruachan; bad orders that good men died following.

Across the battlefield I saw Medb, fighting as fiercely as if she had been of my blood. She swung her sword around her head, slicing throats, slashing chests and taking heads clean off the necks of the first wave of Ulaid men who came for her. Ten, twenty, thirty men fell beneath the tip of her blade till none dared approach. Her face was speckled in the dying breaths of men and her golden armour was red as rust.

'Conchobar!' she bellowed, her voice carrying over the screams of the dying. 'Will you not face me? Or do you only attack women unarmed and alone?'

She spun her sword in a quick, neat circle, flicking the viscera of Ulaid men to the ground. Wading through the battle she called out Conchobar's name, her swift sword taking out three men with each stroke. She slashed and hacked her way through the melee, seeking out the man who had once been her husband, but she could not find him in the bloodshed.

For my part, I killed a hundred, two hundred men. But with each death, I grew more and more weary. All around me, the men of Ireland were dying. We were losing. The four armies, united by a gossamer-thin thread, had forgotten why they were fighting beyond survival. But the men of Ulaid were fighting to defend their land. They were fighting to avenge their sons. They were unstoppable. And yet Medb fought on, calling out for Conchobar.

'Come and fight me!' she cried out, between hacks of her sword. It was growing heavier with each blow. 'You let these men die in your stead? How can you call yourself king?'

A warrior stepped forward and lowered his shield. Blood flowed from a cut on his forehead, and his once tightly coiled curls were matted in mud and shit. And yet there was no mistaking the King of Ulaid.

'I should have killed you that night in Tara,' Conchobar said.

'You did.'

She struck out with her sword quick as a wolf. It sliced across Conchobar's chest, cutting through his armour and opening up a wound like a smile. He roared and swung his sword over his head, bringing it crashing down. But Medb dodged and it met only soil. Again she struck, piercing between his ribs. Again he cried out in pain and swung for her head. She threw herself to the ground, rolled and came up once more. Every move and trick that I taught her she displayed, though she made it look like a dance.

Sweat and blood poured into Conchobar's eyes, and each swing of his weapon was wider and wilder. He staggered back, trying to wipe it away with the back of his hand.

Medb hovered before him. He was unguarded. Now would be the time.

'Finish him,' I shouted. For Medb was surely playing with him now, as a cat with its prey.

There was a sound like a distant wind. I looked up to see a volley of spears cutting through the air like hail. Each black tip was headed for Medb.

I blew out a hurricane of air. It circled Medb, her hair and cloak whipping around her. One spear pierced her through the shoulder, pinning her to the ground. The others thudded in a ring around her. She was trapped in a wooden cage. With her uninjured arm, she hacked at the shafts around her, but it was like trying to hack her way out of a forest.

'Ha!' Conchobar roared. 'See how we have you caught like the she-wolf you are.'

Medb roared, shaking the spears.

Conchobar stepped closer. 'Hmm, I wonder, should I kill you now, or have you thrown to my men for their sport? Or shall I take you for my own again?'

Medb spat in his face. Reached her hand through the spear shafts and tried to claw at him.

I would have to kill Conchobar myself. It was not the death I had seen for him, but I knew that fates could be as easily unmade as they were made. I summoned up what little strength I had and leapt into the air, dancing across the tips of spears and the edges of swords, and made my way to Conchobar. Perhaps it was destined that it would come to this. The day he forced me to run for his sport, he had set himself on a track that came to this.

Before I could lay so much as a finger on him, another got there first.

'Let's see how you like facing a man for once.' It was Fergus.

His clothing shone white and his skin glistened as though newly bathed and oiled. How he had managed to stay so clean in the filth of the battle, I could not tell.

'You're no man,' Conchobar said. 'I should have killed you, not sent you into exile along with the dogs and foxes.'

'And I should have known your word is worth less than a hinny's ball sack.'

They moved in circles, sizing each other up. Had they trained together, I wondered, did they know one another's weaknesses, strengths? Fergus was the larger man by far, and the blade he wielded a death-dealer. But Conchobar was quick and his shield and helm better made. As they fought, I flew to Medb. With a slice of my talons, I cut through the spears holding her captive.

'This will hurt,' I said, as I yanked the spear free of her shoulder and threw it aside.

She bit back her cry of pain.

'Go,' I said.

'But Conchobar . . .'

'He does not die today. But if you don't get out of here, you will.'

I pulled a passing Ulaid man from a chariot and placed Medb on it. With a slap of the horse's rear, I sent her racing beyond the battle lines.

I turned once more to Fergus and Conchobar. Fergus swung his sword with all his strength, aiming for

Conchobar's head. The king met the blow on his shield, though it knocked him back, sliding through the mud. The blow must have broken his arm too, as he dropped his shield, his limb hanging loose as a skinned rabbit by his side. He pushed his chest out and tried to look brave. Tried to use his position as ruler as a desperate last weapon. He stared at the man who had once been his dearest friend as though he were a worm crawling through dirt, as though he were no longer a man.

'Would you kill your king?' Conchobar said.

'You're not my king.'

Fergus raised his sword above his head. The noon sun reflected off the oiled blade, sending rainbows dancing. He cleaved it through the air, with all of the weight of his anger behind it. All of Conchobar's feigned bravery drained out of him and he squealed, actually squealed, as Fergus's blade came cutting through the air, aiming for his head. With a ringing clang, the blade met not flesh, but metal, not bone, but wood. A shield, shattered and shredded, and yet still strong.

The arm that held the shield was bloodied and bruised. A white bone pierced the skin where it had been broken. The arm of a man, though barely. Strips of hazel bound his stomach, and dark blood seeped through the gaps. He stood back-bent, as though he hardly had the strength to lift his head. But lift it he did. And I looked into the face of Cúchulainn. Broken free of his bonds and come again to the fight.

He stood between Fergus and Conchobar. His two foster fathers, the only two men left alive that he cared about. The boys of the boy troop were dead. Ferdiad, his beloved Ferdiad, was dead.

'I can't kill you, Fergus,' Cúchulainn said.

'You're not wrong there, boy. Look at you. You're full of holes. One more strike and you're dead.'

'You swore you would yield to me.'

Fergus's eyes darted between the boy and Conchobar. Between his two promises. Conchobar was still crouched, cowering on the ground, bleeding. He'd shat himself and the paint he'd had dabbed on his forehead was smudged like women's tears. Cúchulainn stood, bloodied, weak, struggling to keep hold of his shield, but he stood.

Fergus could have killed him. He could have driven his sword through the boy's heart and been done with it all. But what would the poets say about good ol' Fergus then? Would they say he had no honour? That he was a man who broke his word? Fergus couldn't have that now, could he? He wanted to be the big man, remembered for ever as the good guy on the wrong side. A hero. And so he lowered his sword. The fool.

'I yield,' he said.

Fergus left the battle and took three hundred of his men with him, but not, they said, before slicing the tops off three nearby hills in his frustrated rage. The Kings of Mumhain, loyalty already shaken after the Finnabair affair and now seeing they were fighting on the losing side, left too, marching backwards away from the fray.

Cúchulainn crawled on to his chariot and strapped his spear to his arm and joined the men of Ulaid in the fight. Fergus had been right about them. They were ferocious. For every man we killed, they killed ten and soon we were not only outmatched, we were outnumbered. We had lost and yet we still fought like fools. By the time the sun had turned the clouds crimson, so that it was hard to see where the rivers of blood ended and the sky began, what men remained standing were weary beyond words.

Medb took her chance to call a withdrawal, sending her forces back across the border and with them, the Brown Bull. She stood, covering their retreat, and I stood beside her. Her wound had been hastily staunched, though her arm hung loose by her side.

Seeing the men of Ireland getting away, Cúchulainn found a new energy in his rage. His warp spasm took hold once again, and he burst out of the bindings that were keeping his innards inside his body. One, huge, bulging eye settled on Medb and he came for her, wading through the bones of dead warriors.

Medb stood firm, her feet planted, sword raised.

'You can't fight him when the warp spasm is on him,' I said. 'No one can stand against him.'

She dropped her sword and started backing up. There was no escape from the beserking boy. 'What do I do?'

Was there anything that could stop a rage like his? It was god-given, monstrous, unstoppable. Then I remembered the story Fergus had told about him.

'Show him your breasts,' I said.

'What?' Medb said.

'Remember what Fergus said? That when the rage was on Cúchulainn, the women of Ulaid showed him their breasts and it stopped him. That it was the only thing that could.'

She fumbled at the straps of her leather armour. She wouldn't have it off in time. He was just a few steps away. An idea came to her. Medb hitched up her tunic and pulled down her breeches, as if to relieve herself on the floor.

'What are you doing?' I asked.

'If a woman's breasts were enough to stop his warp spasm, let's see how he copes with a woman's blood.'

And right enough, a flow of blood came out of her and spilt on the ground. With a word, I turned the flow into a foul trench of blood. Medb's Foul Place, they called it for ever after.

Cúchulainn stopped, looking down at her, shocked as if he'd never seen a woman's parts before in his life. His eye sucked back into his head, his bones snapped back into place. Blood poured out of his wounds like a mountain stream running down white rocks. He was pale as a week-old corpse and he stank of rotting flesh. His eyelids flickered as he struggled to keep them open.

'I could kill you,' he said.

He spoke true, for I saw that he had enough strength left for one more blow. But it would be the final blow he would ever strike.

'Maybe you could,' Medb said, layering her voice with honeyed sweetness. 'You've caught me at my most vulnerable and I am at your mercy.'

Cúchulainn didn't know where to look. At her bloodied cunt, or at her face, or at the ground where her blood flowed. He decided to turn around and face the opposite way.

'I won't kill you,' he said. 'For I am not a killer of women.'

Not a killer, perhaps. But a defiler. A destroyer. Medb straightened and pulled her breeches back up and pulled her tunic down.

'How did you know that would work?' I asked.

'All weak men fear a woman's blood.'

She really did understand men better than I ever had. With a smile, she waded across the ford which marked the border of Ulaid, while Cúchulainn and I stood watching her go.

'What of you, then?' he said to me, his voice weak. 'Any more tricks from you?'

'No tricks, little hound.'

'Kill me, then? You could. I have nothing left.'

He wasn't wrong. One flick of my finger and it would be over for Sétanta. But that is not how his story ends. Nor mine.

'Not today,' I said.

He nodded. 'Not today.'

I saw in the distance a shimmering golden light. It came from a figure standing on a hilltop. Lugh. He waved to me and then vanished like marsh fire.

Poets would later tell the story of the cattle raid of Cooley and even those who were to write it down knew that much of it was lies and fantasies, told for the enjoyment of fools. Some had it that Medb was the victor, others that it was Conchobar who had won the day. They added new strands, new characters who had not been there, side stories to give the battle purpose where there had been none. The story swelled like a corpse fit to burst till the tale became so unmanageable that one day, centuries after it had ended, none could remember it in its entirety and they had to drag old Fergus from his grave to tell it all. But I remembered. I remembered it all. Though sometimes I wished I didn't.

'Well, that didn't go exactly to plan,' Medb said, when we had reunited with Fergus, safe on Connacht land.

'We should never have followed a woman,' Fergus said. 'For a herd led by a mare is always lost and destroyed.'

Medb laughed. 'It's not my fault you turned from the

fight with Conchobar. You may have failed, but I got what I wanted.'

'How can that be true when you don't have the Ulaid throne, when you don't rule all of Ireland?'

'That is what *you* wanted, Fergus,' she said. 'I wanted no such thing. I swore that I would let no man have power over me, not that I would have power over all men. That is a man's vision of power. Domination. No, all I wanted was to remind Conchobar that there are some women he can't control, some provinces that will not bend the knee to him. So let Conchobar rule his scrap of land. Let his hatred for me and his failure to crush me gnaw away at him like rot.'

She smiled, a bloody smile, then spat out a tooth loose from her battling, and I swear she never looked happier or more beautiful.

'Conchobar still lives. He hasn't paid for what he did,' Fergus said, stamping his foot like a child.

'For what he did to Medb,' I said. 'And to her sister. And Deirdre.' For I knew full well Fergus had been talking about himself.

'Yes, yes, of course. He hasn't paid for what he did to my queen.'

'This is true and it is painful,' Medb said. 'But I was heard. I was believed. And the armies of Ireland followed me into battle against him. Though it is not everything, it is enough. For now, my revenge is to go on and live my life as if I'd never even heard his name.'

With a whistle, she called for her chariot and stepped on to it. Fergus grabbed the reins in his hand, stopping the horses' heads.

'All of this death. All of these men who followed you. They mean nothing to you?'

She looked down at Fergus and smiled. 'You said it yourself, a man who follows a woman is a fool. Come, let's go.'

Fergus looked back across the river border to his motherland, where he was no longer welcome. He had thought he could overthrow Conchobar, return home to Ulaid a victor and take the throne that once belonged to him. Perhaps he even thought he could marry Medb and take the throne of Ireland for himself. But now, he was nothing but the plaything of a queen. He stepped up next to Medb, a man with no choices, as much a captive as the broken horses bridled to the chariot. Medb snapped her whip and the horses raced on home to Cruachan. She truly was a woman without shame.

I had dreamt of seeing Medb become a High Queen, ruling over the whole of Ireland. I had believed she would be the ruler the land deserved. But she had wanted only justice. In truth, all that I had wanted for her was that which had been denied me. I had spent lifetime after lifetime chasing it, and yet now it felt as though it had been someone else's dream all along.

'What a fool,' I said.

'Don't be so hard on yourself.'

I turned at the familiar voice. It was the Dagda, leading my chariot as he had once done on a bright day that had been filled with promise.

'You,' I said.

How had I not realized just how beautiful he was?

'Me.' He smiled, and a little of the heaviness in me lifted. It was good to see a smile that didn't hide a lie.

'What are you doing here?'

'I thought you might want someone to lead your chariot as I did a year ago.' He rubbed the velvet nose of my horse. It snorted with pleasure at his touch.

Had it only been a year since I had ridden out with the Brown Bull for Cooley, full of plans and prophecies? 'It feels longer.'

'A year to the day. It will be Samhain tomorrow.'

I looked to the trees, which were turning golden, to the fields beyond, crops like stubble recently harvested. All the time the raid had been happening, life had still been going on. Farmers had tended to their fields, maids had milked their cows, while the warriors of the five provinces fought.

But it was over and winter was not far away. I stepped up on to my chariot and the Dagda stood beside me. We rode past the rotting bodies of men and boys. For the first time in many a year, I thought of Dian Cécht and his healing wells. If he had been with us, how many of these warriors would still be alive and could I have put aside my hatred of him to save them? If the Dagda, bringer of life, had been with us in the battle, would the army of Ulaid have stood aside? If any of the Tuatha Dé had been with us, would the slaughter have been avoided? But only I had fought, and little good it had done.

I heard an angry shouting carried on the wind across the plain and a sorrowful whickering of horses. I borrowed the eyes of a crow flying overhead to see Conchobar, whipping his chariot horses, their hooves buried deep in the sucking mud, their eyes wild with fear. Each of his strikes opened their flesh, pain pushing them onward till at last they were free. Conchobar, pride bruised, soft skin bloodied, angry as ever, rode home to Emain Macha, King of Ulaid still.

'You got your war then.' The Dagda's voice brought me back.

'All wars are my wars,' I replied, looking at the crows picking at the bones of the dead.

'And did you win?'

It was a good question. Conchobar lived. Cúchulainn lived. Both had paid for their actions, but had they paid enough? Could any retribution truly be enough?

'Not this time.'

'Ah, so,' the Dagda said, with a soft sigh. 'And what does the goddess of battle do when she doesn't win?'

I looked at him to see if he was joking, for the answer was as clear as though it had been carved in stone. There was only one thing that could be done.

'She keeps on fighting,' I said.

The Dagda acknowledged this with a nod of his head, and a click of his tongue set the horses trotting for home.

37.

I wasn't there when the Brown Bull was taken to Cruachan, though I heard the bellowing from within my cave. I heard the thundering of the hooves of Finnbhennach, the white bull, as it came to defend its territory from the invader. If the battle between the men of the raid had been fierce, it was nothing to the battle between the two bulls. Across the land and up and down their battle raged, till at last the Brown Bull impaled Finnbhennach on his horns and tore out his innards. He then staggered his way back to Cooley, blood and entrails falling from his horns on his way. Home at last, his heart broke in his breast like an egg and the Brown Bull fell to the ground, dead.

They said Medb smiled as she watched the bulls tear shreds off each other and that when she heard they were both dead, she smiled broader still. I could imagine that smile. It was the one I had seen in my dream. The smile I had taken to mean victory over the whole of Ireland. But it had only been her fulfilling her promise that no man be above her.

The raid had ended. The bulls had fought and died. Conchobar and Cúchulainn and the men of Ulaid lived. It took Cúchulainn months before he was strong enough to hold a sword again. His scars, without Lugh's magic to heal them, thickened and reddened, like ropes wrapped around his arms and face. His once great beauty was gone for ever.

Medb continued to rule in Connacht, Ailill by her side, Fergus in her bed. Till she tired of him too. We drifted apart, as we no longer had our purpose to bind us. She had got what she wanted, but I was left still unsatisfied. I should have known that she could never have been the ruler I had wanted. For a true ruler, a good, righteous ruler, must be subject to their people. They must put every man, woman and child above themselves, and Medb had sworn against such a thing. Perhaps there would never be a ruler worthy. No man or woman. Perhaps no single individual who wanted power would be worthy of it, or any person who held it could withstand the power of it to corrupt. Or perhaps Lugh was right. Power could only be shared.

Ulaid continued to have petty squabbles with the other provinces of Ireland. Conchobar, twisted by the bitterness of his stalemate with Medb, kept demanding reparations here or portions there. But I couldn't find it within me to care.

Some years later, I heard word that Conchobar had been struck in the head and was now alive but near senseless. He had been hit with a ball made from the lime-preserved brain of Mesgegra, the same King of Laigin whose coronation I had attended when Medb and I first met. Mesgegra's brain had been scooped out and kept preserved in lime as a trophy by the men of Ulaid, then stolen by a warrior of Connacht, who had flung it at Conchobar's head. But it hadn't killed him. It had lodged itself in his head, bulging out of the king's skull.

I had to go and see this for myself.

Conchobar lay in his bed, pillows and furs propping him up. A wrinkled black lump stuck out of his forehead like a gall on an oak tree. His eyes no longer saw and his mouth drooped heavily to the side and he drooled like a baby. I let out a great 'Ha!' of laughter.

'Who is there?' he shouted, his words struggling through twisted lips. 'Who dares to laugh at the king?'

I leant over him, my lips next to his ear.

'Remember me, Conchobar?' I hissed. 'Remember Macha, wife of Crunden, mother of Fir and Fial?'

'No . . . No! A ghost. A nightmare.'

He swiped at the air, trying to wave me away as though I was the smoke from a green wood fire.

'Remember Deirdre? Remember Medb? Remember Eithne? Remember every woman you have ever hurt and shamed and belittled? Well, hear this now. Hear how they laugh.'

And I laughed and laughed. I couldn't stop laughing.

He roared. And as he did, the brain ball burst out of his head and after it a jet of blood as steady as horse piss. He roared till his last breath. I dipped my hands in the pools of his blood and used it to redden my lips and cheeks.

I walked around the walls of Emain Macha and remembered how it had felt to run with the herds of horses. I stopped and laid flowers on the place where I had buried my children, their bones long turned to dust. When the wailing went up that Conchobar had died, I joined it, though mine was a wail not of sorrow but of delight.

I stayed for a while longer, enjoying the turmoil of the province now that their king was dead. Then I gathered up enough lime and burned Emain Macha to the ground.

'I should have done this at the start,' I said to no one in particular, as the flames heated my cheeks, warm for the first time in centuries.

Medb died not long after Conchobar, and her death was

only slightly less strange than his. Her nephew, the boy she had raised as her own, had been poisoned by the stories he'd heard that Medb had killed his mother out of envy. He became a master with the slingshot and one day loaded his sling with a piece of hard cheese and flung it through her skull while she bathed.

I cried at her death, keened along with the women of Connacht, for my friend, my only true friend. My heart, already battered by lifetimes of pain, broke a little more.

Word came to me that Cúchulainn had killed his own son, sent to him by Aífe. His wife Emer had shouted at him to stop and he'd ignored her, just as he ignored all women, and so his only son died by his hand and his line ended with him. I had promised Aífe and Scáthach that the boy would destroy Cúchulainn and I had not lied. When Cúchulainn learned that it was his only son he had slain, whatever was left of the champion in him died; his hero light was extinguished for good. After that, he spent his days drinking and feasting and trying not to sleep for when he slept, he saw the face of Ferdiad and his son and all the boys of the troop of Emain Macha, come to ask him when he would be joining them. He saw me too.

He should have died in the cattle raid. He should have burnt brightly and been snuffed out, not clung on to life, desperate and broken. Better a beautiful death than a sorrowful life.

Seasons passed and I often wished for death myself, as I had when Meche had been taken from me. Wished that I could be stripped of my immortality and simply cease to be. I had lost much of myself. The rage that had kept me going all these many long years was gone and with it, many of my powers. I thought about finally joining the rest of my family in the lands below. The Dagda had promised me I would find peace as the rest of the tribe had done, but I couldn't believe him.

For sixteen years, I wandered the land with no direction, letting the ebbs and flows of life push and pull me like a seed caught on the wind. I mostly took on the form of an old woman, bent-backed and grey-haired, for without beauty I could move among mortals with ease. In this form I was shunned by men, but welcomed by women. They would invite me into their homes, give me a place to warm my gnarled feet by their fires. In my youth, I had spent all my years moving among the world of control-hungry kings and men. Now, the women I chose to spend my time with had little interest in power, other than when it attempted to control them.

I loved the washerwomen the most, how they worked together, laughing and sharing the load. They would scrub the shit out of the breeches of the powerful and poor alike and their only concern was that there be food to eat, a fire to warm themselves by and a story to pass the evenings. Even these were different. They told tales of love and loss, of hope and heartbreak, and while they too were enamoured with stories of heartbreak most of all, their tales weren't soaked in women's blood. They would sigh or cry as the stories ended and prepare themselves for bed. Not one was moved to take up arms and go and kill their neighbours. And yet, when it took them to make a difference, they would come together, and when united, nothing could stand in their way. It was the purest form of power I had known. Shared among many and given away once their goals were met. I passed my days with them, and I was, if not exactly happy, then not restless. Sometimes I would catch my reflection in the waters as I was washing clothes and I wouldn't recognize the face staring back at me. Grey-haired, skin mottled like marble and wrinkled like the bark of an oak. All my sharp edges had been rounded off, and I was soft and undulating. My knees would creak when I stood and every day it took me longer to get out of bed. My spear-hopping days were behind me. I was lucky if I could hop over a stream.

So it was, in this shape as I knelt by the river scrubbing clothes, that Cúchulainn came upon me.

38.

He did not recognize me. Truth was, I hardly recognized him. The youth who had so stunned with his beauty was now a man, average and easily forgotten. Muscles that had once been lean and hard were now soft. Skin that had shone so bright it had blinded his enemies was now grey and blotchy from heavy drinking. His hair was thinning and his eyes had lost their sharp keenness. Had it not been for his hands, I might not have known him at all. His hands and his scars. They cut across his face like a badly repaired cloak.

'Greetings, Mother,' he said.

'Greetings, yourself. What brings you here on this day?'

'I heard the sounds of a battle nearby. Can you tell me where to find it?' He looked around.

'There is no battle here, boy, and believe me, I would know.'

'But I swear I could hear . . .' He looked down at the river. 'What is it you're washing there?'

I looked down to see that the skirts and tunics I had come to the waters with had changed into the armour of a warrior. And it was not chicken shit and dust I was washing from it but blood.

I looked back to Cúchulainn, to see that he was wearing the very same armour.

'Ah,' he said.

'Ah,' I said in return.

'Come.' I reached out my hand for him to help me to my feet. 'I have a stew on the go. You might as well eat. No point in dying on an empty stomach.'

I pushed the clothing I had been washing into his arms and led the way back to my home. He laid the clothes out on a rack to dry and came to sit by the fire. I ladled out two bowls of the stew and handed it to him.

'Bless you, Mother,' he said.

I laughed, for it wasn't the first time he had blessed me, but he was too focused on the stew to notice.

'What is in this?'

'Carrots and celery and onions.'

'And what is the meat?'

'Just meat. Are you so spoilt from the feasting at the king's tables you would refuse simple meat broth?'

No man may refuse hospitality and I knew it. I also knew that Cúchulainn had a geas on him never to eat dog's meat, for after he had killed one and taken its name, all hounds were sacred to him. It just so happened that a wild dog had got into my chickens the day before and so I'd broken his neck and butchered him for my stew.

Cúchulainn paused with the spoon to his lips, caught between two options. Refuse my hospitality or break his geas. He slurped at the stew.

I think he knew what he was doing. I think he knew full well that he was eating the flesh of a dog, and by doing so he was dooming himself. But I also think he was tired and truly had died years before on the day he killed his best friend by trickery, or when he killed his own son. What had been left of him after the raid was but a shell. He finished the food and thanked me and left.

I put out the fire. Tidied up the house, let my chickens

go loose and for the first time in many years hopped into the air as a crow.

There are as many versions of how Cúchulainn died as there are how he lived. But I was there, and I saw it with my own eyes. As he rode through the darkening forest, a band of people followed him from the shadows. There was Lugaid, son of Cú Roí; Erc, son of Cairbre Nia Fir; and Ethnea, Ethlend and Ethnen, the three daughters of Calatin, the first to fall in the Cattle Raid of Cooley. Triplet girls who had been trained in magic by his druid wife. All of them had one thing in common: Cúchulainn had killed their fathers. Though he probably didn't remember the doing of it.

They weren't as stupid as so many others had been to take him on one by one. Instead, they worked together to hunt him down. Calatin's daughters used their magic to create the sounds of battle that only he could hear, luring him further away from his home. When, at last, he came to a lake and could ride no more, Erc and Lugaid struck. They flung three strong spears at him. The first hit his horse, which fell down dead on the spot, half-crushing Cúchulainn beneath it. The other two spears thudded into his belly. He pulled himself out from under his dead horse and tore the spears free, spilling his guts on to the ground. But there was power in him yet. Just enough.

'I'm dying of thirst here, lads. Can I just go to that lake there and get myself a drink?'

Knowing a man doesn't come back from a stomach wound like that, the attackers put down their weapons and allowed him this small mercy. Cúchulainn gathered up his innards and hobbled over to the lake. He lay down and lapped at the water like a deer come to drink. When his thirst was sated, he struggled to get back up again.

'Are you going to die on your belly like a beast?' I said, landing on the soft grass beside him. 'Or on your feet like a man?'

'Give over, woman, I can hardly sit let alone stand.'

'On your feet, you little pup. Or I'll say you died sobbing like a baby.' I taunted him into action, for I had seen his death and knew he died standing. He dragged himself up and limped over to a pillar stone, placed by the lake. He used his own intestines to tie himself to the stone, so that he would die on his feet.

'Come on then,' he shouted. 'Are we going to finish this or what?'

The children of dead fathers gathered around the stone, looking up at the dying Cúchulainn.

'We'll take your head for you took the head of our fathers,' Lugaid said.

Cúchulainn made no answer.

'Is he dead?' Erc asked.

'Check,' Lugaid said.

'You check,' Erc said.

I flew over and landed on his shoulder, for hadn't I said I would stand guard at his death and stand guard I did. I began pecking at his eyeballs.

'He's dead all right.' Lugaid crept forward.

He prodded Cúchulainn in the chest with the tip of his sword. The hero didn't move. I hopped on to the top of the pillar to be out of the way. Lugaid grabbed Cúchulainn by his hair and sliced his head off. The life finally out of him, Cúchulainn dropped his sword and it sliced Lugaid's hand clean off. Always one to have the final blow.

Cúchulainn, Ireland's greatest hero, dead at last.

His death unlocked something in me. As though I had

been wrapped up in the strands of his story and at last I was free. It was my story once more.

I felt my power flood back through me, filling me from my fingertips to my bones, full as a well after a rainstorm. It poured into me and overflowed, endless and bountiful. Everything about it felt different. I felt different. I felt light. Joyful. Free. Before, my power had felt like a burden and I had feared what it could do. Now, it felt like a gift. I had believed my power came from pain, and I'd held on to my pain, tight as a vice. And all the time my power had fought me because I had tried to contain it and to control it when all I needed to do was to let go. It would not abandon me. It would never abandon me. I was alive with the possibilities. I was unlimited. And I was unafraid.

The grief I had carried all those long years shifted too. I could think of my children, my beloved boy Meche, the twins I would never get to know; I could think of my mother, who had wanted me to be happy, and feel love. Endless, enduring, exquisite love that was greater than the pain. I had thought if I let go of that pain, it would mean letting go of them. But they would always be a part of me, woven into the fabric of my being for ever.

I scattered myself to the winds, going anywhere the mood took me. I had no purpose, but that didn't scare me as it had when I had first come to this land. Who needed purpose anyway, when you had freedom? I still had my rage, oh, I still had my rage, for like me, like my love, it was imperishable. But it no longer scorched me. I was its master now and could put that fire to work.

The years turned into decades and decades into centuries. Rulers came and went. Battles were fought and lost and sometimes I played my part in them. I spent my time among women, among the powerless, the voiceless. Gave them some of my fire to keep them going and took a little of their shame away. I became the seed of rage in every woman's heart, ready to catch fire. I was in the passing of weapons in bread baskets. I was in the printing of seditious materials. I was the call for change.

Men have always been afraid of women's anger. Have shushed and shooed us away. And so they should be afraid. For when women realize that raging alone is like screaming into the wind, but raging together, raising their voices as one, is when they can change the world, that is when the time of men will be over.

Sometimes, I visited powerful men on the night of their death to shriek. Those who had taken power and wielded it badly. Those who had used their strength to weaken others. The banshee they call me now. The last of my names. An old woman wailing for the dead. But what they don't know is that I am not wailing out of sorrow or anguish.

When a cruel man dies, I laugh. And laugh. And my laughing is taken up by the birds.

Acknowledgements

This story might begin in darkness, but it ends in light. The burning light of my gratitude for everyone who worked to set this book free. It was born in those grim, grey days of the pandemic and I never knew if it would one day escape into the world. It's thanks to you that it has.

It is no small exaggeration to say this book would not exist without the unfailing encouragement of Amy McCulloch. From nudging me in the right direction towards this idea, to every single WhatsApp and chat that followed, you were the midwife of this book, right down to screaming 'push' at me when I needed it most.

To Bea Fitzgerald, who just GOT what I was trying to do with this story; your belief in it was infectious. Like you, I have a thing about female rage – it was a joy to work together and put our rage to good use. And to the whole team at the Blair Partnership who have taken such incredible care of me and this book, thank you.

To Ruth Atkins, editor extraordinaire. Your knowledge of and passion for Irish myths is unsurpassed and your ability to see into the soul of the book helped make it even better than I dared dream. *Go raibh míle maith agat.*

To my copy-editor, Mary Chamberlain. Knowing the book was in the hands of a woman who knows her das from her fadas was beyond amazing. I am sorry there were so many names for you to triple-check. To Bea McIntyre, Brónagh Grace and everyone at Penguin Michael Joseph, from publishing to comms, thank you for your passion and excitement. And to Vasilisa Romanenko, Jon Kennedy and Lee Motley for the stunning design, thank you for your patience and incredible talent.

To Lisa Paasche and Sarah Devine, a lot of your strength shines through the women in these pages. To Bex Levene and Leila Abu el Hawa, for being both brilliantly smart and wonderfully kind. To El Lam and Katie Marsh for feedback on my agent submission letters. To Hazel Gale, who enabled me to say 'I am a good writer' without cringing. To Jane Tauwhare, for our dog walks and your patience as I tried to explain the tangled world of publishing. To Patrick Ness, for our burgers and friendship. To Juno Dawson for riding the rollercoasters with me, literal and metaphorical. And to those who helped without even knowing: the Story Archaeologists, Candlelit Tales, and Lora O'Brien, your beautiful retellings and translations proved invaluable sources of inspiration.

To my sisters, Heidi and Natasha, and my parents, Deirdre and Malachy, who were perhaps even more excited about this being published than I was. And to the whole Curran Clan back home.

To my husband, who not only read the messy, early draft and corrected my knowledge of iron weaponry but also supported me though the dark times when I didn't think the book would ever see the light of day. To my dog, Domino, I hope you don't eat this book like you have others.

To all the men who have talked over me, down to me, or refused to talk at all: thanks for the fuel.

And at last, to you, dear, fearless reader. This is your story now – take from it what you need, burn everything else to the ground. I hope it makes you rage in the best possible way. After all, that's what the Morrigan would want.